DEADLY REPRISAL

DETECTIVE ZOE FINCH BOOK 5

RACHEL MCLEAN

Ackroyd Publishing

ackroyd-publishing.com

READ ZOE'S PREQUEL STORY, DEADLY ORIGINS

It's 2003, and Zoe Finch is a new Detective Constable. When a body is found on her patch, she's grudgingly allowed to take a role on the case.

But when more bodies are found, and Zoe realises the case has links to her own family, the investigation becomes deeply personal.

Can Zoe find the killer before it's too late?

Find out by reading *Deadly Origins* for FREE at rachelmclean.com/origins.

Thanks,

Rachel McLean

CHAPTER ONE

"NOT THAT ONE."

Kayla felt her chest tighten as her friend Lin raised a hand to knock on the door.

Lin turned to her, eyes flashing into the camera lens. "Yeah. Let's leave that one. For now." She smiled, injecting a note of breeziness into her voice and lifting her chin for the most flattering angle. "We'll start at the far end of the corridor and work our way along."

Kayla let out a short breath, glancing back at the door as they headed towards the other end of the corridor. It had just gone midnight and they were stalking the corridors of Boulton Hall of Residence. Lin was on the hunt, as usual, for material for her YouTube channel. Bass reverberated through the building from the party three floors below and Kayla could hear distant laughter.

Lin cleared her throat, raised a fist to the last door in the corridor and turned to the camera.

"Hey party people, welcome to *Lin's Lens*. Tonight is the

Valentine's Ball at Boulton Hall and we're expecting plenty of dirt." She leaned in, her eyes wide. "And you can expect us to dish it out for you!"

Lin knocked on the door, her gaze still on the camera. She winked, and Kayla suppressed an eye roll. Lin was in her element recording for her channel; she spent far more time on this than she did on her studies.

"Aw, shucks!" Lin exclaimed. She liked to broaden her mild Texas accent for the videos. Her mum was from Hong Kong and her dad from Austin, but the fact that she'd grown up in Hemel Hempstead wasn't something she shared with her audience. "No one home." She turned to check the name plate on the door. "*Susy* must be partying downstairs with the rest of them."

"Which is where we should be," muttered Kayla. Knocking on doors like this, spying on people. It made her uneasy. Especially since they'd eventually have to knock on the door she'd persuaded Lin away from.

"Come on." Lin waved an arm in a *follow me* gesture and hurried along the corridor, knocking on doors and pushing on each to check if any had been left unlocked. At the second, they were yelled at by two guys. Lin sliced at her throat, gesturing for Kayla to hit pause.

The fourth door was open, and she went inside without waiting for an invitation. Kayla's toes curled in her shoes.

"Huh, no one home," Lin shrugged. "Nice wall art though." She swept a hand behind her and Kayla followed with the camera, taking in the occupant's collection of soft porn. *Ew*, she thought.

"Ha!" Lin said. "We can talk to Dan about his collection in another episode. Let's see if we can find anyone at home."

Kayla knew what Lin was looking for. Couples she could interrupt, threesomes even better. Capturing drug-taking on camera. She didn't upload everything she filmed; sometimes it suited her to have her subjects know she was keeping the footage for a future date. As a result, Lin never paid for her own drinks, and even text books materialised from nowhere. Kayla wasn't sure how she felt about being a conspirator in what could only be described as extortion. But one thing she *was* sure about was that she didn't want to be Lin's next victim.

Eight doors and one snogging couple ('dull', Lin pronounced) later, they arrived back at the first door.

"Now to see what Boulton Hall's biggest creep is up to," Lin said. Kayla put a hand out to stop her but it was too late. Lin had knocked.

Laurence Thomms, the room's occupant, would be in there. No one had seen him at the party. No one had seen him anywhere other than mandatory tutorials for a month now. And they all knew why.

"It's open!" Lin's eyes gleamed as she pushed on the wood. Kayla swallowed the lump in her throat.

"Let's see what he's up to, huh?"

Kayla squeezed her eyes shut, not looking at the image on the camera's screen. Laurence's face was all too familiar to her. It haunted her nightmares.

She heard Lin's footsteps as her friend walked into the room and stumbled after her, the camera pointing ahead but her eyes not following. Lin made a low sound and stopped. Kayla crashed into her friend and opened her eyes. The room was dark.

"Where are you, creep?" Lin whispered. "Hope you

haven't dragged some poor girl up here and drugged her into submission."

Kayla winced. She knew the possible consequences if Lin accused Laurence of a crime on video. But then...

"Shit." Lin's voice was breathy.

"What?"

"I felt something. Open the fucking door."

"What?"

"It shut behind us. There's something on my foot. Laurence, is that you?" Kayla felt Lin's hand on her arm. "Open the door, Kay. I don't like this."

Part of Kayla registered that this would make a great video. She wondered if Lin's fear was genuine.

"Didn't you hear me? Open the fucking door!" Lin's voice was sharp.

Kayla stumbled backwards, her body slamming into the door. She yanked on the handle, but her own weight was keeping it shut.

"Hurry," came Lin's voice. Kayla heard a groan: Lin, or someone else?

Kayla shifted to one side and hauled the door open, then turned back to look at her friend. Lin had crashed onto the unmade bed. Her face was pale and her breathing ragged.

At her feet, curled up like a sleeping child, was Laurence. Kayla recoiled at the sight of his thin frame and sharp cheekbones.

"Is he...?" she breathed.

Lin blinked. The young man at her feet wasn't moving. Lin prodded him with her toe, rolling him to face upwards. His eyes were open.

Lin retched. Kayla stepped towards her. "Come on. Let's get out of here. He's taken something."

Lin looked up at her. She shook her head, her skin now almost as pale as Laurence's. "He's stone cold."

Kayla forced herself to look back at the man. His jaw had fallen open and drool ran down his chin. She shuddered.

"He's dead, Kay. He's fucking dead."

CHAPTER TWO

THE SAFE HOUSE Ana-Maria Albescu was being held in wasn't much better than the building she'd been forced to live in while being sold for sex.

DI Zoe Finch sat on the oily sofa, arranging her feet on the threadbare carpet and telling herself not to move. Opposite her, DS Mo Uddin perched on a high-backed chair that looked like it might collapse under his weight.

"It's a disgrace," Mo said, breaking the silence.

"What is?"

He raised his arms in a gesture to indicate the room. "You know what these women went through. They should be in a sanctuary now. Not... this." He wiped a finger along the top of a chest of drawers and screwed up his nose.

"At least they're safe," Zoe pointed out. Mo grunted.

The women living in this house in Bearwood had been victims of an organised people-trafficking and prostitution operation. They'd been persuaded to come to the UK from less wealthy countries in search of new lives, then forced to earn money for the men who'd paid for their passage.

One of those women, Andreea Pichler, had died in Zoe's arms. Another, whose name they still didn't know, had died when she'd set off a nail bomb in New Street Station. And Ana-Maria, the woman they were here to see, was the only link they had to the bomber. After two weeks of silence, Zoe was hoping she might give them information that would help them discover who the bomber was and why she'd sacrificed herself.

The door opened with a squeak. A chubby woman with curly blonde hair walked in with an apologetic look on her face: Tina Galton, the administrator.

"I'm sorry." She twisted her mouth in frustration – or perhaps apology. "She won't leave her room."

"Not again," Mo breathed.

Zoe slumped in her chair, wishing she hadn't bothered sitting down. It was the fourth time this had happened.

"She's scared," Tina said. "She thinks that if she tells the police anything, the men will hurt her. Or her son in Romania."

Zoe nodded. The woman was probably right. Trevor Hamm's organised crime operation had tentacles that reached into more places than they'd previously thought. If he could traffic women from Romania, he could most likely hurt people there too.

"It's all anonymous," she said. "Ana-Maria will never be named in court. Any records we keep, notes we take, we'll use a false name." She held out her notepad, indicating the *Daniela* she'd written at the top. "See."

"I've told her that." Tina shrugged.

"Yeah, course you have."

"Why would she believe us?" Mo said. He stood up and

wiped the dust off his fingers. "No one in this country has proven exactly trustworthy."

"She'll be going home tomorrow," Tina said.

"We know," Zoe told her. "All the more reason to persuade her to talk now."

"Sorry. I know it's important, but my responsibility is to the women."

Zoe stood up. "Important doesn't really cover it."

Tina met her gaze. "I know you've got a terror investigation to pursue, Inspector, but that's not my priority."

"Hmm." Zoe eyed Mo. "Come on then. Let's get back to the office."

She followed Mo from the room, peering up the stairs as they passed them and wondering if Ana-Maria was listening in. Once the woman was back in Romania, she'd vanish. And their only lead to the bomber would be gone.

Outside, she yanked open the door to her Mini, her mind racing. "We'll need to track down Hamm's lot directly."

"You know what he's like, boss. We'll never pin anything on him."

"Maybe if Ian talks."

Mo let out a sigh. "DS Osman's not going to tell us anything."

DS Ian Osman had been Zoe's sergeant until he'd got himself caught planting evidence at the scene of a second terror attack. Now they were hoping he'd lead them to the gang that had played a part in both attacks, and done so much damage to so many people – the women in this house included. But so far, he was keeping his thoughts to himself.

She shook herself out. "Come on, I've got a shedload of paperwork to get through. And the DCI wants me to revisit the files from those robberies in Chelmsley Wood."

"Fun."

"Yeah." Zoe landed in the driver's seat heavily and turned the ignition. Her phone rang as she was about to put the car in gear.

"Connie?"

"Boss. Where are you?"

"Hall Green, the safe house. Why?"

"The DCI wants you at a murder scene."

Zoe raised her eyebrows at Mo and switched to speaker-phone. "Where?"

"Birmingham University. Kid called Laurence Thomms. They thought he'd OD'd but now they think it's suspicious."

"Give me details." Zoe started driving as Mo took down the address: Boulton Hall.

Zoe glanced at Mo as she turned right off the Hagley Road. "Let's hope this one's a bit more straightforward."

CHAPTER THREE

BOULTON HALL WAS AN ANGULAR, modern building surrounded by bare trees and flanked by two small car parks. Zoe drove around each of them in turn, cursing the lack of parking spaces.

"I'll drop you at the front," she told Mo. "One of us might as well go in."

She pulled up to the front of the building and let Mo out. Reversing, she thought better of driving away, and instead parked her car halfway up the pavement outside the entrance. She was investigating a murder; they'd hardly begrudge her some inconsiderate parking.

Inside, Mo was talking to a large man in a black uniform.

"We're from West Midlands Police. Investigating a suspicious death."

"I don't care, mate. You leave your car out there and it's an obstruction. What if a fire engine needs to get past?"

"We're police," Zoe told him. "Emergency services, too."

"I don't see no blue lights."

She narrowed her eyes at him. "Tell me where to leave my car then. And it'd better be nearby."

The security guard squared his shoulders, pleased with himself. He had a name badge sewn onto his sweater: Mark Jenks. *Jobsworth*, she thought.

"Well?" she asked, resisting an urge to grab the man by the lapels.

"There's a staff spot round the back." He made a circling motion. "You can put it there."

"I'll do it," said Mo. He held out a hand and Zoe passed him her keys.

"Thanks," she said.

The last time a detective sergeant had driven her Mini it had been Ian Osman, and he'd been trying to cover up his crimes. Mo was different, thank God.

"Right," she said to Jenks. "Show me the way."

He grunted and led her to a bank of lifts.

As they rode upwards she realised what had been bothering her since she'd entered the building.

"Where is everyone?" she asked. It was half past ten on a Monday morning, even students would be awake by now. She thought of her son Nicholas, about to go off to uni himself, and not known for early rising.

"We've confined them to their corridors," Jenks replied.

"Can you do that?"

"In cases of emergency, yes. A kid's been killed. What if the killer's still in the building?"

Heaven save me from over-zealous security guards, she thought. "Whose idea was that?"

He smiled. "Mine. The warden was in agreement."

"Oh he was, was he?"

"She. Yes. She was. They're all tucked up safe in their corridors."

"What if they need to go to lectures?"

He shrugged. "There's been a murder. That's more important."

Zoe sighed as the lift doors opened. The door closest to them hung open, voices spilling out beyond it, forensic floor protection plates leading inside. Zoe pulled on her overshoes and gloves and cleared her throat. Jenks hung behind her.

"Thanks," she told him. He nodded.

"I mean, you can go now," she said.

He wrinkled his nose and stepped back into the lift. Someone would have to interview the man later, find out what he knew. She hoped it wouldn't be her.

"Hello?" she called.

A white-suited tech with their back to her stood up and turned. The eyes, the only part of the human inside visible, crinkled at the sight of her.

"Zoe!"

"Adi," she replied. "What have you got for me?"

"Good to see you too," said Adi Hanson, Forensic Scene Manager. After a pause he turned back to the room. A young man lay slumped against the bed, his face raised towards the ceiling and his mouth hanging open. White foam surrounded his lips and his skin was turning blue. On the carpet next to him was a splash of vomit.

"Looks like an overdose to me," she said.

"You'd think so, wouldn't you?" said Adi. "But look at his wrists." He pointed.

Zoe leaned forwards. The victim's wrists were ringed with purple-yellow bruises. "You think that's connected?"

"Not my job to put two and two together, Zoe. But

there's marks in his nostrils too, scarring. And on his tongue and gums. Recent, I reckon."

"You think someone forced drugs into him?"

"At first glance it looks like an overdose," Adi said. "But apparently the girl who found him was a medical student, and she decided to take a look."

"Great," Zoe said.

"Tell me about it. But she may have done him a favour. The knuckle-dragger calling himself a security guard would never have called us out if she hadn't."

"That's a bit rude," Zoe told him.

Adi turned to her, eyebrows raised. She suppressed a snort. "OK, so what did this medical student tell you?"

"She's along the hall," he said. "You can ask her yourself. Name's Lin Johnson."

"I'll get to her in a minute. First, tell me about the scene. Any signs of a struggle, someone forcing their way in?"

"No forced entry, but if these students are anything like I was back in the day, no one locks their door anyway." Adi pointed to a folded-up sheet of cardboard next to the door, which was now propped open with a chair. "Wedge them open, like."

"OK. So someone came in, but he didn't want them here, and he certainly didn't want them shoving drugs into him."

"Hi." Mo hurried in, bringing a cloud of cold air with him. "Your car's bloody miles away. Sorry."

Zoe took her keys from him and shoved them into the pocket of her jeans. "That's OK. Adi's telling me about signs of a struggle."

"Well, it's not all that cut and dried," Adi said. "I mean, the kid could just have been a slob. And if he had been using, then he might have done himself some damage. But there's books all over the floor, and that mug..."

He pointed to a mug which lay on its side beneath the bed, liquid puddling beneath it.

"What about the body?" Mo asked. "Defensive wounds?"

"We've got bruising on the wrists," said Adi.

"Could have been self-inflicted," Mo said. "If he was an addict..."

"They're fresh," Adi said. "But the pathologist will be able to confirm."

"Where is Adana, anyway?" Zoe asked.

"She's sending one of her team," Adi said. "This is small beer, for her. Especially as I couldn't convince her it definitely wasn't an overdose."

"Maybe she's right," said Zoe.

"The only way to be sure is for a pathologist to take a look," said Adi.

"Do I detect professional tension?" Zoe asked.

"Ignore me," Adi said. "I just want them to take him away so we've got a bit more room in here."

He did have a point. The room couldn't have been more than two and a half metres square, and it housed a bed, a desk, a wardrobe, two detectives and three FSIs. As well as a body.

"OK," Zoe said. "I'll get out of your way. Mo, let's go talk to this Lin girl."

CHAPTER FOUR

KAYLA CLAMPED her hands over her knees, trying to stop the trembling. She'd fled to her room after they'd found Laurence. Lin had tried – and failed – to calm her down.

His room had stunk. Vomit, and shit, and something else she couldn't identify. She'd been in there before, of course. It hadn't smelled good before, but it had been nothing like this.

An image of his pale face on the floor flashed through her head, and she let out a whimper. She jerked her face up to check the door. They'd confined the students to their corridors, which meant she was alone. The other students on her corridor were wary of her: they knew she was somehow damaged, and they didn't want to find out more.

But she couldn't risk anyone coming in.

Kayla pulled herself up, pushing past the weakness in her legs, and stumbled to the door. She leaned against it as she turned the lock. Someone was outside, talking.

"He had it coming," said a voice. Kayla leaned against the door, trying to still her breathing.

"You can't say that," said another. "No one deserves that."

"Maybe he did. He was bad news." A third voice, lower. This one was male, the other two female.

"They're saying he took an overdose."

"You reckon he killed himself?"

"Maybe. What with it all hanging over him..."

Silence. Kayla pictured the three people outside: Dawn, Shavon and Ricky. They'd be staring into space, trying to make out like they were affected by it all. Trying to pretend they cared.

Well, she cared. She'd been there when he'd been found, and she'd known what he was like. For weeks. She should have told someone...

She brushed tears from her cheeks and staggered back to the bed. There was movement outside. Her doorknob turned.

"Kayla? You in there?"

She stared at the door. She shook her head.

"Kayla?"

"Leave her. She doesn't want to talk to us."

"Yeah, we might give her the plague or something."

Laughter. Kayla tensed, wishing she had the courage to go out there and talk to them. To tell them what she knew.

She couldn't. She would take it to the grave.

She let herself fall back onto the bed and curled into a ball. She grasped her legs, hugging herself, and allowed the sobs to rip through her body.

CHAPTER FIVE

"LIN JOHNSON?" Zoe stepped into the room, a smile on her face. The student sat on the bed with a female constable beside her: PC Lark.

"That's me." The young woman straightened and met Zoe's gaze.

"How are you doing?"

"I'm good." A slight American accent.

"You from the US?"

Lin stared at her for a moment then shook her head. "My dad is. But I'm from Hemel."

"Hemel?"

"Hempstead? Outside London?"

"I know where it is."

Lin nodded and wiped her face with her sleeve. Despite the bravado, her cheeks were blotched with tears.

Zoe nodded at the PC who gave the girl a reassuring rub on the shoulder and stood to leave the room. "I'll get you a cuppa," she said.

Zoe exchanged glances with Mo, who was still standing

in the doorway: cups of tea, the family liaison officer's answer to everything. She doubted the students drank much tea.

"Why not make that something stronger?" Zoe suggested. Lin looked up at her, a smile flickering across her lips. "Vodka?"

"There's a bottle in the wardrobe." Lin replied.

PC Lark frowned. "It's only eleven o'clock..."

"I think Lin's been through enough of an ordeal to justify a drink," Zoe said. "Have you slept?"

Lin shook her head. The PC grunted and opened the wardrobe door.

After the vodka had been found and the student had downed two generous shots, Zoe sat on the chair opposite the bed. Mo was still hovering at the door. PC Lark had left.

"My name's Detective Inspector Zoe Finch. This is Detective Sergeant Mo Uddin. You don't need me to tell you why we're here."

Lin shook her head. "There were contusions on his procheilon. Lacerations to the frenulum. I can write it all down, or make a video for you..."

Zoe put a hand up. "It's OK, Lin. To be honest, I don't understand half of what you just said anyway. And the pathologist will be able to figure all that out."

"So why...?"

"You found him. We need you to describe what happened."

Lin slumped into herself. She was short and slender, with cropped dark hair. Zoe thought of Andreea Pichler, the Romanian woman who'd died in her arms. Superficially the two young women were nothing like each other, but there was something in this girl that reminded Zoe of Andreea.

"He was lying on the floor, next to his bed," Lin said.

"Wait a minute," said Mo. "We'll need you to start at the beginning."

Lin frowned. "From when I opened the door?"

"Before that. Why did you go to his room? Did you see him beforehand?"

"Uh-uh. No one had seen him for days."

"Days?" asked Mo.

"Yeah. He was... kinda reclusive, you might say. Attended tutorials, the ones he had to, but that was it. The uni has started putting lectures online, helps overseas students they say. But really it encourages introverts to stay in their rooms and everyone else to get up late."

"So when did you last see him, Lin?" Zoe asked.

A shrug. "About a month ago. I guess." Her face darkened.

"So why did you go to his room?" Mo asked.

"We were making a video. *Lin's Lens*. I'm a creator, that's my channel. I was looking for dirt. You usually get a lot of it when there's a party on. People making out, taking drugs. That kind of shit." She clapped her hand to her mouth. "Sorry."

Mo scratched his head. Zoe gave the young woman a smile. "We're police. We're used to swearing, you know."

"First hand, in her case," Mo added.

The student blushed and nodded. "Sorry."

Zoe leaned towards her. "So you went to his room thinking you might be able to catch him on camera taking drugs?"

"I don't know why I went to his room. Not really. Guy's a creep. Kayla didn't want me to go, I think she's allergic to him. Don't blame her."

"So is Kayla the other person making the video?" Mo asked.

"Yeah. She was behind the camera. Always is."

"Anyone else there?" Zoe asked.

"Place was deserted, they were all downstairs, at their pathetic party."

"You're not a fan of university parties?" Zoe asked.

The girl shrugged. "They're OK, I guess. Plenty of material, for the channel. But... yeah. Not a fan."

"OK," said Mo. "So you came to his room with your camera and...?"

Zoe raised a finger. "Wait. Where's the footage?"

"Oh. Yeah, Kayla's got it," Lin replied.

Zoe turned to Mo. "We're going to need to speak to her, asap. In fact, can you go to her now, get that tape."

"It isn't a tape," Lin said. "No one uses tape anymore."

"File," Zoe said. "You know what I mean. Where is Kayla?"

A shrug. "In her room, I guess."

Zoe sighed. "Any chance you might give me her room number?"

Lin eyed her and recited a number. Zoe gestured at Mo, who left the room.

"Right," Zoe said to Lin. "So you went to his room and you found him on the floor. Did you see anyone else around?"

"No one. We passed his door about ten minutes earlier, too."

"OK. Where did you go in those ten minutes?"

"Along the corridor. We were filming, seeing what we could get."

"Were you in sight of Laurence's door the whole time?"

"Sort of. Kayla would have been, but she was looking at the screen. Filming."

"She didn't say she'd seen anything? No one coming or going?"

"You'd have to ask her."

"We will. Let's go back to when you found him. What did you do?"

Lin swallowed. "I took a look at him."

Zoe nodded, slowly. It wasn't this student's job to do her own post-mortem, but there was no point in berating her for it now. "Describe that."

"I'd already rolled him over with my foot." Lin looked into Zoe's eyes. "I was careful not to touch him. I had gloves in my pocket."

"You always carry surgical gloves?"

"We'd been doing anatomy that afternoon. I'd put them in my pocket instead of handing them over for disposal."

Great, Zoe thought. Now they had a body contaminated by whatever Lin had brought in on those gloves. She clenched a fist and nodded for Lin to continue.

"He had foam coming from his mouth, and he'd vomited. So I took a look at his lips and his gums. He had bruising and lacerations, small cuts. The frenulum." She opened her mouth and put her finger on the webbing between her gum and upper lip. "And on the lower gums and the procheilon. Here." She shifted her finger to her own upper lip.

"You talked to my colleague about this, the crime scene manager?" Zoe said.

"The cute guy in the mask? Yeah. I think he was impressed."

Zoe tightened her fist. She wondered if Adana's

colleague had arrived yet. They needed a professional autopsy, not the ham-fisted efforts of a medical student.

"What year are you in?" she asked.

Lin blushed. "First year."

Of course, Zoe thought. Keen, but inexperienced. Maybe Adana not being here was a blessing: she could only imagine the pathologist's reaction to Lin.

"OK," Zoe said. "So what did you do after that?"

"I went looking for Kayla."

"Kayla had gone?"

"I hadn't noticed, I was too busy looking at Laurence. I found her in the bathroom at the end of the hall. Shitting herself, she was. Well, not literally, but you know what I mean..."

"Then what?"

"Jenson appeared. He's our pastoral tutor. S'posed to look after us. I guess he'd heard Kayla, she was shrieking by that point. And I told him."

"Did anyone else go into Laurence's room?"

"No. Jenson shut the door. He sent everyone away, and he told security. I didn't see anything else."

CHAPTER SIX

Zoe leaned against a wall outside the hall of residence and took out her phone. The area was quiet, no students coming or going. She wondered how long it would be before they rebelled.

"Hey, boss." DC Rhodri Hughes's voice was perky.

"Rhodri. You got Connie with you?"

"Both here, boss. Awaiting your command."

"Put me on speakerphone." Zoe wondered if she should wait for Mo. But she had no idea which part of the building Kayla's room was in.

"Boss." Connie's voice came on the line.

"OK, you two," Zoe said. "We've got a nineteen-year-old male killed by what might be an overdose, but could be suspicious. Signs that someone may have forced whatever killed him into his mouth. I'm waiting for the pathologist to get here" – *and where is Adana's colleague?* she wondered – "but in the meantime I want you to check out our victim. Laurence Thomms. Comes from Leeds, studying Chemistry, in his first year. A bit of a recluse, from what I've been told. Find out if he's got a record, if he's reported any threats or attacks. Anything you can dredge up."

"No problem," said Rhodri. "You want us to liaise with university security?"

Zoe could imagine that Mark Jenks guy responding better to the constables than to her or Mo.

"Yes. The guard on duty is Mark Jenks. Rhodri, you get out here and talk to him. Find out what you can from him and his colleagues about the students involved, whether there's anything suspicious we need to know about."

"There's more than one of them?" Connie asked.

"He was found by a Lin Johnson and a Kayla Goode. I've spoken to Lin, Mo's talking to Kayla right now. There's something that made me wonder about Lin. I want to know about their relationship with Laurence, if they had one, and any other students. There'll be staff at Boulton Hall who might be more willing to tell us what's going on than the students."

"Boss," Rhodri said.

"I'll call you back when the pathologist has turned up," Zoe said. "Let you know if there's anything you can follow up on."

She heard Rhodri make a guttural noise.

"You want to go to the post-mortem, Rhod?"

"Er..."

Zoe laughed. "Don't worry, Constable. It's Connie's turn."

"Really?" Connie sounded hesitant.

"We all have to do it at some point. Believe me, Connie, this one won't be as bad as some you'll see."

"OK." Zoe heard the two constables mutter between themselves.

"What is it?" she asked.

"Nothing, boss. I'll let you know when I'm at the uni," Rhodri replied.

"Good. Keep me informed."

CHAPTER SEVEN

Kayla jumped at a knock on her door. She shrank back onto the bed, her knees drawn up.

"Who is it?"

"My name's Detective Sergeant Mo Uddin. I need to ask you some questions."

She felt ice run down her back. The others would be out there, watching him. Wondering what was going on. They'd have let him in the outer door.

"OK," she whispered, and crossed to the door. She turned the lock and peered out. The corridor was empty except for a middle-aged Asian man with a friendly smile. He held up a police badge.

"Hi, Kayla. Sorry to bother you, but can I come in?"

Kayla's gaze darted along the corridor. Ricky's door was open a crack: listening in. She felt like screaming.

"Come in."

The detective followed her into the room and looked around for something to prop the door open with. *Of course,* she thought. He wouldn't want to risk being alone with her. In case she accused him of something.

"Here," she said. She reached under the bed and brought out the stuffed dog she used to hold the door when she was feeling sociable.

"Thanks." He placed it next to the door and turned to give her a wary smile.

She looked past him into the corridor. They'd all be listening in. But at least if they knew the truth, they wouldn't be able to speculate.

She would just have to be careful what she said.

"Mind if I sit?" The detective put a hand on the back of her work chair. She nodded and he pulled it out and slipped into it. She took her place on her bed, legs drawn up to her chest.

"We've been talking to Lin," the man said. "She says the two of you were making a video."

Kayla nodded.

"Could you let me have a copy?"

"Oh. Yes, of course." The camera was behind him, on the desk. She'd used her phone at first, but Lin had complained that they needed something with higher resolution. The camera had turned up one morning as they were about to film. Kayla didn't know if Lin had got her folks to pay for it, or if she'd acquired it some other way, maybe even stolen it. "It's right there." She pointed.

The detective picked up the camera and turned it over in his hand.

"Here," she said. "There's a SD card." She held out her hand and he passed it to her. She flicked the button to open the card slot and tipped it into her hand, then passed it to him.

"Thanks," he said. "Mind if I take the camera too?"

Kayla frowned: what would Lin say? "OK." She handed it back to him. He brought a plastic bag out of his pocket and put both camera and card inside.

He placed the bag on the desk and turned to look at her. She blinked under his gaze.

"So," he said. "How are you?"

"Fine," she grunted. *Just get on with it*, she thought.

"Your roommates – is that the right term? – were worried about you." He gestured towards the door.

Yeah, right, she thought. "Oh," she said.

"They said you came running in here at around half past midnight and locked yourself in your room. You haven't been out since."

Kayla shrugged.

"What you saw... it can't have been easy."

She pursed her lips but said nothing. Her skin felt hot.

"I'm going to need to ask you what happened."

"It's on the video," she whispered.

He glanced at the camera. "We'll look at that," he said. "And I'm grateful for it. But I'll need your account too."

She shifted on the bed. Her hands felt cold.

"Would you like me to fetch someone? For support?"

She shook her head. He'd get Jenson, the residential tutor. She didn't want that.

"No," she said.

"Can you call your parents? Would they come and take care of you? I'm sure some leave..."

"No." She clenched her fists. "No." She hadn't spoken to her parents since Christmas, and even then she'd returned to Birmingham as soon as she could. Her mum had a way of looking into her face and reading her thoughts, and Kayla didn't want that.

"I'm fine," she said. "Ask your questions." She straightened, shifting her back up the wall and putting her legs out in front of her. She wished she had another chair.

"OK." He smiled. "There was a party on, yes?"

"The Valentine's Ball."

"And you and Lin decided to come upstairs and make a video?"

"Lin likes to record when there's a party on. Capture the stuff that happens in the shadows, she says."

"Had you seen Laurence before you went to his room?"

"No."

"When was the last time you saw him?"

She bit her lip. "I don't know. A while." Truth was, she avoided him. Especially now, after what had happened with that Becca girl.

"OK. Whose idea was it to go to his room?"

"Lin's. I tried to stop her. We went along the rest of his corridor first, but then she said it was his turn." She tugged at her sleeve. "I wasn't keen."

"Why not?"

"He never comes out. I didn't like the idea of... disturbing him." She gazed at her fingers, turning them over in her lap.

"Was his door locked?"

Kayla shook her head. "We wouldn't have gone in if it had been."

"Was it normally locked?"

She felt heat pass through her. "How would I know?"

He frowned at her and shrugged. "Just a question."

She swallowed. "I don't know. Most people don't lock their doors, but he might have."

"Why's that?"

Her back stiffened. "Like I said, he's a recluse. Doesn't like people."

The detective stared at her for a moment, deepening her discomfort.

"OK," he said at last. "So when you found him, what did you see?"

Why are you asking me this? she thought. Surely they could see for themselves.

"He was on the floor. It was dark, Lin hit him with her foot. We opened the door to let some light in, and he was there." She shivered, remembering his body slumped next to the bed.

"It was Lin who opened the door?"

"It might have been me. Sorry, I can't..."

He smiled. "Don't worry. Our memories can play tricks with us, when things like this happen."

Yeah, she thought. *They can.* She stared back at him, trying to keep her face impassive.

"Did either of you touch him?" the man asked.

"Lin pushed him, with her foot. He... he rolled over." She felt sick. "Then... then I left."

"You came back here?"

Her eyes ached, tears fizzing behind them. "Sorry. I shouldn't have left her there."

"It's understandable." He reached into his jacket pocket and pulled out a card. "If you think of anything else, will you call me?"

She nodded.

"And I'll make sure you get your camera back as soon as we're done with it," he said.

"Thanks," she murmured.

He smiled as he stood up. He held out his hand but withdrew it when she didn't respond. "Thanks, Kayla. You take care of yourself, yes?"

She shrugged as he left the room, then fell back against the wall, tears pouring down her cheeks.

CHAPTER EIGHT

"So. What we got?" Zoe asked. She was in her car, Mo in the passenger seat and Rhodri in the back. They were parked in the spot Mo had been directed to, a good ten minutes' walk from Boulton Hall. At least it afforded them some privacy.

"The security guard's a busted flush, boss," Rhodri said. "Didn't even go into the room. I think he was worried he'd get a grilling if he disturbed anything."

"Did he give you any information about the students? Whether Lin or Kayla had any dealings with Laurence? Who his friends were?"

"He told me the two girls are *nosy parkers*. His words. Always creeping around the building, filming people."

"Hmm." Zoe wondered what they'd done to piss Jenks off. "What about Laurence?"

"Kept himself to himself, like your witness said. Hardly came out of his room. I spoke to the bursar and he said the kid hadn't taken any of the meals on his meal plan for two weeks."

"Do they have cooking facilities in the rooms?"

"Each corridor has a communal kitchen and living room," said Mo. "But according to the students on that floor, he never used that."

"So where did he eat?"

"Judging by the state of his room, he was living on a diet of Jacob's crackers and Pom Bears," Mo said.

"Nice." If it hadn't been for Zoe's son and his culinary skills, that wouldn't have been too far off her own diet.

"So was he pals with any of those kids on his corridor, then?" Rhodri asked Mo.

"Nope. None of them had any dealings with him."

"Poor lad."

"He's nineteen. Was," said Zoe. "Hardly a wee laddie."

Rhodri shrugged. "S'pose so."

"So," she sighed. "We haven't got much to go on until the pathologist reports. Where the hell is he or she anyway?"

Her phone rang: Adi.

"Good news, Zoe."

"Tell me it's Adana."

"Not Adana, sorry. Next best thing. Her colleague, Brent."

"Brent?"

"Doctor Brent Reynolds."

"Never heard of him."

"He's new."

"He's also bloody late."

"Had to come from Leicester, apparently."

"Why did Adana send us someone who was in Leicester?"

"Are you coming back here, or what?" Adi asked. "He'll be gone in five minutes."

"On my way."

Zoe hung up and told Mo to head back to the office in Rhodri's car. "I'll be right behind you," she said. "Not much to do here. Find out if Connie's made any progress."

Mo nodded, and he and Rhodri got out of the car. She followed and headed back to Boulton Hall.

Inside, she gave Mark Jenks a cursory nod as she passed his office then called the lift, sighing. She wasn't looking forward to meeting this Doctor Reynolds.

When she arrived at Laurence's room, the pathologist was on the floor next to the body, examining the inside of the young man's cheeks.

"Doctor Reynolds," Zoe said. "Nice of you to join us."

He turned to look up at her, his eyes narrow. "Don't bloody blame me. Fucking pile-up on the M1."

She twisted her lips in irritation. "You could have called ahead. Maybe got a colleague to fill in for you?"

"We're short staffed. I'm only here cos I've been seconded to fill a gap while they do recruitment."

"So. What can you tell me?"

"Rigor's only just setting in and the room's chilly, so I'd say somewhere between eight and twelve hours. I can be more accurate when I do the PM. Judging by the marks inside his mouth, something was inserted into it by force."

"A weapon?"

He shook his head, his back to her. "Fingers, I reckon. We'll take swabs, test for DNA. Look more closely for finger-nail marks. Of course it might just turn out to be him forcing his own fingers down his throat, but the bruising doesn't quite fit with that."

"So you think someone forced drugs down his throat?"

"There's remains of foaming, could be drugs, could be something else. But let's not jump to conclusions, eh, Inspector? I'll run a toxicology analysis when he's safely with us, and then I can tell you. But you might still be looking at a suicide."

Zoe folded her arms across her chest. The kid was a recluse, with no friends. And the way the young women talked about him made her suspect he was an outcast. Suicide would fit.

"Fine," she said. "Let me know when you've got the results."

She gave Adi a nod and turned to leave. She still needed to follow up on the investigation into the New Street bomber, now known as the Magpie case. Then there was the Professional Standards investigation to worry about, not to mention Ian's looming trial. If she'd been dragged into this and it turned out to be a wild goose chase...

"You leaving us?" Adi asked.

"I'll be in the office if you need me," she said. "Failing that, I'll be somewhere along the ten-mile hike back to my car."

CHAPTER NINE

KAYLA KNEW they were out there, talking about her. They always were.

She lay on the bed, her face buried in the pillow, wishing she'd never agreed to do that stupid video. The party had been OK, she'd been chatting to a girl from her course. She'd have been happy staying where she was. But Lin had a way of making you do what she wanted.

Kayla pushed herself up, dragging her dark hair back from her face, and went to the door. She had to escape sometime, and she knew where she'd rather be.

She pushed the door open a crack and peered out. The hallway was quiet, the only sound music coming from Shavon's room. Kayla slipped through the door and crept to the outer door, careful to close it silently behind her.

She hurried to the back stairs, avoiding the main flight down to the front entrance and security office. She raced down, her breathing shallow. At the bottom was a fire door that wasn't connected to an alarm.

Outside, a group of students stood smoking under a tree. She recognised Ricky from her corridor.

"Kayla."

She winced and turned to face him. "Hi, Ricky."

"You OK?"

"Fine. I thought everyone was still shut in."

"Hah! They decided they couldn't imprison us any longer."

"We'd have broken out if they hadn't let us go," said a blonde girl next to him. She shivered. None of them were wearing coats, despite the February cold.

Kayla realised she hadn't stopped to get a coat herself. It didn't matter, she didn't have far to go.

"See you later," she said.

The students nodded and turned back to their huddle. Kayla ran across the damp grass. When she reached Edgbaston Park Road she felt herself breathe freely again, as if the campus had been suffocating her. She hurried towards Selly Oak, ignoring the blast of exhaust fumes from a bus as she rounded the corner to the Bristol Road.

Five minutes later, she was hammering on the front door of a terraced house, her limbs trembling with the cold.

The door opened and a skinny guy with an undercut and blotchy skin stared at her. "What you doing here?"

"Is he in?"

"Dunno. See for yourself."

The man stood to one side and Kayla swept past him and up the stairs. She knocked on a bedroom door then pushed it open without waiting for a reply.

"Kayla." The man inside stood up from his seat on the floor, knocking over an ashtray and shoving something inside his shirt.

"It's only me, Jenson. You're fine."

He winked at her and brought out the object.

"Give me some," she said, holding out her hand. "I need it."

"It's not the usual," he said. "I don't think..."

"Just let me." She yanked it from his hand and brought it to her lips. She inhaled deeply and choked as the sharp smoke filled her lungs.

"Shit, Jenson, what the—?"

"I did warn you." He took the pipe from her hand and guided her into an armchair. Its stuffing was spilling out, but she was glad of the support.

"What was it?" she croaked, her head spinning.

"Meth."

"Shit."

He laughed. "Yeah." He held the pipe towards her. It was made of glass, not ceramic. "Wrong kind of pipe, sweetie. You thought it was hash, didn't you?"

She nodded, placing her hands on the arms for balance. She leaned back. The drug had taken her by surprise, but it felt good to lose herself. To let some of the tension go.

"Thanks," she moaned. He smiled and bent over her, placing a soft kiss on her lips.

She batted him away. "No."

"It's OK." He dropped to the floor and stroked her face. She shuddered, feeling as if some strange creature was pawing at her.

"It's only me," he whispered. "It's fun, makes it more intense."

"I've had a... I'm not in the..."

"Shhh." He kissed her again, deeply this time. She let his

tongue explore her mouth and wrapped her own around it. He was right. It did feel good.

She giggled.

"See?" he said.

"See," she replied. She reached up and linked her hands around the back of his neck. "See."

She felt him smile into her mouth. He smelled of heated metal. It was reassuring, familiar.

"I wanted to talk...," she began.

"Hush." He pulled her up and helped her to the bed. She stumbled as her foot hit its side, then slumped onto it.

"Kayla, did anyone ever tell you you're beautiful?"

"You did," she whispered into his cheek. "Yesterday."

"So I did." He fingered her shirt and pulled it up over her breasts. She felt her bra loosen.

"Laurence. He..."

"Shh."

She stroked his face. His skin was smooth, he'd shaved. "You're soft," she said.

"So are you."

He unbuttoned her shirt and let it fall to the floor. He leaned back and peeled off his own t-shirt. She smiled up at him, her limbs soft. "'S good," she said.

"I told you." He put a finger to her lips. "Don't do it again, though. Dangerous."

She felt a jolt run through her. She pushed him off and turned, leaning against the wall. "He died."

Jenson cocked his head. "Who?" He stared into her eyes, his pupils dilated. She wondered how much of the meth he'd smoked.

She blinked. Her mind was clearing, the memory of

Laurence lying on his floor jerking her back to reality. "Laurence Thomms. We found him. He..."

She sprang off the bed. She needed to puke.

She crashed towards the bathroom, just catching Jenson's sigh of irritation as she flew out of the door.

CHAPTER TEN

DC CONNIE WILLIAMS couldn't decide if she hated being left on her own in the office, or secretly loved it.

She stared into her computer screen, numbers and information washing through her mind, and allowed herself to relax. She knew this was the way the boss felt when she sifted through documentary evidence. For Connie, it was computer files and databases: running through the digital world, she was able to achieve a zen-like calm that let her make connections and spot things others might not.

Her little brother, Zaf, had laughed at her when she'd told him about this. She'd made damn sure not to share it with anyone else since. Not even the DI, who she expected would be sympathetic.

Rhodri had gone off to the university. He liked chatting to people, it was his happy place, his moment of zen. If Rhodri could ever be accused of anything approaching zen. Mo was with the boss, a state of affairs that made Connie want to hug herself with relief. She'd hated DS Ian Osman. From the moment he'd walked into the team room, the two of them had rubbed each other up the wrong way. He'd ordered her to go home in the middle of the investigation into Zaf's abduction, and he'd treated her like an inferior member of the team, someone of less value because she was happier dealing with data and not witnesses.

It wasn't like she couldn't deal with witnesses, too. Amelia Dowd, the nice old lady who lived next door to one of the victims in the Digbeth Ripper case: she'd loved Connie. OK, so she'd loved Rhodri even more. But still.

But the best thing about being shot of Ian was losing the constant nagging feeling that she should be watching him, making sure he didn't get up to no good. She didn't want to be associated with a bent copper and she sure as hell didn't want to be managed by one.

She trawled through HOLMES, checking for any records relating to Laurence Thomms. There was nothing. No arrests, no cautions, no crimes reported against him. The guy was clean as a bell.

He was a student. It wasn't that long since Connie had been a student herself. She hadn't had the privilege of living in halls of residence like Thomms and the girls who'd found him. Her mum had wanted her at home, so she'd gone to Wolverhampton University, travelling back and forth every day and trying her best not to resent Anabelle for it.

When you were a student, the campus security guys were a bigger deal than the police. They were the people who fined you when you parked in the wrong spot or stayed too long. They were the ones who bundled people home after a few too many beers, the threat of informing a tutor hanging in the air. If you so much as stole a library book, they could tell the admin department and withhold your degree.

If Laurence Thomms had any kind of record, or if he'd

reported harassment or an attack, then it would be campus security he'd dealt with, and not the police.

She flicked onto the university website. Security files would be protected, and if she tried to hack into them she'd be traced.

She picked up her phone. "Hey, Rhonda."

"Connie Williams! How's my favourite girl in blue?"

She laughed. Rhonda was an old school friend. She worked for the university, in an administrative role.

"I'm hoping you can help me out with something, Rho."

"Go on." Rhonda was a tall, heavy-set woman who commanded respect because of the way she had of looking at people like she was their mum.

"Can you get some info on a student for me?"

"Depends what kind of *info* you mean."

"Not sure. But his name's Laurence Thomms."

"OK. What's he studying?"

"Er..." Connie checked her notes. "Chemistry. First year. Lived at Boulton Hall."

"Lived? Shit, Con, is this the one they found dead in his room?"

News travels fast, Connie thought. "It is."

"Why aren't you asking the authorities?"

"You know how long that takes. Red tape, and all that."

"I'm not sure I should..."

"Just one little look. I'll buy you a drink."

"You and me know you're way too busy for that, with your fancy job."

"Promise."

"You didn't get it from me, right?"

"Right." Connie mimed zipping her lips, then remembered Rhonda couldn't see her.

"Give me five minutes. I'll call you back."

Connie thanked her friend and hung up. She continued working through HOLMES, her mind elsewhere.

The door opened and Rhodri and the sarge came in. Connie sat up straight in her chair and patted her hair down. "Sarge."

Rhodri gave her a wink and sat at his desk. "How's things back at the fort?"

"Just waiting for some—" Connie's phone rang and she raised a finger: *wait*.

"DC Williams."

"You don't impress me with your fancy title."

"Hey, Rhonda. What you got for me?"

"OK. So it seems he was the subject of an investigation."

"Campus security?"

"Boulton Hall. The warden."

"What kind of investigation?"

"One of the other students made a complaint about him. A girl called Becca MacGuire."

"What kind of complaint?"

"She said he raped her."

CHAPTER ELEVEN

ZOE CLIPPED a photo of Becca MacGuire to the board behind Connie and Rhodri's desks. The picture showed a slender, blonde nineteen-year-old wearing a bulky winter coat that made her look tiny.

"We'll need to find her," she said. "It could be related."

"She won't want to talk to us," Mo said. "Why don't we have a chat with the warden first?"

Zoe nodded. "You go talk to the warden, find out what you can about her investigation. But I still want to talk to Becca. Connie, I want you with me for that. I know it's a cliché, but it'll be better with two women, especially with you being closer to her age."

Connie nodded at the board, her gaze on the photo. She was five years older than Becca, thought Zoe, but close enough.

"OK," Zoe said. "Let's make this quick. Our witnesses are Lin Johnson and Kayla Goode. Neither of them were much help, they say they found him in his room at around half past midnight but neither of them had seen him for days.

"Maybe weeks," said Mo. "Kayla was a bit vague."

Zoe shrugged. "She wasn't friends with him, was she?"

"Not from what she told me."

"So she'd have had no reason to see him."

"They live in the same building," Connie said. "Lived."

"So she might have known him," Zoe said.

"Except for him being a hermit, and that," added Rhodri.

"At least she ran off after finding him," Mo said. "Means she and Lin didn't have a chance to confer on their stories."

"You think there's a reason to suspect them?" Zoe asked. "Looks to me like they were just in the wrong place at the wrong time."

He wrinkled his nose. "You're probably right."

"OK. Adana's lazy colleague is doing the post-mortem this afternoon. At which point we should know if we actually have a murder to investigate at all."

"Could just be a drug overdose," said Mo.

"You reckon?" asked Connie. "With him being accused of rape and that?"

"Maybe he couldn't face the investigation," Zoe said. "Took the drugs to anaesthetise himself."

"Or to escape," said Rhodri.

Zoe chewed her bottom lip. "There is the possibility of suicide."

Mo pointed to the close-up photo of the victim's lips. "Someone did that to him."

"He might have been clumsy," Zoe said.

Mo shook his head. "It feels to me like there's things people aren't telling us." He turned to Connie. "What sense did you get from your friend in the admin department?"

"She didn't know anything more than what was in the file. She hadn't spoken to anyone about it, or overheard anything. Seems it was being dealt with in Boulton Hall and not by the main university authorities."

"A cover-up," said Mo.

"Hold your horses," Zoe told him. "This is a student taking an overdose, not a terror attack."

The room went quiet at the memory of their last case.

Mo let out a long sigh. "You want me to get back to work on Magpie?"

Zoe shook her head. "I want you at the post-mortem. Let me know what happens, and whether we've actually got a job to do here. Depending on that, we can decide what to do next."

Connie breathed an audible sigh of relief: she'd probably been expecting to be sent to the post-mortem. *Next time,* thought Zoe.

The door opened and DCI Lesley Clarke walked in. She'd lost weight since her spell in hospital after the New Street bomb, but her stride was as purposeful as ever.

"Don't stand up," she said.

Zoe looked around. No one had shown any sign of standing, except Mo who was already on his feet.

Lesley barked out a laugh. "What's got into you lot? You look like someone's given you all sleeping pills."

"Sorry, Ma'am," Zoe said. "We've got this case, but we don't even know if it *is* a case yet."

"Laurence Thomms." Lesley approached the board. "Poor kid." She leaned in and peered at the photos of his gums, then winced. "You're thinking he OD'd, topped himself, or that someone forced the stuff into him."

"We'll know after the post-mortem," Zoe told her.

Lesley nodded. "And you've still got our mysterious woman in the green headscarf to track down." She was refer-

ring to the Magpie case and the New Street bomber, who
had been caught on camera but not identified.

"We have."

Lesley clapped her hands then rubbed them together.
"Don't wait for me, then. Get over to the bloody PM,
Sergeant Uddin. Then we'll know what we've got."

CHAPTER TWELVE

"WHO ARE YOU?"

"Nice to meet you too," Mo said. "Detective Sergeant Uddin. DI Finch sent me."

The pathologist gave Mo a look of disdain then went back to washing his hands. "You're here for the Thomms kid."

"I am. What's the status?"

Dr Reynolds shook his hands out, not caring about the stray droplets landing on Mo's jacket. He grabbed a paper towel and wiped his hands, then tossed it into a bin. "Just finished."

"Excellent. Can I take a look?"

The pathologist raised an eyebrow. "I trust you have a strong stomach?"

"I've been in CID for almost twenty years."

Reynolds looked him up and down. Mo stood very still, determined not to let this man intimidate him. He had a voice like cut crystal and the attitude to match. Behind his face mask, large brown eyes seemed to be appraising him, a gaze that spoke of confidence and privilege. Mo normally resisted making snap judgements about people, but this guy wasn't easy to like.

"Better get your clothes covered up, then," Reynolds said. "Unless that's your protective gear..."

Mo pursed his lips. Under the pathologist's scrubs, he imagined the man was wearing expensive suit trousers and a silk tie. None of that mattered, though. What counted was whether the man could do his job.

Mo pulled himself up. At five feet eight inches, the same height as Zoe, he was an inch shorter than the pathologist. "Give me a minute." He turned and left the examination room in search of an overall and boots.

Thirty seconds later, he was back. The pathologist stood at the examining table, Laurence Thomms's body laid out before him. The young man's chest had been cut in the distinctive Y form, and sewn up again. Despite the scar, he looked calm in death. The skin on his back and limbs had darkened where it made contact with the bench, and his face had paled.

"Let's start with the mouth," the pathologist said. Mo kept his eyes on Laurence's face, wondering what this kid had looked like in life. People looked smaller after death, especially the young.

Reynolds bent over to open Laurence's mouth. "There's bruising on the procheilon, this fleshy bit here." He placed a finger on the victim's upper lip. "And small cuts to the frenulum." He lifted the young man's lip to reveal the flesh joining it to the gum. "There's bruising here too."

Mo thought of Lin Johnson, the way she'd used medical language as a shield to protect herself from the reality of what she'd seen. Or maybe it was habit.

"Caused by what, you think?" Mo asked.

"Give me a minute, will you?"

Mo shifted between his feet.

After a moment, the pathologist spoke again. "There's scratching on the inside of the mouth, here." He pointed but his hands were in the way and Mo couldn't see. "Looks like it might be from fingernails."

"Could he have done that to himself?"

"He could. But we can find out for sure." Reynolds lifted an evidence bag from a side table. It contained a swab. "Once that's been tested." He put it down and lifted another bag. "Then there's this."

Mo took the bag off him. Inside was a sliver of glass.

"I found this in his throat, almost at the opening to the oesophagus," the pathologist said.

"How did it get there?"

"He could have swallowed it by mistake, or it could have been pushed down his throat. It didn't go far or it would have caused more damage. I didn't find anything else deeper down."

Mo peered at the glass. "What's it from?"

Reynolds straightened, hands on hips. "Doctor Adebayo told me that CID like us to do their job for them. She wasn't wrong."

"Where *is* Adana?"

"Adana? *Doctor Adebayo* is on leave."

Mo sniffed, wondering if Zoe knew her preferred pathologist was away.

"So," the pathologist said, "I checked my notes from the scene. His pupils were dilated and his airways constricted. But there's no sign of long-term use of stimulants: teeth are fine, nasal cavity intact. His heart was previously in good shape, he was young and hadn't done any damage to it. But his blood samples showed presence of stimulants, specifically methamphetamines. Concentrations twice what you'd expect from normal use, if there is such a thing."

"Crystal meth?"

"Yes."

"But you don't think he was a user?"

"I don't."

"So he either overdosed the first time he took it, or..." Mo said.

"Or someone forced it into him."

"What would that shard of glass have to do with it?"

"Methamphetamines can be smoked via a glass pipe."

"Do you think the bruising might be consistent with that?"

"It could be. But then you have the fingernail scratches."

"Can you tell from the blood concentration what form he ingested it in?" Mo asked.

"Get you." The pathologist smirked. *"Blood concentration. Ingested."*

Mo said nothing, but waited for an answer to his question.

"The answer is no, I can't. Given that it could have entered his system at any time in the previous twenty-four hours, it's impossible to tell. If he smoked or snorted it, it would have been more recent. It builds up quicker that way. But it depends on the amount, too. Methamphetamines stay in your system for longer than many other illegal drugs. You haven't asked me what killed him."

"I assumed the drugs."

"Yes, and no. Actual cause of death is myocardial infarction. A heart attack, in your language. There's rupturing to the heart muscle consistent with a spike in blood pressure. An overdose can do that to a person."

The pathologist raised a finger to keep Mo from asking more questions. He turned back to the body and lifted the right hand off the bench.

"See this?" He turned the hand to reveal small reddish-brown marks on the inside of the wrist.

"Bruising," Mo said.

"Finger marks. What look like thumb prints on the insides of the wrist and finger marks on the outside." He lowered the right hand and raised the left one. "Matching marks on both wrists. The orientation suggests they weren't self-inflicted."

There were four distinct bruises on one wrist and three on the other. The pathologist was right: they were arranged in the way he'd described. Mo tried grasping his left wrist with his right hand and observed the pattern of contact.

"Look." Reynolds peeled off his gloves. He reached out and grabbed Mo's wrist. His fingers landed at very different angles, similar to the marks on the body.

Mo shook his grip off and stroked his skin where the pathologist had dug into it with his fingers. "Any other marks?"

"Nothing. I'd imagine the attacker was known to the victim. For him to have been able to grab the wrists just once and leave such neat marks... there was no run-up to this, no struggle. It would have taken the victim by surprise."

"You say him."

Reynolds shook his head. "The attacker had to be strong. But it *could* have been a woman, if she took him by surprise. If he wasn't ready."

"So you think that the attacker grabbed Laurence by the

wrists then shoved something down his throat? He'd have to have let go."

"Maybe there was another reason why the victim didn't struggle."

Mo nodded: he'd seen plenty of crimes where the victim had been too scared to struggle, or where they thought they'd come out of it better if they didn't.

"Are you saying this is definitely a murder?" he asked.

"It's definitely an overdose. And the bruising to the wrists would indicate that someone grabbed him. Of course the clincher will be the swabs from inside his mouth. If it's not just his DNA in there, then you might infer that someone else put the drugs that killed him in his mouth."

"Did you find any residue?"

"Nothing on his skin. Your FSIs might have found evidence of it at the scene, I imagine."

"So he was grabbed by someone with strong fingers, possibly had methamphetamines pushed into his mouth by force, and wasn't a user."

Reynolds flashed his eyes at Mo. "You really do want me to do your job for you, don't you?"

CHAPTER THIRTEEN

"THAT WAS FUN," Mo said.

Zoe was in her Mini in the car park next to Boulton Hall, much closer to the building this time. Connie was in the passenger seat beside her. Mo was on speakerphone.

"What did she say?" Zoe asked.

"Not she. He. Reynolds did the PM."

"Did he say where Adana is?"

"On leave, apparently. Sooner she comes back, the better."

"I got enough of him at the scene. What kind of leave?"

"I wasn't about to pry. So d'you want the verdict, or not?"

"Go on." Zoe glanced at Connie, who stared at the speaker, her expression intent.

"He died of a meth overdose," Mo said. "But he wasn't a habitual user."

"First time taking it?"

"His mouth and lips are bruised. Someone might have forced the drugs into him. There's fingernail damage to the inside of his cheeks. We'll need a DNA check to know if they were self-inflicted or not. And there were finger marks on his wrists which by the pattern, look like someone restrained him."

"Any other marks? Defensive wounds?"

"Nothing. Looks like there was no kind of struggle. If there really was another person involved."

"That's still in doubt?"

"It's not one hundred percent," Mo told her. "But going by the fact that he wasn't a habitual user of methamphetamines, and the bruises, I don't think this was self-inflicted."

"How long before we get the DNA results?"

"That's my next call."

"Good." Zoe eyed Connie. "We're going to have a gentle chat with Becca."

"You think that's wise?" Mo asked. "She'll be fragile."

"Her alleged attacker gets killed two weeks after she reports a rape? We have to at least check her alibi."

"Go easy on her," Mo said.

Connie nodded. "We will." Zoe gave her a reassuring smile.

"Wish us luck," Zoe said, and hung up before Mo had a chance to respond.

The two of them sat in silence for a few moments. A pair of students walked past the car.

"They've let the students out of their rooms," Connie said.

"There's no reason to think they're in danger," Zoe told her. "And it takes time to identify who we need to talk to. Let's just hope Becca is still here."

Connie nodded and opened her door. Zoe climbed out and they strode towards the front entrance of Boulton Hall.

Zoe was relieved to see someone other than Mark Jenks

on duty. This one was an older man, with thinning grey hair and a tired expression. She showed her ID.

"We're here to interview Becca MacGuire. Can you tell me which room she's in?"

"239."

"Thank you." Zoe and Connie exchanged a glance: *that was easy.*

They made their way to room 239 and Zoe knocked on the door. The outer door to the corridor had been unlocked and this one wasn't fully closed. But she wasn't about to enter uninvited.

The door opened and a young woman stared back at them. She seemed larger without the bulky winter coat in the photograph, and her blonde hair had been cut short. The sides were uneven and it looked like she'd done it herself.

"Becca MacGuire?" Zoe asked.

The woman tensed. "Yes." She frowned at Connie then looked back at Zoe.

Zo held up her warrant card. "My name's Detective Inspector Zoe Finch. This is DC Connie Williams. I'm sure you can imagine what we're here about."

Becca's shoulders slumped. "*Him.*"

Zoe sensed Connie shifting her weight, uneasy.

"We're investigating Laurence Thomms's death. I hoped you might have a very brief, very informal chat with us."

"You heard."

"I'm sure you'd rather have this conversation inside," Zoe said. The other doors on the corridor were closed, but she was sure everything she said could be heard by their occupants.

Becca stood back to let them in. She closed the door

behind her and leaned against it. Zoe and Connie stood in the centre of the room looking back at her.

"We've been told that you alleged an assault by Mr Thomms," Zoe said, keeping her voice low.

Becca nodded. She curled her lip as she met Zoe's eye. "He raped me."

"Did you report it to the police?"

Becca's gaze was unwavering. "I told my residential tutor."

"Who is...?"

"Jenson Begg. He told me I had to report it to the warden. Seeing as we're both residents."

"And did you?"

Becca nodded, her hand on the door handle. "I spoke to her ten days ago."

"What did she do in response?" Connie asked.

Becca turned quickly towards the constable, as if she'd forgotten Connie was there. "She said she'd investigate."

"She didn't contact the police?" Zoe asked.

Becca shook her head.

"Why not?"

"Because I asked her not to."

Zoe clenched a fist. She understood how hard it was for rape victims to report their assaults, but wished more of them would. She nodded, slowly. "Why didn't you want the police involved?"

"I slept with a few boys. In fresher's week. Three, to be precise. I knew how that would look in court."

"Juries can be instructed to ignore a victim's sexual history," Connie said.

Becca snorted. "Yeah, right."

"Becca, is there anyone else you talked to about the

alleged rape?" Zoe asked. "Any friends, other members of staff?"

"Alleged. Even you don't believe me." Becca scratched her nose. "No. I couldn't face it. Didn't even tell my mates."

"Were you satisfied with the investigation the warden was carrying out?"

Becca shrugged. "She hasn't reported back to me yet."

"And when are you expecting that?"

"Friday."

"Do you know what kind of investigation she's undertaking?"

"She wouldn't tell me. Said it had to be impartial." Becca almost spat out the last word.

"I'm sorry to ask you about this, Becca, but where were you last night? Were you at the party?"

"No."

"Can anyone else corroborate that?"

"I was working the students' union bar. I guess if people are going to talk about me, they might as well do it out in the open."

"People know about your allegations against Laurence Thomms?"

"*Allegations.* Yes, they know. Everyone knows. That's why he's dead, I imagine."

"You think someone killed him because he raped you?" Connie asked.

Becca turned to her, her face hard. "I think someone killed him because he was a parasite."

CHAPTER FOURTEEN

RHODRI PLACED the mug of coffee – white, three sugars – on his desk and sat back in his chair. He'd found the *Lin's Lens* YouTube channel and discovered a video that had been posted two hours earlier. Ten hours after Lin had found Laurence dead.

Nice kid, he thought as he slurped his coffee. A splash spilled over the rim and onto his jacket. He cursed and brushed it off with the back of his hand.

First, there was the SD card. He took it from the bag on his desk and stuck it into the side of his computer monitor. He flicked to the file manager and checked what was on it. Five video files dating between early this morning and ten days ago. He clicked on the most recent one and sniffed as the video came up onscreen.

Lin stood in front of the camera, a closed door behind her. Her hand was raised as if she was about to knock.

"Not that one," came a voice. Kayla, presumably.

Lin's face fell. She looked back at the door then shrugged. She leaned forward, her eyes bright. She looked like she'd been drinking. "Yeah, let's leave that one. For now." She flashed a smile, then turned to walk along a corridor. The camera followed her, the movement jerky as Kayla walked.

Lin stopped at the last door on the corridor and turned to the lens. She grinned as she knocked on the door.

"Hey party people, welcome to *Lin's Lens*. Tonight is the Valentine's Ball at Boulton Hall and we're expecting plenty of dirt." She leaned in, her eyes wide. "And you can expect us to dish it out for you!"

After a few moments, Lin shrugged. "Aw, shucks! No one in, I guess."

"They're all at the party," said Kayla from behind the camera.

She moved to the next door and pushed it lightly. It gave way.

Lin raised an eyebrow at the camera and walked into the darkened bedroom. Two young men were inside. They didn't look pleased to see her.

"Fuck off, Lin! We don't want to be on your bloody channel."

Lin left the room, giving the men the finger as she walked. Rhodri allowed himself a chuckle. He'd never gone to university, he'd joined Uniform after leaving school, but he knew from his mates the kind of things that went on. It seemed like it was less about studying, and more about taking drugs and copping off with as many people as you could manage.

After a few more door knocks – some fruitful, some not – Lin arrived back at the first door. Rhodri straightened in his chair, his hand on the empty coffee mug.

"Now to see what Boulton Hall's biggest creep is up to,"

Lin said. She pushed the door. "It's open," she added. Watching, Rhodri wrote her words in his notepad.

Lin pushed the door a little further and stopped, hesitating at the threshold to the dark room. Rhodri heard a whisper from behind the camera. Kayla trying to stop her, perhaps.

"Let's see what he's up to, huh?" Lin disappeared into the shadows. Rhodri heard muttering: something about dragging and drugging.

The screen went dark. "Shit," came Lin's voice.

"What?"

"I felt something," Lin said. "Open the fucking door."

There was a rustling sound, more muttering, and then knocking. Rhodri heard a yelp.

"Open the fucking door!" Lin's voice, if it was hers, had changed. The bravado and drunkenness were gone, replaced by panic.

After more rustling and dim movement onscreen, the screen lightened. The camera was pointing downward. Rhodri could make out the lower half of a man's body. He wore black jeans and red socks and his feet were almost hidden by the bed.

The angle changed and the body enlarged as the camera was dropped next to it. All Rhodri could see was a close-up of the man's ankle in its red sock.

He could still hear voices.

"Is he...?" Kayla said.

"Come on." Kayla's voice again. "Let's get out of here. He's taken something."

The ankle shifted: Laurence moving, or one of the girls kicking him?

"He's stone cold." Lin this time. "He's dead, Kay. He's fucking dead."

A shadow crossed the screen. One of the girls moving past the camera, Rhodri supposed. He turned the volume up.

"Did he take something?" said Kayla.

"He's foaming at the mouth. Eurgh, that's gross." Lin's American accent had gone.

"We need to get out of here, Lin. What if they think we did it?"

"They won't think that, dumbass."

A pause.

"They might."

"Oh come on, for fuck's sake."

The camera moved. Someone was lifting it off the floor. Laurence's body flashed past, and then the camera was plunged into a pocket and the screen went almost black.

"She killed him, didn't she?" said Lin.

"She can't have."

"He didn't do this to himself. That's not his style. Come on, let's tell someone. She fucking killed him."

Rhodri heard shuffling noises and a mass of dim redness appeared in the image. A hand. He held his breath as the video ended.

CHAPTER FIFTEEN

"A PARASITE, SHE CALLED HIM." Zoe stood next to Connie's desk, leaning against the wall beside the board.

"Who?" asked Rhodri. He'd just finished telling Zoe and Connie what he had heard on the video.

"Becca MacGuire. The student that Laurence allegedly raped."

"Well I guess it's not surprising," he said.

Connie shook her head. "There's more to it than that."

Zoe nodded. "She told us she wasn't the first."

"He's raped other girls?"

"Women," said Connie. Rhodri shrugged.

"That's what Becca claimed," Zoe said. "She couldn't give us any names, though."

"Typical," Rhodri said. Connie flashed him a look of irritation.

"We need to talk to the warden," Zoe said. "She might have uncovered more information."

"Problem is," Connie added. "She's away on a research trip."

"Where?"

"Iceland. She's taken a group of Geography students to observe the geysers, apparently."

"A student in her hall has died," Zoe said. "Surely that takes priority."

"Her assistant said she's trying to get her on a flight, but there aren't many at this time of year."

Zoe sighed. "Have we at least got a phone number for her?"

"Better than that." Connie grinned. "Her Skype account."

"OK. Let's just hope she's got good wifi out there in the wilderness."

"I've made an appointment to talk to her in the morning," Connie said.

"That's not soon enough."

"Her assistant wasn't exactly helpful."

"What's the time difference?"

"Same time as here."

The door opened and Mo entered. "Any news?"

"Laurence was a multiple rapist," Rhodri said.

"Allegedly," Zoe added.

"Who told you?" Mo asked.

"Becca did," Zoe told him. "She doesn't know the names of any of his other alleged victims, though."

"What do the university authorities say?"

"We're talking to the warden first thing tomorrow. I guess we'll find out then."

"That's off," Rhodri said. "They can't dick us around like that."

Zoe raised her eyebrows at him.

"He's right," Connie said. "I'll call my mate at the uni. She might know if there's been any other allegations."

"Good," replied Zoe. "You do that. Mo, when will we get the DNA results?"

"Not till tomorrow."

"Looks like this investigation's on hold overnight," Zoe said. She lifted her watch. "Blimey, is that the time? Connie, you make that call. Then I want everyone to head home. We can pick this up in the morning."

"What about Becca?" Rhodri said.

"What about her?" Zoe replied.

"Well, if he raped her, she had a motive..."

"She was working the student bar. We can check that out, but she didn't strike me as someone who'd just committed murder."

"Not that easy to tell," Rhodri said. The phone rang on his desk. Zoe waited for him to pick it up, and gave him a fierce stare as he dithered. He grimaced and grabbed it. "Sorry, boss," he whispered.

"Force CID, DC Hughes... yeah... yeah, she's here... no problem." He held out the phone. "Adi Hanson, boss."

"Good." Zoe took the phone from him. "Adi, what you got for me?"

"Good evening to you too," he replied.

"You and I have known each other long enough for..."

"I was joking."

"Ha ha." She wound the phone cord around her finger.

"OK, so we've taken prints from various surfaces in the victim's room. Most of them match the victim himself, but there are others. Two other people, we think."

"Any idea who?"

"One of them's Lin Johnson."

"Makes sense." Her prints could have got there when she found him. Or they might have got there another way. "Where in the room did you find her prints?"

"On the headboard of the bed. Consistent with her stumbling and catching herself on the bedframe.

"Hang on. I'll put you on speaker." Zoe pressed a button. "Can you repeat that?"

"We found Lin's prints on the bed headboard, in a pattern that fits with her stumbling and catching herself on the bed, to stop herself falling."

Zoe turned to Rhodri. "Does that fit with what you saw on the video?"

He shrugged. "It was dark when they entered the room. Think the door closed behind them. There was something that sounded like someone falling over, but I can't be sure."

She nodded. "Adi, did you find her prints anywhere else?"

"No."

"And the other person's prints?"

"On the desk. Where we also found a few trace crystals of methamphetamine."

"That fits with the pathology report," said Mo.

"Does it look like the owner of these prints might have brought the drugs in?" Zoe asked. "Maybe forced Laurence to take them?"

"They're too random to be able to conclude anything like that," Adi replied.

"OK. Send over the files with these prints and we'll see if we can find a match. Have you taken prints off any of the other witnesses? Neighbours?"

"All of them. Kayla didn't touch anything, it seems. And

none of his neighbours ever went in his room, or if they did they were careful not to touch anything."

"He was a recluse," Mo said. "From what we've been told, he didn't have much to do with the other students living on his corridor."

Zoe remembered what Mo had learned from the bursar and the other students: Laurence hadn't used the shared kitchen, and he hadn't taken his meals in the canteen. Now they knew why.

"So either he withdrew into himself because he was ashamed of what he did to Becca and the other possible victims," she said. "Or he suspected the other students were watching him."

"Maybe he did take an overdose," Connie suggested. "If he was living like that..."

"Don't forget the bruising," Mo said. "His wrists. Those injuries were sustained within twenty-four hours of the post-mortem, and that was at lunchtime."

"Eww," said Rhodri. "A post-mortem at lunchtime." He shuddered.

Zoe laughed. "Come on, folks." She noticed Connie placing her phone on the desk. "You tried your mate?"

"No answer, boss. Sorry."

Zoe turned to the board. *What did you do?* Laurence's photo was in the centre. He had dark, straggly hair and wore an Adidas t-shirt. They had to know if he'd raped those girls, and if that was why he'd died.

CHAPTER SIXTEEN

KAYLA SAT in the corner of the Boulton Hall canteen. Dinner had long since finished but she couldn't bring herself to move. The room was empty, one of the dining staff turning out the lights half an hour ago without spotting her.

She still felt fizzy from the drugs she'd taken with Jenson. He'd wanted to have sex, he'd said it would be more stimulating than usual. She wanted none of it. In the last twenty-four hours she'd seen a dead body, lied to the police, and accidentally smoked meth. She just wanted to sleep.

The swing doors to the canteen opened and a dark shape entered. Kayla tensed. It could be Lin, the two of them sometimes met in here after everyone had disappeared to their rooms or the bar. But the shape was too large.

Kayla shrank down, hoping she wouldn't be seen.

"Hello?" the person called. It was a woman with a Yorkshire accent. Not Lin, with her feigned Texan drawl.

Kayla tried to stop breathing. If she kept very, very still, then the woman wouldn't see her. She knew it was dark in this corner of the room, she'd sat here plenty of times.

"I don't want to hurt you."

Kayla stared at the figure heading her way. Why would she say she wasn't going to hurt her, unless she *was* going to hurt her? She considered bolting for the door, but the only way out was between the two rows of tables and that would take her right into the woman's path.

The woman was closer now. Dim light filtered through the blinds at the windows on the opposite side of the room and Kayla could just make out her features. She was heavy-set, with spiky orange-red hair and pale skin. She wore blue jeans, a torn grey t-shirt that might once have been white, and black boots that squeaked on the polished floor.

Kayla huddled further into her chair, causing it to shift beneath her. She winced at the sound of the legs scraping along the floor.

The woman paused a moment, facing Kayla.

Shit.

"Hi." The woman walked towards her, smiling. "I saw you in here on your own. Wanted to check you were OK."

It was too late to pretend she wasn't here. "I'm fine."

"You don't look it."

How do you know how I look? Kayla thought. *You don't even know me.*

The woman pulled out a chair opposite Kayla and sat down. Kayla looked past her, towards the door, unwilling to make eye contact.

"I won't bite."

Kayla shrugged, still not meeting the woman's gaze. She smelled of fried food. Kayla didn't remember seeing her in Boulton Hall. She was older than Kayla, a third-year or a postgrad maybe.

"Please, leave me alone."

"Must be pretty tough, what you saw last night."

Kayla felt her spine tingle. She forced out a breath, slow and steady.

"I'm fine. Please..."

"Especially given who it was."

Kayla's gaze darted to the woman's face. "I don't know what..."

The woman shrugged. "I know what he was like. I know what he did."

"To Becca."

"And the others. To you, maybe?"

Kayla shook her head. "I don't know what you're talking about."

"Look." The woman leaned back and delved into the pocket of her jeans. She brought out a folded-up leaflet. Kayla watched her hands as she unfolded it and smoothed it out on the table between them. Her nails were painted a perfect shade of wine-red, dark against the pale skin of her fingers.

The woman pushed the leaflet across the table. It was for a women's support group.

"I don't need any help."

"I didn't say you needed help. But there are others who might."

"How d'you mean?"

"Every time a woman fails to report an assault, it puts more of us at risk."

Kayla shifted her gaze to look past the woman's shoulder again, towards the doors. She could see people moving around in the hallway beyond. Could she make a run for it?

"You do know that, don't you?" the woman said.

Kayla shrugged. "Like I say, I don't know what you're talking about. And besides, he's dead."

The woman licked her lips, her fingers drumming on the leaflet. "If one of them gets away with it, it tells the others they can, too."

"I'd hardly say he got away with it." Kayla felt heat rise to her face. She wondered what Lin would say if she was here. If she'd film this woman for *Lin's Lens*.

"I'd say he did," the woman said, "if no one knows what he did. Why he died."

Kayla tensed. "You're saying he was killed because of what he did to Becca?"

The woman shrugged. "I'm not saying anything. But if you want to talk, come to us." She pushed the leaflet closer. "I'm Gina."

Kayla stared into the woman's face, trying not to display emotion. She said nothing.

The woman drummed her fingernails on the leaflet twice then stood, leaving it on the table. "Email's on here. Mobile too. Goes straight to me. Gina." She moved away from the table, still facing Kayla. "Call me, if you want to prevent it happening again."

CHAPTER SEVENTEEN

ZOE STOOD in the lift of West Midlands Police HQ at Lloyd House, watching the floor numbers light up. She was alone, no one to interrupt her thoughts or force her into awkward conversation as she rose to the fifth floor.

The corridor outside was quiet except for a woman who stood in front of the doors, waiting for her. Detective Sergeant Layla Kaur of Professional Standards. The woman who'd questioned her in the Ian Osman case.

"DI Finch."

"DS Kaur."

"Thanks for coming so late."

"Better than having to account for myself in the daytime."

"That's what I thought."

"Let's get this done, then. My son's waiting for me."

DS Kaur nodded and turned to lead Zoe along a dark corridor. After some time, they came to an interview room. DS Kaur opened the door and waited for Zoe to pass her.

"Just you and me?" Zoe asked.

"This is an informal interview," the DS said. "You aren't under caution."

Nothing's informal with Professional Standards, Zoe thought, but instead of objecting she nodded. She had nothing to hide, after all.

"Coffee?" DS Kaur went to a side table where a coffee pot sat. Zoe wondered how long it had been sitting there, spoiling.

"OK." She needed all the stimulation she could get, even if it would taste like crap. "Thanks."

DS Kaur passed her a mug and put it on the table.

"You not having one?"

The other woman pulled a face. "No."

Zoe took a sip as she sat down. The coffee was tepid and bitter. She pushed it away. "Don't blame you."

"I recommend bringing your own, next time."

"I'm hoping there won't be a next time."

The DS nodded. "We'll see." She sighed as she sat down opposite Zoe and opened a file. "So. DS Osman."

"DS Osman."

"Start from the beginning, will you DI Finch? When did you first meet him?"

"His children were abducted in October last year. The first time I met him was at his home, with his wife, Alison. The evening after they were taken."

"And was he a suspect at that time?"

"Only in as much as parents always are when you don't have anything else to go on in a child abduction case. We didn't have any concrete reason to suspect him or his wife at that stage."

"Was he cooperative?"

"Not really."

"How so?"

"When we did talk to him, he would answer our questions. I don't believe he ever told me or my team any outright lies. But he was evasive. He kept disappearing without good reason. His colleagues at Kings Norton nick told us he had a habit of doing that."

"Where do you think he was going?"

"I didn't have any idea at that point. I was too focused on finding his children."

"You didn't think he had his kids hidden somewhere, and that was where he was going?"

"It was a consideration. The investigation did lead us to suspect him and his wife of orchestrating the whole thing. We had a link to a cleaning firm. There was a woman working there, using Alison's name and looking a lot like her. We were sufficiently convinced that I arrested her."

"And you arrested DS Osman too, is that true?"

"He was arrested by DI Whaley. I sat in on the interview the two of you conducted with him."

DI Carl Whaley was Zoe's boyfriend. Or at least, he had been.

"So you did," DS Kaur said. "Took him quite a bit of smooth talking with our bosses to persuade them to let you in that interview."

"I was grateful for that." Zoe looked around the blank grey room, wondering if there was a camera somewhere. *Carl, are you watching this?*

"But in the end you released both of them."

"That's not entirely true," Zoe said. "We at Force CID released Alison. We discovered another woman had been using her identity, and had the children. It was Professional Standards who released DS Osman."

She didn't mention the fact that PSD had done a deal with Ian: he was to spy on organised crime and on her own boss, Detective Superintendent David Randle, in return for being allowed back to work. And he was moved to her team in Force CID, so she could report to Carl on his movements.

None of which had turned out well.

The DS leaned back, her hands behind her head. "At what point did you suspect DS Osman might be involved in corrupt activity?"

"He booked a DNA test, but that turned out to be because he wasn't sure if he was the kids' dad. And then there was the work he had done to his house. The contractor was Stuart Reynolds, who worked for organised crime."

"And you reported this to DI Whaley."

"I did."

"You didn't talk to DS Osman about it."

"I did not."

"Sure about that?" DS Kaur cocked her head.

"Positive."

"So how is it that he seems to know you were watching him, and that you believed he was involved with organised crime?"

"I have no idea." Zoe wiped her palms on her jeans. Informal chat, she'd been told. "Am I under investigation?"

DS Kaur shook her head, smiling. "Just an informal chat. If it wasn't for the sensitive nature of this conversation, I'm sure we'd be doing it in a pub somewhere. Or a coffee shop maybe."

Zoe narrowed her eyes. She shouldn't have come here alone. "Is this being recorded?"

"I'm taking notes, as you see. But no, there's no recorder."

Zoe looked up. "No camera?"

"DI Finch, you know I'd be required to tell you if there was a camera in the room. We aren't filming you. No one is watching." She blushed a little. Thinking of her boss no doubt, and Zoe's relationship with him. How much did she know about that? Did she know that Zoe hadn't spoken to Carl for three weeks, since he'd made it clear that he couldn't be sure she wasn't bent?

Zoe sighed. "I said nothing to Ian about my suspicions. I told DI Whaley everything that concerned me. Including any activity Ian was undertaking under the terms of his agreement with DI Whaley."

"We aren't here to talk about that," DS Kaur said, too quickly. "Let's move on to the terror attack in January. You and DS Osman were both at the airport, yes?"

"You've already questioned me about this."

"This isn't a questioning. I just want to get a few things straight in my head. Like why DS Osman was there when it was his day off."

"I did wonder that myself."

"He didn't tell you?"

"He told me he'd had a call from the office. He was out shopping with his wife and kids. I had no reason to doubt him. Until..."

"Until the Forensics team found evidence that he'd planted explosives residue on an innocent victim of the attack."

"I couldn't have put it better myself." Zoe licked her lips. "Can I have a glass of water?"

DS Kaur placed her hands flat on the table. "Not enjoying the coffee?"

Zoe smirked. "I think you know the answer to that."

The other woman stood up. "Fair point. Wait one

minute." She rounded the table and left the room. Zoe heard the lock turn behind her. Locked in, for a friendly chat?

She stood and walked round the table a couple of times. DS Kaur had taken her folder with her, too cautious to leave it in the room with a witness who still wasn't sure if she was being treated as a suspect.

The door banged open and DS Kaur came in carrying two plastic cups of water. She placed one in front of Zoe and drank from the other before crumpling it and dropping it into a bin.

Zoe sipped at her water, hoping she wasn't going to be here much longer. "You wanted to know why Ian was at the airport. I've told you before that apart from what he told me, I don't know. He was assigned to work with me on securing the scene and preserving evidence as best we could while the rescue attempt was underway."

"Did he do that?"

"Neither of us did, really. It became clear that the fire-fighters' work had to take precedence."

"And the two of you weren't together the whole time."

"I tried to board the aeroplane. When I came out, that was when I saw him near the bodies."

"Including the body of Nadeem Sharif." Layla checked her file. "The man he planted evidence on."

"Allegedly. We hadn't identified the bodies at that stage."

"So you didn't see DS Osman leaving any residue on Sharif's body?"

"I didn't." She'd already told them this: DS Kaur, and her boss Detective Superintendent Malcom Rogers.

A phone buzzed in Layla's pocket. She took it out and listened, her eyes on Zoe, silent.

After a few moments she hung up and put the phone

face down on the table. "Thank you, DI Finch. You can go home to your son now."

Zoe looked up at the ceiling, but there was no sign of a camera.

"Good," she said. She downed the rest of the water, tossed the empty cup into the bin, and yanked the door open.

CHAPTER EIGHTEEN

RHODRI STOOD at the student's union bar, a pint of Foster's in his hand. He'd gone home and got changed, knowing that his Top Man suit would make him stand out like a ballerina at a rugby match. Instead he wore a black t-shirt with blue jeans and a black leather jacket. But even in this gear, he knew that he didn't fit.

The girl working behind the bar was young and pretty. She laughed with the punters as she served drinks. It was quiet tonight, and she was the only one behind the bar most of the time. There was an older man who kept appearing and then disappearing through a narrow door at the back. It looked like he was replenishing stocks.

Rhodri considered finding a table and sitting somewhere he'd be less conspicuous, but then he wouldn't be able to watch people. Or talk to the barmaid. Who cared if they rumbled the fact he was a copper? No one would say anything, and he'd be gone once he'd finished this pint.

He downed his pint and banged his glass on the bar to get

the girl's attention. She flashed him a smile and approached, her hand out for the glass.

"Same again?"

"Please." He grabbed a fiver from his wallet. He should drink here more often, he thought. It was bloody cheap.

He sidled along the bar to stand in front of her as she poured his pint. He held his gaze on the glass, not wanting to look like a weirdo.

At last she placed the glass in front of him and he handed over his money.

"Haven't seen you here before," she said as she gave him his change. "You a mature student?"

"Yeah," he said. "Chemistry."

She shrugged. "Enjoy your pint."

"Hang on a minute."

She turned back to him. Two girls were at the other end of the bar, trying to get her attention.

Rhodri flashed her the best smile he could. "You work here every night?"

She folded her arms. "You trying to chat me up?"

"Just making conversation." One of the girls at the other end of the bar cleared her throat loudly. "S'pose I'd better let you do your job," he said, hoping she'd come back afterwards.

She served the girls – two gin and tonics – and then a man who wanted a pint of Guinness, and a girl who looked too young to be drinking. Anywhere else, she'd have been carded. Rhodri cursed himself. *Stop thinking like a copper. You're supposed to be a student.*

He cursed himself for picking Chemistry. He'd dropped it in Year 9 and knew nothing about anything scientific. But he knew Chemistry was Becca's subject. And Laurence's too. It might give him an in.

When the barmaid got closer again, he spoke. "I'm in the same tutor group as Becca MacGuire. I was hoping she'd be here."

The girl's face darkened. "No." She turned away from him, polishing beer taps that already gleamed.

The man he'd seen earlier appeared through his door and grunted something at her. She pointed to the optics at the back of the bar and he squinted at them, then left again.

"He your boss?" Rhodri asked.

She shrugged.

"So, no Becca tonight?"

She gave him a pointed look. "What d'you think?"

"She didn't show up?"

The barmaid ran her tongue over her teeth, then shook her head. "I'm not saying anything."

"I guess she must find things tough, what with what happened to her."

The girl stopped polishing. "She told you."

He nodded, watching her reaction. He wondered how many people knew about Laurence raping Becca. How many people might have wanted to see him pay for it.

"Terrible, what he did to her," Rhodri said.

"That's one way of putting it."

"And him, last night..."

"If you ask me, he got what he deserved."

Rhodri swallowed. "You think so?"

"The guy was a creep. Before all the trouble with Becca, he used to come in here. I had to kick him out more than once."

"What was he doing?"

"Hassling women. What d'you think? I refused to serve him alcohol."

"What did your boss make of that?"

"He's not my boss. He's just... but he was OK with it. No one wanted Laurence in here."

"So if everyone knew about it, why did no one go to the police?"

She leaned back. "Who are you, again?"

"Told you. Mature Chemistry student."

"In Becca's tutorial group."

His mouth felt dry. "Yeah."

"Who's your tutor?"

"Erm... Professor Drake."

"Who?"

"She's new. They changed it last week."

The barmaid placed a fist on the bar. "I suggest you leave."

"I didn't mean to..."

"Look. If you're a mate of Laurence's looking to get some kind of sick revenge out of all this, you can fuck off. And if you're campus security..." She eyed him. "Or a copper. If you're a copper then you need to know Becca was here all night last night, working her shift. There's no way she would have had time to sneak off and kill him. If that's what you're thinking."

"You've got me wrong."

"Whatever." She pointed to his pint. "Why don't you take that to a nice quiet table, and then leave?"

CHAPTER NINETEEN

KAYLA SAT AT HER DESK, trying to focus on the words on the page in front of her. She had an essay to hand in tomorrow, on the role of satire in Jane Austen's novels. She was never going to do it.

She heard the outer door to her corridor open, followed by voices. She pushed the book away, her senses alert.

Ricky was in the corridor, talking to a man. Kayla froze. It was Jenson.

"Is Kayla in?"

"Er, yeah. She's studying though. Told us not to bother her."

"I won't take up much of her time. I wanted to check if she needed any support."

Jenson was a residential tutor for Boulton Hall. He had a flat on the second floor which he lived in when he wasn't at the house in Selly Oak, and he was supposed to provide emotional support to the undergraduates.

No one knew she was seeing him.

She closed her copy of *Emma* and walked to the door.

She opened it a crack and gave Ricky a smile. "It's OK. I'm nearly finished."

Jenson turned and smiled at her. His pupils were dilated. "Kayla. I came to see if you were OK, after what happened last night."

She shrugged. "I'm fine."

"You got a minute? I can give you details of support services?"

Kayla glanced at Ricky. He didn't seem suspicious.

"Yeah. Sure."

She opened the door and Jenson walked in, his gait casual. She closed the door and leaned against it while he took a seat at her desk.

"*Emma*." He picked up the book and leafed through it. "God, I hated this book at school."

She snatched it off him. "I love it. What are you doing here?" She glanced back at the door.

"I told you. I wanted to check on your welfare." His voice was loud; he wanted to be overheard. "I have the details of a helpline for people who've been through traumatic events. And there's the student switchboard, if you need to talk to someone."

"I don't need support." She slumped onto the bed, her voice low. "I just want to forget about it."

He swivelled the chair to face her. "You were in a bit of a state earlier." His voice was low now, his lips barely moving. "I wanted to check you hadn't done anything silly."

"Silly? What kind of silly are you thinking?"

He shrugged. "Dunno." He blinked at her a few times. She turned the book in her hand. Jenson had this way of looking at her that made her feel soft inside. But she needed to study.

He slid off the chair and took a seat next to her on the bed, their thighs touching. "I was worried about you."

"Thanks." She pushed a lock of hair out of her eyes. "I'm fine."

He put a hand on her knee. "If you need to talk to someone, you come to me, OK? Not the police. Not the warden."

"I don't understand what you think I'm going to go to the warden about."

"You found a guy dead of an overdose. And not just any guy. I guess you'll have things you want to tell people." He moved his hand up her thigh, making her skin tingle. "I'm here for you Kayla, if you need someone to talk to."

"This morning you thought the answer was to give me drugs."

His hand halted on her leg. "That's not quite true, is it sweetie?"

She turned her head to look at him. His eyes were dark and his lashes long. He had pale skin with a smattering of freckles on his nose. She had an urge to kiss them.

"You grabbed that pipe off me," he said. "You thought it was hash."

"I won't make that mistake again."

"No."

"I didn't know you smoked meth."

He shrugged. "I don't. Not really."

"Your pupils are dilated."

He took her chin in his hand. "That's because I'm with you."

She allowed herself a smile as he kissed her. He brushed his lips over hers then worked down her chin and onto her neck. She felt herself shudder as he covered her skin with soft kisses.

"That's nice," she said.

"Mmm."

"Helps me relax."

His head came up. "That's the point. It's my job to look after the undergraduates. And this is how I'm going to look after you."

CHAPTER TWENTY

ZOE SAT in front of the TV, gazing absentmindedly at it. Nicholas was watching some documentary about Turkey. She tried to focus on it, to summon up some interest, but it was beyond her.

"Can we turn this off?" she asked.

"I'm watching it."

"I just want to watch something easy."

"It's only got another quarter of an hour."

She sighed. "Fine. I'm putting the kettle on. Want one?"

"Tea, please."

She prised the cat off her lap and shifted it to her shoulder. Yoda, their six-month-old silver tabby, meowed into her ear. She liked being carried around like this, riding on shoulders like a parrot. It gave her a good vantage point to steal food when Zoe tried to put it into her mouth.

She filled the kettle then grabbed her espresso pot. She filled the base with water and scooped yesterday's grounds out of the filter. Yoda shifted around on her shoulder as she moved, constantly adjusting her weight and keeping her balance.

While the pot bubbled on the hob, Zoe opened the fridge and grabbed a pack of ham. The cat meowed at her and she held up a slice for her to grab. Yoda stuck out her head and seized it, swallowing it instantly.

Zoe stroked the cat as it nuzzled her neck. "You're too greedy. You're going to be a fatty."

As the coffee pot finished its work, the doorbell rang. The cat stiffened on Zoe's shoulder and she scooped her up and lowered her to the ground.

"Go and see who it is," she muttered as the cat scooted out of the door.

Zoe poured Nicholas's tea and her own coffee and went back to the living room, expecting to find Nicholas's boyfriend Zaf. There had been tension between the two of them lately, but they seemed to be working through it. She was glad: Zaf was a great kid, and he was also Connie's little brother.

"Oh," she said as she saw the man standing with Nicholas in the doorway. "What brings you here?"

Inspector Jim McManus turned to her, a hand on his son's shoulder. "I wanted to talk to Nicholas about the trip to London at the weekend."

Zoe wrinkled her nose. "Shula and Geordie going too?"

"Of course."

She turned to Nicholas. "You definitely want to go?"

"Mum, don't fret. It'll be fine."

She knew that Nicholas didn't get on well with his half-brother Geordie. It was hardly surprising, given Geordie and his mum had known nothing about Nicholas until Geordie was thirteen and Nicholas eleven. When she'd sent Nicholas to stay with his dad last October, he'd complained that Geordie had punched him.

"As long as you're sure."

"Course I'm sure. Dad's bought tickets for Cirque du Soleil."

Zoe handed Nicholas his mug. "Cirque du Soleil?"

"It'll be fine," Jim said. "He'll enjoy it."

Zoe eyed Nicholas. She hadn't known he was interested in that kind of thing, but it didn't hurt to try something new.

"Good." She dredged up a smile. "You'll enjoy it. Maybe I'll get a chance to take you somewhere nice in the summer, before you go off to uni."

Nicholas almost spat out his tea. "Mum, you've never been on holiday in your life. You're not about to start now."

"You never know. If Jim can do it..."

"It's not a competition, Zoe," Jim said, his voice low.

"I never said it was." *And besides, you lost years ago*, she thought.

She yawned. "OK. I'm going to bed. Early start tomorrow. Big case." She wasn't about to tell Jim she was tired because of her grilling in Lloyd House.

"Not all that big," Jim said. "Not compared to the last one."

"OK, small case. But the victim's parents won't be thinking that when they arrive from Leeds tomorrow."

Jim grunted. Zoe was reluctant to say more. She didn't like thinking about a first-year student dead of a drugs overdose when her son was heading off to university in less than six months.

"Let your dad out when he's done, will you?" she told Nicholas.

"No, I thought I'd imprison him here and feed him to Yoda." Nicholas looked down at the cat who mewed up at him.

"Whatever. See you in the morning."

CHAPTER TWENTY-ONE

Zoe stood in the lobby of the university Chemistry department, watching as staff hurried past and students ambled.

This would be Nicholas in eight months' time, she told herself. University was a privilege she hadn't enjoyed: with an alcoholic mum and a dad who struggled to hold the family together, there was no way she'd have buggered off to study for three years. Police college had been enough.

There was no sign of a reception desk or anywhere she could ask for the right person to speak to. She decided to head upstairs, past the lecture halls and towards where she hoped the offices might be.

At the top of the stairs she pushed through a set of double doors and came to an area flanked by low chairs. A couple of students sat in them, laptops on knees: studying, or checking social media, perhaps. There was a wall of glass on the far side with what looked like a reception desk behind it.

Zoe waited for the young woman behind the partition to finish her call, then held her ID up to the glass.

"I hope someone here can help me," she said.

The woman looked worried. "What's happened? Did someone call 999?"

"Nothing like that. I'm here about the death of Laurence Thomms, on Sunday night. Early hours of yesterday morning."

"Sad business."

"Did he have a tutor?"

"All undergraduates have a tutor. Let me look for you."

The woman turned to her computer screen and frowned into it. "Here. He's with Professor Beauman. Was. Sorry."

"Is Professor Beauman available?"

"Hang on..." the woman raised a finger to stop Zoe going anywhere, not that she was planning to. "She's in a lecture right now." She looked up at Zoe. "You can sit in, if you want. Grab her at the end."

"I'd rather wait."

"She has a habit of sneaking out for a cigarette after lectures. I'd sit in, if I were you."

"OK. Where will I find her?"

"Lecture theatre seven. It's downstairs, second door on the left as you come to the bottom of the stairs."

"Thanks." Zoe turned for the stairs.

"Hang on."

Zoe turned back. "Yes?"

"She's already started. You don't want to go in that door. Come with me."

The woman left the reception area via a door at the end. "I'll show you how to sneak in at the back. It's on this level."

Zoe followed her along corridors, scanning the walls as she did so. They were lined with Chemistry-related posters: graphical representations of chemical reactions, a poster advertising graduate job opportunities, a periodic table or two. Eventually the woman stopped at a door.

She put her fingertips on the door's surface. "Be careful with this. It bangs. Just take a seat at the back and then you can go down and grab her when she's finished."

Zoe nodded thanks and opened the door. She was at the top of a steep bank of seats, at the back of a lecture theatre. Below her, lit by two spotlights, was a woman in her forties who paced the area at the front of the room as she talked animatedly. Between her and Zoe were rows of students, bent over notepads or laptops or whispering to each other.

The door banged behind Zoe and two girls looked round.

"Sorry," she muttered, and took a seat. The woman at the front, Professor Beauman, paused and looked upwards, a hand shading her eyes.

"There's an awful lot of you hiding out at the back," she said.

Muttering began amongst the students. No one moved.

"Not much I can do about it, I suppose. But this isn't school, you know."

The professor went back to her lecture. She was using a laptop on a lectern to one side, displaying images that made no sense to Zoe. Zoe watched, more interested in the woman's energy and enthusiasm than in her subject matter. The students around her seemed less impressed. Two had started kissing and one was asleep.

At last the lecture ended and the students rose with an urgency that surprised Zoe. She waited as they crowded past her, voices buzzing.

Professor Beauman was packing away her notes, unplugging the laptop. She patted her jacket pocket, looking for her cigarettes no doubt.

Zoe hurried down the steps, anxious not to let her get away. When she was three-quarters of the way there, she called the woman's name.

The professor turned, startled. "Yes?"

"I wonder if I could talk to you."

"You've got a follow-up question? Happy to help." Professor Beauman leaned against the large desk and smiled at Zoe.

"Sorry, it's not about that." Zoe showed the woman her ID. "DI Finch, I'm here about Laurence Thomms."

Professor Beaumont's face darkened. "Poor kid. Bloody tragedy."

Zoe nodded. "You were his tutor."

"Yes." She bristled.

"I'd like to ask you about him. Who he was friends with, what his habits were."

"He was a first year. I don't know much."

"No?"

"He'd been one of my students for a little more than a term, Detective. I had hardly any contact with him."

"Surely you had tutorials?"

"My postgrads take some of those. And he didn't always turn up."

"That didn't worry you?"

"If I worried about every student who doesn't show up for a few tutorials, I'd have no time to do my job."

"Other students have told me he was a recluse. I'm trying to find out why."

The professor sighed. "Come to my office."

They left the room and went back towards the reception area. Before they got there, though, Professor Beauman opened a door and passed through it, with Zoe following half a step behind.

The professor had a large office with a view of Old Joe, the university clock tower. In one corner was a set of low chairs and a coffee table, and near the window was a desk piled with paperwork. Shelves lined the walls: books, ornaments and what looked like models of molecules.

The professor sat behind her desk and motioned for Zoe to sit in one of the two chairs opposite. "I'll tell you what I can, but it's not much."

"Please."

"Laurence Thomms was a quiet student. He barely spoke in tutorials, didn't show up for group work, and as far as I could tell he didn't seem to have any friends."

"Was he friendly with Becca MacGuire?"

The professor shook her head. "No idea. She's not one of mine."

"Sorry?"

"I mean, she isn't in my tutor group. I do know the name though. High achiever. Nothing like Laurence."

"You don't know if Becca and Laurence had any kind of relationship?"

"Sorry. I don't keep tabs on that kind of thing." She flicked her wrist to check her watch. "I've got a faculty meeting in five minutes, so..."

"One more question."

"OK."

"Would anyone here have access to the equipment or materials needed to make methamphetamine?"

"Crystal meth?" Beauman leaned across the desk. "Bit of a cliché, isn't it?"

"You haven't answered my question."

"The constituent chemicals used to manufacture crystal meth would be stocked by this department, yes. But that doesn't mean any students or staff had access without authorisation. We're very careful to control access to any substances we think people might want to steal. I'm sure you are aware that Ephedrine, for example, is a controlled substance."

"So you can account for all of your supplies?"

"Of course we can. I'll get the faculty administrator to confirm it with you, if you want. If any of our students are taking meth, it's going to be manufactured in someone's bedroom in Selly Oak, not on our campus."

CHAPTER TWENTY-TWO

CONNIE YAWNED as she entered the team room.

"Late night?" Rhodri asked. She shook her head.

"Early morning. My mum's got herself a dog and the bugger keeps waking me up."

"He doesn't wake your mum up?" Zoe asked.

"He knows it's easier to wake me up." She dumped her bag on her desk. "Ignore me. What's the plan today?"

Zoe was at the board, her eyes roaming across it. They had photos of Laurence pinned up: one from his Facebook profile, several others from the crime scene. To one side were Lin and Kayla. Becca's photo was alone at the bottom of the board.

"What subjects were they all studying?" she asked.

"Laurence was doing Chemistry," Connie said. "Becca too."

"I know those ones. I was there this morning." Zoe wrote *Chemistry* under Laurence and Becca's names. "What about the other two?"

Connie picked up her notebook. "Kayla's studying..."

"English," Rhodri interrupted. "And Lin's doing Medicine."

Zoe wrote the subjects on the board. "Laurence and Becca could have known each other through their course. But they weren't in the same tutor group."

"They all lived in Boulton Hall," Connie said.

"All first years," Zoe said.

"Aren't they all, in those halls of residence?" Connie asked.

"Most of them," Mo replied. "But there's at least one postgrad. Jenson Begg, their residential tutor."

"You and I are going to see him today," Zoe told him. She wrote his name on the board.

"I checked out Becca's alibi," Rhodri said.

Zoe turned to him. "You did?"

"I went to the university bar. Spoke to one of her colleagues. She was working all night Sunday night."

"Did you find out what time they closed?"

"Er..." Rhodri blushed. "Sorry."

"There was a party going on," Connie said. "Surely the bar would have been open till that was over."

"We'll need to check," Zoe said.

"The other barmaid seemed pretty certain Becca didn't do it," Rhodri muttered.

"It's looking like she couldn't have," Zoe agreed. "But let's just check what time the bar closed, yes?"

"Sure thing."

"Laurence's tutor, in the Chemistry department," Zoe said. "She didn't know him from Adam."

"No?" Mo asked.

"He was one of twenty first-years she had responsibility for. She clearly hadn't bothered to get to know him, or any of the rest of them, I imagine. I tried to find out from her what he was like, if he'd been attending lectures. Who his friends were on his course. She knew nothing."

"Hopefully his residential tutor will know more," Mo said.

"Let's hope so. I asked if anyone might have stolen the ingredients for the drugs from her department. She was insistent they wouldn't have."

"They'll keep some of them under lock and key," Mo said. "The controlled substances."

Zoe nodded. "We still need to find out where the drugs came from. Rhodri, can you speak to Adi and find out if they're able to get a fit on that from the residue they found. And see if he's anywhere with those DNA results while you're at it."

"Sure thing, boss."

"Good. Mo, let's head over to Boulton Hall. I want to talk to that residential tutor, see what he can tell us."

"You've got your Skype call with the warden in ten minutes," Connie said.

Zoe eyed her watch. "OK."

"Actually, eight minutes."

"Where?" she said.

"I've emailed the details to you. Just click the link, and it'll hook you up."

"Thanks. Mo, let's go into my office."

"What d'you want me doing while you're interviewing?" Connie asked.

"Try to get your mate in university admin again."

"I already did. There was one other complaint made about Laurence, but it was dropped."

"You get a name?"

"She couldn't give it me. Sorry, boss. Said it was more than her job was worth."

"You think it's someone we need to worry about?"

"I just think she was thinking of the fact it was dropped. The girl's anonymity would need to be protected..."

"I still want to know how many girls he might have assaulted. If he did, of course. Hopefully the warden will be able to shed some light."

"So...?" Connie asked.

"Check social media. Becca's accounts, and Laurence's. Any mention of either of them. Find out who their friends were, are. Someone other than Becca might have wanted revenge. See if anyone else knew."

"Right, boss."

CHAPTER TWENTY-THREE

ZOE CLICKED the link in Connie's email to find the warden already online and waiting for her. She was a middle-aged woman with a double chin and short blonde hair, wearing a pink shirt and matching lipstick. She stared into the camera, looking uneasy.

"Doctor Edwards," Zoe said, checking her notes. "My name's Detective Inspector Finch and this is Detective Sergeant Uddin. Thanks for taking the time to talk to us."

"I've been trying to get a flight back, but they're all booked. I can't quite believe..." The warden had a soft Welsh accent. Zoe couldn't tell if it was this, or genuine emotion, that made her sound concerned.

"We need to talk to you about the investigation you were conducting into rape allegations made against Laurence Thomms by Becca MacGuire."

The warden paled. "The boy's just died..."

"This might be relevant."

"You think Becca killed him?"

"We don't. But it might be related."

"We kept the whole thing highly confidential. I don't believe many of the other students knew about it."

"Many of them?" If just one person knew a secret as explosive as this in a closed community like a hall of residence, it wouldn't be long before everyone knew.

"Well, there was Jenson, of course. Becca's residential tutor. He was the person she reported it to. And then I imagine she told one or two of her friends. She needed someone to lean on, Detective."

"I can understand that. So when did she report it?"

"It was at the beginning of this month I was told about it."

"And Jenson?"

"She told him the day before he told me. Let me see." The warden leaned back and reached behind her. She returned with a phone in her hand. "Damn. It's not in here. I'll have to ask my secretary for the exact dates. But it was ten, eleven days ago, I think. Around the fifth."

"That was when Jenson told you?"

"Yes."

"And what did you do?"

"I opened an investigation. Spoke to Becca, and Laurence, and a few other students who lived in the rooms around the one where the alleged rape took place. I was circumspect, Inspector. Apart from the ones Becca had spoken to, the students would not have known who was involved."

"So she said he raped her in Boulton Hall?"

"In one of the communal lounges on floor three."

"But Becca lives on the second floor."

"Yes. And Laurence on the fourth floor. One of the

things I was trying to ascertain was why they were both on the third floor."

"Did you find out?"

"Becca has a friend in that corridor. She'd gone to the kitchen to get a coffee for the two of them. She said Laurence was there, waiting for her."

Mo was out of sight of the camera, next to Zoe. She felt his weight shift.

"Did any of the neighbouring students hear anything?" Zoe asked.

"One of them said he heard shouting. That's all."

"And was there any physical evidence? Did you ask a medical professional to examine Becca, or take samples?"

"It was six days before she told her tutor. It would have been too late for that."

Zoe balled her fist on the desk. "Doctor Edwards, why didn't you call the police?"

"Becca asked us not to."

"Did she give a reason why not?"

"She didn't want to go to court. Didn't think she'd be believed. She was insistent."

That fitted with what Becca had said.

"So what did your investigation find?"

"The evidence was inconclusive."

I bet it was, Zoe thought. How could a university lecturer possibly hope to investigate a serious crime like a rape?

Mo put a hand on her arm. She frowned at him. He shook his head.

She looked into the camera. When Doctor Edwards arrived in Birmingham, they would need to speak again. "Is there anything else you want to tell me?"

"Laurence came to me a week ago. He said he was being victimised."

"In what way?"

"Other students were calling him names. Leaving things under his door. Spitting on him."

"Did he have any idea why?" Zoe asked.

"I imagine word got out about the alleged rape."

I bet it did, Zoe thought. "And what did you say to him, when he told you this?"

"I told him not to worry. That it would blow over."

Zoe plunged her hands under her thighs and pushed down on them with all her weight, to stop herself from punching the screen. "Again, you didn't report anything to the police?"

"DI Finch, I know this looks bad. But you must consider that you are viewing events with the benefit of hindsight."

The woman was right, Zoe knew. But the refusal to take responsibility irritated her.

"Doctor, can you answer a question for me?"

"Of course."

"Have Laurence's parents come to the university yet? Because I know they've been to the morgue to visit his body."

"I have an appointment with them tomorrow. If I manage to get a flight."

"Well you tell them about the benefit of hindsight from me, won't you? I'm sure that will be very reassuring."

CHAPTER TWENTY-FOUR

DETECTIVE SERGEANT IAN OSMAN sat on the low chair he'd been directed to, his hands clasped between his knees. A woman sat at a desk opposite, occasionally glancing up at him. The first time, she gave him a tight smile.

The door next to him opened and DI Carl Whaley emerged.

"Detective Sergeant Osman. Come in, will you."

"I'm waiting for my solicitor."

Carl checked his watch. "Will he be long?"

"I've had a text. Five minutes."

"Five minutes it is, then."

DI Whaley disappeared through the door. Four minutes later a woman in her early forties hurried up the nearby stairs, panting.

"I'm so sorry, Sergeant Osman. I got stuck in traffic."

"Where's Edward Startshaw?"

She paused for breath. "My name's Jane Summer." She handed him a card: *Jane Summer. Criminal law specialist.* "Edward called me. Asked me to take on your case."

"Nobody told me."

She shrugged. "For the best, he said. His caseload is overwhelmed."

For the best. It probably was. Edward Startshaw was Trevor Hamm's lawyer. Hamm liked to use him as his eyes and ears in legal cases that touched him. And he was good at his job. But Ian knew that had Startshaw represented him, it would indicate suspicion by association.

He stood up, hand outstretched. "You can call me Ian."

She took it. "And you can call me Jane."

Her handshake was firm. "They're waiting for us," Ian said.

"Good." She nodded at the woman behind the desk, who stood up and knocked on the door. DI Whaley re-remerged.

"About time."

Jane had caught her breath by now. She gave DI Whaley a level stare. "Jane Summer. You are?"

"Detective Inspector Whaley. My colleague is DS Kaur. What kept you?"

"I got stuck in traffic. You haven't been waiting long."

DI Whaley said nothing, but instead looked at Ian. "Come on in then."

Ian wiped his hands together and followed the DI in, his lawyer walking behind him.

The room was similar to the one Ian had been questioned in last time: small, blank, anonymous. It was nicer than the rooms he was accustomed to questioning suspects in.

"Take a seat, DS Osman. Ms Summer."

The two of them sat at the table. DS Kaur was already there, waiting. She pursed her lips as she sat down.

"So," DI Whaley said. "You've already given evidence

about the residue you planted on Nadeem Sharif at Birmingham airport on the twenty-fifth of January."

"My client has been most cooperative," Jane said.

DI Whaley eyed her. "Indeed. And you've told us that you were instructed to plant that evidence by Trevor Hamm, who Force CID are still looking for."

"Hamm told me I had to incriminate a random individual from the plane. Preferably someone Asian. Preferably a man."

DI Whaley leaned back. "Did he?"

Ian met his gaze. "He did. And you told me that any information I provided to help you convict organised crime would be favourable to my case."

"We did," Whaley said. "There will have to be a formal hearing, once we've completed our investigation. You'll be dismissed from the police service, of course, but the nature of any criminal charges against you is still to be determined."

"I understand." Ian's chest felt tight. He hadn't told Alison that he was going to be sacked. All she knew was that he'd been suspended.

"But I don't believe you," DI Whaley said.

Ian gripped his leg under the table. "Why not?"

Jane put a hand in front of his, on the table. *Calm down. Don't let him rile you.*

DS Kaur opened a file and brought out a photo of a green Ford Focus. "Is this your car?"

"It is."

"The car you used to drive to Stuart Reynold's industrial unit on the twenty-eighth of October, when Force CID were investigating the disappearance of your children. And again on the tenth of December."

Ian felt the hairs on his neck bristle. "Yes."

"You visited Reynolds because he was your contact in the organised crime gang you were working for."

"He passed me messages from Hamm, and he did renovation work on my house."

"Which was how you were paid for services rendered."

"Yes."

DI Whaley leaned forward. "So how come we have no evidence of you visiting Reynolds, or indeed Hamm, after that date?"

"Maybe you weren't following me."

"We were, DS Osman. And you took great care not to go anywhere or meet anyone from the organised crime gang."

Ian shrugged.

"So how did Hamm get these instructions to you? The ones about planting evidence on a body at the airport?"

"By phone."

"See, that's not right either, is it?"

"Hamm called me."

"Himself?"

"Why not?"

Whaley wrinkled his nose. "One thing we do know about Trevor Hamm is that he lets his subordinates do that kind of thing. And he avoids using the phone."

"He must have used a burner phone."

Whaley shook his head. "Could you maybe have got those instructions from someone else?"

"I didn't get them from Reynolds, if that's what you're—"

"I'm not talking about Reynolds."

Ian pulled at his collar. He was sweating. "I'm entitled to a glass of water."

"So you are." DI Whaley turned to DS Kaur. "Can you do the honours, please?"

Her shoulders slumped, but she stood up and left the room.

Whaley watched Ian while they waited. Ian stared back at him, trying not to blink. He felt light-headed.

DS Kaur reappeared with a plastic cup of water. She placed it in front of Ian and he gulped it down.

"Better?" Whaley asked.

"Thank you."

"So. You didn't get your instructions direct from Hamm, and you didn't get them from Reynolds. We have no evidence of you visiting anyone in Hamm's organisation close to the time of the attacks. So who did tell you to plant this evidence?"

Jane leaned forward. "I don't think this is re—"

Whaley raised a hand. "If DS Osman helps us, we can tell the CPS." He turned his gaze on Ian. "You know we're after someone bigger than you, Ian. And I'm not talking about Trevor Hamm. Help us, and it'll work in your favour."

"I don't know what you're talking about."

Ian knew damn well what, and who, they were talking about. Detective Superintendent David Randle. But if Whaley didn't have enough evidence to name him, Ian wasn't about to.

Whaley sighed. "You're being stupid, Ian."

"I'm telling the truth."

"No. You're trying to protect someone. How are you more scared of him than you are of Trevor Hamm?"

Ian turned to his solicitor. "I don't have to say anything, do I?"

"You don't," she confirmed.

He cleared his throat and turned back to DI Whaley.

"No comment."

CHAPTER TWENTY-FIVE

RHODRI SHUFFLED in his chair as he waited for Adi Hanson to pick up the phone. He'd been up late last night, he had a new girlfriend and they'd been snuggled up – and the rest – in front of Netflix till one am. The thought of it made him glow inside and yawn simultaneously.

"Adi Hanson."

Rhodri straightened in his chair and rubbed his eyes. "Adi, it's DC Hughes."

"Rhodri. You'll be wanting a progress report on the substance that killed Laurence Thomms."

"Couldn't have put it better myself, mate."

Adi laughed. "I'm not as slow as some people like to think."

Rhodri frowned; *slow* wasn't a word he'd have used to describe Adi.

"OK," Adi said. "So they've analysed the residue we found on Laurence's lips, as well as the contents of his stomach."

Rhodri put his hand to his own stomach, which gurgled. He hadn't eaten breakfast, and now he was glad of it.

"The stuff he was given was muck," Adi said.

"Muck?"

"Dreadful stuff. If the drugs themselves hadn't killed him, the crap they mixed in with it would."

"Like what?"

Adi winced. "Chalk. A bit of washing powder. They used flu tablets as a base, then added all sorts of crap to them." He pulled in a breath. "Jesus, Rhod. These bastards are going to kill the kids they push this stuff on with household cleaners, not with actual drugs."

Rhodri nodded. "So does it help us identify where the ingredients came from?"

"I'm pretty sure they didn't come from the university Chemistry labs, if that's what you've been thinking. This isn't *Breaking Bad.*"

Rhodri stifled a chuckle. He'd watched a couple of episodes in the hope it might teach him something about how Laurence had died. Instead it had just made him depressed.

"So we don't need to search the Chemistry department for missing supplies?" he asked.

"You don't. These are low-grade street drugs. Whoever forced them on Laurence got them from a shabby dealer somewhere. I suggest you talk to the Drugs team."

"I will." Rhodri had a mate in that squad: Detective Constable Arjun Metha.

"Good."

"What about the DNA results?" Rhodri asked. "You know who it was scratched the inside of his mouth yet?"

"That won't be with us for a few hours at least. You know what it's like with DNA."

"Yeah. OK, thanks, Adi."

He hung up.

Connie looked up from her screen. "News?"

"Yeah. The crystal meth that killed Laurence was impure. Very impure. Adi says it came from the street, not from the Chemistry lab."

"No surprise there."

"No. Which means we've got to talk to the Drugs team before we can go any further."

"Surely we need to start at the other end."

"How d'you mean?"

"Well, instead of how they got the drugs: why they got them. Who'd have motive to kill him?"

"Becca. Half a dozen other women, by the sounds of it."

She nodded. "Any of them could've bought street drugs."

"We aren't going to know till we get that DNA result," Rhodri said.

Connie shook her head. "You think the boss is going to authorise getting DNA swabs from every student in the place?"

"Maybe every student living in Boulton Hall."

"Maybe. But I think we need to work out who else had a reason to kill him. Find out which other women he attacked."

"Any clues on social media?"

"Would you believe Laurence didn't have a single social media account? No Twitter, no WhatsApp, no Snapchat."

"Facebook?"

She wrinkled her nose. "The guy was nineteen. No he wasn't on Facebook. And yes, I did check."

"Maybe under a false name."

"I can't find anything on his laptop, or his phone. So I'm

going to check Becca's public social media. Then I'll move on to Kayla and Lin. You never know."

"Public? That's not like you." Connie had a reputation for breaking into suspects' private social media accounts.

She frowned. "Feels too intrusive, right now."

"The boss has been warning you off."

"No. But I know what the sarge would say." Connie dipped her head back down to focus on her screen.

Rhodri watched her for a few moments, then picked up the phone to call Arjun. All they had was illegal drugs in Laurence's system, and a rape allegation. Maybe he wasn't even murdered, Rhodri thought. Maybe they were all wasting their time.

CHAPTER TWENTY-SIX

Mo and Zoe stood outside Boulton Hall. Mo was still bristling from the call with the warden. The woman wasn't taking this case as seriously as she should.

"Ready?" he said.

"You bet," Zoe replied. She yanked open the door, eyes on the security office. Wondering if Jenks was on duty, no doubt.

The security office was empty. They passed it, heading for the apartment on the second floor allocated to Jenson Begg. Zoe's phone rang.

"Shit," she muttered. She shoved it to her ear.

"I'm about to go into an interview," she said. Mo watched her, realising she was as riled up as he was.

Her expression dropped. "Sheila. Thanks." She put a hand over the phone. "Sheila Griffin," she whispered to him.

DS Sheila Griffin was an Organised Crime detective. She was working with them on Magpie.

Mo raised his eyebrows: *news?* Zoe shrugged and listened.

She nodded her head. "Uh-huh... OK... that's good. I'll be right there." She closed her eyes briefly as she hung up.

"Sorry, mate. They've got a lead on the Magpie case. I need to go."

"That's great news."

"I don't like doing this without you, but we can't leave Jenson Begg too long."

"It's alright, Zo. I'll take this one. Just keep me posted, yeah?"

"I will." Zoe and Mo had been working on the bombing case together since he'd rejoined her team a few weeks ago. He didn't want to miss out.

Zoe placed a hand on his arm. "Good luck. Hopefully he'll shine some light on what Laurence Thomms was really up to."

Mo flashed his eyes in response: *hope so.*

Zoe headed outside, not pausing to suggest how Mo might get back to the office. They were only a mile away. He could walk.

He took a breath and flexed his shoulders. He needed to push all thoughts of what Zoe was doing from his mind and focus on this interview. He made for Jenson's apartment, ignoring the student staring at him as he passed.

He knocked on the door to the apartment.

Silence.

Damn. He checked his watch: ten thirty-six. The man would be in class. Or whatever it was postgrads did.

The door flew open. "Kayla?... Oh."

Mo held up his warrant card. "Jenson Begg?"

"Er, yeah." The man wrinkled his nose. He was medium height, thin, with hair that looked like he'd just got out of bed. He wore nothing but a pair of boxer shorts. "That's me."

"I need to ask you a few questions about Laurence Thomms."

The man glanced back into the flat. "Yeah. Course." He stood back and let Mo pass.

Inside was a large room with high windows overlooking a football pitch. To say the place was untidy would be an understatement. It looked like no one had cleaned up for at least a year.

Jenson pushed in front of Mo, picking up discarded clothes and hurling them into a corner. "Sorry, it's a bit of a mess. Here." He grabbed a pile of books off a low, institutional chair, and pointed to the vacated space. "Take a seat."

"Thanks." Mo lowered himself into the chair. The room smelled of stale milk. He breathed through his mouth, eyeing the window. "Can you open a window, maybe?"

"OK. I'll need to get dressed, though."

"Be my guest."

Jenson stared at Mo for a moment, then forced the window open with a hard push and disappeared through a door. A bedroom, Mo assumed. He could only imagine the state that would be in.

This room was littered with discarded takeaway cartons, food wrappers, clothes and Chemistry books. Another Chemistry student, he thought. Like Laurence and Becca.

He bent to peer under the desk in the opposite corner and pushed a dirty t-shirt aside with his foot to see what was hiding in amongst the mess. There was no evidence of drug-taking.

Jenson reemerged wearing a crumpled pair of jeans and a blue t-shirt with a Nike logo. "Sad news," he said.

Mo nodded. "Did you know Laurence well?"

"I spoke to him a few times. But he... he kept himself to himself."

So we've been told, Mo thought. "Do you know why?"

"I can hazard a guess."

"What kind of guess?"

"You'll know about the allegations Becca MacGuire made against him. We – that's me and Doctor Edwards, the warden – we tried to keep it confidential. But you know what these places are like."

"What *are* they like?"

"It's a closed community. Secrets don't stay that way for long."

"So the rest of the students knew about the allegations?"

"Reckon so."

"You know that for sure, or are you assuming?"

A flush rose up Jenson's neck. "One or two of the girls told me they knew about it. They were worried."

"Which girls?"

A frown. "Can't remember. I tried to reassure them. The warden was investigating. If she'd upheld Becca's complaint, he'd have been kicked out of the hall."

"And the university?"

"That too, probably. Not good for your record, raping a fellow student."

"Did you think of going to the police?"

"Becca made it clear she didn't want me to." A pause. "I respected her wishes."

"If it had gone far enough for Laurence to get thrown out of Boulton Hall and off his course, surely the police should have been involved. We're talking about an alleged crime here."

Jenson shrugged. "The rule with the residential tutors is

confidentiality. If Becca told me not to tell the police, that isn't my place."

"But you did tell the warden."

"She said that was OK."

Mo nodded. "Did the warden talk to you about her investigation?"

"Nah. Once I'd passed it to her, that was it."

"But did you talk to Becca? Provide support?"

"I tried. She wasn't too keen on the idea."

"She came to you to report the rape in the first place, but then she didn't want your support?"

Jenson tugged at his t-shirt. He shrugged. "Who knows what makes women act the way they do." He grinned at Mo, who didn't return the smile.

Mo wondered what kind of relationship this young man had with Becca. He was good-looking, in a slightly battered kind of way, and Mo could imagine the female students being attracted to him. He wondered whether Jenson took advantage of that.

"How well did you – do you – know Becca?"

Another shrug. "She's one of my students. I invited her to my coffee morning in Fresher's Week. After that I hardly saw her."

"But she trusted you enough to come to you."

"I'm a trustworthy kind of guy."

Mo eyed him, trying not to show his irritation. "Jenson, when you opened the door to me, you said the name Kayla."

"Did I?"

"You did. Is that Kayla Goode?"

"She's one of my students."

"You were expecting her?"

Jenson scratched his neck. "She'd asked if she could come

and talk to me. I think she was pretty freaked out, finding Laurence like that."

That made sense. "You were expecting her at around this time?" Mo glanced at the door.

Jenson tugged his t-shirt again. "She didn't say a specific time. This morning. That's all."

"You often meet your students dressed in boxer shorts?"

"You caught me by surprise. I wasn't doing anything illegal."

"No."

Jenson held Mo's gaze. "Anyway, Kayla will be along soon. And I've got data to write up. Are we done here?"

"For now." Mo stood up.

"Good."

"Before I go... you're a Chemistry student, right?"

"I'm doing a PhD on Perovskite Photocatalysis."

"That means nothing to me."

"It's related to solar cell technology. Solar power. Important work."

"You know anything about how to make methamphetamine?"

Jenson pinched his nose. "Very different branch of Chemistry, mate."

Mo said nothing. Jenson looked him up and down and laughed. "You think I'm cooking meth in this apartment?"

"I just asked if you knew anything about it."

"You can search the place if you want. You won't find anything."

"It's fine. Thanks for your time."

CHAPTER TWENTY-SEVEN

"Sheila," said Zoe. "Sorry I couldn't get here quicker."

"It's fine," said Sheila. "I hear you're working on that death in Boulton Hall."

"Nineteen-year old man. Allegations of rape against him."

"Ouch. I'll try not to keep you."

They were in Sheila's office in Lloyd House, two floors below the room where Zoe had been interviewed by Layla Kaur the night before. Two floors below where Carl worked. Zoe had been on alert since arriving in the car park, imagining how she'd react if she bumped into him in the lobby or a corridor or even the lift. She'd run through half a dozen possible meetings in her mind, and she still wasn't sure if she was hoping to see him or not.

"So what you got?"

Sheila pointed at her computer monitor. "Interview with Ana-Maria Albescu."

"She not back in Romania yet?"

"We had a word with the airline."

"So you got her to talk."

"To some extent. Watch this."

Zoe grabbed a chair and pulled it to Sheila's desk. The two women sat next to each other, eyes on the screen. The office held three other desks, all of which were empty.

"You in on your own today?"

"The others are out on a surveillance job. Sorry."

"I'll have to go to my DCI," Zoe said. "But if Ana-Maria's provided useful information, I'm sure I'll be able to free up at least one of my team."

"Good. Here." Sheila clicked her mouse and the video started playing. Onscreen were Sheila and a male colleague, their backs to the camera, Ana-Maria opposite them, flanked by two women Zoe didn't recognise.

"Two lawyers?"

"Lawyer and translator. Both appointed by us."

Zoe nodded. So Ana-Maria wasn't important enough for Trevor Hamm to send her a lawyer.

She leaned back and watched as Sheila led the introductions onscreen. Then she went into the questions.

"Ana-Maria, we have a photograph that was sent to you via Instagram on the day of the New Street bomb." She pushed a photo across the table. "Do you recognise this?"

Ana-Maria waited for the translation then shrugged.

"It's the woman who we believe set off the bomb."

Ana-Maria's gaze shot up to look at Sheila, then back down to her hands, which twisted on the surface of the table. Zoe wondered how much English she understood.

"I understand that you're scared," Sheila said. "You were taken advantage of by some pretty scary men. But if you can help us establish that your friend was forced to do what she did by those men, it will be very helpful. You aren't in any trouble, Ana-Maria. We'll let you go once this is over."

Ana-Maria looked at her translator, who spoke fast. As she listened, her eyes narrowed. She said something in Romanian.

"I do not know her name," the interpreter said.

"We don't need a name," said Sheila. "But we do need to establish how the two of you knew each other."

A pause for the translation.

"I prefer not to say."

Onscreen, Sheila leaned forwards, her hands clasped on the table. Ana-Maria moved hers beneath the table. Next to Zoe, Sheila adopted the same position as in the recording, her hands on the desk.

"Like I say Ana-Maria, I understand that you're scared. But if you can tell us what you know, we will be able to put these men in prison for a very long time. Much longer than if we prosecute them for human trafficking."

As the interpreter spoke to Ana-Maria, the woman swallowed. She wiped under her eye.

Ana-Maria turned to Sheila. "I do not know name," she said in English.

Sheila glanced at the interpreter then nodded. "But you knew this woman?"

Ana-Maria blinked back across the table at the DS. She put her hand to her mouth and pulled at her lips. "Yes," she said as she pulled it away.

Onscreen, the DC next to Sheila shifted in his seat. Zoe could feel the tension emanating from the screen. "When was this?" she whispered.

"This morning," Sheila said. "About an hour ago. I called you immediately."

"Thanks." Zoe rehearsed what she would say to Lesley. Was Ana-Maria going to provide the missing link? Given that Trevor Hamm had seemingly disappeared off the face of the earth, would it make any difference? And would there be any chance of her appearing in court?

"How did you know her?" Sheila asked onscreen. Her voice was low.

"We... live together."

"In the Hotel Belvista?" Zoe had found Ana-Maria there along with Sofia Pichler, Hamm's girlfriend at the time, and other women who were being held there.

Ana-Maria shook her head. "No. First place."

"Curton Road?"

A nod.

"We know that Trevor Hamm and his men forced you to provide sexual services to men at the Curton Road house. Did they do that to your friend as well?"

"Yes. I hear her cry. Crying." Ana-Maria wiped her face again.

"Did you hear anything else? Did the men force her to set off the bomb?"

Ana-Maria narrowed her eyes. She looked at the interpreter, who spoke to her in Romanian. She chewed her lip, staring back at the interpreter in silence. Then she said something in Romanian.

The interpreter turned to Sheila. "I heard man talking to her. Man called Adam. He tell her if she go to station with rucksack, her family will not be hurt."

CHAPTER TWENTY-EIGHT

Kayla sat at the back of the lecture theatre, slumped in her chair. At the front, Doctor Tanaka was droning on about Jane Austen and Regency England. Kayla loved Austen's books, but sometimes the level of analysis was just too deep. She wondered if the author had intended to insert all those layers of meaning into the text, or if academics just liked imagining a few of them.

At last the lecture was over. Kayla yawned and stood abruptly, sending the back of her collapsing chair crashing backwards. A woman next to her gave her a sharp look and she shrugged.

She shuffled along the row behind the other students. As she reached the exit, she heard her name being called.

"Kayla?"

She turned, her stomach dipping. She just wanted to go back to her room and sleep. She'd managed to get that essay finished at 1am, after Jenson had left. He'd been in an odd mood, telling her how to arrange her hair, standing behind her facing a mirror and styling it.

"Kayla, I wondered if I could have a quick word."

It was Dr Tanaka who'd been calling for her. Kayla pushed her shoulders back and approached the front desk.

"Is it about that essay? I'm sorry it was an hour late, I..."

"It's not about the essay, Kayla. Frankly I'm surprised you managed to get it in at all. I'd have understood if you'd felt the need to ask for an extension, you know."

Kayla shrugged. It hadn't occurred to her.

"How are you?"

"I'm fine. Tired, after staying up to write that essay. But I'm fine."

"You don't look it."

Kayla felt her legs weaken. She looked back at the doctor, wondering just how bad she looked. She couldn't remember if she'd brushed her hair this morning. Even if she'd cleaned her teeth.

"I heard about Laurence. That must have been horrible for you."

Kayla balled her fist in her thigh. "Oh, that."

"Did you know him well?"

Kayla pulled at her collar. "No. He was a recluse. I don't think anyone knew him."

She wasn't about to tell this woman the truth. She'd lied to the police and to Lin. How many more times?

"If you need someone to chat to, my door's always open."

"Thanks." Kayla looked at the floor between them. "I've got my residential tutor, he's helping." *Although not quite in the way you imagine*, she thought.

"Good. That's good. Anyway, if you need to talk to another woman. Someone removed from it all..."

"I will. Thanks."

Another lie.

Dr Tanaka brushed Kayla's arm with her fingertips as Kayla walked away. Kayla resisted an urge to wipe it, instead waiting until she was outside the lecture theatre before she grabbed her arms and threw herself against a wall, shaking.

Leave me alone, she thought. *Everybody, just leave me alone.*

She caught movement along the corridor and looked up. A woman was walking away from her, turning the corner.

Kayla frowned. It was that Gina woman, the one who'd approached her in the canteen. She hadn't seen her in Boulton Hall before, and she'd never spotted her in the English department.

Was she being followed?

CHAPTER TWENTY-NINE

Zoe knocked on Lesley's door.

"Come in."

Lesley was alone at her desk, her shoes kicked into a corner. She had a mug of coffee on her desk and a pile of chocolate digestives beside it. Her eyes flicked to the pile when she saw Zoe eyeing them.

"I haven't had any breakfast."

"I didn't say anything."

"You thought it... oh what the hell. I can eat what I want, can't I? What d'you need, Zoe?"

Zoe stood in front of the desk, unaccustomed to Lesley being so brittle. Her boss had always been eccentric in her eating habits. Yoghurts in briefings, Pot Noodles in meetings, chocolate bars stashed in her pockets for emergencies. Why the boss thought Zoe would be worried about a few biscuits, she wasn't sure.

"So. How d'you like having DS Uddin back on the team?"

"I like it very much. He's a damn good DS."

"I don't need you to tell me that. Good to see the two of you working together again. Just wasn't right, you with DS Osman."

"No, Ma'am." Zoe hesitated, thinking of her interview with DS Kaur. "I've just come from DS Griffin."

"I hope that means good news." Lesley gestured for Zoe to sit down, and leaned back in her chair. She grabbed a biscuit and plunged it in her mouth.

"Ana-Maria Albescu, one of the women from the brothel in Hall Green, said she knew the woman who set off the bomb. She said she was at the Curton Road brothel. That she heard her crying."

"Yes." Lesley punched the air. "We're going to get that fucker, you see if we don't."

"It gets better."

"Zoe, you might turn into my favourite person if you carry on like this. Tell me more."

Zoe smiled. The DCI had been withdrawn since the New Street bomb and it was good to see her cheerful again.

"She told us she heard Adam Fulmer telling the bomber she had to do it. Her words were – she opened her notebook – 'if she goes to the station with a rucksack, her family will not be hurt'."

"Adam Fulmer?"

Zoe frowned: the DCI knew who Adam Fulmer was. "One of Trevor Hamm's lot. He killed Sofia Pichler's sister, and was at the airport when they smuggled those women off the plane from Romania."

"Ah, I remember." Lesley rubbed her chin. "He was arrested by Organised Crime two weeks ago."

"Currently on remand at HMP Birmingham," Zoe added.

"Sheila tracked *him* down, but not Hamm?"

"Hamm's clever," Zoe said. "He's got people to help him hide. His sidekicks seem to be dispensable."

Lesley sighed. "This is useless in court of course, hearsay and all that, but it's something we can use to give Adam a bit of a grilling. Let's get him in for an interview, eh?"

"Sounds like a plan, Ma'am."

"You know who you want to do the interview with?"

"I was thinking DS Uddin, Ma'am."

Lesley winked. "Right answer. Although DS Griffin's bosses won't be happy."

CHAPTER THIRTY

Zoe walked back into the office to find Mo, Rhodri and Connie gathered around Connie's desk.

"I like seeing you lot like that," she said.

Rhodri and Connie exchanged nervous glances. "Like what?" Rhodri asked.

"When the three of you are all at one person's desk, it means the person whose desk it is has just unearthed something useful. Connie?"

Connie nodded. "It's Kayla. She's going out with Jenson Begg, the postgrad counsellor guy."

"What does that have to do with anything?"

"She lied to us about it, boss," said Mo. "So did he. Neither of them mentioned it, and both of them were asked about the other."

"They're keeping a secret. I don't think that means they murdered Laurence Thomms."

"There was something about him..." Mo wrinkled his nose and leaned against the desk. Zoe noticed that Jenson Begg's photo had been added to the board.

"I know your hunches tend to be pretty accurate, Mo. But for once we might just be dealing with a creep who uses his position of authority to get women into bed."

"Nothing new there," said Connie.

"Come on, like." Rhodri looked sheepish. "We're not all like that."

Zoe gave him a smile. "I can't imagine you ever using your position of authority to get women into bed, Rhodri."

He blushed. "Course not."

Zoe laughed. "Oh, Rhod."

"There's more to it, though," said Connie.

"Go on." Zoe approached her desk. She had an Instagram profile page open: Jenson Begg. She'd stopped on a photo of him and Kayla.

"OK." Zoe leaned in.

"Yeah," Rhodri said. "You know what that is."

"I do, Rhodri."

The photo pictured Jenson with his arm slung around Kayla's neck in the proprietorial way some young men had. They sat at a restaurant table, remains of Chinese food in front of them. On the table, poking out from under a napkin, was a glass pipe.

"Kind of pipe they use to smoke crystal meth," said Rhodri.

"And a fair few other things," said Zoe. "You reckon Jenson's using?"

"I talked to Adi Hanson," Rhodri said. "He says there's no way the stuff that killed Laurence was brewed in the Chemistry lab. Rough as shit, it was. He says it's street drugs."

"Which means we need to find the dealer. Who's got someone they can talk to in the Drugs team?"

"Already done it," Rhodri replied. "He's putting out some feelers for me now."

"You're having a good day, aren't you, Rhod?" Zoe said.

"Jenson could be dealing," said Mo. "He's got access to all those students..."

"Doesn't necessarily mean he was the one who shoved it down Laurence's throat," she said. "But it does mean he'll know where the students are getting their supply from."

Connie gave a long nod. Rhodri winked at her.

"You haven't solved the case, you know," Zoe told him. "We've got a creepy postgrad sleeping with undergraduates and taking hard drugs. It might be a coincidence."

"Doesn't hurt to talk to him again," Mo said.

"You up for it?" Zoe asked him.

Mo sighed. "Perk of the job."

She gave him a tight smile. "Thanks."

"Taking one for the team, as they say."

"Don't," she said. "It doesn't suit you, talking like that."

Mo widened his eyes. "OK."

"So..." Zoe approached the board. "We've got street drugs. Cut through with with... Rhodri?"

"Washing powder. Chalk. And a base of flu tablets."

Zoe winced. "Ouch. OK, so we've got Jenson, Kayla, and Becca. We've got the rape investigation, which sounds like it was mismanaged. And we've got Kayla and Jenson seeing each other."

The door opened behind her and she span round. "Adi."

Adi hurried in, bringing in a gush of cold air. "Hello, favourite Force CID team."

"Stop that," Zoe said. "It won't get you any of Rhodri's Hobnobs. What have you got for us?"

"The DNA results from inside Laurence's mouth."

Zoe felt her breath catch. "And?"

"There's more than one pattern. Not just Laurence. Someone left their DNA inside his cheek."

"Tell me you've got a match."

"No such luck."

"Gender?"

"Male."

Zoe turned back to the board, her eyes on Jenson's photo. He knew about Laurence raping Becca. Perhaps he felt protective towards the students in his care. Would he really...?

"OK," she said. "We're going to need to talk to Jenson Begg again."

CHAPTER THIRTY-ONE

KAYLA LEANED back against the wall of Jenson's room, her head light. She'd had most of a bottle of cheap Lambrusco and felt like she might float away.

Jenson was on the floor in front of her, rifling through his pockets.

"Where is the bloody thing?" he muttered.

"What?"

"I think I left my phone at the house."

"I still don't understand why you have two places. How do you afford it?"

"I get this place free in return for the pastoral support work." He pushed himself up and gave her a firm kiss on the lips. "Meeting the needs of undergraduates. You know the kind of thing."

"I hope you don't meet *everyone's* needs the way you do mine."

He pulled away. "Don't be silly."

She raised her eyebrows. "You aren't denying it."

He shifted so his eyes were inches in front of hers. "You are the only student I'm fucking."

"Good." She slapped his cheek, just lightly.

He raised a hand. "Don't do that."

"I was joking."

"Just don't. Alright?" He frowned at her then retreated to the floor, where he continued looking for his phone.

"You already said you thought you'd left it at the house. Let's go over there."

"Dave and Kal are there. I don't want to disturb them."

"But you need your phone."

He grunted. "What's that t-shirt you're wearing?"

She tugged at her top. She'd bought it from a charity shop in Selly Oak the week before. "You like it?"

"It's too revealing."

"I thought you'd appreciate that." She pulled it up a little. The t-shirt was cropped, exposing her stomach. She'd been cold all day, but now, in his room, she was warm.

"I don't like the idea of other men looking at you like that."

She laughed. "They can look." She pulled the top up a little higher so it skimmed her bra. "But they can't touch."

He grabbed her wrist. "You aren't a piece of meat for men to ogle at."

"OK. I won't wear it." She grabbed the collar of the t-shirt and yanked it over her head. "Better?"

"That's not what I meant."

She stared at him. She'd been trying to get him to lighten up, maybe turn him on. What was with him?

There was a knock at the door.

"Who's that?" he muttered, his voice rough.

"You want me to open it?"

"Put this back on." He shoved the t-shirt into her hands. "And put this on top." He grabbed a scrunched up shirt of his own from the floor.

She curled her lip. "This is filthy."

"We don't know who it is. You need to cover up."

She didn't like him talking to her like this. But he wanted her to himself, not being looked at by other men. It was romantic, she supposed. Flattering.

He sprang up and opened the door. "Again?"

"Sorry, but we have a few more questions. Kayla. You're here too."

"It's gone eight," Jenson said.

"Day's only just beginning for you, I imagine." The male detective was at the door. "You remember me, Kayla? DS Uddin."

She nodded, silent.

"I wanted to have another chat with Jenson. It would be good to talk to you too, if you don't mind."

She swallowed. "What about?"

"I'd rather not say right now."

"Are you arresting us?"

"Nothing like that. Just a few questions. We can do it here, but I'll need to talk to each of you separately."

She pushed herself off the bed. "I'll go to my room. Room 512."

The detective nodded. "Thanks. I can call my female colleagues, if you'd prefer."

She shrugged.

"OK," he said. "I'll see you shortly."

She gave Jenson a last look and left the two of them together, wondering why this police officer wanted to talk to her boyfriend.

CHAPTER THIRTY-TWO

"OK," said Rhodri. "I've got it."

"I told you to go home." Zoe emerged from her office.

"Just needed to wait for this file."

The office was quiet, Mo and Connie both gone for the night. Zoe had assumed Rhodri would follow Connie out – it wasn't like him to be in when everyone else had left. Maybe he was trying to impress.

"What is it?" She hid a yawn behind her hand. "Sorry."

"CCTV, from the bar where Becca works."

"Night of the murder?"

"Yup."

"Let's see it then." She dragged up a chair. "Hang on."

She went back to her office to fetch the mug of coffee she'd been drinking. It was tepid and bitter but she needed the caffeine.

"Right," she said as she plonked back down in the chair. "Fire away."

Rhodri gave her a puzzled look, then clicked his mouse. "There she is."

The shot was from overhead, showing two young women working behind the student bar.

"Have we got a time and date stamp?" Zoe asked.

Rhodri put a finger on the screen. "Sunday night. 10pm."

"Let's go back a bit. Check the whole evening."

He rewound the video. The two women moved around the space, heading out into the bar to collect glasses, occasionally joined by a man.

"Who's he?" Zoe asked.

"Manager," Rhodri said. "Doesn't seem to do much front of house, too busy stocking up and doing whatever it is you do to run a bar."

"I thought you'd know all about that," Zoe said.

He pursed his lips and said nothing.

The video began at 7pm. Rhodri hit fast forward and they watched a woman moving around beneath the camera.

"That's the other barmaid," Rhodri said. "The one I spoke to."

"Barmaid? Does anyone say barmaid anymore?"

"I don't know what else to call her, boss."

"Fast forward to when Becca turns up."

He whizzed through to 8pm, when Becca came through the door.

"Right," said Zoe. "Now we need to work through to the time that Kayla and Lin found Laurence."

"About twenty minutes before, I'd reckon," said Rhodri. "She'd need time to get to Boulton Hall. D'you think you could get close enough to shove meth down someone's throat in a hurry?"

"Good point," Zoe said. She let the images wash over her, watching for the moments when Becca disappeared into the main body of the bar or through the door. Each time, she was back within a few minutes.

"Either she was very quick, or she didn't do it," she said.

"She didn't do it, boss."

"You're right." Zoe dragged a hand through her hair. She'd known Becca MacGuire was innocent. But she had to be sure.

Becca finally left at 1am. Half an hour after Lin and Kayla had found Laurence. The video ended fifteen minutes later.

"Go home, Rhod. I'll see you in the morning."

CHAPTER THIRTY-THREE

KAYLA STOOD OUTSIDE BOULTON HALL, shivering in Jenson's thin shirt. Instead of going to her room, she'd come straight to the main entrance. She had no interest in talking to that detective again.

She knew she couldn't avoid it for ever, but that made no difference.

The coward's way, she told herself, then stomped the pavement with her foot. She wasn't sure who she was more annoyed with: herself, Jenson or that detective. Or Laurence.

She was more drunk than she'd thought. The streetlight above pulsed in her eyes and she felt an urge to curl up against the wall of the building. Instead, she picked up her phone.

"Gina Lennon."

"It's Kayla. We met at Boulton Hall last night. In the canteen."

"Kayla." The woman paused. "What a nice surprise."

Kayla sniffed and pulled Jenson's shirt tighter. The alcohol was making her feel reckless.

"Why did you follow me today?"

"I'm sorry?"

"You followed me to the English department."

"I'm sorry, Kayla. I don't know what you're talking about."

The door to the building opened behind Kayla. Two girls came out, laughing between themselves. She huddled closer to the wall.

"I saw you. You're not in my class."

"I'm really sorry, Kayla. But I can't help you... Are you OK?"

"I'm fine." She was telling a lot of people that lately.

"Would you like to come over? There's a few of us here, chatting."

"You got wine?"

"Er... coffee mainly. But yes, we've got some wine."

"Where are you?"

Gina gave her an address in Selly Oak.

"OK," Kayla said. "I'll be about half an hour."

"It's dark. Are you sure you'll be OK? It's not safe for a woman out on her own."

"It's fine. See you in a bit."

Kayla hung up then leaned back against the wall. Her legs felt loose and the streetlamp above her was pulsing more frequently now. It gave her a headache.

Where was she going?

Yes... an address in Selly Oak. She hadn't written it down. Couldn't remember it.

"Kayla? What you doing out here? It's freezing."

Kayla felt a hand on her shoulder. She shrugged it off.

"Hey... it's me. Lin. I thought we could do some filming.

There's a new exhibition over at the Barber Institute, it's having a special opening."

Kayla turned to her. Lin's eyes narrowed.

"You look rough."

Kayla frowned at her. "Just a bit drunk."

"Here. Forget the art installation. Let's get you to bed."

Kayla shook her head violently. "Not my room."

"We'll go to mine then." Lin took her elbow. Kayla let her weight fall into Lin's hand, just slightly. It felt good.

"Yeah," she said to her friend. "Let's go to your room."

"Good." Lin pulled Kayla to her and supported her weight as the two of them walked inside. Kayla scanned the foyer as they passed through, anxious not to bump into that detective.

Lin's room was on the first floor, not far from the lift. The two women stumbled in together and crashed onto the bed. Kayla let herself slide back, her head hitting the wall.

"Ouch."

"Careful, dummy." Lin stood up and went into the bathroom. She emerged with a pint glass of water. "Drink this."

Kayla pulled a face.

"Drink it." Lin pushed it under her nose.

Kayla took the glass and sipped. She shuffled along the bed to make room for Lin, who sat next to her.

"What happened to make you like this?" Lin asked.

"What d'you mean?"

"You're not just drunk."

"I had a bottle of wine. I'll be fine." Kayla sipped more water.

"You seem... down."

"I'm not." Kayla closed her eyes and took a longer sip. She should have stayed outside. She should have found Gina.

"I met this woman," she said.

"OK."

"Gina. You know her?"

Lin shrugged, her expression tight. "There's two hundred students in Boulton Hall."

"I don't think she lives here, but she was in the canteen last night. And she followed me to my lecture today."

Lin laughed. "Now you're being paranoid."

"I saw her. I'm sure of it."

"Maybe she's got the hots for you. You are kinda cute." Lin gave Kayla a friendly shove.

"Don't. I'll be sick."

"Ew. Sorry." Lin moved off the bed and sat in the chair at her desk. "So they question you? The cops?"

"The police. Yes. There was a man, a detective."

"What kinda things he ask you?"

"Didn't they talk to you too?"

"Yeah. Some woman. But I wondered if they asked us different things."

Kayla shrugged. She downed the last of the water and bent down to place the glass on the floor. When she pulled back up she felt dizzy.

"I shouldn't have drunk that bottle."

"They ask you about his injuries?"

"I... yes. They asked about what I saw. I couldn't tell them much. You're the medic."

"They got any theories, you think?"

"They've been talking to Jenson. They came back to talk to him again tonight. I'm supposed to be waiting for them."

Lin straightened. "Where? Is it the woman or the man?"

"A man. He said he'd see me in my room."

"Which is why you don't want to go there."

Kayla blinked in response.

"You worried about what they'll ask you?"

Kayla reached to the back of her neck and rubbed it. She wanted to sleep, but didn't want to impose on Lin.

"I don't know. I just... I wasn't in the mood."

"You knew Laurence, didn't you?."

"No, not really." She spoke sharply, surprising both herself and Lin.

Lin licked her lips. "I don't mean to pry."

Kayla stared back at her. "Then don't."

"Did he do something to you, Kayla? Like he did to Becca?"

Kayla shuddered. "Don't be daft." She stood up, placing a hand on the wall. "He'll have gone now. I'll head home."

"It's alright. Stay, Kayla. You can talk to me."

"Nothing to talk about." Kayla pulled the door open. She could smell frying food from along the corridor. She put a hand to her mouth.

"Kayla, don't be—"

Kayla shut the door behind her. She walked back to her room, her head heavy.

CHAPTER THIRTY-FOUR

"HEY," Zoe said when Carl answered the phone. She was sitting on her bed at home. Nicholas was downstairs, watching one of his documentaries.

"Hey," he replied. "I heard you saw DS Kaur."

"She gave me quite a grilling."

"Come on, Zoe. You know it was just an informal interview. You'd have been entitled to a police friend other—"

"It's OK, Carl. I don't want to argue with you."

"Good. Nor do I."

"Where are you?" She lay back on the bed, staring up at the ceiling. There was a crack running from above the head of the bed to the far corner.

"I'm at home. Eating a takeaway."

"What kind?"

"Curry. Lamb Jalfrezi."

"You don't normally like them hot."

"You inspired me."

She relaxed into the duvet. "I miss you."

"I miss you too."

She listened to him breathing.

"No one said we couldn't see each other," Carl said.

"No," she replied.

"So..." he said. "Could I buy you a drink?"

"That depends." She felt her chest tighten.

He sighed. "On what?"

"On whether you still think I helped Ian."

"Zoe. I don't think you helped Ian."

"You don't think I definitely didn't."

"You know what it's like. You have to keep all options open until you know exactly what's—"

"Has Ian said I was working with him?"

"No."

"Has he even hinted at it?"

"You know I can't talk to you about what DS Osman has told us."

Zoe sat up. "Dammit Carl. This is me you're talking to. I was there the first time you questioned him. I let you plant him in my team so you could keep an eye on him."

"The idea was for him to keep an eye on Randle, as I recall."

"Whatever."

"Which he failed to do."

Zoe closed her eyes. She had no doubt that Ian had been watching Detective Superintendent Randle. But what she did doubt was that he'd reported what he'd seen to Carl and his colleagues in Professional Standards.

"I'm sorry, Carl. But I can't see you until I know you trust me."

"I know."

"And I imagine you don't want to see me until you can be one hundred percent sure I'm not bent."

"I don't think you're bent, Zoe. Not really."

"Well call your bloodhound off then."

"You know I can't do that."

She dug her thumbnail into her palm. "I'm going to hang up now."

"OK. Take care, Zoe. Look after yourself."

"You too." She put the phone down, her skin tingling with frustration.

CHAPTER THIRTY-FIVE

THE WARDEN'S study was a large room lined with book-shelves and filled with plants. To one side was a bank of floor-to-ceiling windows. Zoe sat across the mid-century-style desk from her, waiting for an answer to her question.

"I'm not sure I can tell you that," the warden replied. She wore jeans and a crumpled denim shirt and looked like she hadn't slept. Her plane had only landed two hours earlier.

"We need to know everything about your investigation into Laurence's alleged rape of Becca. This is a murder investigation, Doctor Edwards."

"I'm not trying to withhold information, Inspector. I just don't know."

"You have no idea who knew about your investigation?"

"I know who should have known. But this is a tight-knit community. People talk. Things get out."

"Surely you would have done what you could to keep things confidential?"

Doctor Reynolds leaned forwards, her hands clasped together on top of a desk diary. Her desk was neat, everything at right angles. "Jenson Begg knew, of course. He was the one Becca went to in the first place. He's pretty trustworthy. But I have no idea who else Becca might have told."

"In her statement to me, she said she hadn't told a soul."

"Imagine being in her situation. She's nineteen years old. She's just accused a fellow student of rape. If that was me, I'd want to confide in someone."

"She confided in Jenson."

"I mean a friend. Another girl."

Zoe nodded. The warden was right. She hoped that when Nicholas went to university, he'd have friends he could share his problems with.

"Do you know who her friends were?"

The warden jumped at the sound of something hitting the window. She leapt up from her chair and strode to it, thumping the glass.

"Damn football pitch. Why they put it so close to the building..."

Zoe looked out of the window. A group of four young men in black football kit stared back in, looking sheepish. The warden clenched her fists and walked back to the desk.

"I was asking if you knew who her friends were," Zoe said.

"I don't keep tabs on all the relationships among my students. Over time I get to know some of the groupings. But you'd have to ask Becca. Do you think one of her friends might have killed Laurence by way of revenge?"

"We can't rule anything out yet. I also need to talk to you about the drugs."

"We've already conducted a search of student rooms. When a drugs-related incident occurs, we have the authority to do random checks."

"Any joy?"

"None. The students know to hide anything illegal before we have a chance to do the rounds." The warden shook her head. "Or to leave it with friends off-campus."

"Are you aware of any dealing taking place in the Hall, or between the students?"

"There'll be a small amount of cannabis changing hands. We're not too worried about that."

"Not worried?"

"You're a police officer, Detective Finch. I'm sure you take a different view of these things."

"I'm sure the university authorities do too."

"The university authorities know that it's impossible to prevent marijuana use, and to concentrate on the harder stuff."

"So was there any dealing of that going on here? The harder stuff, I mean? I assume you'd have spoken to the police if you—"

"No, Detective. There has been no dealing of Class A drugs in this building as far as I or my staff are aware. And don't worry. I know full well what kind of penalty we'd pay if we allowed that to go on."

"Maximum fourteen years' imprisonment," Zoe said.

The warden's eyes flashed. "Six months as a summary offence."

Zoe cocked her head. "You know the law."

"I'm an academic. I have friends in the School of Law."

"You've asked them about the punishment for drugs offences?"

"I talk to them about all sorts of things, Inspector. Don't get too excited."

Zoe realised she was grinding her teeth. "So. You found the case against Laurence Thomms to be inconclusive."

"I did. Becca came to us too late. If she'd made the complaint earlier on, if she'd gone to the police and submitted to an intimate examination... it was just her word against his."

"In court that would be a not guilty verdict."

"Reasonable doubt. Yes, I know that, Inspector. But we aren't in court. So I found the case to be inconclusive. I was planning to give Laurence a warning and I have already told Becca to accept counselling. It's all I can do."

Zoe scratched her neck. She knew how hard it was to prove rape cases, especially when there was a gap between the alleged rape and the complaint.

"OK," she said. "So it's quite possible that the whole of Boulton Hall could have known that Laurence might or might not have raped Becca. And you can't say for sure if he actually did. And as for the drugs..."

"I'm sorry I can't be more help."

I bet, Zoe thought. She knew how much the woman would want to divert scandal away from Boulton Hall. Not easy, when a student had been murdered.

"I'll let you know if I have any more questions."

The window banged again and the warden turned to it, fist raised. This time it was a bird that had hit the glass and tumbled to the ground below.

"Oh my God." Doctor Edwards rushed to the window. She peered down at the bird, watching it pick itself up. Eventually it shook itself out and flew away. She jerked her head up to look past it at the football players.

Zoe made for the door, wondering how this woman, who cared more for a clumsy bird than for a dead student, had been put in charge of two hundred of them.

CHAPTER THIRTY-SIX

"How DID it go with Jenson Begg last night?" Zoe asked Mo. They were in the team room: Mo, Connie and Rhodri at their desks and Zoe perched on Rhodri's.

"What d'you expect? He denied it all. Not taking drugs, not involved with any students. Kayla was in his room when I got there, though."

"Which confirms that he's seeing her."

"He denied it. Said she was there for advice. Traumatised by finding Laurence's body."

Rhodri laughed. "He's a bloody bad liar."

"There might be restrictions on him having relationships with undergraduates," Zoe said. "He is in a position of trust, after all."

"Which is why he'd lie," said Mo. "Kayla was drunk, though. She didn't look like she was there for counselling."

"Poor girl," Connie said.

"I asked her if I could have a chat with her, too," Mo continued. "She said she'd be in her room, but when I got there, there was no sign of her."

"Maybe she'd gone out," said Rhodri.

"Maybe she was avoiding me."

"Why?" Zoe asked. "Why would Kayla not want to talk to us?"

"She could be protecting Jenson," Connie said. "She'd want to talk to him before Mo got to her, get their stories straight."

"She didn't strike me as that calculating, when I spoke to her on Tuesday," Mo replied. "Maybe she's scared."

"What of?" asked Rhodri.

Zoe shrugged. "Jenson maybe?"

"Poor girl," repeated Connie.

"Maybe she knows something about Laurence's murder, more like," said Rhodri.

"OK," said Zoe. "We need to track Kayla down. And we need to find out how widely known Becca's rape allegations were. The warden says she didn't tell anyone but she seems to think that would make no difference."

"Jenson swore blind he kept it under wraps," said Mo. "But he also reckoned the whole building knew about it."

"He have an idea how?"

"Gossip. Bush telegraph. Two hundred students living in one building, something like that's bound to get out."

"So we can assume it was common knowledge," Zoe said. "Which means someone might have wanted to take revenge."

"A vigilante?" Rhodri asked.

She shook her head. "What if he assaulted more than one woman? If there was another student who'd gone through the same thing but not reported it, I can imagine she'd have been pretty pissed off."

"Understatement of the century," said Connie.

"Which takes us back to the DNA sample. I'll have a word with the DCI, see if we can get screening samples taken from the students."

"The DNA was from a man," Mo said.

Zoe rapped the desk with her knuckles. "Of course it was. So we're not looking for a potential victim of Laurence's."

"It could have nothing to do with the rape," said Connie.

"Alleged rape," said Rhodri. "The boss says they didn't have enough to find him guilty."

"It wasn't exactly a professionally-run police investigation, Rhod," Zoe pointed out. "Even if he didn't rape Becca, if everyone thought he did, it amounts to the same thing."

"OK," said Mo. "So where does that leave us?"

"I'll talk to the DCI. Mo, can you go back to Adi. See if there's anything else he can tell us from the DNA sample, anything that might narrow it down."

"Sure."

She nodded. She'd slept badly the night before, the conversation with Carl spinning in her mind. "Hang on."

"What?" Mo looked worried.

"I need you in another interview with me." She checked her watch. "Eleven o'clock. Adam Fulmer. One of Trevor Hamm's lowlifes."

"OK. What about?"

"A witness from the Hotel Belvista heard him talking to the New Street bomber."

"That's promising," Rhodri said.

"Let's hope so," Zoe replied. "You call Adi, will you? You were the one he spoke to yesterday."

"Will do, boss." Rhodri grabbed his phone.

"Good. Connie, I want you at the university. Talk to Kayla first. Then find out who Becca's friends were. Chat to them, find out what people were saying about Laurence. There might be something we're not aware of."

Connie stood up. "Now, boss?"

"Yes, now." Zoe turned to Mo. "Come on then."

CHAPTER THIRTY-SEVEN

ADAM FULMER HAD thinning red-blonde hair and a face that looked like it had been in a fight or two. His nose was crooked and the faint trace of a scar ran across his chin. He sat in the interview room chair, his arms folded across his chest, his solicitor beside him.

Zoe shared a look with Mo as she recognised the solicitor: Edward Startshaw.

"Adam," she said. "Thank you for coming to see us."

"Didn't have much choice," he muttered.

"I've been told you're questioning my client as a witness in the New Street bombing enquiry," Startshaw said. "Which means you won't be attempting to pin anything on him, I trust."

"We wouldn't *pin* anything on anybody, Mr Startshaw. We might accuse suspects of committing crimes, but that's a very different thing, and in this case, it rather depends on what your client may or may not have done," Zoe told him with an insincere smile.

Fulmer tapped Startshaw on the arm and leaned towards him. Startshaw nodded and muttered in his ear.

Zoe sat down, piling files in front of her. Half of them were full of blank sheets of paper but the two men opposite her didn't need to know that.

Mo switched on the tape.

"In attendance, DI Zoe Finch," Zoe said.

"DS Mohammed Uddin," Mo added.

"Edward Startshaw and my client Adam Fulmer," Startshaw said with a sniff.

Zoe eyed Fulmer. "Good. Now we all know who everyone is, let's get down to business, shall we?"

Fulmer returned her gaze but didn't adjust his expression.

Zoe nodded at Mo, who brought a photo out from his own thick file. He pushed it across the table, narrating his actions for the benefit of the recording.

"Do you know this woman?" Zoe asked.

Fuller glanced at the photo and shrugged. It was the selfie that the bomber had sent to Ana-Maria on her way to New Street Station.

Zoe sighed. "She was living at the brothel in Curton Road. We have a witness saying you knew her."

Adam's eyes hardened but he said nothing.

Zoe leaned forwards and placed her hands on the table. He glanced down at them, then looked back up at her.

"OK," she said. "Let's get this clear. We're after someone bigger than you, and you know it." She jabbed the photo. "We also need to know the identity of this woman."

He pursed his lips.

"Our witness knew her," Mo said.

"Good for 'er," Adam replied, his eyes still on Zoe.

"She says she overheard a conversation between the two of you."

Fulmer turned to Mo. "Dunno what you're talking about."

Zoe clenched her fists on the table. "If you cooperate, Adam, you know it'll work in your favour. We can have a word with the CPS about recommended sentencing..."

"I haven't been found guilty of anything."

"You were photographed driving away from the airport with a van full of women who were being trafficked for prostitution. You were at the house where these women were being held. We have your fingerprints on some of their passports. You don't need me to tell you you're not walking away from this."

He turned back to her and shrugged.

Zoe tapped Mo's file. He brought out another photo: a CCTV still from inside the station. She placed the photos side by side. "Same woman."

"This woman detonated the bomb," Zoe said. "Our witness told us that you said if she took a rucksack to New Street station, her family would be unharmed."

"Those birds are all thick. They'd tell you anything."

"So you're admitting you know her?"

Fulmer blinked once, but otherwise showed no reaction. "Knowin' someone's not a crime."

"Forcing them to have sex with men for money is. And we have statements from thirteen women saying you and your associates did just that."

"Romanian birds. Full of shit."

Zoe felt heat rise from her gut. *Don't react.*

"Come on, Adam. Do yourself a favour and help us out here. What's the name of this woman?" She jabbed the photo of the bomber. "And why did you make her take a bomb to the station? Who put you up to it?"

Fulmer leaned towards Startshaw, who nodded. He stared at Zoe, unblinking.

Startshaw cleared his throat. He was in his late sixties, wearing a shabby suit, and the lines on his face gave him the look of someone who should have retired years ago.

"You've told my client that if he cooperates then you'll take that into account for sentencing."

"We can recommend it."

"But the questions you're asking my client require him to incriminate himself."

Across the table, Fulmer flashed his eyes at Zoe. She ignored him and looked at the solicitor. "You know that defendants who coorporate generally receive—"

"I don't know 'er," Adam said. He pointed at the CCTV still. "Never seen 'er in my life."

Zoe sighed. "Very well. If you're not going to tell us who this woman is, at least tell us where Trevor Hamm is."

He laughed.

"If you give us information that helps us find him, that'll help your case more than anything."

"No comment."

Zoe handed the photos back to Mo. "Are you going to tell us *anything*, Adam?"

He smiled. "No comment."

"You can go back to Winson Green then. I hope you like it there."

CHAPTER THIRTY-EIGHT

"Hi Adi, it's me again."

"I'd recognise that accent anywhere. Howya doing, Rhodri?"

Rhodri felt heat rise up his neck. He didn't like being teased about being Welsh, even if it was good-natured.

"I'm after anything else you've got on that DNA result. Does it tell us anything more about the suspect, apart from he's a bloke?"

"Ah, good thinking. Zoe ask you to call me?"

Rhodri hesitated. "Yes."

"Let me get it up onscreen."

Rhodri chewed his biro while he waited, then spat as he bit through the plastic and got a mouthful of ink. He tossed the pen onto the desk. Connie, about to leave the office, turned to him and sniggered.

"Right," said Adi. "You're expecting me to tell you how tall he is, aren't you? Shoe size, colour of his skin, where he grew up?"

"Well, maybe not quite..."

"I'm playing with you, Rhod. DNA isn't quite as magical as some people think it is. I'm afraid I can't tell you any of that stuff."

"Ah. OK." Rhodri went to hang up.

"That stuff's all in the genes. It's the trash in between that we use to identify people. The stuff no one knows what it's there for. But I can tell you his blood type, and that he had size seven shoes."

"But you just said..."

"We found a shoe print on a ring binder we'd removed from the scene. It was fresh, and Laurence was a size nine. Nothing to do with the DNA, sorry."

"You said blood type."

"A. So not rare, but not the most common. Not much use to us though, seeing as we've got the DNA."

"Is there anything else that could be helpful? Anything the killer left behind, or touched?"

"Sorry, Rhodri. We did find a few strands of hair on Laurence's trousers but they turned out to be dog hairs."

"He lives in a hall of residence. How can he have dog hairs on him?"

"Not difficult, if you've been anywhere near someone with a dog. I know I get them on my jeans every time I go to the park, dogs seem to like me. You might want to check it out though."

"You know what kind of dog?"

"Short-haired, brown. Similar colour to Laurence's hair, which is why we didn't think much of them at first."

"OK."

"OK. See ya, Rhodri."

"See ya. Thanks."

CHAPTER THIRTY-NINE

Connie knocked on Kayla's door. Loud music was playing behind it: Wiz Khalifa. Connie smiled: Zaf's favourite.

The door opened and Kayla stared back at her, her face reddening. "Oh."

"I don't think we've met."

"No."

"I'm DC Connie Williams. I just wanted to have a chat with you, if that's OK? We can do it here."

Kayla scratched her nose. "OK." She turned back into the room. "Sorry Fi."

"That's OK. Come over later, yeah?" A tall, willowy girl with waist-length mousy hair wriggled past Kayla, giving her a squeeze on the shoulder as she went. She eyed Connie but said nothing. Connie gave her a tight smile.

"What d'you need?" Kayla said as she turned the music down. Connie closed the door and took a seat by the desk. Kayla sat on the bed.

"How are you?"

"Jeez, why does everyone keep asking me that? I'm fine."

Kayla folded her arms.

"Sorry. It must be irritating for you. Does everyone know it was you and Lin who found Laurence?"

"Course they do. Everyone knows everything around here." Kayla stiffened for a moment then blew out a long, controlled breath.

"Like everyone knew about Becca?"

Kayla's eyes widened. "What about her?"

Connie surveyed the younger woman. What she knew about Becca was confidential, but she was sure Kayla already knew.

"I can't tell you. But if you know anything about her, I'd be grateful if you'd tell me."

Kayla's shoulders dropped. "She said Laurence... she said he attacked her."

"What kind of attack?"

"Rape. She said he raped her." Kayla licked her lips. She'd paled.

"Are you friends with Becca? Do you know her?"

"I know her. Spoke to her once in Fresher's Week, she was at Jenson's coffee morning. But I'm not friends with her, no."

"So how did you find out about her alleging Laurence raped her?"

Kayla shrugged. "Same way you find out about everything round here. You just do."

"You can't remember who told you?"

Kayla shook her head.

"It wasn't Jenson?"

Kayla blushed. "It definitely wasn't Jenson. I know that he knew, cos of the investigation and that. But I'd remember if he told me."

"But you can't remember who *did* tell you."

"I can't see why it's relevant. I mean, everyone knew." Kayla started clicking a pen against her teeth. "You think someone killed him cos of what he did to Becca. Or that Becca did."

"We don't think anything right now."

"You must think something." Kayla lowered the pen. "Who else have you spoken to?"

"Just Becca, Jenson and Lin. I'm going to speak to Lin again next."

Kayla nodded. "It definitely wasn't Lin who told me. I remember that, cos normally I get all my gossip from her."

"So she didn't know about Becca and Laurence?"

"Oh, she knew alright. She made a video about it. Still hasn't uploaded it, God knows why. It'd go viral. But she just didn't tell me."

"Any idea why?"

"You're probably better off asking her that."

"I will."

"Yeah."

"Another question, Kayla. How well did you know Laurence?"

Kayla stiffened. "Not well. He wasn't exactly sociable."

"So you didn't meet him at this coffee morning, or anything else."

Kayla held her body very still. "I didn't know him. I mean, he was doing Chemistry and I'm doing English. He lived two floors away. So..."

Connie nodded. She watched the young woman's body language, her senses tingling.

"Thanks, Kayla. I'm glad I managed to catch up with you."

"Yeah."

"My colleague tried to talk to you last night, but you were out."

A shrug. "I went to Lin's."

"Despite the fact you'd told DS Uddin you'd be in your room."

Kayla looked up at Connie. "I bumped into her. We went to her room."

"You weren't avoiding DS Uddin?"

"Why would I do that?"

"You tell me."

Kayla stared back at her, her mouth a thin line. She shook her head. "No reason. I wasn't avoiding him."

"OK. Here's my card. If you think of anything else, if there's anyone who might have had a reason to hurt Laurence, can you call me?"

"I've already got your boss's number."

"Well, now you've got mine too."

"Yeah." Kayla let the card fall to the bed.

Connie stood up. "I'm off to find Lin. You know if she's around?"

"She's a medic. She'll be at lectures."

"She come back for lunch?"

"Sometimes. Depends what they're doing."

"OK. Maybe I'll go over to the medical department."

"School of Medicine."

"Sorry?"

"That's what they call it. Lin's very particular about it."

Connie smiled at the young woman, who seemed to have released some of her tension. "OK. I'll go to the School of Medicine. You look after yourself, Kayla. And call me, if you think of anything."

CHAPTER FORTY

ZOE WALKED into the team room, her head full of everything Adam Fulmer had refused to tell her. He'd admitted to knowing Ana-Maria, and the forensics made it clear he was at the hotel where she'd been kept with the other women. If he'd handled her passport, a good lawyer would use that to prove he at least knew about the trafficking.

But the bomb was the important thing. A police officer had been killed, and civilians injured. The bomber herself had died. If Adam had coerced the woman into doing that, he'd be looking at a solicitation of murder charge. If he was prepared to tell them he'd been told to do it by Hamm, there might be the option to reduce that to voluntary manslaughter.

But she knew how these things worked. Trevor Hamm would have routes into the prison system. Adam Fulmer wouldn't be safe there, and he knew it as well as Zoe did. His only credible option was witness protection, and that didn't come easy.

She needed to talk to Lesley, and to Sheila. And she still

hadn't asked Lesley about getting DNA samples from the male students.

She put her hand on the doorknob, ready to leave. Connie was out conducting interviews. Rhodri was alone at his desk, frowning at the screen.

"Rhodri, I'm going to see the DCI. You OK here?"

"Yeah. Boss, I spoke to Adi."

"OK." She took her hand off the door. "Anything useful?"

"The DNA can't tell us any more about the suspect, something to do with it not being the genes they use. But they did find a footprint and some dog hairs."

"Footprint?"

"Size seven. Laurence was a nine."

"They think it's from the time of the murder?"

"Apparently it was fresh."

"So a man with small feet, or a woman with large feet... what about the dog hairs?"

"From a brown, short-haired dog."

"Find out if Laurence had a dog."

"Pets aren't allowed in halls of residence."

"His family might have one. He might have gone home to visit, or just not washed his clothes all that often."

"How d'you want me to get that?"

"By talking to his parents." She saw his look of alarm. "It's OK, I'll get Mo to do it."

The door opened behind her and Mo walked in, two cups of coffee in hand. "Thought you might want this," he said to her.

"Thanks. I need to see Lesley, but leave it on my desk, will you? And I'd be grateful if you could call Laurence's parents."

He nodded. "Are they in the city?"

"Ask the warden, she'll have been in contact with them. If they're here, go and see them. If not, send someone from their local force."

"Anything specific you want to ask them?"

"For starters, they might know if their son had fallen out with anyone."

"He was living away from home..."

"He might have talked to them. No harm in asking."

"Of course. Must be awful for them."

She nodded. "And ask them if they've got a dog, will you?"

"A dog?"

Zoe gestured to Rhodri.

"Adi found dog hairs on Laurence's clothing, Sarge."

"Right. And you think the killer might have had a dog."

"You never know," Zoe said.

"I'm on it."

"Good," she replied. "I'll talk to the DCI about getting DNA samples, let you know how I get on."

CHAPTER FORTY-ONE

KAYLA WAS RIGHT: Lin wasn't in her room. Connie checked a map of the campus on her phone and grabbed her bike from outside Boulton Hall to cycle over to the School of Medicine. It was a chilly February morning with mist still hanging in the air at 10am, and she shivered as she pulled on her helmet. By the time she arrived at the medical school, she was warm from the exercise and the mist was lifting.

Connie found a toilet and checked the mirror, anxious to present a professional image. After a minute tweaking her hair and rubbing under her eyes, she was ready.

She had no idea where Lin would be.

She went to the reception desk. "Hello, my name's Detective Constable Williams. I need to talk to one of your students."

The young man behind the desk was skinny with wild blonde hair and a tie with pictures of fish. He flushed as she showed him her warrant card.

"Hang on a minute." He ducked out from behind the desk and half-ran up a flight of stairs.

After a few minutes he reappeared with a grey-haired man who eyed Connie with irritation.

"I'm Doctor Ian Hassel, Student Liaison. What can we do for you?"

"I need to speak to Lin Johnson, she's a first year student."

"Can't it wait?"

"My inquiries are part of a murder investigation." She straightened. The man was four inches taller than her, but she was a police officer. "So no, it can't wait."

He pushed his glasses up his nose and surveyed her, then sighed. "Very well. I suggest you wait here."

"Thank you."

He grunted and went to the desk where he conferred with the fish-tie man in a low voice. The younger man peered round him at Connie as they spoke, then picked up a phone.

Connie stood in the centre of the space, determined not to shrink into a wall. Medics in white coats walked past, occasionally giving her puzzled stares. A door banged open towards the back of the reception area and students crowded through it, pushing past her to get to the exit. She felt herself buffeted by them and wondered if they'd even registered her presence.

At last the crowd had dispersed, and she spotted Lin coming down the stairs. She wore a lab coat and her hair was tucked behind her ears. She looked nervous.

At the bottom of the stairs, she painted on a false smile and approached Connie, her hand outstretched.

"Hi, I'm Lin," she said in an American accent.

Connie held up her ID. "DC Connie Williams. Is there somewhere private we can talk?"

"Er..."

"Lecture theatre nine's empty for the next five minutes," the fish-tie man said. "I won't tell if you won't."

"Thanks," Lin shot him a bright smile very different from the one she'd given Connie. She turned to Connie. "Come on."

Connie followed the young woman through the door the students had emerged from, her footsteps echoing on the hard floor. Once inside, Lin closed the door and slid into a seat on the second row. Connie followed her, sitting three seats away and facing her.

"I was in an anatomy class," Lin said.

"Sorry to disturb you."

"I hate anatomy."

"Really?" How could you be a doctor, and hate anatomy? It was one of the more interesting aspects of the forensics training Connie had received.

"Gruesome. We're working on an old guy who died of myocardial infarction. We call him Dave."

"You don't know their real identities?"

Lin shuddered. "That would make it even worse."

"Well, I won't keep you. I just need to ask you a few more questions about Laurence."

"I thought you might."

"Did you know about the allegations of rape against him?"

A shadow crossed Lin's face. "I did."

"Did you know who made them?"

"Where d'you wanna start?"

"There was more than one woman?"

"Laurence was a creep," Lin said. "It's why he never came out of his room. It's why Kayla didn't want to film him on Monday night."

"Because he was a creep?"

"Exactly."

"Anything more specific? Did anything happen between Kayla and Laurence?"

Lin held Connie's gaze. "You'd have to ask Kayla that."

"I have. She says not."

"There's your answer then."

Connie leaned back. "You said *where d'you wanna start?* Does that mean Laurence assaulted multiple women?"

"Look, the guy's dead, alright. Not that anyone'll miss him."

"I imagine his parents will."

"No one in Boulton Hall, I mean. I'm not going to start throwing around accusations when he ain't here to defend himself."

"But you would, if he was still alive?"

Lin's tongue darted out between her lips. Her pupils were dilated. "That's not my place," she said.

"But you think there are other women whose place it would be to say something?"

Lin shrugged.

Connie eyed her. "Did Laurence ever assault you? Did he make unwelcome moves on you?"

"Unwelcome moves?" Lin laughed, her eyes cold. "What is this, Saturday Night Fever?" She blew out. "No. He never tried it on with me. I was lucky, I guess. Doesn't like East Asian women. Didn't."

"So you're saying the women Laurence came on to were white?"

"I dunno. I'm not saying anything. Look, I don't want to stir up trouble. Just forget I ever said anything."

"I can't do that, I'm afraid."

"I guess you can't." Lin dropped her gaze to her finger-nails. They were bitten.

"Do you know of any specific women who might have reason to want Laurence dead, Lin?"

"The whole of Boulton Hall knew what he was like. It was an open secret. We knew the warden was investigating what he'd done to Becca. We knew there were other girls, before her."

"But none of them made a complaint."

"I don't blame them, do you? Doctor Edwards has hardly mounted a thorough inquiry."

"They would have the option to go to the police."

Lin raised an eyebrow. "Bit late for that now."

"Lin, I want you to tell me the names of anyone you think might have wanted Laurence dead. I need to talk to them."

"There are two hundred students in Boulton. Where d'you want me to start?"

"You know what I mean."

Lin stood up. "Look. Becca was popular, yeah? *Is* popular. She's one of those girls who somehow manage to combine being naturally pretty with being really nice. Makes you sick, but there you have it. I guess half the straight guys in the hall have got a crush on her. Any one of them might have wanted to do it, defend her honour, y'know?"

"And the women?"

"Well that's not just cos of Becca. There are a few who'd have wanted rid of him for their own reasons."

Connie stood up to bring their eyes level. "I need names."

"I don't know nothin' for sure. And I'm not about to land people in it on the basis of hearsay. You need to put your nose to the ground, see what you can find."

"That's what I'm doing."

"Good. You carry on doing it. I need to get back to class."

"How's Kayla been? Since the two of you found Laurence?"

Lin stared off into space. "The truth? Pretty freaked out."

"Is she seeing Jenson Begg?"

Lin's head whipped round. "That's her business."

"It's a simple question."

"I don't see what it has to do with Laurence dying."

"Jenson was involved in the warden's investigation. He had information he might have passed to Kayla."

Lin narrowed her eyes. Behind Connie, the door to the lecture theatre opened: time was up.

"She's imagining things," Lin said.

"Hallucinating?"

"Nah. Just imagining things." Lin was having to shout now over the sound of students taking their places around the two of them. "She's got it into her head that some woman is following her."

"Which woman?"

"No idea. But Kayla reckons she's being stalked. Maybe she is, who knows. But I think she's losing it."

CHAPTER FORTY-TWO

KAYLA'S PHONE rang as she walked across campus. Her head felt full of mush and her feet were heavy. Talking to that policewoman had left her irritable and confused.

"It's Kayla," she snapped as she answered it.

"Hi Kayla, it's Gina. How are you?"

Kayla clenched her fist around the strap of her bag. "I'm fine. How are you?"

"I'm good thanks. Just wondered if you fancied grabbing lunch."

Kayla was passing Old Joe, the iconic university clock tower. It was five past eleven. She was running late for her lecture on eighteenth century women novelists.

"I've got a lecture now, but I'll be free at quarter past twelve."

"Perfect. I'll be in the Costa at University Centre."

"OK." Kayla wasn't sure how she felt about Gina paying her so much attention, but lunch with someone not from Boulton Hall could be just what she needed. She picked up pace and hurried to her lecture.

An hour later she was in the basement of the Costa, peering through the crowds and looking for Gina. At last she found her at a long table with four other women. They were huddled together, talking in low voices. Then Gina laughed and leaned back in her seat, her eyes creased. The other women laughed with her. Kayla smiled.

"Er, hi." She stood behind Gina, her stomach clenching. She hadn't been expecting company.

Gina turned round, wiping her eyes. "Kayla, lovely to see you. Here, grab a chair." She yanked a chair out from under the table and patted it. "Folks, this is Kayla. I met her in Boulton Hall."

The woman opposite Gina, who had dark skin and bleached-blonde hair that was almost white, winced. "Nasty business you've got going on there."

Kayla felt herself stiffen. She nodded, unable to speak.

"Kayla was the one who found him," Gina said in a low voice. The women around the table adopted expressions of concern and sympathy: narrowed eyes, cocked heads, down-turned mouths. Kayla shrugged, wishing she hadn't come.

"We can help you," said a tall blonde woman wearing a vibrant green jacket. "That's what this group is for."

Kayla frowned and looked at Gina. She'd been expecting a simple lunch.

Gina smiled at her. "We're a women's support group. We've all had unpleasant experiences at the hands of men. Jane over there" – she gestured at the tall blonde woman, who smiled at Kayla – "she got out of an abusive relationship ten months ago."

Jane nodded gravely, her eyes on Kayla. "And Sukhi's still trying to stop her dad running her life."

"He's a monster," muttered a skinny Asian woman in a

blue and white tunic top. "Fuck knows how my mum puts up with him."

"We got together cos we knew there would be no judgement," Gina said. "Some of us are still battling our demons. Others are through to the other side. Me, for example. But I believe it's the responsibility of a woman who's survived trauma to make herself available to others going through it." She tapped the empty chair again and Kayla slid into it, her rucksack on her lap.

"I'm not sure I've been through trauma," she said.

The other women exchanged glances. What had Gina told them about her?

The white-haired woman reached across the table and grabbed Kayla's hand. "It's hard to admit to it. You blame yourself. You think you could have stopped it, or avoided it."

"I found a... body. There wasn't much I could do to stop that."

The woman raised an eyebrow. "You look like you've suffered worse than that."

Kayla shuffled in her seat. "I don't see how..." She didn't like this.

Gina put a hand over the white-haired woman's wrist. "Go easy on her, Berni. She's new. Let's just let her get to know us, then when she's ready, she might want to open up."

Kayla felt a shiver run down her back.

"Anyway, d'you want a coffee, Kayla?" Gina said. "My treat."

Kayla shrugged. Anything to end the discomfort of this conversation. "Thanks. Soy latte please."

"Coming right up." Gina gave her hand a quick squeeze then left her alone with the other women. They started talking between themselves, leaving Kayla feeling like an interloper in the middle of a crowd of strangers.

CHAPTER FORTY-THREE

Mo sat in the lobby of the budget hotel, trying to ignore the fact that the man behind the reception desk wouldn't stop staring at him. He'd asked for Laurence's parents and been told to wait for them to come down from their room.

He couldn't imagine what they were going through. Summoned from Leeds to identify their dead son not five months after waving him off to university. Being stuck in this soulless place couldn't help.

The lift doors slid open and a grey-haired couple walked out, scanning the space. Mo stood up and gave them a sympathetic smile, aware that his face was a cliché.

"Mr Thomms, Mrs Thomms. Thank you for seeing me."

Mr Thomms was short and slim, dressed in a pair of loosely fitting jeans and a blue shirt. His skin was pale and he looked like he hadn't slept. He held out a hand and shook Mo's. "David Thomms," he said, his voice cracking.

His wife stood a pace behind him, her eyes roaming over Mo. Sizing him up, working out if he was up to solving her son's murder. She was just as slender as her husband but looked less drawn, perhaps because of the perfectly applied makeup. Her pink sweater looked like it had been ironed.

"Mrs Thomms," Mo said. "I'm so sorry for your loss."

She nodded. "Thank you." She eyed the hard sofa Mo had been sitting on and glanced at the receptionist. "Let's not stay here."

"Good idea," Mo said. "There's a place we can get coffee."

They were near the canals, in an area behind the old Royal Mail building, now known as the Mailbox. This part of the city centre was devoted to restaurants, bars and coffee shops as well as a few hotels. Early afternoon on a Thursday, it was starting to get busy.

Mo led the couple to a bar that looked quieter than most and advertised coffee. He found an isolated table near the back and gestured for them to sit down.

"What can I get you?" he asked.

"Two white coffees," Mrs Thomms said. "Just filter. David will have sugar."

"No problem."

Mo collected the coffee as quickly as he could, grabbing a herbal tea for himself, and returned to the table. The couple sat in silence, each of them darting their gaze around the bar as if expecting to spot something of interest. Maybe they thought Laurence had been in the habit of coming here. Mo doubted it.

Mo sipped his tea while Mr Thomms stirred his coffee and Mrs Thomms stared at hers, almost as if she was wondering what it was.

"Before I start," he said, "I want to make sure we don't go over the same ground more than once. Who have you spoken to?"

"We spoke to a uniformed sergeant when we arrived," Mr Thomms said. "He told us the circumstances of Laurence's passing."

Mo nodded. "Did he tell you we're treating it as a murder?"

Mr Thomms nodded, not meeting Mo's eye. His wife scratched her cheek and dragged in a trembling breath.

"We have DNA evidence that we think shows someone forced your son to take illegal drugs in a concentrated form. We're working on identifying this person."

"What kind of DNA evidence?" asked Mrs Thomms.

"There were scratches inside your son's mouth. We found his DNA in the cheek swab we took, but also the DNA of one other person."

"Could he have got that some other way?" she asked. "Kissing, maybe?"

Mo smiled. "You can find DNA from saliva in the mouth of someone who has been kissing. But the fact that this DNA was concentrated around the scratches suggests that it wasn't so well-intentioned."

Mrs Thomms stared ahead of her, past Mo and at the wall behind him, her eyes glazed. After a moment, she nodded slowly. "Why would someone want to kill him?"

"That's what I'm hoping you can help us with. Did Laurence talk to you about falling out with anyone at university? Anyone who might have wanted to hurt him?"

"Nothing," said Mr Thomms. "No."

His wife put a hand on his knee. "He didn't call home much. I spoke to him a few times in the first month, but then contact tailed off." Her voice broke on the *off*.

"When was the last time you spoke to him?" Mo asked.

Mrs Thomms reached inside a slim blue handbag and

brought out a pocket diary. "I always wrote it down." She held her breath for a moment, her eyes wet. She blinked and shook out her head. "Sorry. Here." She held the diary out. On 18th January she'd written *Laurence* at the top of the page, along with a time: 8:20pm.

"That's when he called us."

"That's the last time?"

She nodded, her lips pursed. She blinked a few times.

"I know this is hard," Mo said. "But what did you talk about?" He watched the couple trying to retain their composure. Interviews with family members were always a mix of sympathy, dread and suspicion. In this case, the parents had been over a hundred miles away when their son died, so all he felt was overwhelming sadness for them. He realised he didn't know if Laurence had siblings.

"I can't remember," Mrs Thomms said. "Not much, I imagine. He never said much of substance. If you know what I mean."

Mo nodded. He knew what his own conversations with his parents could be like: plenty of words, no depth. "Did he talk about any of his fellow students? Or any staff members?"

"Not that I remember. He was struggling with an assignment, he was stressed about that. Not that I understood a word he said about it." She sniffed.

"Did he mention a girl called Becca MacGuire?"

Mrs Thomms frowned. "No."

"Why?" asked her husband, his voice rough.

Mo ignored the question. "Kayla Goode? Lin Johnson?"

"He rarely talked about girls, Detective," Mrs Thomms said. "I'd remember if he mentioned any of those names. Were they his friends?"

"They were living in the same hall of residence."

"Have they been hurt as well?"

"No." *Not in the way you think*, Mo thought. He wondered how much the couple knew about the allegations against their son. Would the warden have contacted them? The students were adults; he doubted that would be necessary.

"Did he seem happy at university?" he asked.

"I don't know," said Mr Thomms. "I mean, you can't really tell, can you?"

Mo drew a breath, thinking of his own daughters. Fiona was eleven now, and Isla eight. He hoped he would always know if they were happy or not. "So he gave no indication of his mood?"

"You think he might have killed himself?" Mrs Thomms' voice was sharp.

"We've ruled that out."

"Good."

"I have one final question, and it might feel a bit odd."

Mrs Thomms raised herself up. "Go on." She looked like a woman who expected worse to be piled on top of already devastating news.

"Do you own a dog?"

"A dog?"

"Do you own one?"

"Three cats. Never had a dog. Why?"

"Nothing for you to worry about. Thank you for your time." Mo gulped down the last of his tepid tea and stood up, glad to be leaving the deep sorrow that emanated from the couple.

CHAPTER FORTY-FOUR

"Zoe, how you getting on with our mystery drug death?"

"We've got DNA from inside his mouth, Ma'am. Adi reckons it's from the person who pushed the drugs down his throat."

Lesley swivelled in her chair, her skirt crackling against her tan tights. "And you want me to authorise DNA sampling from all the students in Boulton Hall."

"Just the men."

"It's male DNA?"

"It is."

Lesley held her fingers against her chin and drummed once, then twice. "Is there a risk of this killer striking again?"

"It depends. If it's someone trying to get revenge on Laurence because he assaulted female students, then either no, because they've done what they set out to do... or yes, because Laurence won't be the only man on campus who's done that. And if it's nothing to do with the assaults but it's drug-related, then there's a credible risk of something similar happening again."

"You not got any potential targets in mind, though."

"No. But I think there is a risk the perpetrator might do it again."

"Maybe we should get the good Doctor McBride back in," Lesley said.

"I'd rather we didn't."

Lesley laughed. Petra McBride was a psychologist who'd been drafted in to help identify the person who'd come to be known as the Digbeth Ripper. She'd been short, Scottish, and bolshy. Zoe had grown to quite like her by the time the case was solved, but she wasn't sure she had the energy to square up to the woman on this one.

"Don't worry," said Lesley. "We don't have the budget. Wrong time of year. So. You want to get DNA samples. How many male students are there in Boulton Hall?"

"Ninety-four."

"I can stomach that many. Make sure you do staff, too. Not just academics: cooks, cleaners, the people behind the scenes. Can't afford to miss anyone."

"Thanks, Ma'am."

"My pleasure." Lesley coughed. "I heard you'd had a grilling from Professional Standards."

Zoe clenched her fists. "DS Kaur."

Lesley rifled in her desk for a pencil, then started exploring her mouth with it. Zoe looked away, spotting a McDonalds bag in the bin.

"Don't worry about it," Lesley said, pulling out the pencil.

"She gave me quite the going over."

"It's what they do. You know what we're like with our suspects."

"I'm not a suspect."

Lesley waved a hand. "You know what I mean. They see us like we see the shits who come in here having burgled people and started fights in pubs. Impossible to have any respect when your perspective on the bright and shiny West Midlands Police Service is the small minority of bad apples."

"I'm worried they still think I was working with Ian."

"They don't really think that. They're just tightening the screws, in case you know anything you're not telling them."

"I've been frank and honest from day one."

Lesley raised an eyebrow. "Have you? Told that boyfriend of yours everything you knew about Ian? About David?"

"We try not to talk about work. We're not talking at all right now."

"Exactly." Lesley coughed, bending over to hack for a few moments. She waved an arm in front of her: *ignore this.*

"Are you alright, Ma'am?"

"Me?" Lesley sat up straight and cleared her throat, her hand on her chest. Her eyes were bloodshot. "Never better. Right. I'll get that paperwork for you and you can get onto Uniform and organise this sampling circus."

CHAPTER FORTY-FIVE

KAYLA's last lecture finished early. In truth she'd spent half of it trying not to doze off, and was relieved to be released.

She strolled back through campus, enjoying the thin sunshine that had replaced the morning's fog. As she passed Costa Coffee, she wondered why Gina had invited her to join the women's support group at lunchtime. Did she think Kayla needed supporting? Did she know things about her?

She made a tsking noise to banish the thought from her head. She wanted to get her wits back, to wake up. She'd hardly slept the last two nights; the image of Laurence's dead body kept floating in front of her eyes as she was about to drop off. She yawned, attracting the attention of two men who sniggered as they passed her. She resisted the urge to tell them where to get off.

Back at Boulton Hall, she took the stairs to the second floor and Jenson's flat. He'd have finished his counselling sessions for the afternoon but wouldn't have left for the Selly Oak house yet.

As Kayla rounded the corner to his corridor, she saw his

door open, and the back of a woman's shoe just inside. She could hear a low murmur, but not the words, just that this woman was talking to him.

Kayla hung back, not wanting to invade the woman's privacy. She waited, occasionally peering round the corner. She heard laughter: Jenson's, and then the woman's. Followed by more muttered words.

Kayla hopped from foot to foot. She needed the loo but didn't want to draw attention to herself by moving. She leaned against the wall and waited for Jenson to finish his conversation. What was it that needed so long? It was four fifteen, quarter of an hour after he should have finished.

At last she heard his door close. She retreated towards the lift so Jenson's visitor wouldn't see her. Footsteps approached: firm, steady. She heard low singing: Lady Gaga.

The woman emerged, walking towards the stairs. She was East Asian, wearing cowboy boots over red leggings. She had short dark hair and a gait that smacked of confidence.

It was Lin.

Kayla stepped forward to speak to her friend, then thought better of it. Lin hated Jenson. She thought he was bad news, terrible for Kayla. So what was she doing visiting him in the afternoon, laughing with him in the corridor?

CHAPTER FORTY-SIX

ZOE STOOD up to leave Lesley's office just as the door opened. It would be Mo, reporting back from his interview and checking progress on the DNA sampling.

"I'll be right there," she said. "We've got the OK for the sampling."

"What sampling's that, then?" Detective Superintendent David Randle closed the door and waggled his eyebrows at Zoe in a way that made her feel six years old.

"Sir. The Laurence Thomms case. We have DNA, we're running checks on the students."

"Good, good." He turned to Lesley. "You got a minute?"

"Of course, sir." Lesley slipped her shoes back on and arranged her feet in front of her chair.

Randle nodded then eyed Zoe. "Don't let me keep you."

"Sir." Zoe waited for him to move to one side then left the room, sharing a brief glance with Lesley. When she was halfway down the corridor, she heard raised voices. Was Randle shouting at the DCI?

She stopped walking, desperate to go back and eavesdrop. But she respected Lesley too much for that. She forced herself to put one foot in front of the other, making her way slowly back to the team room.

The three of them were waiting for her. Mo stood next to the board, his finger on Jenson Begg's photo.

"Hi," Zoe said. "How did it go with the parents?"

Mo shook his head, his eyes lowered. "It was heart-breaking just being in the same room with them."

"Must be rough. Did they give you anything useful?"

"Seems he hardly rang home. Last time they spoke to him was a month ago."

She winced. "If Nicholas does that to me when he's at uni I'll be straight over there to tell him what's what."

Mo smiled at her. "No, you won't."

She shrugged. "So did you get anything useful?"

"Sorry. Connie's got something though."

Zoe turned to the DC, who was biting back a smile. "Connie. Tell us what's making you look so pleased with yourself."

Connie held up a file. "Jenson Begg's got history."

"OK." Zoe grabbed the file from her. "What kind of history?"

"The university authorities gave him a warning after he was found in possession of a Class A drug, two and a half years ago."

"When he was an undergraduate."

"Yes. And he received another warning after a student said he stalked her."

"Stalking?" Zoe skimmed the file.

"He was in his third year. He'd been going out with her, April Hulse was her name. She dumped him but it seems he wouldn't accept it. Eventually she reported him to her tutor."

"You get this from your mate...?"

"Rhonda. Yes."

"Good old Rhonda. What came of it?"

"He got a rap on the knuckles and a warning not to do it again. By the time it came to a head, he and the woman had both graduated."

"And she'd buggered off back home or off to her new graduate life."

"Yes."

"Meaning he got to stay at the university as a postgrad, counselling vulnerable students and with no comeback for what he supposedly did."

Connie nodded. "I bloody wish these girls would come to us instead of the university, boss."

"You and me both, Connie. So does the warden know about this? She did give him a position of responsibility, after all."

"She can't have. He wasn't charged with anything. Didn't have his degree withheld, obviously. The woman didn't press charges."

"OK," said Zoe. "I'm not sure if the stalking's relevant, or if it just makes me bloody depressed at the mindset of these young men, but the possession definitely is. You find out how much he was carrying?"

"Sorry, boss. Rhonda didn't know that."

"Exactly which Class A substance was it?"

"Cocaine. Not methamphetamine."

Zoe punched the desk. "We should talk to him. Even if he isn't a suspect, he might know where the drugs that killed Laurence came from."

"You want me to go again, boss?" Mo said.

"I want Rhodri this time."

"Me, boss?" Rhodri looked alarmed.

"You're a young guy. See if you can strike up a rapport with him. A bit of banter. Maybe he'll open up. Brag. Don't go pulling any tricks like you did in the bar, though."

"No, boss."

"You tell him you're a police officer, right? This isn't an undercover operation."

"No, boss."

"Glad that's got through." Zoe turned to Mo. "Right. Can you get onto Uniform and start the ball rolling with the DNA sampling? We'll need to find a room in Boulton Hall we can use, I'll speak to Doctor Edwards."

"No problem, boss. You want it to start tonight?"

"What time is it?"

"Half six, boss," said Connie.

"We get things set up tonight, leave Uniform to work their magic, then start the testing tomorrow. Connie, I want you to liaise with Boulton Hall. Get a list of all male students and staff. Trans women too, if there are any. We're looking for someone with a Y chromosome."

"I already rang them to set up another interview with the warden, boss."

"When you found out about Jenson's record."

"Yes."

"You knew I'd want to talk to her."

"I thought it was a reasonable assumption."

"Nice one, Connie. I do love having a team who're able to think ahead of me."

Connie smiled.

"So have you already got the list?"

Connie's smile dropped. "Didn't think of that, sorry. But I do know they've gone home for the night."

"No bother. We'll talk to them first thing. You OK to come in early?"

"Course I am."

"Good. You and Mo can coordinate that. Rhodri, you want a lift to Boulton Hall?"

"It's OK. I've got my Saab."

"Your trusty Saab, of course." Zoe thought of the time it had broken down when they'd been following Ian. "Let me know how you get on with Jenson, and I'll see if I can pin down the warden at home."

CHAPTER FORTY-SEVEN

"Sir. This is a rare honour." Lesley leaned across her desk, listening to Zoe's footsteps recede along the corridor.

"Don't give me that crap, Lesley."

Lesley sighed. She didn't have the energy for this. "I've got no idea what *crap* you're talking about."

"*Rare honour.* You don't have to sweet-talk me."

"Fair enough. What can I do for you?"

"Ian Osman."

Lesley felt her stomach dip. She didn't like being reminded of the fact she'd agreed to have him in Zoe's team. The guy had been a square peg from day one, and she wished she could take that decision back.

"What about him?" she asked.

"I don't like it."

Lesley regarded her boss. She didn't like it either: the fact that there'd been a bent copper in her team, and the fact it tainted everyone. She had a feeling Randle didn't like it for different reasons.

"You'll have to clarify, sir."

"It reflects badly on Force CID," he said. "DS Osman was given access to sensitive investigations. He was trusted."

Lesley raised an eyebrow. Her recollection was that Ian had been the opposite of *trusted*. And she still believed it was Randle who'd summoned him to the airport where he'd planted that evidence.

"Force CID is the department that works on the most high-profile, sensitive cases," she said. "I can imagine it's a magnet to bent coppers."

"You think you've got more of them?" He sat down in the chair Zoe had vacated, his eyes not leaving Lesley's face.

"No, sir. Not as far as I'm aware. But of course, if Professional Standards have got their eye on anyone, they're more likely to liaise with you..."

"What about DI Finch? You think she was working with Osman?"

A shooting pain ran down the back of Lesley's neck. She'd been having these pains intermittently since the New Street bomb, and agitation set them off.

"I certainly don't," she said.

"Professional Standards don't seem to think so. They interviewed her on Tuesday evening. Very secretive, it was."

"It can't have been all that secretive. Seeing as you know about it and I know about it."

"She told you?"

Lesley shoved the paperwork on her desk to one side. "Of course she bloody told me. My officers come to me when they have problems. When there's anything that might affect their work."

Randle crossed one leg over the other, his ankle perched on his knee. "You're right."

"Not sure what I'm supposed to be right about."

"The investigation will affect DI Finch's work. What have you got her on right now?"

"She's SIO on the Laurence Thomms murder, and she's still working the Magpie case."

"I want her taken off that."

"Which?"

Randle gave her a look. "Magpie. If she's under investigation for potential involvement in the corruption case, then she shouldn't be anywhere near associated investigations."

"We already identified the organisation that planted the bomb at the airport. Or rather, Anti-Terror did. We don't believe the New Street one is the same bunch."

"I don't care. It's linked, it all is. Organised crime, people trafficking. She shouldn't be anywhere near it."

"She's my best detective."

"DI Dawson has six years' more experience as a DI."

"Experience isn't everything. And his team has a full caseload right now."

"Take her off the Magpie investigation. She's got enough to focus on with this murder."

"DS Uddin's been working with her, he's got a good relationship with DS Griffin in Organised Crime. I'll second him to Dawson's team, just part-time while they're working on this case."

"I don't think so."

"He knows the case. He's been working on this for months."

"He's Zoe's oldest friend. He'll tell her what he's working on."

Lesley felt heat rise up her neck. She scratched the skin. "You underestimate him."

"I'm being realistic. Take both of them off the case, DCI Clarke. That's an order."

CHAPTER FORTY-EIGHT

JENSON WASN'T in his flat. Rhodri knocked on the next door along, which was opened by a shirtless man rubbing his eyes.

"Hey." The man stretched his arms above his head. "You after Jenson?"

"Yeah. You know where he is?"

"Probably at his place in Selly Oak."

Rhodri worked to conceal his surprise. "Right. Course. Remind me the address, will you?"

"Er..." The man yawned. "240 Umberslade Road. Tell him he owes me a fiver, will you?"

"Sure."

Once again, Rhodri had changed his clothes before coming here. He'd brought his grungiest t-shirt and a pair of jeans as well as a battered leather jacket into work and stashed them in his locker. He could pass for a civilian, not that he was planning on lying about it.

"Thanks."

"Yeah." The man closed the door and Rhodri heard another loud yawn behind the wood. He yawned himself.

"Get a grip, Hughes," he muttered to himself.

He hurried out of Boulton Hall and towards his Saab. The boss's Mini was parked a few spaces along; she would still be with the warden. *Rather her than me.*

He started the car after a couple of tries then drove to Selly Oak. Umberslade Road was lined with narrow terraced houses and there were no parking spaces. He drove round the block twice, wishing he'd left his car on campus and walked. Eventually he found a spot three streets away.

It was a chilly night, the air fizzy with the threat of rain. Rhodri pulled his collar up as he walked towards Jenson's house. Why would a man with a free flat on campus need a house? It made Rhodri more suspicious.

Number 240's front door had flaking green paint. The windows were made of cheap PVC, the seal broken and the panes misted up. A grimy lace curtain was drawn in the downstairs bay.

Rhodri rapped on the knocker, then took a step back to look at the upstairs windows. A light came on on the first floor. He looked back at the door, waiting.

A short man wearing a blue shirt threw the door open: Jenson.

"I'm not in," he snapped.

"Looks like you are, mate."

Jenson scowled. "You're not Vic."

Rhodri held up his ID. "DC Rhodri Hughes. My boss sent me for a quick chat, like. You got a mo?"

Jenson eyed him then shrugged. "Come in."

Rhodri followed him to a narrow kitchen at the back of the house. Something foul-smelling bubbled on the stove and dishes were piled up in the sink. Jenson opened the fridge and grabbed a beer, then flicked the top off and swigged from it.

"Not offering me one?"

"You're on duty. It would be immoral of me."

Rhodri laughed. "Fair enough."

"What is it this time? I've had the tall redheaded woman, then the little Asian guy. Now I've got you, the Welsh wonder."

"We found out some stuff about you."

"Yeah?" Jenson swigged at the bottle. "What kind of stuff?"

"The drugs, and the stalking."

"Both untrue."

Rhodri raised an eyebrow. "Really?"

"You see anything on my record? You see them stopping me being a residential tutor? Course not. There's no way they'd give you a job like that if you were a stalker."

"And the drugs?"

Jenson shrugged. "Someone got their wires crossed, mate. I don't do drugs."

"None at all? Not even the occasional joint?"

Jenson stared back at Rhodri, saying nothing.

"Fair enough. You're pure as the driven snow. Tell me about April Hulse."

"She was some bitch on my course. Fancied me, and got pissed off when I didn't return the favour. So she decided she'd try to wreck my life."

"You didn't go out with her?"

"One date. Bloody disaster."

Rhodri surveyed the young man as he swigged from the bottle again. The boss might want him to track April down, check Jenson's story.

"So because you dumped her after one date, she told the university you were stalking her?"

"Women, eh?" Jenson sniffed loudly then spat onto the floor.

"What about Kayla Goode?"

Jenson bristled. "What about her?"

"You seeing her?"

"What difference does it make if I am?"

"You're her residential tutor."

"We're both adults."

"You like to sleep with women you're supposed to be looking after?"

A shrug. "I live in a hall of residence, mate. Plenty of women, you'd be tempted too."

"So not just Kayla."

"I'm not a monk, if that's what you're saying."

"OK. So is this your house?"

"It's my mate's. I crash here sometimes, when I want a bit of freedom."

"Does the warden know you've got two addresses?"

"Like I say, this is my mate's place."

Rhodri wondered what it would be like to have this snippy man as your residential tutor. If Laurence had been victimised, if Kayla and Becca had been scared, would he have given them support? Or just made them feel worse?

"Anything else you want to grill me on?" Jenson tossed the bottle into a bin and grabbed another from the fridge.

"Becca MacGuire. Did you tell anyone about her?"

"About what she said Laurence did?"

Rhodri nodded.

"My job involves keeping confidences, mate. What do you think?"

"That's not an answer."

Laurence leaned in. "No. I *did not tell anyone.* Happy?"

"So how come everyone knew?"

"Maybe Becca told them. I dunno."

"Was Laurence being victimised?"

"Victimised? Because he got too handsy with the women?"

"If everyone knew what he'd allegedly done, it would have made him unpopular."

"I don't get involved in that stuff. The undergrads can sort out their own little soap operas. I only wade in when I have to." Jenson gulped down more beer, his Adam's apple bobbing. "Now if you don't mind, Constable, I'd like to get back to my evening."

"Fair enough." Rhodri turned away from Jenson and walked to the front door. The door to the front room was open a crack. He could see a bed inside and a couple lying on it.

"Which is your room?" he asked Jenson.

"I told you. Not my house."

Rhodri nodded, not believing him. He turned to Jenson.

"Thanks for your time."

Jenson grunted. "My pleasure."

Rhodri swallowed down his irritation and walked out to the street. He had a frozen pizza waiting for him in his new flat, and no company as Izzy was out with her mates tonight. There was a six pack of Foster's in the fridge, at least. Watching Jenson drinking had made him thirsty.

As he turned in the direction of his car, he spotted movement in the shadows opposite the house. He stopped, his eyes adjusting to the dark. The house opposite had a rambling hedge in the front garden. Someone was behind it.

Rhodri considered crossing the road to see who it was, then thought better of it. Probably just someone coming home after a few too many in the pub. He took a deep breath and walked to his car, wishing he had something better than Papa John's to look forward to.

CHAPTER FORTY-NINE

THE WARDEN LIVED in a modern house tucked in behind Boulton Hall. Zoe hadn't known these houses existed: perk of the job, she supposed. She wondered if any of the students ever got to see inside. Or postgrads like Jenson.

She pressed the buzzer and peered through the glazed front door, seeing movement beyond. After a moment of what sounded like keys being sought out, a tall black man with light grey hair opened the door.

"I'm here to speak to Doctor Edwards." Zoe held up her warrant card. "DI Finch, West Midlands police."

The man nodded, his breathing shallow. "I'm Doctor Edwards, but I imagine it's Sheila you need. The other one."

"Is she at home?"

"We're eating our dinner."

"Sorry to disturb you. It is important."

"Sure it is." He grimaced. "That poor boy. Come on through, she won't mind."

Zoe followed the man through a narrow hallway into a wide kitchen that had clearly been knocked through or added to the house. Full-height windows filled the wall ahead of her and the bright lights of the room reflected back at her. She blinked in the glare.

The warden sat at a long kitchen island, a bowl of pasta and a book in front of her. She folded over the corner of a page and placed the book next to her bowl.

"DI Finch."

"Sorry to interrupt. I need to ask you a few more questions."

Dr Edwards sighed. "Of course you do. Mind if I finish my meal while we talk?"

"Not at all." Zoe approached the island.

"Can I get you a drink?" the male Dr Edwards said. "We've got a bottle of Sancerre open if you'd like some."

"A coffee please, if it's going."

He tipped his head. "Good idea. Probably should stay off the vino myself. Not quite the weekend yet, huh?"

He turned away to pour water into a complex looking machine and Zoe pulled out a tall chair along from the warden. She raised her eyebrows at the woman, who nodded for her to sit.

Zoe waited, her gaze on the marble worktop, while the warden's husband brewed coffee. The warden sat beside her in silence, eating her pasta. The couple weren't speaking to each other, but it didn't feel awkward: one of those relationships where the two of them could be at ease in conversation or in silence.

After a few moments, the male Doctor Edwards placed a mug in front of Zoe. "Enjoy."

"Thanks." She took a sip: it was good.

He placed another mug in front of his wife and kissed the top of her head. She nodded acknowledgement and cleared her plate. She pushed it away from her, grabbed a tissue out of her pocket and wiped her mouth.

The door closed as her husband left them alone.

"So," said the warden, "what's so urgent it can't wait until the morning?"

"We've been given more information about Jenson Begg."

"Jenson? What's he got to do with it?" Doctor Edwards sipped her coffee and closed her eyes momentarily.

"He was given a warning after being found with Class A drugs, and he was accused of stalking by a fellow student."

"Stalking? When?"

"A year and a half ago."

"He would have been an undergraduate. Final year."

"Did he live at Boulton Hall then?"

"No. He lived in for his first year, then he shared a house. Selly Oak somewhere, I think. Most of them do."

"I know. I live on Tiverton Road."

The warden winced. "Poor you."

"I like it."

A shrug. "So you're wondering why I gave Jenson the residential tutor job when he'd been accused of stalking."

"Did you know about it?"

"I did *not*. Did the young woman involved go to the police? I assume it was a woman?"

"It was. And no. She reported it to her tutor. Not the police."

"So it can't have been upheld. Otherwise it would be on his record, and he wouldn't have been eligible for the tutor role."

"I thought that would be the case," Zoe said. She watched the warden closely for signs she might be lying.

Doctor Edwards gave her a look as if she'd been reading

her mind. "I knew nothing about this. It would be beyond my integrity to—"

"I believe you. What about the drugs? Have you seen any evidence that Jenson might be using or supplying drugs to students?"

"Don't be absurd. If I had, d'you think he'd still be in that flat?" She jerked her head in the direction of the main building.

"Are you aware of any drug dealing or possession in Boulton Hall?"

"You've already asked me this. We did a sweep the day after Laurence died. Found a couple of bags of grass, small quantities for personal use. Nothing more. No meth."

"What happens to students who are caught with drugs in the building?"

"They're given a warning the first time. If it happens again, there's a process. Outcome depends on how much, and if they're dealing."

"And did you search the postgrads too?"

"The postgrads helped with the search."

"So you didn't search them."

"No."

"Does it occur to you that maybe you should?"

"Detective, those young men and women are in a position of trust. They receive board and lodging in return for their work, it's an employment contract. The protocol for searching their homes for illegal substances is quite different from with the undergraduates."

"By their homes, you mean their flats in Boulton Hall."

"I do."

"Which you have jurisdiction over."

The warden scratched her head. "Jurisdiction is a strong word. I have a duty of care."

"Very well, Doctor Edwards. Would you be amenable to conducting a search of Jenson Begg's flat for drugs now?"

"On what grounds?"

"On the grounds that he knew about the allegation against Laurence, and more importantly that he's previously been caught with drugs."

"He was never charged."

"A slap on the wrist. I think it's gone a little further than that, don't you?"

"I'll happily talk to him, ask him if your people can look. But I'm not mounting surprise searches on the postgrads." The warden sharpened her gaze on Zoe. "If we did him, we'd have to do them all."

"In that case, I'll get a warrant." Zoe held the warden's gaze, knowing that Lesley would never give her one on the basis of a years-old case that wasn't taken to the police and led nowhere. But the warden didn't know that.

"You do what you want, Detective. Remember, I have friends in the Law School. You can't pull the wool over my eyes."

Zoe felt her heart grow heavy. Why was this woman protecting Jenson Begg? Did they even have proper grounds to suspect him?

Either way, she wanted to know more about Begg and his relationships with the female undergraduates he had responsibility for.

"Very well, if you aren't going to cooperate."

The warden slid down from her stool. "I'm cooperating fully, Detective. But I'm not about to let you railroad me into subverting my student's legal rights."

"What can you tell me about Jenson Begg's relationships with the students he looks after? What about Kayla Goode?"

The muscle under the warden's left eye twitched. "What about Kayla Goode?"

"Is he seeing her?"

"There's no reason a residential tutor can't date an under-graduate."

"So he is."

The warden turned to Zoe. "Detective Finch, I have no idea. Don't you think I've got enough to worry about with all these students in my care and a subject to teach? Especially now that one of those students is dead." She lifted her wrist, revealing an expensive watch. "It's getting late and I've got a seminar to prepare for. Is there anything else?"

Zoe dug her thumbnail into her palm. "No."

The warden nodded. "Thanks. Frank will see you out."

CHAPTER FIFTY

"IT's ALRIGHT, I'M COMING." Kayla heaved herself up from her bed and opened the door. She'd been trying to read *Persuasion* but had dozed off.

Jenson was on the threshold, looking agitated. "Let me in."

"OK. What's up?"

He shoved past her and slumped onto the bed. "Fucking police again, that's what's up." He stood up to stand a few inches in front of her, looking down at her. "Did you give them my address?"

"What? What address?"

"The house in Selly Oak. I don't want the police there, that's the whole point."

"I don't know what you're talking about." She raised her hand to his shoulder.

He grabbed it. "If you're lying to me..."

She tried to yank her hand away but he held her wrist tight. "Why would I lie to you? Let go."

He jerked her hand upwards, making her wince. She

stared into his eyes. His chest rose and fell, his breathing heavy.

"I saw you with those ballbreakers."

"What? What ballbreakers?"

"That women's group."

"What's that got to do with the police?"

Jenson flung her arm away and she grasped her wrist. It was reddening.

"Keep away from them. They're bad news. Extremists."

"I think you're overestimating the—"

"You had lunch with them, today."

"You were at Costa? Why didn't you come over and say hi?"

"I saw you leaving. You came back here. At least you didn't go anywhere with them."

"You followed me and didn't speak to me?"

He shrugged and threw himself into the desk chair. "I was on my way back here."

"Why didn't you catch up with me?"

He picked up the book that she'd placed face down on her desk and surveyed it like it was contaminated. "I want you to keep away from them. They'll pour stupid ideas into your head, fill it with crap." He flung the book to the desk. Kayla shifted her weight as if to grab it, but with the mood he was in, she didn't want to get too close to him.

"Jenson, I know you're pissed off. But that's the police you're angry with. Don't take it out on me, please." She hesitated. "Why were you with Lin, earlier?"

He turned to her. "You're pathetic, you know that?"

Kayla blinked. "What?"

"I've seen the way you've been mooning about since

Laurence died. He was an arsehole, Kayla. Why are you so upset about it?"

She tried to catch her breath. "I found a dead body, Jenson. Lin and I did. And you haven't answered my question."

"I'm Lin's residential tutor, for fuck's sake. This isn't about me. You're being paranoid."

"Finding Laurence like that was... I don't know what it was. But I think I've got a right to be a bit freaked out."

"Nothing else to it? You and him didn't have a thing going?" He leaned forward, hands clasped in front of his knees.

She pulled back, her stomach clenching. "Don't be ridiculous."

"Don't call me ridiculous." He stood abruptly, sending her book to the floor. She stayed on the bed, anxious not to touch him.

"Get a grip, Kayla. Sort yourself out and decide who your real friends are." He yanked the door open and swept out, leaving her gaping at the door behind him.

CHAPTER FIFTY-ONE

ZOE WOKE to the sound of doors banging in Nicholas's room. She dragged herself in, yawning.

The room was even messier than usual. As well as the usual plates piled up on the desk and dirty clothes littering the floor, half his clean clothes were strewn across the bed.

Zoe watched him, her arms folded across her chest. "It's only two nights, you know." She checked her watch. "Can't you do this later? You've got to leave for school in twenty minutes."

He shook his head, rifling through the clothes. "It's fine. I want to have options."

"You'll need a bigger suitcase if you carry on like this."

He turned to her. "Can you get it please?"

"You've got just the right one there. You don't even need to fill it, not for two nights in London."

"You don't understand."

She sighed. "I'll leave you to it." Nicholas was eighteen years old, perfectly capable of packing for a long weekend away with his dad without supervision. She just hoped he managed to calm down before they left. Nicholas being agitated would set his half-brother Geordie off.

As she walked down the stairs, her phone rang.

"Morning Mo. You want to get breakfast? I need to escape Nicholas's packing antics."

"I'm two streets away from you."

"I'll grab my coat."

"No. I'm at Umberslade Road. An address Rhodri got for Jenson Begg last night."

"OK." Zoe didn't go into the living room but instead pulled her coat from the hook by the door. There was something in Mo's voice that made her think her presence was going to be required.

"What's up?"

"He's dead, boss. Jenson Begg has OD'd."

"What?" Zoe clutched her coat. "I didn't know he was..."

"Rhodri had an idea. Said he was acting suspicious."

"Is Rhodri with you?"

"Not yet."

"OK." Zoe put her hand over the phone and called up the stairs. "I've got to go to work, love. Don't forget to go to school. Have a good weekend."

She heard a muffled shout from upstairs and returned to Mo.

"You think it's just an accident, or it's related to the case?"

"The pathologist isn't here yet, but it looks very similar to the Laurence Thomms crime scene."

"I'm on my way."

CHAPTER FIFTY-TWO

KAYLA YAWNED as she closed her door behind her. She had a lecture at 9am, but had to stop off at the library to return a book that was due.

She glided along the corridor, barely awake, and didn't notice Lin until the two women stumbled into each other.

"Lin. Sorry, I was half asleep."

"That's OK. You alright?" Lin turned and fell into step with Kayla.

"Just knackered. Got to get a book back to the library or they'll fine me."

"I thought you'd be staying home."

"I've got lectures at nine and ten. Shouldn't you be on your way over to the medical school?"

"I just wanted to check you're OK."

"I'm fine."

"I mean, with Jenson and everything..."

Kayla stopped walking. "I'd rather not talk about it."

"If you're sure."

"I'm sure."

"OK." Lin lay a hand on Kayla's shoulder. "I'm here, if you need me."

Kayla pulled her rucksack higher onto her shoulder. She wasn't in the mood for talking, She'd drunk most of a bottle of wine after Jenson had left the previous night, and her head was throbbing. She was worried she might be sick in her first lecture. But she had to keep moving, to get on with her studies. She had to distract herself.

She arrived at the lift and waited for it to appear. Lin stood next to her, shuffling awkwardly.

"You OK?" Kayla asked her.

"Me? I'm fine."

"You seem a little... off."

"Well, I guess...." Lin turned to Kayla. She had that sympathy look, the one Kayla recognised from her parents splitting up when she was fourteen.

She didn't need sympathy today. She especially didn't need Lin, who'd hated Jenson all along, telling her *I told you so* about going out with a postgrad. She wanted to ask her what she'd been doing at his room yesterday, but she didn't have the energy.

"See you later," she said as the lift arrived. She slid inside, hoping Lin would get the hint.

She avoided her friend's eye as the lift doors closed.

CHAPTER FIFTY-THREE

Zoe double-parked outside the address Mo had given her. Two squad cars were outside, as well as a Volvo she recognised as belonging to her favourite pathologist. In spite of the circumstances, she couldn't help smiling at the prospect of working with Adana Adebayo rather than Brent Reynolds.

She showed her ID to the constable on the door and walked inside, careful not to touch anything. The house was dark and dirty, a smell of mustiness and grime pervading the space. She coughed.

"Hello?" she called out.

"DI Finch?" came Adana's voice. "Through here."

Zoe walked past the steep staircase and through a door with one pane missing into a narrow kitchen. It, too, stank of neglect, pots piled in the sink and the surfaces coated in a layer of grime. Jenson Begg's body lay in the middle of the cramped floor, Dr Adebayo crouched over it. Zoe stood on one of the protective plates and peered over the pathologist's head.

"How long has he been here?" she asked.

"Anywhere between three and ten hours, I reckon." Adana turned to look up at Zoe, her mask hiding her expression.

"Cause of death?"

"Drugs overdose. Methamphetamine, by the looks of it. Powder residue around his nostrils and on his fingers."

"Another one."

Adana shrugged. "This one doesn't look suspicious."

Mo came through the door and stood next to Zoe. He held up an evidence bag containing a bag of powder.

"Jenson's room?" Zoe asked.

"Rhodri's cordoning it off," Mo said. "We'll wait till Adi's team gets here before we can say for sure. But yes, it looks like it belonged to him." Mo looked down at Adana, who was feeling inside Jenson's mouth with gloved fingers. "He was keeping two addresses, Rhodri reckons."

"How come?"

"He went to interview him last night. A neighbour at Boulton Hall sent him here."

"Rhodri's been here before?" Zoe's chest slumped. That wouldn't look good for the chain of evidence.

"He didn't go upstairs. But he was in here. We'll need to make sure Adi knows that. I've kept Rhodri out of here since getting here this morning."

Zoe turned back to Adana. "Any scratches inside his mouth?"

"It's not the same, Inspector," Adana said. "This guy just took too much."

"Too much of the stuff he was supplying, if this is anything to go by," Mo said. "A dose of this stuff would be quarter to half a gram. He was dealing into the hall of residence, the little bastard."

"He's dead," said Zoe.

"Doesn't change what he did," Mo replied. "That warden gave him responsibility for two hundred undergraduates. What the hell was she thinking?"

"She told me she knew nothing about it," Zoe said.

Mo snorted. "She needs to grow a pair of eyes if you ask me."

Zoe put a hand on his arm. "You OK?"

He shook his head. "It's just... I don't know. All these young people being sent off by their mums and dads to get an education. And then we have Laurence allegedly raping Becca, and this one dealing drugs to them. How are they supposed to cope?"

"We'll need to talk to the warden again."

"Too bloody right we will. I hope she loses her job."

"There'll be an inquiry," said Adana. She stood up with her hands in the small of her back and stretched. "Don't forget I'm based out of the QE. It's affiliated to the university. I've seen how these things work."

"Good," replied Mo. "I hope they hang, draw and quarter her."

"OK," Zoe said. "Adana, we'll still need the post-mortem report. I want to know what's in these drugs, how Jenson got hold of them, and whether they're the same as the ones given to Laurence."

"My thoughts exactly." The pathologist pulled off her mask and scratched her nose. "I'll have him taken to the morgue this morning and I'll have the report to you by tomorrow lunchtime."

"No quicker?"

"I'm sorry, Zoe. It's bad enough I'll have to ask one of the technicians to work on his day off tomorrow."

"Tell me as soon as you have it, yes?"

"Of course." Adana nodded to the detectives and squeezed past them into the hallway.

Zoe turned to Mo. "The question is, is Jenson still a suspect in Laurence's death?"

"Was he ever?"

"He was a person of interest."

"Let's find out how he died and if they're the same drugs, then we can draw some conclusions."

"I just hope that's quick enough for the DCI. The university's going to be on our backs now, with two students dead."

Mo nodded, gazing down at Jenson's body. He frowned. "Hang on."

"What?" Zoe followed his gaze.

"We'll need Adi to preserve that." Mo pointed past the body towards the door leading into the house's back yard. On the floor was a muddy shoe print: narrow, pointed.

"That's not his shoe," Zoe said. Jenson was wearing trainers, size eight at least.

"I'll get Adi to work out the size, and see if we can match it to any known brands. It's not ridged, though."

"Not a trainer," said Zoe. "Or a work boot."

"Looks like a woman's shoe."

"Maybe Kayla came visiting. Maybe a female student came to buy drugs."

The door opened behind them and two men walked in. "Dr Adebayo has given us instructions to move the body, ma'am."

"Not yet," Zoe said. "Wait till Forensics have examined the area." She turned to Mo. "Does Adi know?"

"He does."

"Do I know what?" Adi stuck his head into the doorway, giving Zoe a lopsided smile. "Jeez, it's crowded in here." He looked at the pathologist's assistants. "Guys, can you give us a bit of space?"

The two men shuffled out, leaving space for Adi to join Zoe and Mo in the kitchen.

"Poor kid," he said.

"He was dealing drugs," Mo grunted.

"Even so." Adi crouched down. "Can't see any injuries. Has the pathologist been?"

"You just missed Dr Adebayo."

"Damn. I always enjoy seeing Adana." Adi leaned further forward. "You seen that?" He pointed at the shoe print.

"Yes," Zoe said. "Looks like a woman's."

"Not necessarily. But we'll take a gander and see what we can get." He stepped over the body and peered back at it from the rear. "Wait a minute." He placed a gloved hand under Jenson's back and moved him very slightly. "There's another one. Smudged."

"Smudged by the body landing there?" Zoe asked.

"It's dry now, but unless it's a hell of a coincidence, I'd wager that yes, it was smudged when he landed on the floor. Which could mean the prints were fresh at the time of death."

"Someone was with him when he died," said Mo.

"They could have been in here shortly beforehand," Zoe said. "Adana says there's no reason to suspect foul play."

Adi reached into his toolkit and brought out a pair of tweezers. He plucked something from Jenson's greying t-shirt and held it up to the light. "This looks familiar."

"What is it?" Zoe bent over to get a better look, but couldn't make out what Adi was holding.

He stood, careful not to move his feet. He pushed the tweezers into an evidence bag and held it closer to the detectives.

"Hairs," Zoe said.

Adi nodded. "Not his."

Jenson had thick, curly brown hair. These hairs were brown too, but shorter, and straight.

"The woman who was here with him?" Zoe asked.

"Uh-uh. I've seen these before," Adi said. "These are dog hairs."

CHAPTER FIFTY-FOUR

Kayla approached the library, ferreting in her bag for her security pass. The authorities liked students to wear them, but she felt uneasy walking through campus with it hanging around her neck.

She crouched down and placed her bag on the ground. She needed to get a smaller bag, or at least give this one a clearout. Her pass was lost somewhere among books and sheets of paper. At the bottom of the bag was a muffin in a paper wrapper. She pulled it out and grimaced. It wasn't going back in there; she'd have to find a bin.

"Hi, stranger."

She looked up to see Gina standing over her. "Hi."

"You OK?"

"I can't find my pass. I need to give this library book back."

"Can't they scan it in, find it on the system?"

"They won't let me in without it."

"Ah. Bit of a problem, then."

"Don't you use the library?" Surely Gina knew how the system worked.

"Most of the books in there don't speak to me."

Kayla stood up. *Don't speak to me?* What did that mean? "I never asked you what you're studying."

Gina shrugged. "I'm not. Not anymore."

"You're a postgrad?"

"I said I'm not. Postgrads do the most studying of anyone. Poor saps."

"So you work here?"

"Bingo. I graduated two years ago and now I work in the student welfare team. I patch up women who've been abused by their boyfriends. Who've been threatened by a fellow student." She gave Kayla a meaningful look.

"Sounds interesting."

"Traumatic, but worthwhile."

Kayla nodded. "Anyway. I've really got to get this library book handed in..."

Gina grabbed her hand. "Don't worry about that."

"They can withhold my degree if I don't return library books."

Gina looked down at Kayla's bag. "You got the book with you?"

"Yes."

"Well, then. It's not as if you aren't going to hand it in, then. I mean, you've got over two years."

"No, but..."

"Lighten up, Kayla. You need to decide what's really important. You need to let us help you."

"I don't need help."

"I've seen the way you look when you think no one's watching you. You're damaged. I know what that looks like."

Kayla tugged at her sleeve. She didn't like this. "I'm fine. Shall we meet for lunch again, later?"

"I'm free now, if you'd like a coffee."

"Don't you have to work?"

"I'm on lates today. We're open till midnight."

"I'm sorry, but I need to go to a lecture."

Gina rolled her eyes. "Like I say, priorities."

Kayla heard a shout. She looked past Gina to see another woman running towards them. It was Berni, one of the women from yesterday.

Kayla forced a smile.

Berni grabbed Gina by the arm. "Are you telling her?" she muttered.

Gina glanced at Kayla, then at her friend. "What are you talking about?"

Berni looked at Kayla, her eyes wide. "You know, don't you?"

"I'm sorry. Know what?"

Berni's mouth fell open. "I'm so sorry." She tugged at Gina's arm. "Tell her."

"I don't know what it is you want me to tell her."

Berni frowned. She took a deep breath, staring at Kayla like she was scared of her. She hadn't been like this yesterday; she'd tried to tell Kayla how to live her life.

"What?" Kayla said. "What is it? You're freaking me out."

"It's your boyfriend," Berni said. "Jenson."

Kayla felt heat rise up her neck. She hadn't told these women about Jenson. She hadn't been sure they'd approve. "What about him?" she whispered.

"He's dead."

CHAPTER FIFTY-FIVE

Zoe watched as the two men from Adana's team slid Jenson's body into a dark van. Mo was behind her, his arms folded across his chest.

"Is it connected?" she wondered aloud.

"Could be. Might not be. We'll know more when we've got the pathology report."

"Those dog hairs..." she said.

"Plenty of people have dogs."

"No sign of one in the house."

"That doesn't mean he wasn't in contact with someone who had one. We'll have to check. Find out who his friends were."

"Talk to his family."

Mo sighed. "Another family."

"Yeah." Zoe turned and put a hand on Mo's arm. "I'll do this one, if you like."

He shrugged. "I know it has to be done, Zo. I'm not going to shy away from—"

"Just because I'm a DI now doesn't mean I don't muck in

with the crappy jobs. I'll do it. I'll get Connie to track them down." She grabbed her phone.

Rhodri came out of the house with Yala Cook, Adi's second-in-command. They were smiling.

"You enjoying yourself, Constable?" Zoe asked.

Rhodri's cheeks paled. "Sorry, boss."

"It's alright. You have to find a way to deal with stuff like this. Just don't let the public see you doing it, OK?"

"Boss." Rhodri lowered his gaze.

"Anything else helpful?" Zoe asked Yala.

"We've bagged up all the drugs paraphernalia. Looks like he might have been cooking it himself."

"On his own?"

"Can't be sure. There are signs of two other men living at the property, but they're nowhere to be seen."

Zoe turned to Rhodri. "Rhod, you came here last night. Was anyone else in?"

"I saw a couple on the bed in the front room downstairs, boss."

"Two men?"

"A man and a woman."

"OK. Mo, you talk to Uniform. Make sure whoever's on the front door keeps an eye out for any other residents. We need names and contact details."

"Boss."

"Rhodri, tell me everything you saw here last night."

"Course." Rhodri took his notepad out of his inside pocket.

A crowd was gathering along the pavement, people wanting to know what was going on. Zoe glanced at them, then gestured towards her car. "Let's do this in my car, Rhodri."

"Yeah." He nodded.

"Shall we go back to the station?" Mo said.

"I want to stay here in case Rhodri thinks of anything we need to tell Adi. Or anything we can look into while we're here."

She pushed through the growing crowd towards her Mini. There were half a dozen students, an elderly man with a dog and two young women holding onto pushchairs. They all turned to watch her as she passed through.

"Detective!"

Zoe turned to see Kayla Goode running towards them from the Bristol Road.

"Shit," she muttered. She pulled on a tight smile.

Kayla skidded through the crowd and stopped in front of Zoe. She was panting. Her face was pale and her hair wild. "Is it true?"

Zoe swallowed. "Come and sit with me in my car." She turned to Mo. "Can you and Rhodri wait in your car?"

Mo nodded and walked to his car with Rhodri trailing behind. Zoe took Kayla by the elbow and steered her towards her car. One of the pushchair women had her phone out and was filming.

"Please don't do that," Zoe said.

The woman shrugged but didn't lower her phone.

Zoe felt heat rise inside her. "Have some respect, will you?" She wanted to grab the woman's phone, but she knew how that would look on YouTube. After a moment's hesitation the woman lowered her phone and placed it in her pocket, not meeting Zoe's eye.

"Thank you. Come on, Kayla. Let's talk in my car where these gawpers can't overhear."

"Is it true?" Kayla breathed. "Is he dead?"

Zoe had the passenger door open. She pushed Kayla in and closed the door behind her, then hurried round to the driver's seat. She was glad of the quiet when she closed the door.

Zoe turned to Kayla. "I'm sorry to tell you this, but Jenson is dead, yes."

Kayla made a squeaking sound. "No."

"It happened overnight."

"How?" Kayla raked her fingernails up the inside of her arm.

"He overdosed."

"Deliberately?"

"We don't know anything like that right now. It might have been an accident, a mistake. Did you ever see him taking drugs?"

Kayla stiffened. "No."

"It's OK, Kayla. You can't get him into trouble. Or yourself. I just need to know if his body was used to them."

Kayla nodded, her eyes on her hands, which twisted in her lap. "Yes."

"Which drugs was he using?"

"Cannabis."

"Anything else?"

Kayla looked up. Her neck was bright red. "I found some meth in his room once."

"In his room in Boulton Hall?"

Kayla shook her head. "Here."

"He had a room in this house?"

"Yes."

"Do you know why he kept two places, Kayla?"

The young woman shrugged. "For privacy, maybe? I don't know."

"He never told you?"

"Not really."

"Not really. Are you sure?"

"I suppose he just wanted somewhere away from the pressure. He gets fed up of people knocking on his door at all hours." Kayla collapsed into herself. "Got."

Zoe rubbed her chin. "I know this is hard, Kayla. I'm sorry. But can you tell me where he got the drugs?"

"I don't know. I really don't. Sorry."

"OK. I believe you. Do you know who else was living in this house?"

Kayla's gaze shot to the front of the house. A female PC stood outside, staring ahead impassively. The crowd was starting to dissipate, just the two mums still standing there with their toddlers sleeping. The two of them chatted, occasionally looking over to Zoe's car.

"You already have my card, Kayla," Zoe said. "If you think of anything relevant please call me."

"Was Jenson murdered, like Laurence?"

"We don't know yet. It might just have been an accident."

"He was... he was a good man, you know. Really. Underneath it all."

"Underneath what?"

A shrug. "He didn't let people in. He came across as... shallow, I guess. That's how he wanted people to see him. But that's not what he was like." A blush. "Not once you got to know him."

"How long have you been in a relationship with Jenson?"

"Two months. Since just before Christmas."

"Did he talk to you about the allegations against Laurence?"

"Your sergeant already asked me this. No. He was professional. He kept confidences."

"I'm sorry to ask this, Kayla. But did he have any other girlfriends? Anyone he was close to?"

Kayla looked horrified. "No. Of course not."

"OK." Zoe gave her a sad smile. "Thanks. I may need to talk to you again."

"I know."

"Good." Zoe grabbed her door handle.

"There is one thing," Kayla said.

"Yes?" Zoe stopped moving.

"I saw him with... no. It's nothing."

"Let me be the judge of that. Who did you see him with?"

"It's nothing, really. She would have been getting counselling, after finding the body."

"You saw him with Lin? That was unusual?"

"She hated him. Said he was a bad influence. But she was at his flat yesterday. In Boulton Hall. Probably getting emotional support." She gave Zoe a teary smile. "That's all."

Zoe nodded. "Well, thank you for telling me. And if you think of anything else, call me. Day or night."

CHAPTER FIFTY-SIX

ZOE WATCHED as Kayla walked back towards the Bristol Road. Her steps were hurried and she was almost tripping over herself as she walked.

"Poor girl," she muttered. She gave the two mums watching her a disdainful look, and slid into the back seat of Mo's car.

"Sorry, boss. I'll get in the front," Rhodri said.

"You're taller than me. Let's get this over with. Tell us what you saw last night."

"I've just been telling the sarge. He was in a really shitty mood. Didn't like that we'd sent two detectives to talk to him, one of them twice."

"D'you think he was high?"

"No sign of it in his eyes. But his mood was all over the place."

"You saw another couple in the front room."

"I only saw their legs. Sorry."

"Did you see anyone else?"

"There was no one else in the house, as far as I could tell."

"Which rooms did you go in?"

"Just the kitchen, boss."

Zoe raised an eyebrow. "The room he died in."

"Yeah." Rhodri looked uneasy.

"Did you see any footprints on the floor? Mud?"

"Sorry, boss. I weren't looking at the floor."

"No. What shoes were you wearing?"

"My Nikes, boss."

She nodded. "You'll have to let Adi have them, just to eliminate the prints. We'll make sure the fact you were in the building is noted on the forensics report. Did he seem suicidal to you?"

"Pissed off, but not suicidal. Too chippy."

"Right." Zoe turned to Mo. "What do you think?"

"I think it all hinges on that shoe print and the dog hair. We just have to wait and see what Adi says."

"You're right."

"You don't think it's just an accidental overdose?" Rhodri asked. "If he was using..."

"It is a possibility," Zoe said. "But there's evidence someone else was in the room around the time he died. And if those hairs match with the ones we found on Laurence, that changes things completely."

"Right."

Zoe stared out of the window. The two women were still nearby, alternating between peering into their pushchairs and staring at the car. "So you didn't see anyone else?" she asked Rhodri.

"There might have been someone sneaking around outside."

"In the back yard?"

"Out front. In the garden opposite. I thought I saw movement, but I assumed it was just whoever lived there."

"What kind of movement?"

"A hedge being shifted to one side. Not much, really."

"Come on." Zoe sprang out of the car and hurried across the road. Opposite the house in which Jenson had died, there was a thick evergreen hedge in the centre of a front garden, surrounded by scruffy grass. It didn't give the impression of a place that anyone looked after very much.

"Why is this street such a mess?" she said. "I only live two roads along, and it's nothing like this."

"If they were doing drugs..." said Mo.

"Yeah, but the house opposite?" Zoe turned to Rhodri. "Is this the hedge you mean?"

He nodded.

"Show me." She drew back and gestured for Rhodri to stand by the hedge. "Show me what you saw."

Rhodri shifted uneasily, then moved to stand between the hedge and the house's front window. The curtain shifted to one side and a young woman peered out. She frowned at Rhodri then yanked the curtain shut.

"Mo, can you knock on the door, talk to her," Zoe said. "Find out if she saw anyone in her garden last night."

"It might have been her," said Rhodri. "I just thought it was probably someone coming home."

"Now that a man in the house opposite has died, I think we have to entertain all possibilities. Show me what you saw."

Zoe stood in the middle of the street, next to the cordon Uniform had placed between the cars. Rhodri disappeared behind the hedge, then grabbed it and shifted it from side to side.

"That all?" she said.

"Sorry, boss."

"I can see your head. You sure you didn't see the person?"

"Pretty sure I didn't."

"OK."

Mo emerged from the front door with the young woman who'd been looking out at them. As she passed Rhodri, Zoe compared their heights.

"Stop a moment." She shifted to one side so the hedge was between her and the woman. She was a good eight inches shorter than Rhodri, which meant she was entirely obscured by it.

Zoe nodded to herself, then approached the woman.

"I've told your colleague, I didn't see anything," the woman said. She had a broad Scottish accent.

"Are you a student?" Zoe asked.

"Yeah. Mary Stewart."

"Do you know the people in that house, Mary?"

"I avoid them."

"Why?"

"Drugs."

"They're dealing?"

"Reckon so."

"You've seen evidence?"

"You can just tell, can't you?"

"Why didn't you report it?"

Mary hesitated. "Didn't want to cause trouble."

Zoe sighed. "Were you here at around... Rhodri, what time did you leave last night?"

"Eight seventeen, boss."

Zoe nodded. "Were you here at that time last night?"

"Sorry. I was in The Country Girl, with some mates."

Zoe knew the pub well; Nicholas often drank there. "What about the rest of your household? I assume you don't live alone?"

"There's five of us. We were all in the pub. Together."

Zoe looked at Rhodri. His eyes shone.

"What time did you get home?" she asked Mary.

"Me and Lydia came home at about half ten. The others got back after us, about half eleven. They came via the chippy."

"Thank you. You've been very helpful." Zoe looked at Rhodri. "I think you might have seen our killer, Rhod."

CHAPTER FIFTY-SEVEN

CONNIE WATCHED the slowly advancing line of male students, feeling satisfied. She'd managed to find a helpful member of Boulton Hall's admin team and had been allocated a room for the task. The FSIs had three tables set up, with help from Uniform, and they were getting through about twenty students each hour. All of them would have been swabbed by the end of the day, and Adi's team would have the information they needed to match the DNA in Laurence's mouth with one of these young men.

The students chatted between themselves as they queued up, no one apparently worried about the process. At the moment this was voluntary, but if anyone didn't show up, that would change. Making it voluntary had meant they could get started quicker, with less paperwork.

The room they were in was large, with ceiling-height windows and modern artwork on the walls. Tables and chairs had been pushed aside to make room for the line of students, which snaked towards the door. Tom Fenton, a member of the admin team, had helped with a list of students and he was still there, flitting between the tables and trying to make himself useful.

Connie approached him. "Tom."

"DC Williams, hi. It seems to be going well. Have you got everything you need?"

She wished everyone at the university was this helpful. "We have, thanks. Can you do me a favour, though?"

"Yeah."

She gestured for him to follow her to the side of the room.

"I really appreciate your help," she told him. "But our guys need to get on with their work. I'll come and get you if we need anything else, OK?"

"Oh." His face fell. "I have to stay. You might need to check students against the list."

She shook her head. "We're asking them for ID when they come through. It's all in hand."

"I'll sit to one side, keep an eye on things. I won't get in your way."

Connie stared at him. "Have you been told to keep an eye on us?"

He flushed. "I..."

"It's OK." She smiled. "I understand your boss might be uneasy about all this. But we'll keep her in the loop. I promise."

He pushed his specs up his nose. "I shouldn't leave. She'd..."

"If she gives you trouble, tell her to talk to me, OK?"

"With all respect, you're just a constable. She'll never listen to you."

Connie felt her warmth towards the man cool. "I've been given responsibility for getting this sampling operation off the ground, and that's what I'm doing. Tell Dr Edwards it makes no difference what my rank is."

"I didn't mean to be rude."

"I'm sure you didn't." He had his instructions, she thought. But she did too. Zoe didn't want the university staff interfering with this process. They'd ballsed things up enough as it was. No point making it worse.

"Sorry, Tom," she continued. "But I've got a boss, too. And she's told me we need to work independently. We can't have anyone suggesting the university might have tried to steer the investigation one way or the other."

"That's not what we're trying to do."

"I'm not saying you are. But like I say, we don't want anyone suggesting you are." She cocked her head. "I'm sure you understand."

He let out a long sigh. "OK." He shuffled towards the door.

"Thanks." Connie felt guilty. She knew what it was like having to do things you weren't comfortable with. She'd had enough of that when DI Dawson had been in charge of their team.

Stop being such a softie, she told herself. He was just being nosey. Sticking his oar in. She shook herself out and approached the constable on the nearest table. He was packing a sample away, labelling it with the name of the student who'd provided it and stowing it in a box. Yala Cook, one of Adi's team, was moving between the tables, keeping an eye on things. There was a low hum in the room, the combined sound of students chatting in the queue and police getting on with their job.

"How many now?" Connie asked the PC.

"Twenty-three at my table."

"Fifty-two altogether," said Yala.

The PC looked smug. His was one of three tables and he'd processed almost half the samples.

"Don't rush it," Yala said, looking down at him. "We need to do this properly."

"I'm not rushing it, ma'am."

"I'm a civilian," Yala told him. "You don't have to call me that."

He stiffened. "Fair enough." He beckoned the next student forward and handed him a sampling kit and a leaflet.

The door that Tom Fenton had left by opened and DCI Clarke entered. Connie stood straight, almost to attention. She blinked at the DCI, waiting for her to approach.

She went to the farthest table first, exchanging a few words with the constable there. The two of them laughed quietly.

Connie held her breath, watching the DCI as she worked the room. At last DCI Clarke was standing next to her.

"DC Williams," she said. "Zoe got you working alone on this one?"

"I've got Yala and Uniform helping me."

"Even so. Everything going OK?"

"Fine."

"No one here from the university?"

"DI Finch told me not to—"

DCI Clarke put a hand on Connie's shoulder. "That's exactly right, Connie. Thanks." She blinked and her face paled.

"Ma'am? Are you alright?" Connie's stomach dipped. She'd heard rumours about the DCI's health since the New Street bomb, but she hadn't been this close to her without the boss in the room.

The DCI gave her a thin smile, but her face was pale. Sweat beaded her forehead. "I'm fine, Constable. Don't you worry about me. Just keep on as you are. I'm going to have a word with the warden."

"Ma'am." Connie watched as the DCI left the room, accompanied by a besuited man she didn't recognise. She wondered what DI Finch would make of this. Was the boss being checked up on?

"DC Williams."

Connie turned. "Yeah?"

Yala was staring at her. "I need you to check something with the university. We don't have any postgrads on this list."

"Oh." Connie wasn't sure how many postgraduate students were living at Boulton Hall.

"Can you find out who we're missing and make sure we've got a complete list, please?"

"No problem." Connie hurried out of the room towards Tom's office, hoping she didn't bump into the DCI.

CHAPTER FIFTY-EIGHT

"I want to check it's all going OK with the sampling," Zoe said. "Can you two go back to base, liaise with Adana over Jenson's post-mortem?"

"Course," said Mo.

"Ta." Zoe climbed out of Mo's car and walked back to her own. The gawpers had gone now, seemingly bored.

She drove to Boulton Hall and parked on the double yellows outside, tired of having to drive in circles to find a parking space. She wouldn't be long.

Inside, a security guard she didn't recognise was in the office. She held up her ID.

"Can you tell me where they're doing the DNA sampling?" she said.

"Sure," said the woman. She pointed past Zoe. "Room 105, down that corridor there."

"Thanks." Zoe turned in the direction she'd pointed.

A group of male students passed her as she walked. They were talking about the sampling. One of them poked inside his mouth, saying something unintelligible. They quietened as she passed, giving her wary looks.

As she rounded a corner, Lesley was coming the other way. Zoe stopped in her tracks.

"Ma'am. I didn't know you'd be here."

Lesley was with a man in a suit. She had a hand on his arm, and looked pale.

"Are you alright, ma'am?"

"Will people stop bloody asking me that? I've already had your DC on my case."

"I'm sure she was only trying to help."

"Yeah, yeah. I'm sure she was."

"Is there a problem?" Zoe asked. Why had the DCI come to check up on her team?

"I wanted to talk to the warden. Do a bit of community outreach, you know what it's like."

"Have you seen her?"

Lesley sighed. "The woman's in the Geography department this morning, apparently. You'd think she'd be here looking after the students."

"I don't imagine it's easy to get out of lecturing commitments." Zoe was secretly relieved the warden wasn't here to interfere.

Lesley grunted. "Seems like I had a wasted trip." She closed her eyes for a moment and cleared her throat. Zoe resisted the urge to ask if she needed help.

"Is there anything you need from me?" she asked.

"Just tell Doctor Edwards I was here, when you see her. I guess I'll give her a call sometime."

"Of course."

"And I haven't told you about some changes to the Magpie investigation."

"Oh?" Zoe's pulse accelerated.

"You're busy with this one, I want you to focus. I'm putting DI Dawson on the other case."

"But ma'am, I've been—"

Lesley raised a hand. "Don't argue, Zoe. Ask DS Uddin to sit in on the meetings, share what you've been doing."

"I can do that."

Lesley screwed up her face. "I'm sure you can, but you're busy here. Talk to DS Uddin. Brief him, if you need to."

Zoe pushed down her anger. This wasn't like Lesley. But she had to show even-handedness between her DIs. "I'll talk to Mo."

Lesley patted Zoe on the arm. "You're doing a good job. You'll catch this one, I'm sure."

"We may have two to catch now."

"You think the Begg kid was murdered too?"

"Not so much of a kid, he was twenty-four." Zoe looked up and down the corridor. She stepped closer to her boss. "Adi found a dog hair on him that was very similar to the ones on Laurence Thomms."

"The kid was a junkie, Zoe." Lesley sniffed and pulled a hankie out of her pocket. "It's just a dog hair." She blew her nose. "Let's not jump to conclusions."

"I'll let you know when we have the forensics in detail."

"Yes. You do that." Lesley pinched Zoe's arm. It hurt. "Right, I'm off."

"Ma'am." Zoe stepped to one side to let her boss and her companion pass. She wondered why they hadn't been introduced.

She pulled her shoulders back and carried on walking. What room number was it again? She'd find it when she got there, surely.

Room 105. Zoe stood outside it. The door was glazed and she could see Connie inside, talking with Yala Cook from Adi's team. Zoe observed her for a moment. Connie was doing a good job.

There was a crash from behind her. Zoe turned, but the corridor was empty.

"Need some help here!" a man called out. Zoe ran towards the voice.

She skidded round the corner. The suited man was hunched over, looking around him with the air of someone who didn't have the faintest idea what to do. In front of him, slumped on the floor, was Lesley.

Zoe ran to her. "Ma'am!"

Lesley's eyes flickered. She'd landed clumsily and her face was grey.

"Call a bloody ambulance," Zoe told the man. "Who are you, anyway?"

"I'm Kit." He pulled out a phone.

I'm Kit. What was that supposed to tell her? And what kind of name was Kit, anyway?

"I'll do it," she snapped. She grabbed her phone and hit 999.

CHAPTER FIFTY-NINE

"Some fucker blocked the double yellows."

Shit. "I'll move it," Zoe said.

The paramedic gave her a look that would have melted steel. "Too late now. My partner's parked up, she'll be with me in a minute. You don't want her knowing what you did."

Zoe pulled out her ID. "I'm SIO on a murder investigation. I needed access to the building."

"I don't care if you're the Queen of bloody Sheba. You parked a Mini on double yellows and you made it harder for me to do my job."

Lesley was propped against a wall between Zoe and the paramedic. Her breathing was shallow and her skin damp. The paramedic was pulling equipment out of his bag and attaching it to Lesley: a heart rate monitor, an oxygen mask.

"She had a brain injury six weeks ago," Zoe said.

The paramedic's eyes widened. "A brain injury? What's she doing here?"

"She's my boss. DCI Lesley Clarke."

"I know that." He looked down at a monitor that beeped at him. He shook his head.

"What?" Zoe said. "What's happened to her?"

"Her BP is low," he said. "And her O2 levels aren't great either. What kind of injury?"

Zoe put a hand to the back of her neck. "She was attending the attack at New Street. She was injured. Glass lodged in her neck, she was lucky it didn't embed in her spine."

"She bloody was." The paramedic held Lesley's hand. "She's cold." He turned towards the door. "We need to get her to the QE."

"What can I do?" Zoe asked.

Another paramedic hurried in, lugging a heavy case.

The first paramedic turned to her. "We need to get her to A&E, right now."

The woman nodded. "I'll get the chair."

Moments later Lesley was in a wheelchair being pushed towards the doors. She groaned at Zoe, her eyelids flickering. Zoe felt sick, watching her boss's face. As they reached the doors she glanced out at her car, cursing herself. The ambulance was parked behind her.

"I'll move it."

The female paramedic looked up from Lesley. She gave Zoe a sharp stare.

"Leave it," the male paramedic said.

His colleague bent over the DCI. "Lesley love, we're nearly at the ambulance and then we'll have you at the hospital in two ticks."

They held the doors open for the wheelchair. A group of male students were crossing the reception area. They stopped and stared at the commotion.

Zoe waved them away. "Go to room 105," she said. "Nothing for you here."

They exchanged looks, then hurried away, their footsteps loud. Zoe's heartbeat rushed in her ears.

Lesley was in the ambulance now. The man who'd been with her, Kit, stood to one side, looking helpless. He looked at Zoe as if she had all the answers.

The paramedics secured Lesley's wheelchair, then slammed the doors and drove away. Zoe's phone rang.

"DI Finch." She watched as the ambulance turned out of the driveway towards the street.

"Zoe, it's Carl."

"It's not a good time."

"I wanted to let you know we've got a trial date for Ian Osman."

The ambulance drew out of sight, blue lights faint above the tree line and siren blaring. Zoe wondered if she should follow behind, go to the QE. She'd need to call Lesley's family.

"What?" she said into her phone.

"Ian's trial. It's next month."

"Oh."

"I imagine you'll be called as a witness."

"All the more reason for you not to be calling me, then," she replied.

"Don't be like that."

The sirens dimmed until she couldn't hear them anymore. "Lesley's just been rushed to hospital. I'll talk to you later."

"What happened?"

"I don't know. She collapsed."

"Her injury from the bomb?"

"I don't know, Carl." Zoe put her hand to her forehead. She still needed to speak to Connie, to check on the sampling. And then there was Jenson's murder to follow up on.

"She's taken me off the case," she said.

"What case?" Carl asked.

"The bomber. Look... I don't... you don't need to know about this. I'll call you when things have quietened down a bit."

"I hope the DCI is OK."

"Yeah. Sorry I snapped at you, Carl."

She heard him breathe out heavily. "It's OK, Zoe. You're under a lot of stress."

"Yeah." She hung up and dialled Rhodri.

"Rhod, I haven't got long. The DCI's been taken ill, she's been rushed to hospital. Find out her husband's number and make sure someone calls him, will you? She's at the QE."

"Err..." The man who'd been with Lesley, the one who'd introduced himself as Kit, was at Zoe's side.

"What?" she asked him, irritated.

"I can take care of that. I work with her."

Since when?

Zoe clutched the phone. "OK Rhod, ignore that."

"Is the DCI going to be OK, boss?"

"I don't know. I'll be back as soon as I can."

"No problem."

Zoe turned to Kit. "Who are you, anyway?"

"Senior management wanted someone from the support team working with DCI Clarke, to provide..."

"Support?" Zoe suggested.

He shrugged. "Yes." He looked in the direction the ambulance had gone. "Has this happened before?"

"Surely you know."

"The New Street bombing, yes. But I thought she was OK."

"So why were you brought in to babysit her, then? And where are you from?"

He held out his hand, which Zoe ignored. "Kit Singh. I'm normally based at Lloyd House, in Force CID Support."

"You're civilian."

"Yes."

"And you work for Detective Superintendent Randle."

"Not directly."

"But that's your team." Zoe clenched a fist. Was he here to babysit Lesley, or to spy on her?

"Well," she said. "There's nothing for you to do here now. You might as well toddle off back to Lloyd House."

"I'm sure there's something I can..."

She shook her head emphatically. "Nothing. You leave us to the police work. I'm sure your bosses will tell you when the DCI is out of hospital."

"I'm sure it's not—"

"I'll see you around, Kit Singh." She stood with her hands on her hips and raised her eyebrows at him.

"Fair enough." He walked towards a grey Hyundai that was parked legally, unlike her own Mini.

She watched him leave, and turned back into Boulton Hall. She didn't like the idea of Randle having a spy watching them, even if PSD had done the same thing to him. She also didn't like being taken off Magpie. She could pretend she hadn't received that instruction, couldn't she? With Lesley in hospital and Kit Singh an irrelevance, no one need know for now.

CHAPTER SIXTY

Zoe walked into the team room. Mo turned to her, his face full of concern.

"How is she?"

"I don't know. I was hoping you might."

He shook his head. "We haven't heard anything."

She slumped into Connie's chair. "I thought she'd recovered." She leaned back, her stomach hollow.

"Why was she at the university?" Mo asked.

"Seeing how the sampling was coming on, doing a bit of community outreach with the warden. And she..."

"What?"

"Nothing. The warden wasn't even there."

"She'll be fine, Zo. You know what she's like."

"You should have seen her, Mo. It was scary."

They stared at each other, both imagining Force CID without Lesley in it and not liking the idea.

Zoe screwed up her eyes and leaned back. She pushed out a breath between her gritted teeth, then looked at Rhodri. "Right. How's it going with Jenson?"

"Still no word on the hairs, boss," Rhodri said. "And I'm going to attend the post-mortem."

"You volunteered?"

He smiled. "I did."

"Get you." It wasn't long ago Rhodri had turned green at the thought of attending a post-mortem. "When is it?"

"Five o'clock."

"Call me afterwards, let me know if there's anything I need to be aware of. We know he was a habitual drug user but I want to know if the drug that killed him was new to him. Or if not, was it in his system in significantly larger quantities than he was used to."

"He might have committed suicide," Mo said.

"We can't rule anything out yet," Zoe agreed. "But the boot print and the hairs steer us away from that. Tell me as soon as we have anything from Adi."

"Where are you going?" Mo asked.

"I'm going back to Jenson's house. I had a call from Uniform, one of his housemates has turned up."

"Where were they all?"

"Lectures, maybe. Hiding out, maybe."

"Hiding their stash, more like," said Rhodri.

"How's Connie getting on?" Mo asked.

"She's doing fine," Zoe replied. "I spoke to her after Lesley was taken away. She was nearly halfway through. Apparently there was a problem cos they didn't have the names of the postgrads living there, but she's got it in hand."

"Good," Mo said.

Rhodri was making notes on the board: time and nature of Jenson's death. He drew a line between the photos of Jenson and Kayla.

"Rhod," said Zoe. "You get to the post-mortem. I'll call

Adi, tell him he can reach me on my mobile. Mo, you come with me to the house."

"Sure." Mo grabbed his jacket from the back of his chair and stood up.

"Good." Zoe looked back at Mo, but her vision was clouded. Seeing Lesley like that had thrown her. "Come on."

CHAPTER SIXTY-ONE

Zoe drummed the steering wheel with her fingertips as she waited for the lights to change and let her onto the Bristol Road. She came through this junction every day; Jenson's house was only two streets away from her own.

"There's something we're missing, I'm sure of it," she said.

"Something at the scene?" Mo replied.

"Adi went over both of them, if there was anything else he'd have found it. It's the relationships. We've got Laurence raping Becca—"

"Allegedly."

"Whatever. Then we've got Becca telling Jenson about it, him reporting it to the warden, her investigation. Then there's Kayla and Lin finding Laurence, and the fact that Kayla's sleeping with Jenson. It all feels too cosy. Too tight."

"That's why you think the two deaths are connected."

"I don't know. But what I'm wondering is whether Jenson's death has got anything to do with the fact that it was his girlfriend who found Laurence. Not to mention his involvement in the investigation."

"You think he knew something about Laurence's murder? Kayla told him something?"

"We've interviewed her twice. Her story tallies with Lin's, and we got the two of them alone before they'd had a chance to confer on Tuesday morning."

Zoe drove into Umberslade Road. The cordon had been reduced and no longer stretched across the street but surrounded the pavement in front of Jenson's house. A white-suited tech emerged from the house and put a bin bag in the boot of a car.

"Maybe we should talk to the girls again," said Mo.

Zoe shook her head as she scanned the street for some-where to park. "We know Becca didn't do it, Rhodri estab-lished her alibi. But I think the whole thing goes back to what happened between her and Laurence. And the fact that Jenson knew about it."

"OK. You want me to talk to Becca, you talk to the warden again?"

"We're going to have to see the warden again. One of her postgrads is dead and she'll know more about him than she's told us, I'm sure of it."

"Maybe his housemates can shed some light."

"You'd think so," Zoe said. "But I'm not holding out much hope."

She found a space that had been marked with police bollards and sat back in her seat after turning off the ignition. "OK. Let's do this."

"You're worried about the DCI."

Zoe nodded. "Still got a job to do. Come on."

She strode to the house, flashing a smile at the constable

on duty along with her warrant card. Mo followed behind, exchanging pleasantries with the man.

Two students stood in what passed for the front garden. One male, one female. The man was white, in his early twenties, with skin so pale Zoe thought she might see right through him, and a patchy beard that made him look like a vagrant. The woman was black, younger than him, with dreadlocks down to her waist.

Zoe showed them her ID. "I'm Detective Inspector Zoe Finch. This is Detective Sergeant Uddin. Thanks for waiting."

"When are we gonna be let back into the house?" the man asked.

"Our forensics team are working through it right now. We'll let you back in as soon as they've finished."

"I've got books in there I need for this afternoon," the woman said.

"Tell us what they are and someone will fetch them for you." Zoe told her.

"I can't remember, can I? Let me in there for five minutes and I'll get them. I won't touch anything."

"I'm sorry, we can't do that. While we wait, can you let me have your names?"

"I'm Shonda," the woman said.

"Surname?" Mo asked. He had his notepad out.

"Taylor."

"Thanks." Mo looked at the man, a question on his face.

"Will Bulmer."

"Right. Give me a moment and I'll find out how long they'll be." Mo turned to Zoe. "Boss?"

"That's fine."

Mo went inside and Zoe faced the two students. "We'll

need to talk to each of you separately, so we have independent statements. Were you both here last night?"

The woman nodded. She grabbed the man's hand. "Will came round for the night."

"Good."

Mo emerged. "You can go in. You're in the front room, downstairs?"

The woman frowned. "How d'you know that?"

"There's a photo of your boyfriend next to the bed."

She blushed. "Oh. That." She tightened her grip on Will's hand.

"Right," said Zoe. "Will, Sergeant Uddin will talk to you out here. Shonda, let's go inside."

"You can't go past the front room," Mo said. Shonda looked worried.

"We won't," said Zoe. She gestured for the woman to follow her.

Zoe stepped inside the house, aware of faint voices from the kitchen at the back. Adi had the most important items of evidence, but they would be checking all the surfaces, just in case. She held out a hand, gesturing for Shonda to go into her room. The girl slipped inside and Zoe closed the door.

Inside, the double bed was unmade, a duvet piled up in its centre. In the window sat a graffitied wooden desk and an uncomfortable-looking chair.

"Mind if I sit down?" Zoe asked.

"Er, yeah."

Zoe took the desk chair. Shonda sat on the bed, tweaking the duvet to tidy it a little. She looked embarrassed at the state of her room. On the opposite wall was a bookcase, most of the books on the floor in front of it. Shonda had been right;

there was no way one of the techs would have been able to find the right book.

"Shonda," Zoe said. She gave the woman a smile. "Thanks for talking to me. I'm sure this is all a nasty shock."

Shonda nodded. She shuffled on the bed.

"How much do you know about what happened to Jenson?"

"Only what your guys told me. He died last night."

"You know how he died?"

A shrug. "An overdose?"

Zoe leaned back. "Was he a habitual drug user?"

Shonda stiffened. "I wouldn't know."

"It's OK," Zoe said. "It's not like you're going to get him into trouble."

"He did smoke sometimes, yeah."

"You know what he smoked?"

"Not sure."

"OK." Zoe was sure the techs would uncover more of Jenson's supply in his bedroom. "Did you see him dealing?"

Shonda's eyes widened. "No. Never."

Zoe sighed. "Again, you can't get him into trouble. I just need to know where the drugs came from."

"Look, I don't know. He might have been. I think he had a few mates he shared it with. I don't know if he was dealing, though."

"Did those mates pay him for the drugs he shared with them?"

"I don't know."

"You lived in the same house as him. Surely you'd have seen what he was doing."

Shonda shook her head. "He was hardly here. He's got a flat on campus. To do with being a postgrad."

"So how often was he here?"

"He used to come nights, mostly. Sometimes in the afternoon. Never before 3pm."

"3pm?"

"Normally he was here later, but sometimes I saw him here then."

"Did you talk to him, when he was here?"

"He kept himself to himself."

There were a lot of people doing that round here, Zoe thought. "He stayed in his room?"

"Mostly."

"Did he use the kitchen? Did he eat here?"

"Not much. He went in there sometimes for coffee, but I never saw him eat here. I think he got free meals at Boulton Hall."

Zoe nodded. "Did you see him last night?"

"I saw him early evening, before me and Will went out. He had a visitor."

"What kind of visitor?"

"A copper, by the looks of him. It made Will jumpy."

"Why would it do that?"

Shonda looked like she'd put her foot in it. "Nothing like that, Will's not broken the law. Just, it's a bit odd having a copper come in your house."

"Can you describe this man you thought was police?"

"Tall, skinny. Mousy hair. Welsh."

Zoe suppressed a smile. "DC Hughes. He's a member of my team."

"Why was he here?"

"We're investigating a death at Boulton Hall."

"Laurence."

"You knew Laurence?"

"Only by reputation."

So Laurence's reputation had spread beyond Boulton Hall.

"What kind of reputation?"

"He raped a girl, she never went to the police, but everyone knew about it. Then there was Jenson's girlfriend. Well, I say girlfriend. It was a pretty toxic relationship, if you ask me."

"Kayla? In what way toxic?"

Shonda shook her head. "He was her tutor. He shouldn't have... I heard her complaining sometimes. It sounded like he... maybe not forced her, but coerced her."

"To have sex?" Zoe asked.

"What else?"

"You mentioned Kayla when I asked you about Laurence."

"I'm not s'posed to tell anyone."

"This is confidential, Shonda. I need to know. What happened to Kayla?"

Shonda licked her lips, her eyes on Zoe. "Laurence assaulted her. She came to see Jenson after it happened. He was out, I was here."

"When was this?"

"Last term. Around Bonfire Night, I think. Yeah, it was two days before Bonfire Night cos Will was building a guy in the garden and Kayla kicked it to bits."

"When you say assaulted, did Kayla accuse Laurence of raping her?"

"No."

"No?"

"She got away. He never got the chance."

CHAPTER SIXTY-TWO

Zoe's phone rang as she slumped into her car.

"DI Finch."

"Ooh, that doesn't sound good."

"What's up, Adi?"

"You OK, Zoe?"

"The DCI's been taken to hospital. What can I do for you?"

"She going to be OK?"

"I don't know. Sorry, Adi, I don't feel up to chatting right now. What d'you need?"

"I got a lead on the Magpie forensics."

Zoe thought back to the conversation she'd had with Lesley. Clearly Adi hadn't got the memo. "Go on."

"There's a match to one of the passports we picked up in the hotel in Hall Green."

"The Hotel Belvista. Where Trevor Hamm's people were keeping those women."

"That's the one. Anyway, one of my team found a hair stuck under a stamp in one of the passports. In the name of

Alina Popescu, not been matched to any of the women your guys found there yet."

"Half the passports we found haven't been matched up." Zoe didn't like to imagine what might have happened to the women they hadn't tracked down.

"I heard. Shall I send you a photo of the passport?"

"Does it look like the bomber?"

"Not really. She changed her hair, and she was wearing a headscarf in that selfie she sent. But the forensics don't lie."

"Is that the only passport with matching DNA?"

"It is. They're all covered in Adam Fulmer and Kyle Gatiss's prints, so they must have taken them from the women. But this hair definitely doesn't belong to either of them."

"Thanks Adi. Send it over."

Zoe hung up. What would she do with this information? The best thing would probably be to give it to DS Sheila Griffin. She was in a separate team, not involved in the politics of Force CID.

She checked her phone: no email from Adi yet. She'd wait till she had that, then give Sheila a ring.

CHAPTER SIXTY-THREE

Rhodri wriggled his fingers inside his pockets, trying to distract himself from the nausea playing at the pit of his stomach. He'd promised himself he'd hold it together this time, that his guts would obey him. But the sight of Jenson Begg's insides opened up to the world was making him feel iffy.

"Right," said Dr Adebayo. She looked at him. "Oh hell, Constable, I thought you'd be able to hold it together this time. Here." She put a hand on his elbow and steered him away from the body. She stopped next to a metal trolley holding jars containing items Rhodri would rather not dwell on.

"I conducted blood tests and examined his liver and kidneys," she said. "Unlike your last guy, this one had been using for some time. There were traces of cannabis, cocaine and methamphetamine in his blood."

"D'you know which one it was that killed him?"

"The methamphetamine. There's ten times what you'd expect based on a normal dose."

"Can you tell when he took it?"

"Hard to be sure. But I also can't be sure he *did* take it, voluntarily, that is, or if it was forced on him."

"I thought there wasn't any evidence of that."

"Follow me." Adana gave him a wary look then walked back to the body. Rhodri focused on the man's head, which was intact. At least, it looked intact.

The doctor placed her gloved hand inside the mouth and pulled it open, wider than Rhodri thought a mouth could be opened. He wrinkled his nose.

"I didn't spot it at the scene, but there's damage to his epiglottis." Dr Adebayo spotted Rhodri's expression. "The flap at the top of his oesophagus, stops food and anything else going down when you breathe. It's less obvious than last time. To be honest, if I hadn't been looking for it, I'd have missed it."

"Have you swabbed it for DNA?"

"I have. I'm not so sure you'll get any this time round, though."

"Why not?"

"The scratching isn't so pronounced. The skin hasn't been broken."

Rhodri swallowed. His stomach gurgled.

The pathologist shook her head at him. "You'll get used to this eventually, Constable. Zoe make you come?"

"Actually, I volunteered."

She laughed. "Well done you. You surprise me."

He felt heat creep into his cheeks. "Has the swab gone to the lab?"

"I thought I'd keep it here, maybe display it on my desk as a keepsake. Yes, of course it's gone to the lab. Should be back tomorrow."

"Thanks."

"Only doing my job."

"Yeah. Anyway, cheers."

"Anything else you need from me?"

"The written report..."

"Already winging its way to your DI. The damage to his epiglottis had to be caused by some sort of object. You could never get your fingers in this far."

"You know what kind of object?"

"Not sharp. There are no fragments. Sorry."

"OK. Ta."

"You keep saying that. You got a stuck needle or something?"

Rhodri opened his mouth to speak, then thought better of it. He left the morgue, glad to escape.

CHAPTER SIXTY-FOUR

Kayla looked up at the sound of a knock on her door. She'd skipped her lectures and locked herself in her room. That policewoman had treated her like she was a suspect. Surely they couldn't think she'd kill Jenson?

"Go away." She slumped onto the bed and pulled her pillow over her head. Her eyes were sore and her stomach ached.

"It's Gina. I came to see how you are."

Kayla propped herself up. *God.* It was probably all over campus by now.

She heaved herself up and unlocked the door. "Come in." She trudged back to the bed and let herself drop onto it.

Gina closed the door and stood by the window. "I thought you might want to talk about Jenson."

"I bet everyone is, by now."

"You were close to him."

Kayla shrugged. "Yeah."

Gina perched on the end of the bed. She put a hand out but didn't make contact. "How are you?"

"How d'you think I am?"

"It's been a rough few days for you. First Laurence, then this."

Kayla gulped in a breath. "I'm fine."

"You don't look fine."

She shrugged. She didn't much care what she looked like.

"He was bad for you, you know."

Kayla felt her muscles clench. "You don't know."

"I heard... rumours... about him."

"He was a good man. He helped people."

Gina put a hand on Kayla's foot. Kayla tensed but didn't pull away.

"He preyed on undergraduates, Kayla."

Kayla jerked away from Gina's touch. "What are you talking about?" She sat up, pushing her hair out of her eyes.

"Tell me how you got involved with him."

"I wasn't *involved* with him. I was his girlfriend."

"Did you ever go on a date? Did you go anywhere together outside his room?"

"I went to his house in Selly Oak."

"Did he ever come here? Did you sit together in the canteen?"

"He was a tutor. He had to look like he was available, to talk to people. He couldn't..." Kayla drew a hand across her cheek. *Shut up*, she thought. She wished she'd never answered the door.

"So you were never together in public."

"He wasn't ashamed of me, if that's what you mean. It wasn't a secret."

"I'm not saying that, Kayla. Just... I've known men like him. Fuck, I used to go out with one."

Kayla looked at the other woman. Her vision was blurred

by tears. "Why are you hanging around me? I'm so much younger than you."

"You looked like you'd benefit from some support. You've met our group. We can help."

"I'm fine."

Gina looked at Kayla, her eyes dark. After a moment, she pulled a hand through her short brown hair and shook her head. "You're not though, are you? You really aren't."

Kayla leaned towards the other woman, her body hot with anger. "You don't know how I feel. Yes, I'm pissed off he's dead. Of course I am. But I don't need *support*. I'll be fine."

Gina stood up. "You're better off without him, you know."

Kayla thumped the bed. She wanted to physically kick Gina out, but she didn't have the strength. "Fuck off."

"You know where I am. Call me, if you want to talk."

"I won't."

Gina put a hand on the doorknob. "I'm sorry you had to go through this, Kayla. But one day you'll realise it was for the best."

CHAPTER SIXTY-FIVE

ZOE PARKED her car outside Harborne police station, her mind full of contradictions. If Laurence had assaulted Kayla, and she'd been in a relationship with Jenson, then she was the person with the most obvious motive. Was it enough to formally question her, though?

She needed to talk to Lesley. The DCI had a way of looking things that cut through all the crap and helped her see straight.

She got out of her car and walked to the front entrance of the police station, giving Sergeant Jenner a curt nod as she passed the reception desk.

She would go back to the team office, talk to Mo about her concerns. Hopefully someone would be able to tell her how Lesley was.

Rhodri was at his desk, looking uneasy.

"Everything OK?" asked Zoe. "How did the post-mortem go?"

Rhodri opened his mouth, then closed it again. He looked towards Zoe's office. Mo was inside, with DI Dawson.

"Shit. What's he want?"

Rhodri shrugged. "Dunno, boss. He came charging in about twenty minutes ago and all but dragged the sarge into your office."

"OK. I'll be right back, I want to know if there's anything useful from the PM."

"Dr Adebayo said she sent the full report to you."

"I'm sure she did. But I want to hear it from you."

"No problem, boss."

Zoe pushed open the door to her office. Dawson was in her chair, leaning over the desk and talking to Mo in a low voice. Mo's body language was tight and uncomfortable.

"What's going on?" Zoe asked. "I'd like my office back, please."

Dawson leaned back, a smile flickering on his lips. "It's not as simple as that."

"No? Fill me in, then." She took a step forward and placed a hand next to his on the desk. Mo shifted in his chair.

Dawson stood up. Zoe was as tall as him, although not as broad. Their eyes locked.

"You're reporting to me until further notice," he said.

"What? No, I'm not. I'm a DI too, in case you hadn't noticed—"

He shook his head. "The DCI's not going to be back for a while. I'm acting up until... well, until we know what's happening."

Zoe's chest hollowed out. "She's that bad?"

Dawson shrugged. "Randle told me she'll be off for a few weeks at least. Maybe longer."

"D'you know what it is?"

"Sorry, Zoe. You'll have to find out for yourself. I know how you like getting distracted from your real work."

"Give it a rest, Frank. I'm just concerned about the boss, is all."

"You can call me Sir."

"You're acting DCI? For real?"

"I'm your line manager for the time being, and that's what counts."

That wasn't an answer. Zoe exchanged glances with Mo. He looked pissed off, too.

She sighed. "Well, I guess you'd better sit in with me and my team while we go over the latest in the Laurence Thomms case."

"Rhodri got something at the PM," Mo said.

"Why didn't he say?" Zoe looked out of the glass separating her office from the team room. Rhodri quickly looked away.

"I think he was a bit preoccupied, boss," Mo muttered.

She grunted. "OK. Come on then." She looked at Dawson, expecting him to follow. Acting up or not, there was no way she was letting him boss her around.

"Before you drag me into your cosy little briefing, we need to have a word," he said.

"Go on."

"The Magpie case. You've been taken off it, but I hear you're still poking around."

"I don't know what you're talking about."

"You're too close to it, Zoe. What with Ian Osman being one of your team. Not to mention your involvement with DI Whaley."

She wondered what would happen if she punched Dawson right now. "Are you saying I'm not professional enough to handle this?"

"I'm saying you're off the case. Mo, too. Leave it with my

team and focus on this one. You've got two murders to deal with now, that should keep you busy."

She glared at him. Randle would have spoken to him, and Randle had his own reasons for wanting Zoe off Magpie.

"Fair enough," she said. "Let's get this over with, then."

CHAPTER SIXTY-SIX

ZOE WALKED TO THE BOARD, aware of Rhodri's gaze flitting between her and Dawson. She perched on the edge of his desk and waited for Mo to sit at his own desk. The sight of Dawson, hunched in Connie's chair, was enough to make Zoe want to push him out of it.

"Right," she said. "We've got the post-mortem report, and I've been speaking to witnesses. Let's start with the PM."

Dawson cleared his throat. "I think you're forgetting something."

She dug her thumbnail into her thigh. It would bruise later. "Frank."

He gave her a look of annoyance. She wasn't going to start calling him Sir.

Dawson walked to the board. He looked at Rhodri.

"Shouldn't we do this when Connie gets back?" asked Mo.

"You're right," said Zoe. "Frank, if you want to make a speech, why don't you save it for when the whole team's here? Maybe bring your team in, too?"

"I'm sure Fran would welcome the opportunity," said Mo, referring to DC Fran Kowalczyk, his former colleague in DI Dawson's team.

Zoe suppressed a smirk and stopped herself from meeting Mo's eye. She turned to Dawson, adopting a look of innocence. "What do you say?"

He blew out a heavy breath. "Very well. Where is DC Williams?"

Zoe checked the clock. Five-thirty pm. "She'll be finishing up at the university, she's been supervising the DNA sampling."

"Good. We can go over that when she returns."

"I doubt we'll have any results tonight."

Dawson nodded. "No. Well, why don't you get on with briefing us on where we're at, then?"

Zoe allowed herself a subtle smile in Mo's direction. "No problem." She turned to Rhodri. "Rhod?"

"Yeah. Er, thanks, boss." Rhodri looked at Dawson, his shoulders hunched. "What d'you want me to cover?"

"Anything important from the post-mortem, Rhod," Zoe said. "I know there's a report sitting in my inbox but I want the summary."

Rhodri grabbed a couple of photos from his desk and joined her at the board. He pinned them both up. The first was of Jenson's head, his eyes closed, his skin pallid. The second was a close-up of internal organs. Zoe couldn't work out what they were.

Rhodri pointed to the second photo. "This is his epiglottis. It's the flap that stops stuff going down when you breathe."

"You learn that today?" asked Mo.

Rhodri blushed. "Well yes, actually. But..."

"Carry on." Mo smiled at him, shifting in his chair.

"Well, see here?" Rhodri grabbed a pen and touched a point in the centre of the photo. Zoe leaned in but couldn't make out what he was indicating.

"What is it?" she asked.

"Damage, boss. At the scene, Dr Adebayo didn't think there was any internal damage to his mouth. But in the post-mortem she found this. There's scratching on his... epiglottis."

"You can't get that naturally?" asked Mo. "Choking, eating something spiky?"

Rhodri shook his head. "Not according to the report."

"You've read it," Zoe said.

"I thought it'd help me make sure what I told you was as thorough as possible."

"Good. So the pathologist says the scratching got there how?"

"Foreign body. And the epiglottis is a long way down so there's no way you'd be able to do it to someone while they were alive, or at least not with them able to resist. Not without the gag reflex forcing the object back up."

"OK." Zoe looked at the photo. She couldn't make out any scratching but she was happy to trust Adana. "She have any idea what type of foreign body did it?"

"She didn't know, boss."

"I take it swabs have been send to Adi?"

"They have."

"Good." Zoe nibbled a fingernail. "So we've got two dead men, both with damage inside their throat, both with dog hairs found on them. Neither owning a dog. And both of them preying on Kayla Goode."

"She found Laurence, but that's hardly—" said Mo.

Dawson coughed. "Preying? Pretty emotive language isn't it, DI Finch?"

"That's the word that Jenson's housemate gave me. She said he" – she poked the photo of Laurence – "was a predator. He attempted to rape Kayla in early November. And she didn't think Kayla's relationship with Jenson was entirely consensual."

"That's not what Kayla told us," said Mo.

Zoe sat on the edge of Rhodri's desk. "He was in a position of authority, Mo. Yes, they were both adults. But what if he was taking advantage of her? What if the attack by Laurence and then the abuse by Jenson tipped her over the edge and she decided to kill them both?"

"So you've got an overemotional teenager who another teenager says might have been assaulted or maybe abused. Doesn't sound like much to me," said Dawson.

Zoe looked at him. She wished Lesley was here.

"I want to know more about these allegations about Laurence and Kayla," she said. "And I want to get to the bottom of her relationship with Jenson."

"If we ask her directly, she'll just lie to us," said Mo.

"I know. That's why we need to talk to Lin again."

"OK. You want me to...?"

"I'll send Connie. She's talked to her before, she might be able to get more from her."

"What about the dog hairs and the damage to the throat?" said Dawson. "I'm sure DCI Clarke would tell you to stick to the facts of the case."

Zoe looked across at him. Rhodri and Mo's eyes were on her. The way she behaved around him would be their cue.

"I know full well what the DCI would say," she told him. "But I'm SIO on this case and I say we pursue both angles.

And besides, we won't get anything concrete on the forensics till tomorrow at least. You want us to twiddle our thumbs until then?"

"Of course not," Dawson replied.

"Good. I'll talk to Connie."

CHAPTER SIXTY-SEVEN

CONNIE WATCHED as the FSIs packed up their gear. She reached her hand behind the back of her neck and leaned back, stretching out her muscles. It had been a long day and she'd been on her feet for most of it, but it had been worth it.

They'd taken samples from every male student on the list, including the postgrads once she'd got the extra list from Tom. The samples had already left, Yala Cook taking them away in an insulated case.

They had ninety-seven samples. It would take days to go through them all, Yala had told her, but they'd asked the lab to work as fast as they could. They could run quick preliminary tests targeting one area of the DNA, to spot any samples that might be a match and then go back to analyse them in more detail. That would speed things up.

Connie had left her bike outside, in the students' bike shed. It was dark outside and she knew it would be cold, but she was used to that. The ride home from here wasn't much different from her commute into work. She'd be fine.

She went to the corner where she'd left her gear and grabbed her helmet. Her phone rang: DI Finch.

"Hi, boss. We're just finishing up here."

"Thanks for everything you've done today. I'm impressed with how smoothly it's gone."

Connie waved at one of the FSIs who was leaving the room. "It was Yala and her crew that did most of the work, boss. And Uniform."

"You should take credit where it's due, Constable. You heading home?"

"I was just putting my cycle helmet on." Connie held her helmet. She had a feeling she wasn't going home anytime soon. "You need me to come back to the office?"

"I need you to stay in Boulton Hall. Can you go and see Lin again? I've been talking to Jenson Begg's housemate, and she says his relationship with Kayla might not have been consensual. That even if he didn't actually assault her, he was abusing his position of authority. And that Laurence assaulted Kayla in November."

"What?" Connie dropped her helmet.

"We have no way of knowing if it's true or just a rumour, but I want you to dig around."

She bent over to pick up her helmet. One of the FSIs, a guy called Rav, was watching her. "Shall I talk to Kayla?"

"She'll just lie to you," the DI said. "She hasn't exactly been forthcoming so far."

"You want me to quiz Lin instead."

"She's over at the Medical School in the day, she's more likely to be at Boulton Hall now. You're not in a hurry to get home, are you?"

Connie strapped her helmet to her rucksack. Her mum

would be annoyed with her, she'd been expecting her home for dinner.

"It's fine. I'll go and find her now."

"Thanks, Connie."

"They've just finished dinner here so she should be in her room. If she hasn't gone out."

"I'll let you go so you can grab her before she goes anywhere."

"You want me to call you when I'm done?"

"If you get anything new, yes. If not, we'll talk in the morning."

"No problem."

Kayla followed Rav, the last FSI, out of the room and walked towards the main entrance. Lin lived on the first floor. If she was going out, she'd be more likely to come down the stairs than use the lift. Connie made her way towards them.

She turned as she reached the stairs. Rav was behind her, heading for the door. He nodded farewell to her.

"Rav, can I ask you a favour?"

"Sure."

"Can you stay here for five minutes, just keep an eye on the lift? If you see an East Asian woman come out, ask her name, and if it's Lin, get her talking."

"What if I don't?"

"Give it five minutes, then you can go. Is that OK?"

He wrinkled his nose.

"Sorry, Rav. I know you're about to leave..."

He threw her a smile. "It's OK, Connie. Seeing as it's you." He winked.

She smiled, her cheeks warm. "Thanks, Rav." She turned and took the stairs two at a time.

She was halfway up the first flight when she heard a voice.

"Constable?"

Connie turned. Doctor Edwards was standing at the bottom of the stairs, Kayla next to her. Connie looked between the two women.

"Can I help you, Constable?" the warden asked.

"I need to speak to a witness," she said. "I won't be long."

The warden took a step towards her. "I can't allow that."

"Sorry?"

They'd already spoken to plenty of students. They'd been getting DNA samples from them.

"You've finished the sampling. I think you've impinged on us enough for one day. Wandering the corridors and frightening my students isn't going to help anyone." Dr Edwards took a step up, towards Connie, lowering her voice. "Especially given this morning's events, don't you think?"

Connie stared back at the woman, then looked past her at Kayla. The girl had been crying. Not surprising, really.

"I would like to talk to one of your students," she said. "It's important."

"I'm sure it is." The warden stepped back. "But so is the welfare of the student population. Now, I'm sure it can wait till the morning and be done properly, in my office."

Connie breathed in. She didn't have a warrant, and this was private property. There was nothing she could do.

"Very well." She walked down the stairs past the warden. Rav was watching her. She avoided his gaze.

At the main entrance, Connie turned to the warden. "We'll be in touch. First thing tomorrow."

"I'm sure you will." The warden turned away, a hand on Kayla's back.

CHAPTER SIXTY-EIGHT

Zoe sat in her office, her skin itching and her heart racing. Dawson lording it over them like this reminded her of the bad old days. He'd been her boss for three years, before he'd gone on his secondment to the Met and she'd been told to act up for him. Then when he'd come back she'd been kept on as a DI, replacing Carl when he'd moved away from his undercover job in Force CID.

She'd hoped the stint away from Birmingham would do Dawson good. That maybe he'd smooth off some of his rough edges and learn how to treat people nicely. Especially her.

Wishful thinking, she thought.

Outside, Mo was on the phone and Rhodri peered at his computer screen. She'd told Mo about the match between the DNA on the passport and the New Street bomber, and asked him to call Sheila. Mo had a good working relationship with Sheila and was happy to work on the case. Zoe's eyes flitted between his back and the door. She hoped Dawson wouldn't come in.

She yawned and checked her watch. Six forty-five. There

wasn't much they could do until Adi came back with more forensics tomorrow. She might as well send the team home. Maybe she'd drop by the university on her way, check Connie was doing OK. She felt as if she'd abandoned her today.

The outer door opened and Zoe sucked in a breath. Mo placed a hand over his phone and stopped talking, his eyes going to the newcomer.

Zoe allowed herself a breath. It was Adi. He waved at her through the glass and knocked on her door. She beckoned him in.

"Give me some good news," she told him. "I need it."

He beamed as he sank into the chair opposite. "Happy to oblige." He slapped a file on her desk and pushed it forward.

Inside were photos of the two bodies, close-ups of the dog hairs found on them, and two DNA analyses.

"They match," Zoe said.

"They certainly do. Either both those men were in contact with the same dog, or the people who killed them were."

"Or one of the victims was in contact with the dog, along with the killer of the other man."

"Blimey Zoe, you do like to complicate things." He leaned back and crossed his legs, an ankle resting on a knee.

"Got to entertain all possibilities. What d'you reckon?"

"In both cases there's no sign of a dog having been at the scene. Laurence lived in a hall of residence where pets aren't allowed, and his parents didn't have a dog. Jenson's a bit less clear cut. But we've found no evidence of dog hairs anywhere in the house, just on his body."

"That could mean he had contact with the dog."

"We didn't find any hairs on his other clothes. We took some from his room, both at the house and at Boulton Hall."

"Did you do the same for Laurence?"

"Yup." Adi smacked his lips, pleased with himself.

"So some other person introduced the dog hairs to both bodies, at or not long before the time of death."

"I don't see any other explanation."

"We're looking for a dog lover."

"A dog owner. Or someone who works with dogs. With this dog in particular."

"Can you get the breed from the hairs?"

"You're the third person who's asked me that today. 'Fraid not, sorry. It's a short-haired brown dog, with quite wiry hair. But that doesn't narrow it down by much."

"Thanks anyway." Zoe closed the file.

Adi stayed put, surveying her.

"Something else?" she asked.

He licked his lips and shifted position. "You might be wondering why I came in to tell you this, when I could have called you or just sent an email."

"I know you like dropping in here, Adi. It's like a second home for you."

He continued staring at her, his eyes losing their brightness. Zoe tugged at her sleeve.

"Adi, you're making me nervous," she said. "Is something wrong?"

"I heard you'd stopped seeing DI Whaley."

"Well... it's not quite like..." She shook herself out. "It's not really your business, Adi."

He leaned forward. "I was wondering if you'd like to go out for a drink."

Zoe laughed then slapped her hand over her mouth. "Oh

Adi, I'm sorry. I'll happily go for a drink with you. But not... like that."

He raised an eyebrow. "Like what?"

"You're asking me about my relationship with Carl and then you invite me out for a drink. Like I say, I'll go for a drink with you anytime. It's not as if we haven't before. But I can't go on a date with you, if that's what you're asking."

He paled. "What made you think I was asking that?"

"I... I just... let's forget we had this conversation, eh? I'll see if Mo and Rhodri want to join us in the pub."

Adi stood up. The colour had returned to his face but he was struggling to meet her eye. "That sounds like a plan."

CHAPTER SIXTY-NINE

CONNIE STOOD in the bike shed, her eyes on the front of the hall of residence. A group of students walked out, laughing between themselves. One of them wolf-whistled and another slapped him.

She fiddled with her bike lock, taking her time. The warden had told her she couldn't 'wander the corridors' to find Lin, but there was no reason she couldn't talk to her if she bumped into her out here.

She would wait.

She couldn't stay too close to the main doors; someone might spot her. But she needed a vantage point.

The bike shed would do. How many people would be coming to retrieve bikes in the dark? And if they did, she could pretend she was picking hers up.

"See ya, Connie," Rav called. He stood next to a blue car, another man in the driver's seat.

"Bye, Rav. Thanks for your help today."

"My pleasure."

Connie couldn't see his face, but she was sure he was

smiling. Rav was cute. She'd worked with him on a case last summer. And there'd been that wink...

She stepped out of the bike shed. Did she have the courage to ask him out for a drink?

He gave her a final wave and slid into the car. She cursed herself.

She had to wait here, to find Lin. The boss had given her a job, and she didn't want to let her down. Besides, Rav was with a colleague.

She'd find an opportunity to see him again. She could volunteer to go to the forensics team and fetch the sampling results.

She turned towards the building. She needed to focus. *Don't let yourself get distracted.*

The building was quiet. Connie could see people moving around inside, the lights in the reception area bright against the dark night. She shivered. It had started to rain, and the bike shelter gave her some protection, but not as much as she'd have liked. She hoped Lin would emerge soon.

She heard voices coming from behind her and turned. Three people approached, their footsteps brisk. Trying to get out of the rain. As they came closer, she recognised one of them.

Connie stepped forward. "Lin?"

Lin raised a hand over her eyes. "Yeah. Who is it?"

Connie realised she was silhouetted by the light over the bike shed. She took a step back so it would illuminate her face and brought out her ID. "It's DC Williams. I've just finished taking DNA samples."

"Oh. Cool." Lin started walking. The other two students had gone on ahead and were at the door to the building.

"Could I talk to you?" Connie asked, falling into step beside her.

"Again?" Lin sighed. "I missed dinner. I'm planning on ordering a pizza, I'm bloody starving."

"I'll buy you a pizza." Connie hesitated. "Sorry, I'm not sure if I can. But I can buy you a drink, if you like."

"I'm not thirsty. I need food and I need my bed."

"It's about Kayla and Jenson."

Lin stopped walking and turned to Connie. "What about them?"

"Was their relationship consensual?"

"That's a hell of a question."

"Was he taking advantage of her?" Connie asked. "He was her tutor, he was five years older than her."

"They were both adults." Lin's voice was sharp.

"Was she happy with him?"

Lin snorted. "You'd have to ask *her* that, buddy." She shook her head and started to walk away.

"Did Laurence assault Kayla?"

Lin stopped walking. She stood still, facing away from Connie. Rain drummed on her head and shoulders.

"Lin? You know something, don't you?"

Lin turned. She plunged her hands into the pockets of her coat. "I don't know anything, OK?"

"Whatever you tell me will be strictly confidential. I just need to know—"

"Leave it. Just leave it alone."

Lin turned away from her and half-walked, half-ran, into the building.

CHAPTER SEVENTY

ZOE PUT a hand on Mo's shoulder. "I'll see you in the morning."

"See you, Zo."

She turned to Adi. "And you, Adi. Thanks for the drink."

Adi looked up at her. "Sure thing, Zoe. Thanks." He gave her a lengthy look which she tried to ignore.

She picked up her Diet Coke and downed the last of it, then checked her watch again. Nine o'clock.

"I'd best get home. Get my beauty sleep."

Adi looked away. Zoe rolled her eyes. Normally Adi would take a statement like that as an opportunity to make a joke. She hoped this new awkwardness wouldn't last.

"See you tomorrow, guys."

She turned and headed out of the pub. They were in the White Swan, not far from the office. She'd hoped that going out with Adi and Mo would lighten the air between her and Adi, and make it clear she wasn't about to start dating him. She liked Adi, she'd always liked him, but she'd never been attracted to him. She'd watched him flirt with every woman he worked with, always good-natured, never threatening. She'd never thought he meant it.

The cold air hit her lungs as she left the pub. It had started to rain. She ran to her car and dived inside.

She pulled out of the car park, looking forward to a couple of hours in front of the TV with Yoda on her lap. Nicholas was in London and she wouldn't have to sit through one of his documentaries. She wondered how he was getting on.

Her phone rang. Zoe hit hands-free, expecting it to be Nicholas.

"Hey, you."

"That's a bit informal Zoe, even for you."

Zoe straightened in her seat. "Ma'am."

"Who did you think I was?" Lesley asked.

"I thought you were my son. Sorry."

A hoarse laugh. "That's OK."

"How are you? Are you still in hospital?"

Lesley coughed. Zoe listened, her gaze flicking between the phone and the road ahead. That didn't sound good.

She waited for Lesley to catch her breath.

"I wanted to talk to someone who wouldn't nag me about my health," Lesley croaked. "I'm hoping you'll be that person."

"I promise not to ask you how you are again. Although..."

"You can find out about my health from someone else. I'm sure Terry has been on the phone to David Randle." Terry was Lesley's husband; Zoe had met him last time the boss was in hospital.

"Tell me what you're doing, right now," Lesley said.

"Err... I'm driving along Richmond Hill Road. Just left the White Swan."

"Glad to hear you've been enjoying a bit of downtime, Zoe."

"I went for a drink with Mo and Adi. Adi was being... you don't need to know about that. It was good to relax with them."

"I'd give anything to be in the pub with you right now."

"They looking after you, Ma'am?"

"I thought you weren't going to ask after my health."

"OK, how's the food?"

A laugh. "No fucking idea. I was being shunted around from one department to another till an hour ago and I missed dinner on the ward. You think I should ask if they've got leftovers?"

"I wouldn't advise it."

"Not based on the last time I was in here."

"Take care of yourself, ma'am."

"Uh-uh. You promised."

Zoe heard a voice in the background.

"I've got to go, Zoe. But don't let them give you any shit while I'm gone. Yeah?"

"I'll try not to."

"I mean it. Randle. Dawson. I know what they're like. You're a damn good copper, you're worth ten of DI Dawson."

Zoe felt her spirits lift. Coming from Lesley, that was quite something.

"Thank you, ma'am."

"Shush. Come and visit me when you can, eh? I know you're busy. But I'm bored as hell." Zo heard the voices again. "Even with my husband here. Especially with my husband here."

"I will, boss."

"Good. I've got to go, Terry's nagging me. See you soon Zoe."

The line went dead. Zoe stopped at the lights to the Bristol Road and smiled to herself.

CHAPTER SEVENTY-ONE

ZOE FLUNG her coat at the hook, missed, and stepped over it. She wandered into the living room and dropped her bag on the sofa.

The house was a mess. She needed to stop letting Nicholas do all the tidying up. But when she was working a case, even if she did get any downtime, it was hard to focus on anything else. She didn't notice the dishes piling up in the sink and the dirt accumulating in the corners.

She had to get better at this. She didn't want to end up like her own mum, alcoholic and slovenly.

She went into the kitchen and filled the filter coffee maker. There were hours to kill before bed, so no harm in taking her time over a coffee. She was peckish, too.

She opened the fridge and grimaced. A pile of carrots, a lump of cheese, and two cartons of milk. A Tupperware container sat at the back, something pale Zoe didn't recognise inside. It was probably worth eating, possibly something Nicholas had made. But then, it could be anything.

She'd dial out for a pizza. The carbs would restore her energy.

She closed the fridge door and pulled the pizza menu from under the magnet. Not that she needed it; she had the number programmed into her phone and she always ordered pepperoni, extra chilli.

She called the number and ordered. The pizza would be half an hour. Time for a shower.

Twenty minutes later she was in her bedroom, clean and refreshed. She'd felt the grubbiness of Jenson Begg's house on her skin all day. Some people felt that way about her own house, she knew, including Mo.

She pulled on clean jeans and a shirt and tramped downstairs. Her stomach rumbled. Her phone was on the coffee table; two missed calls.

She picked it up, hoping she hadn't missed Nicholas.

It was Carl. He'd left two texts.

The first was brief: *Just checking how you are, Carl.*

The second was less so: *Sorry things are weird between us right now. I'll call you as soon as the trial is over xx*

She dropped the phone on the table. She was tempted to call him, just to hear his voice. But she knew it was a bad idea.

Her phone pinged and she picked it up, her breathing tight.

Hi Mum, London's great. Dad keeps buying me stuff. Taking advantage of it!

She smiled. Good to know Nicholas was enjoying himself. She hoped he was getting along with Geordie. The two of them rubbed each other up the wrong way. Nicholas didn't know how to compensate for Geordie's autism and Geordie didn't know when to leave Nicholas alone. Nicholas had been eleven and Geordie thirteen when the two of them had first met, so they'd never had the chance to become comfortable around each other.

Her phone rang. Zoe put it to her ear.

"Couldn't resist calling me?" she asked.

The voice on the other end laughed. "Don't tell my wife."

"Sorry, Mo. I thought you were Nicholas." This was the second time tonight she'd done that. She had to get used to him not being around.

"He out with Zaf?"

"He's gone to London for the weekend with Jim and his family."

"Oh."

"Oh indeed. He sent me a text, seems to be enjoying himself."

"Good. And you?"

"What about me?"

"I know how you feel about Jim and Nicholas."

"He's his dad, Mo. I can't stop him taking him places."

"Good. So I wanted to check you were OK, after this evening."

"Course. Why?"

"Did something happen with you and Adi earlier?"

Zoe sat down on the sofa. "Was it that obvious?"

"He wasn't flirting with you."

"What's so odd about that?"

"He *always* flirts with you."

"This is between you and me, Mo. Confidential."

"You know me. Zippy's my middle name." He made a zipping sound. Zoe could imagine him miming zipping his lips. She chuckled.

"He asked me out. Thought things were finished between me and Carl."

"I was wondering when he'd get around to it."

"What?"

"Come on, Zo. All that *my favourite detective* stuff? You might not have noticed, but the guy's face lights up when he's around you."

Zoe felt her face heat up. "He flirts with everyone."

"That's a diversion. He's trying to make you jealous."

She laughed. "Don't talk bollocks."

There was silence for a moment. "I take it you turned him down, which is why you dragged me along for protection."

"You weren't protection."

"You didn't want to be alone with him."

"No. And yes. I did turn him down. I've never thought of Adi that way."

"What about Carl?"

Zoe heard muffled voices in the background: Mo's girls. She listened while he spoke to them, unable to make out the words.

"Sorry, Zo. I've got to go. Look after yourself, yeah?"

He hung up. Zoe stared at her phone, feeling empty. She was realising how much she missed Carl. There had been something solid between them, something she'd hoped might grow. Now he thought she was dodgy and she resented him for it.

The doorbell rang. Zoe heaved herself up from the sofa, glad of the distraction. She'd console herself with a pizza and a film instead of the man she'd thought she was falling in love with.

CHAPTER SEVENTY-TWO

DAWSON WAS SITTING at Zoe's desk when she arrived in the office the next morning. She stood opposite him, hands on hips. How was she going to stop him doing this?

He leaned back in her chair, his feet on her desk. She thought of Lesley, the way she sprawled over her own desk. But that was her own desk. Lesley would never do this in Zoe's space.

"Frank. I'd like my desk back please."

"I need a word."

"OK." She folded her arms and tapped her foot. "Can you get your shoes off my desk? Please."

He gave her a self-satisfied smirk and pulled his feet off the desk, straightening up in the chair.

"Haven't you got your own office to go to?" she asked.

"I didn't want to miss you."

"Well, you've got me."

"DCI Clarke told you to pull back from the Magpie investigation."

"Did she?"

"She had a conversation with you when she came to Boulton Hall. Kit Singh witnessed it.

Shit. Her intuition about that Kit guy had been right.

"She did," she said. "Thought I was too busy on this murder case."

Dawson raised an eyebrow. Did he know the real reason she'd been pulled off that case?

"So why did you ask DS Uddin to discuss the case with the Organised Crime unit?" he asked.

Zoe hesitated.

"It wasn't Mo's fault, if you're thinking of laying anything on him. I received a piece of evidence, and I asked him to pass it over to DS Griffin."

"You should have given it to me. Like you were told."

"Mo and I have been working with Sheila on this case. It seemed sensible to pass the information to her."

Dawson stood up and leaned over the desk. "You received a direct order, Zoe. You then failed to tell Adi Hanson that he should have called someone else with this evidence, and you continued liaising with DS Griffin despite knowing that the responsibility had been passed to me."

She met his gaze. "I did."

"Why?"

"You weren't at that hotel, Frank. Those poor bloody women. I watched one of them die, when Adam Fulmer deliberately ran her over. It's hard to leave a case alone, after you've seen something like that."

Dawson shook his head. "I don't give a fuck about your emotional reaction to cases, DI Finch. If you're told to get off a case, you get off it. Understood?"

She licked her lips and took a shaky breath. "DCI Clarke

told me to leave the case alone. I accept that I shouldn't have followed it up, but in my defence Adi came to me."

Dawson opened his mouth. Zoe raised a hand to stop him.

"If I get an order like that from a senior officer again, I will pass on any information immediately, as commanded."

"You're getting that order right now, Zoe."

She stared at him. She wasn't about to say outright that he wasn't her senior officer, but she knew they were both thinking it.

After a moment, he broke the silence. "Very well. I'm glad we're clear. I don't expect to see you within ten miles of this case from now on, Zoe."

"Understood." Zoe clenched her fists, her palms damp. DI Dawson had no idea what was really going on with Randle, Ian and Trevor Hamm, and she wasn't about to tell him. Unless...

No. She had to assume Dawson was clean.

"Right." Dawson stepped around the desk, his arm brushing hers as he passed. Zoe flinched. "I'll be back in twenty minutes, for the briefing."

"I look forward to it."

He pursed his lips, staring into her face. He smelled of sweat. He wanted her to call him *Sir*, she knew it. He blinked at her a few times, then turned for the door.

As he left the outer office, Zoe threw herself into her chair, her heart pounding. Reporting to Dawson again was no fun.

CHAPTER SEVENTY-THREE

Zoe stood in front of the board, her stomach clenched. Mo, Rhodri and Connie were at their desks. They fidgeted in silence. Mo kept checking his phone, Rhodri was clicking a pen. Connie chewed on her bottom lip. No one knew when Dawson would reappear.

"I say we get on with it," said Mo. "He told you twenty minutes, it's been twenty-five."

Zoe looked at the door for the umpteenth time. "You're right. Come on, then. Connie, how did you get on with Lin last night? I take it there was nothing useful?"

Connie shook her head. "She wouldn't talk to me, boss."

"She refused?"

"As good as. I asked her about Kayla and Jenson first, she was snippy with me, said they were consenting adults. Then when I asked if she knew anything about Laurence assaulting Kayla, she shut down on me. Walked away."

"Did she know anything?"

"She said not. Told me to leave it alone."

"Which suggests there *was* something to leave alone," said Mo.

"That's what I thought, sarge," said Connie.

"OK," said Zoe. She used her pen to jab Lin's photo on the board.

"I told you to wait for me." Dawson was in the doorway.

"We did. Twenty minutes, you told me."

"Five minutes late, and you're..." he caught himself. Even Dawson didn't want to be seen arguing with Zoe in front of the team. Not about something as petty as a five-minute delay.

"We were talking about Connie's trip to see Lin Johnson last night," said Zoe. "Lin denies that Laurence Thomms assaulted Kayla Goode, or that Kayla's relationship with Jenson Begg was nonconsensual."

"You still flogging this old horse? What about the forensics?"

"We've got results on the dog hairs. Nothing on the samples yet."

He sighed. "Well bloody well hassle the FSI buggers." He looked around the team. "Go on, then. Get on the phone."

"We're reviewing the evidence."

"You did this yesterday. You've made no progress, and standing around here isn't going to get us anywhere."

Zoe took a step towards him. "This is how we work. We discuss the evidence we have, we confer on conclusions and hypotheses. It means everyone in the team knows what's going on, and gives us more chance of spotting connections."

Dawson grunted. "Well now I'm in charge, and I want you to get on with it. DC Hughes, call the lab. Find out what's happening with the DNA sampling from yesterday and tell them to get a shift on."

Rhodri looked at Zoe. She shook her head. "Before we do that, DI Dawson, there is one piece of forensic evidence we need to discuss. I already mentioned it."

"Enlighten us, then."

She had the photos and printouts that Adi had brought her the night before. She stuck them to the board and turned to face the team.

"We found dog hairs on both bodies. Short, brown, wiry. They're both from the same dog. Neither victim owned a dog, and there was no sign of a dog in Jenson's house. Boulton Hall doesn't allow pets."

"Maybe they both knew someone with a dog," said Dawson.

"I'm not aware of the two of them moving in the same social circles."

"So the killer had a dog?" said Rhodri.

"Not for definite. But it's a good possibility."

"And both of them were given drugs," said Connie. "Both of them had them forced down their throat."

"How many people knew the details of Laurence's death?" asked Mo.

"Good question," said Zoe. "We kept it tight. The warden. Lin and Kayla knew what they saw when they found him. That's all."

"But the public knew that Laurence died of a drugs overdose," said Dawson. "I saw the press release."

"We didn't say what kind of drugs. We didn't say anything about how it was introduced into his system."

"So the second murder wasn't a copycat," said Connie.

"Exactly," said Zoe. "I think we can assume we're looking for one killer."

Mo nodded. "And you think Kayla has a motive for both men."

"If we're to believe what Jenson's housemate said. And Lin's reaction to Connie's questioning makes me more suspicious."

"You don't have grounds for arrest," said Dawson. "There's no physical evidence putting her at the scene of either crime, at least, not at the time of the murders."

"She discovered the first body and was going out with the second victim," said Zoe. "She'll have had legitimate reason to leave traces at both scenes."

"You can't arrest her."

She resisted rolling her eyes. "I'm not going to arrest her. But I would like to talk to her again. Possibly under caution."

Connie turned to Dawson. "After the way Lin was with me last night, I think the boss is right." She blinked. "Sir."

"OK," said Dawson. "But I'm doing it with you, DI Finch. I want to be sure this is done properly."

"I think she should be interviewed by two women," said Zoe. "I was going to suggest Connie—"

"Uh-uh. I don't trust you to not fuck this up. I'll be in there with you."

"Fair enough." Zoe knew which battles to pursue, and which to drop. She turned to Mo. "In the meantime, you and Rhodri go back to Jenson's house. I want to see what we can find out about where he got his drugs."

"I think we should ask around on campus too," said Mo. "If he was dealing, he'd have been doing it in Boulton Hall."

Zoe bowed her head. Jenson Begg was dead, but it was

hard to grieve for him. "I agree. You two head over there. I'll bring Kayla in, interview her with DI Dawson."

"What d'you want me to do?" asked Connie.

Zoe's gaze flicked to Dawson and back to the DC. "DI Dawson is right, Connie. I want you on the phone to Forensics. Make sure we get any match from the sampling the minute it comes in."

Connie sat up straight. Her eyes brightened. "I'll go over there on my bike, boss. Refuse to leave till they give me something."

Zoe shrugged. "Don't make a nuisance of yourself though, will you?"

Connie smiled. "I won't."

CHAPTER SEVENTY-FOUR

KAYLA STARED AT THE CEILING. She couldn't face lectures today. She felt hollow inside, as if someone had scooped out her intestines.

Her phone buzzed. She ignored it. It buzzed again. Cursing, she picked it up from the floor next to her bed.

It was Gina. *How are you? Fancy a coffee?*

Just leave me alone, she thought. She let the phone slide to the floor.

Maybe she should go out. Distract herself. Even if she didn't make it to lectures, getting out of her stuffy room might help. She'd walk into Selly Oak, go to Jenson's house. His housemates would let her in. She felt a need just to be in the house. To be closer to him.

She pulled on her trainers and denim jacket, and yanked the door open. She hadn't put any makeup on and wasn't about to bother. No one that mattered would see her.

She stood outside the lift, scanning the corridor. She didn't want anyone seeing her. The people in the rooms around her knew about her and Jenson. They would be full of smiles and false sympathy.

The lift door opened – empty, thank God – and she slid inside. It rumbled to the ground floor and she crept out, hoping no one would notice her.

Lin was near the door to the canteen, talking to the warden. Kayla's chest tightened. She hurried towards the main entrance, her head down.

"Kayla?"

Kayla paused, then carried on moving. She scuttled towards the door and pushed her way outside. The air was biting cold and she wished she'd put on a better coat. But there was no way she was going back in there.

She rushed up the driveway towards the road. She could be at the house in ten minutes if she was quick. She just hoped the police wouldn't be there still.

A car rounded the corner leading to Edgbaston Park Road. It was a green Mini. She knew that car. She'd sat in that car.

The car pulled up next to her and a uniformed police-woman got out of the passenger seat.

"Kayla Goode?" The constable stood in front of her. Kayla stared back at her. *Leave me alone.* She shook her head and started walking away.

The driver's door opened and a woman stepped out. It was the tall redheaded one, DI Finch. The one who'd been full of insincere concern and friendliness. "Kayla, we need to talk to you."

"I don't want to talk."

She turned away. There was a cut-through up ahead, she could lose them.

She heard the car start up again. It stopped ahead of her.

The detective jumped out on front of her and put a hand on her wrist. "We need you to come to Harborne police station to answer some questions."

Kayla jerked her arm away. The detective looked into her eyes, her grip firm. Could she do this?

"Are you arresting me?"

"I'm cautioning you. It's not the same thing. You're not under arrest and you don't have to agree to questioning, but it's in your interests to do so."

"I've got lectures."

"We'll make sure your department knows where you are."

"No." Kayla glared at her. "They don't need to know."

"Fine. We'll go to the station. I'll have you back here in an hour."

Kayla looked between the detective and the car. The uniformed constable watched from inside, her hand on the door handle.

The detective looked into her eyes. "Please."

The constable got out of the car and pulled the back door open. The detective led her to it.

Kayla drew in a shaky breath and let the woman guide her in, her stomach full of lead.

CHAPTER SEVENTY-FIVE

THE FSIs HAD GONE and the house had been returned to its tenants. Mo pulled up opposite, glancing at the garden where Rhodri had seen a possible intruder.

Rhodri grabbed his door handle. Mo put up a hand to stop him. "Hang on a minute."

He grabbed his phone and called Adi.

"Hi, Mo. How's it going?" Adi seemed to have cheered up since last night, at least.

"Fine, thanks. I called to ask about the boot print you found at the Jenson Begg house."

"We've been working on that this morning. Still trying to identify the brand of shoe. It's not easy."

"Did you do a soil analysis?"

"We did. You're wondering about the house opposite."

"I am."

"Well, I've got good news for you."

Mo threw Rhodri a thumbs-up. "You've got a match?"

"Yup," said Adi. "The mud on the kitchen floor has *Ligu-*

laria seeds and dandelion fragments in it. So has the front garden of the house opposite."

"Could they have got there some other way?"

"The two houses *are* very close. But we sampled the back garden of the house where the body was found, and it was different. Mainly annuals and a few sycamore seeds. They get everywhere."

"What about the front?"

"Yeah, the front's all tarmacked. Nothing but dog shit and remains of old Maccies."

"Surely if someone was in the front garden opposite and then went through the house to the kitchen, they'd have left traces in the front garden of Jenson's house?"

"It's a tarmacked path, and it was trampled all over by the world and his wife yesterday. I'm not surprised we didn't find anything."

"Right," Mo said. "So you think that's enough to conclude that the person who killed Jenson was in the front garden opposite beforehand?"

"I think it's enough to conclude that the person who left that boot print was in the front garden opposite. Not the same thing."

"No. Thanks, Adi."

Mo hung up and turned to Rhodri. "That's encouraging."

"Yeah."

"Right. Let's see who's in, shall we?"

They left the car and walked to the front door. Mo rapped on the wood with his knuckles. There was no knocker or door bell.

A skinny man with a scruffy beard opened after a few moments. Will Bulmer, the man from the downstairs front room. "You again."

"Sorry to disturb you," said Mo. "We need to ask you some questions about the drugs Jenson was taking."

"I told you I don't know nothing about no drugs."

Mo eyed him. The man's face was sunken and his eyes were yellowing. He knew about drugs, alright.

"You're not in any trouble," Mo said. "But I do need to ask you some questions. And if you don't feel able to cooperate, then my colleague here will have no choice but to search the premises..."

"You've got no grounds."

"We found drugs here yesterday, in Jenson's room. We do."

The man muttered under his breath. "Come in." He turned towards the back of the house. Mo and Rhodri followed.

In the kitchen, Will leaned against the stove and cocked his head at them. "Go on, then."

Mo nudged Rhodri, who jolted.

"Look mate," said Rhodri. "We don't want to arrest anyone. Too much bloody paperwork, to be honest. We just want to know where Jenson got his stash from."

"Don't try and talk like that, *mate*. You're a copper."

Rhodri blushed. "Where'd he get his drugs?"

Mo put a hand on Rhodri's arm. "Tell us, and we'll leave you alone."

The young man shrugged. "No fucking idea, pal."

"You sure about that?"

He slumped against the stove. "Honest. I don't know. He was secretive about it, like. Never told no one where he got them."

"Was he dealing?"

A pause. "He shared his stash with his mates sometimes."

"In return for money?" asked Mo.

A shrug. "Yeah."

Dealing, Mo thought. The question was how much, and who had supplied it.

"Did you buy from him?"

"You told me I weren't gonna be in trouble."

"You're not. If I don't find any drugs in your possession, I can't arrest you. And if I don't look, then I won't find anything."

"That good enough?" asked Rhodri. Will nodded.

"Yeah, I bought from him. Don't have it no more, though."

"I'm sure you don't," said Mo. "Did anyone else in the house buy from him?"

"A bit. Sometimes. Just a little bit, though. Nothing major."

"What about Boulton Hall? Was Jenson selling drugs there?"

Will returned Mo's gaze. "He might've been."

"Who to? Undergraduates?"

"The place is full of fucking undergraduates."

"So that's a yes, then."

"You'd have to ask Jenson." The man curled his lip. "Oh no, you can't, cos he's *dead*."

"Trust me, Will," said Mo. "If we find out where Jenson got his drugs, it puts us closer to finding the person that killed him."

"He weren't killed by his dealer, if that's what you think."

"No?"

"Nope."

"And you know that how?"

"Cos I saw him talking to someone."

Mo's skin prickled. "Who? Why didn't you tell us this yesterday?"

"Only remembered this morning. He was out front, chatting to some girl."

"A woman?"

"Yeah."

"When?"

"I dunno. About ten-thirty. She seemed pissed off."

"Was she a student? Did you recognise her?"

"Sorry, mate. I've got net curtains, and it was dark. Their voices were muffled, like."

"Did your girlfriend see this?"

"Shonda was in the loo. I was looking out the window, having a fag. Waiting for her to get back."

"You're sure you can't remember what she looked like?"

"I saw silhouettes. Heard low voices. That's all I got. Sorry."

CHAPTER SEVENTY-SIX

Zoe drove to the office, her fingers drumming the steering wheel. She struggled to pay attention to the road, so focused was she on the silent presence of her back-seat passenger.

They weren't arresting Kayla, so in theory she was free to go. But placing her under caution meant anything she said could be used as evidence.

At last they arrived at the station. Zoe found a parking spot and watched the uniformed officer guide Kayla inside. Zoe sprinted to catch up with them, arriving just as Kayla was being checked in.

"Thanks, guys. I'll take it from here." She turned to Kayla. "We'll go into an interview room and ask you some questions. The interview will be recorded and you have a right to a copy of the tape. Does that make sense?"

"Do I need a lawyer?"

"You are entitled to a lawyer. But you're not under arrest, Kayla."

Kayla was pale, her forehead beaded with sweat. She

carried a rucksack which she held in front of her, her fingers stroking the handle.

"OK. I'll answer your questions."

Zoe gave her a smile. "Thanks. Come with me." She gestured towards an interview room.

The PC who'd come with her to Boulton Hall, PC Jenks, followed them in. Zoe considered calling Dawson, like he'd asked her too. She'd get this done wick, he'd never know.

Inside, Zoe pointed out where Kayla should sit and turned on the tape recorder.

"Thanks for agreeing to this interview, Kayla. I need to ask you some more questions about Laurence Thomms and Jenson Begg." She recited the standard words of the police caution.

Kayla stared back at her, unblinking.

"Can we get you a drink? Water? Cup of tea?"

"Water, please."

"One moment." Zoe poked her head out of the door and asked the duty sergeant to bring in a glass of water.

"Right, it won't be long," she told Kayla. "Are you OK to get started?"

"You said you'd have me back on campus in an hour. I've got a lecture at eleven."

Zoe glanced at the clock: quarter past ten. This would be tight. "I'll do my best."

Kayla nodded. She still held her rucksack. She'd placed it on her lap and was clutching the straps. Her knuckles were white.

The door opened and the sergeant came in with a plastic cup of water. She gave Zoe a questioning look. Zoe nodded towards Kayla and the sergeant placed it in front of her.

"Thanks." Kayla picked up the cup and drank greedily. She wiped her lips and placed it back down.

"Right," said Zoe. "Let's start with Jenson." Hopefully this would be less contentious. "Can you tell me about your relationship with him?"

"We were going out."

"Were you?"

"Yes."

"Only I've been told you weren't really *going out* as such. Just staying in, really."

Kayla blushed. "It was a passionate relationship."

Zoe smiled. "Nothing wrong with that. But were you officially dating? Did other people know about it?"

Kayla gripped the plastic cup. Water splashed onto the table. "People knew."

"Which people?"

"Lin. The people in Jenson's house."

"No one else?"

A shrug. "You don't have to go trumpeting it to the world just because you're in love with someone."

"Did Jenson ask you not to tell people about your relationship?"

"Who told you that?"

"Answer the question, Kayla."

"He thought the warden would have a downer on it. Abuse of power, shit like that." Kayla looked up at Zoe. "I consented. He never coerced me."

"I never suggested he did."

"Good."

"What made you say that?"

Kayla frowned. "You're twisting my words."

"Kayla, did Jenson ever force you into anything you

didn't want to do? Did he make you have sex with him? Did he force you to take drugs?"

"No." Kayla placed her hands in her lap, one clutching the other.

"Did he sell you drugs?"

"No."

"I'm not going to arrest you for taking drugs. Are you sure he didn't sell them to you?"

"He gave them to me."

"For free?"

"Yes."

"Why would he do that?"

Kayla's gaze was steady. "Because he loved me, maybe?"

"Or because he preferred you when you weren't fully in command of yourself."

"Jenson cared about me."

"Like he cared about all his students."

Kayla swigged from the cup of water and crumpled it up. She left it on the table.

"Was Jenson sleeping with any other undergraduates?"

"I don't see why that's relevant."

"So he was."

"I didn't say that. There's no law against having..."

"I know this is hard, Kayla. You loved him, you've told me that. But I believe that Jenson was manipulating people with whom he was in a position of trust."

Kayla shook her head. "I've got no idea what you're talking about."

Zoe sighed. Kayla was protecting Jenson. Maybe she wouldn't be so quick to defend Laurence.

"OK, let's move on to Laurence, then."

"What about him?"

"In your witness statement, you said that you were going to knock on Laurence's door ten minutes earlier than you did, but you decided not to. Why was that?"

"He was a creep. We didn't want to talk to him."

"You, or Lin?"

"Both of us."

Zoe leaned back. "According to your statement, it was you who told Lin to start at a different room."

Kayla pulled at her sleeve. "Yeah."

Zoe watched the young woman's face. Had Kayla considered that if she hadn't done that, Laurence might have still been alive when they went in there?

"How do you feel about that decision now?"

Kayla shrugged. "Dunno."

"Tell me why you thought of Laurence as a creep."

"Everyone thought the same. It's cos he was."

"What happened to give him that reputation?"

"Becca."

"The alleged rape."

"Yeah."

"Was Becca his only victim?"

"How should I know who else that bastard tried it on with?"

Zoe eyed Kayla. The girl really hated Laurence. It felt like it was more than because of Becca. Was this personal?

"When did you find out about Laurence allegedly raping Becca?"

"After she reported it."

"She reported it to Jenson, as her residential tutor?"

"Yeah."

"And he told you."

"Yea— no. I just heard it."

"You're not going to get Jenson into trouble, Kayla. Did he tell you about Becca?"

Kayla sighed. "He did. Not till after he'd talked to Dr Edwards, though."

Well at least that's something, Zoe thought.

"Did he tell anyone else, apart from you?"

"Not that I know of."

"So just you. He confided in you."

Kayla puffed out her chest. "He did."

"Any reason why he might have told you?"

"He was my boyfriend. We talked a lot."

"Did he tell you because Laurence had attacked you too?"

"He might ha— I mean, no. He told me because we talked a lot."

"But he might have told you because of what Laurence did to you?"

Kayla stared back across the table. Zoe said nothing, leaving empty space for the young woman to fill.

"I didn't make a formal complaint. I just told him."

"You told Jenson that Laurence had assaulted you?"

A nod.

"And what did Jenson say when you told him?"

"He said... he said without any evidence, it would be my word against Laurence's."

"So you didn't make a complaint?"

Kayla looked into her lap. "No."

"When did this happen?"

"November," Kayla muttered.

"Did you tell anyone else?"

Kayla shook her head. A tear dripped from the end of her nose. Zoe grabbed a box of tissues and held it out.

Kayla took the box, not looking up. "Don't tell anyone, alright?"

"Why don't you want me to tell anyone?"

"I should've reported it. He might not have... you know."

"He might not have raped Becca."

Kayla sniffed. She nodded.

"Is that a yes?"

"Yeah." Kayla blew her nose. "Can I go to my lecture now?"

Zoe softened. "We won't be much longer, I promise."

Another sniff. Kayla balled up a tissue, shoved it up her sleeve, and grabbed another one.

"Why do you think Jenson told you not to report Laurence?"

Kayla looked up. Her eyes were puffy and red. "I told you. He said I had no evidence."

"Evidence doesn't always have to be physical, Kayla. Sometimes there are witnesses you don't know about. Sometimes there are forensics you aren't aware of. And sometimes, if there's been another victim..."

"I know that, don't I? I fucking know it. If it wasn't for me, he wouldn't have raped Becca, and he wouldn't be dead."

"You think he died because of what happened with Becca?"

"Course he did. Everyone hated him. He didn't take drugs, someone forced them on him. Didn't they?"

"Do you have any idea where that someone might have got hold of the drugs to do that?"

Kayla shrank back. "No."

"Not from Jenson?"

Kayla clenched her fists. She pulled the rucksack closer. "No."

"Kayla, do you have any idea if someone might have wanted to kill Jenson?"

"He died of an overdose. It was an accident."

"That's not what we believe now."

Kayla's mouth fell open. "What?"

"We have evidence suggesting he was murdered. Who might have wanted to kill him?"

The redness had left Kayla's cheeks. She was the palest Zoe had seen her. "I don't. I really don't."

CHAPTER SEVENTY-SEVEN

CONNIE PARKED her bike outside the office where the Forensics Scene Management team were based. It was only three miles from Harborne and the journey had taken her twenty minutes: probably faster than it would in a car. There were no bike racks, so she had to find a lamp post.

She took a deep breath and approached the door, checking her reflection in the glass before she pushed it open. Her hair was frizzy today; she wished she'd put oil in it last night.

She sniffed and went inside. A young blonde woman sat at the reception desk, gazing at a computer screen.

"Hi, I'm Detective Constable Williams." Connie showed her ID. "Here to see the FSIs."

"First floor, on the left. I'll get someone to come down for you."

"It's OK, I've been up there before," Connie lied. "I know my way."

The woman shrugged. "Fair enough." She pressed a button and the security barrier slid back.

"Thanks." Connie shot her a grin but the woman was back at her screen.

Connie took the stairs two at a time, regretting her eagerness when she got to the top. She was out of breath and probably sweating.

She paused in a spot where the receptionist wouldn't be able to see her from below, hidden from anyone beyond the glazed door into the FMS office. She took a few deep breaths, licked her lips and told herself to stop being so pathetic.

She knocked on the door and pushed it open without waiting for a response. She found herself in an open plan space with a bank of desks closest to her and workstations beyond it. Two white-suited techs stood at the workstations and three people sat at the desks. One of them was Rav.

He looked up and grinned when he saw her. She felt her heart leap.

"Connie."

"Hi, Rav. You OK?"

"I'm good, thanks." He leaned back in his chair, swinging it back and forth. "What can we do for you?"

"My boss has told me to come over here, make sure we get the results from the sampling as soon as they're in."

He had a lopsided smile that put a dimple in the centre of his right cheek. "No pressure, eh?"

"Sorry. You know what it's like."

Rav stood up. "Come on. We're making good progress."

He led her to the workstations and the two techs. One of them removed a mask. It was Yala.

"Hi, Yala." Connie felt awkward. Could Yala tell she'd been flirting with Rav?

Had she been flirting with Rav, or had she just been acting like an idiot?

"Connie. Are you psychic, or something?" Yala asked.

"Er, no." Connie's gaze flitted to the workstation. Yala had been working on the DNA swabs. "Does that mean you've got something?"

"We have."

"OK."

Yala looked past Connie at Rav. "Haven't you got work to do?"

Connie could feel Rav's arm just centimetres from hers. She held herself very still, nervous of making contact.

Rav nudged Connie. "See you later, huh?"

Connie felt heat prick her cheeks. "Er, yeah." She kept her gaze on Yala, who was suppressing a smile.

When Rav was back at his desk, Yala leaned in towards Connie. "He's cute, isn't he?"

"Sorry? I don't know what..."

"It's OK. I don't blame you. He broke up with his girlfriend two weeks ago, she moved to Edinburgh or something. Field's clear."

"I don't..." Connie wanted the floor to eat her up. "What about the DNA results?"

"Oh, those." Yala pushed a stray hair behind her ear and turned back to a computer screen. "Afraid we don't have a match between any of the samples we took yesterday and the DNA found inside Laurence's mouth."

Connie felt her chest sink. "Oh."

"So I thought I'd check another sample."

"Oh?"

"Jenson Begg. We have plenty of DNA from his murder scene." Yala flashed her eyes at Connie. "We got a match."

"A match between one of the students and the Jenson Begg scene?"

"No." Yala bit her lip. "Between Jenson Begg and the inside of Laurence Thomms's mouth. It's his DNA that was left at the first scene."

CHAPTER SEVENTY-EIGHT

Zoe dropped Kayla off outside the English department. Her phone rang.

"Mo, how'd it go at the house?"

"Interestingly. We spoke to one of the people living there, he says he saw a woman with Jenson not long before he died."

"Any particular woman?"

"He couldn't say. She was outside and he was looking through his net curtains, which I have to say are bloody grubby."

"What time did he see this woman?"

"Ten thirty. He said she was pissed off, arguing with Jenson."

"Could it have been Kayla?" Zoe looked towards the English building, wishing she still had Kayla with her.

"He says he'd have recognised her. He didn't know this woman."

"And he can't remember anything about her?"

"Sorry. A pissed-off woman."

"That boot print wasn't large. Could have been a woman."

"It could."

"I've just spoken to Kayla," Zoe said. "She seemed genuinely shocked when I told her we were treating Jenson's death as suspicious."

"You believed her?"

She considered. "I did, yeah. So I don't think she was the woman anyway. Or if she was, she didn't hang around, wasn't the one who killed him."

"We need to work through the timeline for Jenson's evening."

"Have you spoken to the rest of the people in the house?"

"Two guys in the upstairs rooms. Both out last night."

"Typical. What about the woman downstairs?"

"Her boyfriend says she was in the loo when he saw this woman."

"Still. She might have seen her come inside, or approach the house."

"We'll track her down."

Zoe's phone beeped. "It's Connie. She might have the sampling results."

"I'll wait."

"Yeah." Zoe pulled her phone from her ear and frowned at it. She wasn't sure how to take Connie's call without cutting Mo off.

She sheeshed in irritation at herself. She could always call Mo back.

"Connie. Give me good news."

"They've got a match, boss."

"The DNA from the sampling?"

"None of them matched. It's Jenson Begg's DNA."

"Sorry?"

"The DNA taken from inside Laurence's mouth. It was Jenson's."

"Shit." Zoe put her hand over the phone. If Jenson had killed Laurence, then who had killed Jenson? And why did the two killings look so similar?

She could hear Connie's voice, faint from the phone in her hand. She lifted it to her ear.

"Connie. You're good at this stuff. Can you bring Mo into this call? I think he's still on hold to me."

"I can boss, but you'll have to hang up from that call."

Zoe shook her head. "Tell you what, I'll hang up from everything. You call me back and bring Mo in."

"Boss."

Zoe hung up and held her phone in front of her, waiting. A group of female students strode past her car. They looked focused, serious. She looked back at her phone. *Connie, where are you?* Maybe she wasn't as clever at this stuff as Zoe thought.

She looked up again to see Lin at the back of the group of women. Zoe checked her watch. Ten past eleven. Surely Lin should be over at the medical school?

Maybe she had a free period. No law against walking across campus with your mates.

Her phone rang.

"Connie, any joy?"

"I've got Mo on the call, boss."

"Hey, boss," said Mo.

"Me too," said Rhodri. "The sarge has got us on hands-free."

Zoe smiled. "Nice one, Connie. OK, so this is what we have. Jenson's DNA was in Laurence's mouth, which suggests it was him that forced the drugs into Laurence. And for Jenson's murder, we've got a woman seen at the house not long before time of death."

"What about those boot prints?" asked Mo.

"Connie?" said Zoe.

"The FSIs are still working on them. Apparently they're not very well defined, makes it harder to match them to a brand. And with them not being trainers..."

Zoe nodded. She knew how hard it could be matching shoes without much in the way of treads.

"So what about this woman at the house? Could she be the one Rhodri saw sniffing around over the road?"

"Could be, boss," said Rhodri. "Whoever it was, they were well hidden. Might mean they were small."

"Or that they were crouching down," said Zoe.

"But if Jenson killed Laurence, then did whoever killed Jenson do it in revenge?" asked Mo.

"That's the best hypothesis we've got right now," said Zoe. "Who would have been upset at Laurence's death?"

"No one, by the sounds of it," said Connie.

"Yeah," said Zoe. "Everyone we've spoken to says Laurence was universally hated."

"Maybe the two deaths *aren't* related?" suggested Rhodri.

"Hell of a coincidence if they aren't," said Mo.

"You're right," added Zoe. "It's too tight for there not to be a link. I just can't see it."

"You want us to talk to the other woman from the house?" asked Mo. "If we tell her what her boyfriend said, it might jog her memory."

"Do that," said Zoe. "But be careful. You can't go putting testimony in her head."

"Come on, boss..." said Mo.

"Sorry. I know you're too smart to do that. I just feel like we're getting evidence that's designed to have us going in circles. Almost like someone wants us to get confused."

"It's DNA evidence," said Connie. "Not much arguing with that."

"Yeah." Zoe sighed. "OK. Mo, you find this woman, see if she can remember anything. I'm going to talk to the warden again. I want to know what she's not telling us about Jenson and Laurence, any interactions they had."

"Jenson was investigating Becca's allegations of rape," said Connie. "He'd have interviewed Laurence, wouldn't he?"

"Possibly, although the warden might have done all that," said Zoe. "Connie, can you talk to Becca again? I want to find out what the investigation looked like from her angle. And if there was anyone who took the other side in all this. Someone who sided with Laurence."

"No problem, boss. I'll need to cycle over there, should take about half an hour."

"Good." Zoe checked her watch. She caught movement out of the corner of her eye: Kayla, leaving the English building. She was with the group of women that had passed Zoe earlier. One of the women had her by the arm, and seemed to be all but dragging her along.

"Boss?" Mo's voice.

"Sorry?"

"I was just asking if you wanted us to check witness statements from Jenson's neighbours?"

"Sorry. Do that, yes. And someone needs to speak to the other housemate."

"Rhod's better with the students than I am," said Mo.

"Really?" Zoe raised an eyebrow.

"Give him a chance, boss."

Rhodri cleared his throat.

"Up to you, Mo," Zoe said. "One of you check the statements, one of you talk to the other housemate."

"I'll let you know if we get anywhere," Mo said.

"Yeah." Zoe eyed the women as they hurried away from the car. She wanted to know why Kayla was being pushed around by these women, and who they were.

She got out of her car and started following them.

CHAPTER SEVENTY-NINE

IAN STARED out of his kitchen window, his gaze unfocused. It was raining outside, he could hear it beating against the glass. He didn't care.

He checked his watch, pushing up the sleeve of his best jacket to do so. Eleven thirty. He had a meeting with his solicitor at 2pm. The woman was coming here, for once. She wanted to see him in his home environment. Not that his home environment was exactly typical today.

"Right." Alison stood in the doorway. "Good luck."

He turned. Suitcases stood either side of her, a pile of teddy bears balanced on top of one of them. She was going to her mum's until this was all over. She said the kids were suffering with the atmosphere in the house. But he knew the real reason: she hated him. He'd lied to her for six years, he couldn't blame her.

He took a step towards her and she shrunk back. He felt his chest drop.

"Say hi to your mum from me," he said.

She shrugged. Her mum hated him even more than she

did. He was the bastard who'd dragged her daughter into police corruption, who was responsible for their kids being kidnapped as far as she was concerned. He and Alison both knew that the kids had only been kidnapped because their birth father had shacked up with a woman who was unhinged. But with Ian facing trial, his mother-in-law didn't believe a word of it.

He leaned against the sink, ignoring the damp seeping through the back of his shirt. "When will you be back?"

"I've talked to you about this, Ian. When the trial's over."

He nodded. That could be weeks away. It was a complex case: terrorism folded up with police corruption. He had no idea who would be called as a witness. Whether his former colleagues would stand by him.

He swallowed, his throat tight. "Look after yourself. Give the kids a kiss from me every night."

Her face softened. "I will."

The kids weren't his, not genetically. But his name was on the adoption certificates. He loved them like they were his own.

If he went to prison, would he ever see them again?

He stretched out his arms. "Please. Just a hug."

She shifted her weight, her eyes on his face. Then she took a few steps forward and leaned in to give him a tentative pat on the back. He tried to draw her closer, but she pulled away first.

"Good luck," she said.

"I love you, Alison."

"I know." She looked back at the suitcases. "I have to go."

Her mum was waiting outside, sitting in that bloody Corsa that dated from 1995. What was it with old people and their cars? The thing should have dropped dead of old age by now.

Ian nodded. "Call me."

"If I get a chance."

Her mum's house was small, a claustrophobic terrace half a mile away. There wouldn't be much room for Alison and the kids, and she'd struggle to find privacy.

Even so, she didn't have to stay in with them every moment of the day, did she?

The door slammed and Ian turned to the window. He watched his wife drag her suitcases up the path to the pavement, thinking of the moment Ollie had appeared out there, been dumped by the madwoman who'd taken him.

Alison's mum climbed out of the car and folded her daughter in a hug. Ian watched the pair of them open the boot and haul Alison's luggage inside.

He stared at her, willing her to turn and acknowledge him. She walked to the passenger door. There was a brief moment when she paused, and he thought she might turn to him, but instead she just pulled the door open and climbed in. He watched her reaching for the seatbelt, clicking it into place, her eyes ahead the whole time.

The car pulled out slowly, indicator blinking. Ian watched as it drove out of sight, his mouth dry. He stood watching the quiet street for a few minutes, until he was startled out of his daze by his phone ringing.

"Ian Osman." It still took concentration to not say *DS Osman*.

"Ian."

He knew that voice. "Sir."

"You don't need to call me that any more, you're a civilian."

"Don't remind me."

A laugh. "I can imagine. You're seeing Jane this afternoon, yes?"

"I am." Ian tugged at his tie. It was damp.

"Good. There's a thing or two we need to go over first. You've got three hours."

"Two and a half."

"That's enough. Come to this address."

Ian grabbed the pen for the magnetic whiteboard attached to the fridge and wrote down an address in Chelmsley Wood.

"I'll never get there and back in time."

"You will. Don't worry. You leave now, and it'll be fine."

CHAPTER EIGHTY

"OK, Rhodri, let me know how you get on. I'll head back to base, go through those statements."

"You sure?"

"I think you're better with these students than I am," said Mo. "I'm going to leave you to talk to Shonda and go back to the office."

"I don't mind working through the witness statements, honest."

Mo turned and gave him a smile. "I know you don't, Constable. And in any other circumstances, believe me, I'd be more than happy to dump that job on you. But right now I think your talents are better used on interviews."

Rhodri beamed. "Thanks, Sarge."

"Don't tell the boss I was so glowing in my praise for you."

"Promise." Rhodri shrugged, still smiling.

"I'll wait while you find out where she is. Be quick."

"Yeah." Rhodri opened the car door and jumped out. He hurried back to Jenson's house. Will answered the door.

"You again."

"Sorry, mate. Look, after what you told me about seeing that woman, it'd be a big help if I could talk to your girl-friend. She's not here, is she?"

"Nah. She's got lectures."

"Any idea where?"

A shrug. "Psychology building, I guess."

"Cool. Thanks."

"Like I said, she was in the loo. She won't be able to help you."

"Best to try anyway, eh?"

Another shrug. Will shut the door.

Rhodri ran back to the car and landed in the passenger seat, making the car shudder. Luckily the sarge hadn't left yet.

"Psychology building, Sarge."

"He tell you where that is?"

Rhodri cursed himself. "I'll look it up. You start driving."

"Fair enough."

As they drove towards the campus, Rhodri scrolled through Google Maps. He gave Mo directions as they approached the university.

Outside the Psychology building, Mo stopped the car. "Call me if you get anything. Can you make your own way back?"

"Yeah. I'll walk."

"Be quick about it, yeah?"

Rhodri got out, bending down to talk to Mo. "No probs."

Mo reached across and closed the passenger door. He drove away.

Rhodri turned to the Psychology building. How was he

going to find Shonda? How was he going to get her attention in the middle of a lecture?

Only one way to find out.

He walked into the building and searched for a reception desk. There was none. He grabbed a passing student.

"Hiya, I'm looking for Shonda Taylor."

The young woman frowned. "Never heard of her."

"Is there someone I can talk to who might?"

"The admin office is over there. They know who's who."

"Ta." He went to the door she'd indicated and knocked, then pushed it open.

Rhodri pulled on his most endearing smile. A middle-aged woman around the same age and build as his mum sat behind a desk, staring at him. "Who are you?"

He pulled out his warrant card. "Nothing to worry about, but I need to talk to Shonda Taylor."

"Why?"

"It's in connection with an inquiry.""

The woman's eyes widened. She looked like she might cry. "That kid who died in Boulton Hall?"

"Can you tell me where she is?"

"Wait a minute." She looked at her computer screen. "She's third year, so she should be in Professor Musa's lecture right now."

"Where is that?"

"Second floor. Room 234."

"Thanks."

"You can't just drag her out of there."

"I'll wait."

"Don't disrupt the lecture. Please."

He gave her his brightest smile. "Don't worry. They'll never know I'm there."

He turned and left the room before she could stop him. He took the stairs two at a time and was soon on the second floor. He followed the room numbers until he got to 234.

He peered through the glass in the door to see a lecture underway. A skinny black man with grey hair stood at the front of the room, waving his arms around. Rhodri scanned the rows of students. Shonda was in the sixth row, near the middle.

There were two exits at the back of the room, higher up. But she was closer to this one. He had to hope she'd come this way when the lecture was over.

He checked his watch: eleven forty-five. Not long.

"Excuse me, do you need help?"

Rhodri turned to see a man behind him, head cocked. He was overweight with pasty skin, wearing a suit that struggled not to rip at the seams.

"I'm fine, thanks."

"You need to go into that lecture? Professor Musa doesn't like it when students are late."

"Just waiting for someone. Cheers."

The man raised an eyebrow, and walked away. Rhodri leaned against the wall, his heart pounding. He was a police officer: why did he feel so out of place here?

He turned back to the door to see the students getting up from their seats. Shonda was hidden by a group of students in front of her. Rhodri stared at the spot where she'd been, hoping she hadn't gone already.

"You after me?"

He turned to see Shonda behind him.

"How the hell did you get there?"

She raised an eyebrow. "Swearing at a witness, Constable? Hardly professional."

"You were in there a minute ago."

"I spotted you through the door. Thought I'd grab you before everyone else saw me being interviewed by the police. It's not a good look, you know."

He smiled. "Sorry. You want to go somewhere?"

"There's a coffee shop in the basement. Follow me."

He followed her along the corridor and through a doorway leading to a set of stairs. She hurried down, her footsteps light. No one passed them on the way down.

"This your private rat run?" he asked.

"It's handy." She stopped at the bottom and held the door open for him. "After you."

"Ta." He walked through and found himself at the edge of a space containing a few tables and chairs and a Costa vending machine to one side.

"Hardly a coffee shop," he said.

"I exaggerated. You paying?"

"I can't, sorry."

"Oh, come on. I'm helping you with your job. Least you can do is buy me a coffee."

"Alright." He'd use his own money. No way the force was stumping up for coffees for witnesses.

She waited at a table near the stairway while he fetched two lattes. He placed one in front of her and sipped his own.

"So?" She leaned back in her chair, legs out straight in front.

"I wanted to talk to you about Wednesday night."

"Thought you might. But what specifically?"

"Did you see anyone come to the house, about ten thirty?"

"What kind of someone?"

"Any kind of someone. Did you hear anyone come in? Anyone talking to Jenson?"

"People came to see Jenson quite a lot. I'm sure you can guess why."

He nodded and took a gulp of his coffee. He hadn't realised how thirsty he was. "So he had visitors on Wednesday night?"

She stared off to one side, thinking. "I'm not sure."

"You were with Will."

"I'm always with Will."

"Maybe you heard someone out the front? Maybe someone arguing with Jenson?"

"You're telling me he had an argy with someone."

"I'm saying nothing of the sort. Just asking if you saw anything like that."

"Which means someone has told you he did have an argument with someone. You think he was murdered?"

Rhodri gripped his cup. "Not officially."

"But...?"

"His death is suspicious."

"Shit. To think I was right next door."

"So did you see anyone?"

"Sorry, mate. Didn't see a thing."

Rhodri slumped in his chair. She'd conned him out of a coffee, and she didn't know anything. He handed over his card. "If you remember anything, will you call me?"

She smiled. "You hitting on me, Constable?"

Rhodri coughed. "No."

"Shame." She winked.

Rhodri blushed. "I'd best be going." He stood up.

"Ta for the coffee. You might want to talk to the nosey bitch at number 245."

"Sorry?"

"Mrs Anderson. Most of the houses on Will's road are students but she's been there since the year dot. She hates us all, thinks we're druggies and troublemakers. She watches us. I've seen her filming."

"Why didn't you tell me this before?"

"Sorry. Didn't occur to me. I thought Jenson died of a drugs overdose, it wasn't exactly…"

Rhodri swigged back the last of his coffee. "I have to go. Thanks for the information."

"Be warned, she's got a fucking big dog."

He laughed. "I don't think I need to worry about that."

"Nasty bastard, it is. Tries to bite anyone who knocks on the door. Don't say I didn't warn you."

"I'll take that under advisement." Rhodri headed towards the main stairs, anxious to speak to the sarge.

CHAPTER EIGHTY-ONE

Zoe walked a hundred yards behind the women, observing their body language. The woman holding Kayla's arm was mid-height with short brown hair. She'd loosened her grip, but Kayla didn't look happy. There were three other women: one tall and blonde wearing a bright orange dress, and the other dark-skinned with white-blonde hair that looked like a halo when it caught the light. They walked purposefully, eyes ahead, and showed no sign of having spotted Zoe.

The final woman was Lin, bringing up the rear. Kayla turned to look at her from time to time, which meant Zoe kept having to slip out of sight. But from what she could see, Lin wasn't meeting Kayla's eye.

At last they arrived at Boulton Hall. They stopped outside and formed a tight circle. Zoe slipped behind a neighbouring building and peered round a wall. The women spoke to each other, Kayla's eyes on the ground. After a few moments two of the women peeled off and headed back the way they had come. Kayla, Lin and the brunette walked towards Boulton Hall.

Zoe watched them walk inside, puzzled. They'd dragged Kayla out of her lectures: for what?

She approached the building and looked through the glazed front wall. The women stepped into the lift.

Zoe dashed inside and watched the numbers light up. They stopped at the fifth floor. Kayla's floor.

Should she go up there, disturb them? Was Kayla in danger?

"Detective?"

Zoe turned to see Doctor Edwards coming out of the canteen.

"Can I help you?"

"Doctor Edwards. I need to go up to Kayla Goode's room. I believe she might be in danger."

"Don't be ridiculous."

"I think she's being held against her will."

"If someone was holding her against her will, I hardly think they'd take her to her room."

"She didn't look like she was going up there voluntarily."

"I don't like you storming around the building. It puts the students on edge."

"It's my job to protect them."

"No, Inspector. It's *my* job to protect them. You wait here."

The warden pressed the button for the lift and stepped into it. "Don't go creeping around my building while I'm gone."

Zoe curled her lip as the lift doors closed and the numbers ascended, stopping at five again.

She wasn't waiting around. She'd seen the look on Kayla's face.

The lift numbers descended and the doors opened. Lin walked out.

"Oh." She looked surprised. "DI Finch."

"Lin. Have you just come from Kayla's room?"

Lin shook her head. "I was in my own room. Why?"

"I thought I saw you on campus with Kayla."

"I'm not on campus now, am I?"

"Did you come back here with her?"

"We walked together, yes. She went to her room, me to mine. She'll be down for lunch in a minute. You need her?"

Zoe eyed the young woman. "It's OK." She turned towards the stairs.

As she rounded a bend in the staircase, she almost crashed into Doctor Edwards coming down.

"I thought you might try this," the warden said.

"Doctor Edwards, I don't think you understand the seriousness of what's happening in this building. You've had two students die in under a week. Kayla is connected to both of them, and I'm worried about her."

"I've just been to her room. She's fine."

"Really?"

"Yes. Look, there she is." The warden pointed down the stairs. Kayla was in the entrance hall, with Lin. Lin gave her a hug which Kayla returned stiffly.

"She came down in the lift," said Doctor Edwards. "I came this way, to intercept you."

Kayla stood between Zoe and the building's exit. No one could stop her speaking to the girl. She hurried down the stairs. "Kayla? Can we have a chat?"

Kayla looked at Lin and then at Zoe. "I'm about to go in for lunch."

"It won't take long."

Another glance at Lin, as if Kayla needed her friend's permission. Lin smiled at her.

"OK," said Kayla. "But I have to be quick, I've got lectures in a bit."

"Don't worry." Zoe put out a hand to take Kayla by the arm, but then remembered how she'd been held in the same way not long ago.

"Let's go outside," she said. Kayla followed her through the main doors.

Outside, it had started to rain. Zoe hurried to an open-sided bike shed and turned to face Kayla.

"Kayla, are you OK?"

"What d'you mean?"

"I saw you with some women, outside the English department. What were they doing?"

Kayla scratched her cheek. "They're my friends."

"They didn't look very friendly to me."

"I don't know what you're talking about."

"Did they pull you out of your lecture?"

Kayla blushed. "The lecturer was sick. They told us to study privately. No point in hanging around."

"But you were in such a hurry to get back when I interviewed you."

"I didn't know he was going to be sick." Kayla turned towards the building. "I need to go now."

"Kayla, tell me if you feel unsafe, will you?"

"I'm fine."

"Two people have been killed, and you knew both of them."

"You think there's a serial killer around, and he's going to target me next?" Kayla gave a shaky laugh.

"You need to be careful."

In the space of a few hours, Zoe had gone from thinking of Kayla as a suspect, to worrying she might be the next victim. "Have you got somewhere you can stay for a while?"

"No. Why? Do I need to?"

"Until we find whoever killed Jenson."

"And Laurence."

"Yes." Zoe wasn't going to tell Kayla about the DNA they'd found.

"I'm fine here," Kayla said. "I've got Lin and Gina looking after me."

"Is Gina one of the women you were with earlier?"

"She might be." Kayla stepped away. "Just leave me alone, OK? I'm fine."

Kayla ran into the building. Zoe stared after her, not sure if she was right to be so worried.

CHAPTER EIGHTY-TWO

Mo STARED AT HIS SCREEN, flicking through witness statements. His phone rang.

"Sarge?"

"Rhodri. You want a lift?" Mo looked out of the window. Rhodri wouldn't have thought to take a sensible coat.

"It's not that, boss. I'm with Mrs Anderson, lives over the road from Jenson."

"You went back there?"

"Shonda told me she was a" – Rhodri lowered his voice – "busybody."

"Every street has one. Does she have information?"

"Better than that, Sarge. She's got video. Camcorder, old-fashioned thing. But it does the job."

"Of Wednesday night?"

"Yup."

"And?"

"Sarge, have you looked at the witness statement from number 245?"

"Hang on." Mo flicked through the files onscreen. "Here.

Mrs Anderson. Same woman you're talking to." He enlarged the text. "How did we miss this?"

"She says the PC who spoke to her was dismissive, Sarge. Thought she was just a nosey parker."

"And you're saying there's more to it than that?"

"Sarge. She's got video. We've got the woman on camera."

CHAPTER EIGHTY-THREE

KAYLA RAN BACK into Boulton Hall and up the stairs. Doctor Edwards gave her a sharp look as she passed, but she didn't slow down.

Her room was on the fifth floor. By the time she got there she was out of breath. She fumbled with her key, her heart racing.

She crashed into the room and slammed the door behind her.

Two women were inside: one sitting on the bed and another in her desk chair.

"Kayla." Lin stood up from her perch on the bed and stepped towards her. Kayla shrank back to the door.

"How did you get in?"

"Don't worry about that. We want to look after you. What did that detective want?"

"She... she just had some questions. Wanted to know about what Laurence did to me." Kayla's eyes flicked to Gina. Gina didn't know what had happened with Laurence. Did she?

She glared at Lin. "Did you tell her? I told you it was confidential!"

Lin shook her head. "I'm sorry, Kayla. But Gina can help you. She's helped other women like you. Victims."

"I'm not a victim!"

Gina gave her a patronising look. "I volunteer at the student welfare office. You were Laurence's victim. You were Jenson's victim."

"I was Jenson's *girlfriend*."

"Did he ever let himself be seen with you outside this building, Kayla?" Lin asked.

"Yes. At the house."

"That doesn't count."

Gina was picking at her trousers. She looked up at Lin. "We don't want to hurt you, Kayla."

Kayla was trembling. "Why do you have to tell me you don't want to hurt me, unless you're planning to hurt me?"

"You can't trust the police."

"What?" Kayla grabbed the door handle behind her. Lin ran to her and put her hand over Kayla's. She pulled Kayla away from the door and pushed her to the bed.

"Why are you doing this?"

Lin sighed. She nodded at Gina.

Gina picked something off her trousers and rubbed her fingers together, depositing it on the bed. Kayla grimaced: dog hairs.

"OK," Gina said to Lin. "You'll be OK?"

"Fine."

Gina gave Kayla a long look then left the room.

"Better?" Lin asked, when they were alone.

"I didn't know you two were friends."

"I used to go out with her. She can be a bit full-on, I know. But I thought she could help you."

"I don't need help."

Lin sat down at the end of the bed, her hands in her pockets. She dipped her shoulders and cocked her head in an expression of concern. "It's OK, Kayla. Why can't you trust anyone?"

"I don't know what you're talking about."

"Have you got lectures this afternoon?"

"I've got an essay to write."

Lin stood up. "I'll leave you to it."

"OK."

Lin went to the door. She looked back at Kayla from the doorway. Kayla shivered. None of this made sense.

"See ya, Kayl." Lin gave Kayla a mock-salute then closed the door. Kayla lay back on her bed, her mind numb.

CHAPTER EIGHTY-FOUR

Zoe headed towards Boulton Hall. Kayla was refusing to speak to her, but that wasn't what she'd come here for. She needed to speak to the warden, find out about the link between Laurence and Jenson.

Her phone rang as she arrived at the doors: Sheila Griffin.

"Hey, Sheila. This isn't a great time."

"I won't keep you. Got an update on Magpie."

"You do know you're not supposed to talk to me about this, don't you?"

"I won't tell if you don't."

"Thanks, Sheila. What you got?"

"We've found Alina Popescu. She came from a village in Romania, seventy miles from Bucharest."

"Great." Zoe stood outside Boulton Hall, trying to will the rain from soaking into her hair. "Adi already told me about that."

"It gets better."

"OK."

"Her flight to the UK was arranged by Trevor Hamm's organisation. Same credit card as paid for the Pichler sisters' flights."

"OK. But we knew that."

"Bear with me, Zoe. I'm passing this on to you because I know who your boyfriend is and I didn't know who else to talk to."

"Carl? He's not really my boyfriend. Not any more."

"Oh. Sorry about that. Maybe I shouldn't..."

"Tell me. I can pass it on to him, we're still in touch."

"Are you sure? This is delicate to say the least."

"I'm sure." Zoe looked into the foyer of Boulton Hall. The warden was inside, staring back out at her. The woman started walking towards her. "Quick, tell me."

"I've found a photo of her with someone we know. At a dinner. Some kind of local business thing. Looks like they had her working as an escort."

"With Trevor Hamm?"

"Closer to home than that."

The doors opened and Doctor Edwards stepped out. "DI Finch, are you still hanging around?"

Zoe gave her a *wait* gesture. "Sheila, who?"

"We've got a photo of her with Detective Superintendent Randle, Zoe. She accompanied him to a party, in September last year."

CHAPTER EIGHTY-FIVE

CONNIE KNOCKED on Becca MacGuire's door and smoothed her damp hands on her trousers. It had been drizzling on the way here and the wet had soaked through her cycling gloves.

The door opened and Connie put on a friendly smile. "Hi, Becca."

Becca shrunk back. "You again."

"I won't keep you long, but I was wondering if we could have a brief chat?"

A door along the corridor opened and a woman looked out. Connie gave her a smile.

"Everything OK, Becs?" the woman said.

"Yeah," Becca replied. "She's just leaving."

The woman stayed where she was, watching Connie.

"I need to ask you about the investigation," Connie said.

"You mean the way they covered up the fact that Laurence raped me?"

"Who did the investigation, Becca? Was it Doctor Edwards, or Jenson Begg?"

"Jenson? Why would he have done it?"

The woman from the other room left her doorway and approached Connie. "Is she bothering you, Becs?"

Connie turned to her. "I'm a police officer."

"And I'm Harry Potter. Doesn't mean you can ask her questions when she doesn't want you to."

"Jules, leave it," Becca said. "I've got nothing to tell her."

"Becca," said Connie, "How much did Jenson know about what happened?"

"I reported it to him. He passed it on to the warden. Far as I know, that's all."

"Did Jenson talk to Laurence about what happened?"

Becca shrugged. "Not as far as I know."

Connie lowered her voice. "Becca, how was it that everyone knew about what Laurence did to you?"

Becca paled. The other woman, Jules, put a hand on Becca's door frame. Her arm separated Becca from Connie. "Time you left."

Becca licked her lips, her gaze moving between Connie and Jules. She nodded.

"OK, Becca," Connie said. "Sorry to have bothered you. Hopefully next time we have a murderer on the loose round here, the other students won't be quite so obstructive." She gave Jules a pointed look and headed towards the lift.

CHAPTER EIGHTY-SIX

"You're here to tell me the results of the DNA sampling, I imagine," Doctor Edwards said. "Unless of course you want to apologise for storming around my building and making the students anxious."

"We do have the results, yes," replied Zoe. "Although they don't relate to the swabs we took."

The two women were in the warden's office, facing each other across the desk. Zoe had her legs crossed and was trying to project calm. In reality, she was furious with the warden. The woman had been obstructive and obnoxious from the start. Did she not want them to catch the killer?

"How's that?" Doctor Edwards asked.

"None of the swabs we took yesterday were a match for the DNA we found inside Laurence's mouth."

"You could have told me that without coming to my office."

"But we did find a match."

Zoe studied the warden's face. She didn't want to miss the woman's reaction when it came.

"Not one of my students, in that case," Doctor Edwards said. She pursed her lips.

"Not an undergraduate, no."

The doctor raised her eyebrows.

Zoe leaned forward. "The DNA inside Laurence's mouth, the DNA left there by the person who pushed drugs down Laurence's throat, belonged to Jenson Begg."

The warden sat back abruptly. "You're mistaken."

"It's DNA. The room for error is infinitesimally…"

"I know the statistics of DNA matching. But what about human error? You got the samples muddled, or the pathologist made a mistake."

Zoe felt her skin bristle. "Doctor Adebayo is the best pathologist I've worked with. She doesn't make mistakes."

"The pathologist who attended the scene was a man."

Damn. "Doctor Reynolds works closely with Doctor Adebayo. I'm confident in his findings."

"Even if you can't remember which pathologist it actually was that you need to have confidence in."

"Doctor Edwards, were you aware of any kind of relationship between Laurence and Jenson?"

"No."

"Was Jenson Laurence's residential tutor?"

"No. Amelia was."

"When Becca MacGuire accused Laurence of raping her, she went to Jenson first. Yes?"

"She did."

"And he came to you."

"Yes." The warden steepled her hands on the table.

"Did Jenson talk to Laurence about it? Was he involved in the investigation?"

"It's not the role of a postgraduate to take part in that

kind of thing. I questioned Jenson, yes, to use your own terminology. I asked him about what Becca had said to him, what kind of mood she was in. But I also told him not to speak to Laurence. I didn't want any interference."

"You thought Jenson might interfere?"

"That's not what I meant, Inspector. I wanted a clear line of accountability. I wanted to know who was talking to who."

"Were you aware that Becca's allegations were common knowledge around Boulton Hall?"

"That did come to my attention. I don't know how it got out. I imagine Becca confided in a friend or two, who were less than circumspect."

Oh yes, thought Zoe. *Blame the undergraduates.*

"How did Jenson react to Becca's allegations against Laurence?"

"I told you. He came to see me, and repor—"

"I don't mean what did he do, Doctor Edwards. I mean how did he react emotionally. Was he angry, upset?"

"He was... introspective. It worried him, that one of his students had been through such an ordeal."

"So he believed Becca?"

"He certainly believed that she was suffering."

"Not that she was raped?"

"Inspector, as you know, I didn't come to the police, and that was out of respect for Becca's wishes. If that means our investigation wasn't to the high standards you uphold, then there's little I can do about that. But we weren't able to find conclusive proof that Laurence did in fact rape Becca."

"No physical evidence. His word against hers."

"Exactly."

"How d'you think that made Becca feel?"

"I guided her in the direction of the student welfare office. They offer counselling for women who've suffered—"

"Once again. I didn't ask you what you did. I asked how you think Becca *felt* about the lack of conclusion."

"She was angry."

"Did she talk to her residential tutor about those feelings, perhaps?"

"I can't tell you that, Detective."

"Did she tell Jenson how disappointed she was that justice hadn't been done? Could he have decided to mete out his own form of justice?"

The warden barked out a laugh. "Now you're being ridiculous."

"Doctor Edwards, did you see or speak to Jenson around the time of Laurence's death?"

"I was away on a field trip, if you recall."

"Did you see him when you returned? How was his mood?"

"Sombre, like the rest of us. A student had died. The entire community was in shock."

"Did he seem agitated, or nervous?"

"If you're asking me if he was wringing his hands and wailing *out, damned spot*, then no. He showed no signs of anything out of the ordinary."

Zoe sighed. They had forensic evidence pointing to Jenson, but nothing else. The party made it hard to establish alibis. Her gut told her the forensics were pointing the wrong way, but it *was* DNA. She'd have to look elsewhere for corroboration.

"Thank you, Doctor Edwards. I'll let you know if I need anything more from you."

CHAPTER EIGHTY-SEVEN

"I can't make it out."

Mo and Rhodri sat in Mo's car, on Jenson Begg's street. Mo held Mrs Anderson's camcorder up in front of him and peered at it. "It's just too grainy."

"We'll have to get Connie to work on it, Sarge."

"Has she said we can take it away? Hopefully we can transfer the film onto digital and then let her have this thing back."

"She has, boss. Right friendly she was."

Mo gave Rhodri a knowing look. "I bet she was." There was something about Rhodri, perhaps his gangly frame and awkward manner, that endeared him to elderly women.

"Come on then." Mo started the car. "Call Connie while we're en route, will you?"

"Right... Connie, it's Rhod. Where are you?... OK, can you get back to the office? I've got a video I want you to work your magic on."

They stopped at the junction with the Bristol Road.

Rhodri laughed. "Yeah, magician, me. Anyway, can you?...
Ta. See ya, Con."

He hung up. "She'll be there in ten minutes, Sarge."

"Good." Mo focused on the road ahead, ignoring the rain-
drops splashing on the windscreen. Rhodri was looking at the
camcorder screen.

"Can *you* make anything out?" Mo said.

"Well there's definitely a woman. And a man."

"Standing in Jenson Begg's front garden."

"Talking by the looks of it."

"Arguing?"

"I can't tell, Sarge. Maybe when we blow it up it'll be
easier."

"You've got young eyes. Do you recognise either of
them?"

'The guy looks like Jenson, but I can't be sure. The
woman... dunno. Could be anyone."

"Could be Kayla."

"Could be Shonda."

"She'd have told us if she had an argy with him, surely?"

"Who knows," said Mo. He turned onto Edgbaston Park
Road and accelerated up the hill. "She could be trying to
muddy the waters."

Rhodri gazed out of the window, tracing a raindrop with
his fingertip. Mo's stomach rumbled. He hadn't taken a break
yet today. Hopefully Rhodri would have one of his biscuit
hauls in his desk.

"You think someone in the house is responsible?" said
Rhodri.

Mo shrugged. "I think people were dealing drugs from
that house and they want as little police attention on them as
possible."

"Not easy, when one of your housemates has been murdered."

"Nope." Mo pulled into the car park of Harborne police station. "Let's get inside and find out, eh?"

CHAPTER EIGHTY-EIGHT

KAYLA DRAGGED herself off the bed and made her way to her desk. She might as well make a start on that essay, even if her brain did feel like someone had pumped rubber into it.

She grabbed her copy of *Emma* from the shelf above her desk and opened up her laptop. *Describe how the respective social standing of Emma Woodhouse and Harriet Smith drives their actions in the novel.* She wasn't in the mood.

Maybe she'd go to the vending machine downstairs, get some chocolate. That would help with motivation. It might boost her mood, too.

She reached up to the shelf where she kept her keys. She fumbled for them, her fingers moving blindly above her head.

She stood up, frowning, and looked at the shelf. A row of books, a postcard from her mum, a spider plant. No keys.

She felt her pockets. No keys there either.

That's odd.

It was early afternoon. She could wedge her door open and pop out without taking her keys. She grabbed a hardback book.

She pulled the door handle. It didn't budge. She tugged again. She rattled it, and turned it, and pulled again.

The door was locked.

Kayla stumbled back to the shelf. She pushed the books and the plant aside, searching for her keys. She swept a pile of papers off her desk, her hands moving across the surface.

Where were they?

She went to the door again. *Be calm.* Maybe she was pulling it the wrong way.

She wrapped her hand around the door handle, gently this time. She concentrated on turning it one way, then the next.

It wasn't going anywhere.

Someone had locked her in.

CHAPTER EIGHTY-NINE

CONNIE DUCKED her head as she hurried towards the bike shed. The helmet would keep some of the rain off, but not all of it.

She'd cope. Getting wet on her bike wasn't exactly new.

She caught movement from the corner of her eye. She turned to see Lin running away from the building.

"Lin! You OK?"

Lin skidded to a halt. She turned towards Connie. "I'm fine. Leave me alone."

Connie raised her hands. "Just asking a question. You look like you're in a hurry."

"I've got lectures."

Lin's hands were empty. She wasn't carrying a bag. Connie stepped out of the bike shed.

"Lin, you seem agitated."

"I'm fine. Leave me alone." Lin started walking.

Connie grabbed her bike. She slung her helmet strap over the handlebars and started cycling to catch the younger woman up. "Lin!"

Lin looked over her shoulder. She was hunched against the rain. "Stop following me! This is police harassment."

"I just want to ask you a couple of questions."

Lin span round. "Go on then. What d'you want to know?" She pushed her hair back and shook her hands out.

"Did Laurence Thomms and Jenson Begg know each other?"

"No. Why?"

"What kind of man was Jenson?"

Lin shrugged. "You'd have to ask Kayla."

"I have. Now I'm asking you."

Lin took a deep breath. Rain poured over both of them. Connie ignored it, but Lin was shivering.

"Did he take advantage of the students he was a tutor for?"

Lin stiffened. "Maybe that's how Jenson knew Laurence, if you reckon he did. Two creeps together."

"Did Laurence try to rape Kayla?"

Lin's expression hardened. "I'm not talking about that."

"Did he?"

"I'm not talking about it." She turned and started walking.

Connie caught up and cycled alongside her. She knew Lin might make a complaint, but she was sick of being pushed away. Why were the students hiding things?

"Lin, did Laurence assault other girls?"

"Probably. You'd have to ask them."

"Did Jenson assault undergraduates?"

Lin closed her eyes for a moment, not breaking stride. "He was a creep. He wanted to control the students he was responsible for. He thought he was being protective." She turned to Connie. "He knew about Laurence, he wanted to stop him."

"Enough to kill him?"

Lin didn't slow down. "I can't answer that. But maybe, yeah."

"Did Laurence have any friends? Anyone who'd want to protect him?"

"No way. We all hated him."

Connie shifted her weight on the bike. She wished Lin would slow down.

"Lin, did either of them assault you?"

Lin flinched. "No. Now leave me alone before I call your boss." She ran towards a grassy area where Connie couldn't follow.

CHAPTER NINETY

ZOE SLID INTO HER CAR, her mind racing.

The interview with the warden seemed an irrelevance after what Sheila had told her.

Alina Popescu, with Randle? Was it a coincidence, or something more?

Did she want to give this to Carl, or do some digging of her own?

She stared out through the rain, fists clenched in her lap. Eventually she came to a decision and picked up her phone.

It rang out five times. Zoe cursed herself: why had she expected it to be answered?

"Zoe."

She straightened. "I hope you don't mind me calling."

"I've got my daughter looking like she's seen a ghost and the nurse that's on today is bloody rough with the cannula. I could do with some distraction."

Zoe smiled. It was always good to speak to Lesley.

"Ma'am. I need to talk to you about something. It's sensitive."

"One of your team giving you trouble?"

"No."

"I didn't think so. Is it Frank? I know he's a dinosaur, but you've dealt with worse than him before."

"It's not DI Dawson."

"Right." Lesley coughed. "What is it, then?"

Zoe hesitated. What was she doing calling her boss with information about the New Street bomber, when that was what had put her in hospital?

"I'm sorry, ma'am. You're supposed to be resting. I'll talk to someone else."

"Oh no you bloody don't."

"It's fine. I can talk to Frank."

"No you can't, and we both know it. This is about David, isn't it?"

"I didn't..."

"Zoe, you have a tone to your voice when you're thinking about that man. It's like a fucking great Belisha beacon on top of your head, it's that obvious. Now spit it out."

"I don't want to upset you."

"Upset me?" There was a pause. "Hang on."

Lesley coughed, the sound muffled. Zoe waited for the coughing to recede. It took over a minute.

"Carry on." Lesley's voice was hoarse. "Is it about Magpie? Is that why you're pussyfooting around me?"

"It is." Zoe gripped the steering wheel.

"Don't keep me in suspense, Zoe."

OK. Deep breath. "We identified the bomber, Ma'am."

"That's the best news I've had all fucking day. Who was she?"

"Alina Popescu. She was brought over from Romania by Trevor Hamm's organisation."

"So far, so predictable. What's this got to do with Randle?"

"There's a photo of the two of them together."

More coughing. Zoe waited for it to subside.

"Ma'am? Are you OK?"

"Fine," Lesley spluttered. "You're saying there's a photo of David with this woman?"

"At a function last September. From what Sheila could tell, Alina was working as an escort."

"OK. You stop talking to me right now. Go back to Sheila and tell her to talk to Carl Whaley. This is too hot for anyone other than Professional Standards."

"She wanted me to call him."

"It'll be cleaner if it comes from her. You don't want to be mixed up in this. Randle was your boss, Zoe. Still is. Step back."

Zoe sighed. She'd been hoping to call Carl next. Any excuse to speak to him. Passing him information like this might bring him back to her.

"Ma'am."

"Do as I say, Zoe. Hang up, call Sheila. Pass it back."

CHAPTER NINETY-ONE

"Guys." Connie stood at the door to the office, dripping wet.

"Connie, you should have called me for a lift," said Mo.

"How would I have got my bike back here if I'd done that?"

"We could have gone back for it."

"It's alright, Sarge. I'm used to it." She shoved her bike helmet under her desk and sat down. "Where is it then?"

Mo grabbed the camcorder off Rhodri's desk. "It's pretty old. Got a cassette in it."

Connie whistled. "That's ancient." She turned it in her hands. "Practically an antique." She looked up at him, her eyes glowing. "A challenge."

He grinned at her. "I knew you'd be able to sort it. We need it blown up, the image improved if possible."

"Yeah." She turned it over, looking for any kind of input or output. "Here. There's an AV out. I can hook this up to a TV." She looked up at Mo. "Not difficult at all."

Mo felt his cheeks flush. "No?"

Connie laughed. "No. But we do need a telly. One with the right input. And some leads..."

"There's the telly in the break room," said Rhodri.

"There is." Connie had her head down, rummaging through her desk drawers. "Bingo." She sat up, a red and white lead in her hand. "See, all those people who tell me not to hoard old leads. They're wrong."

"Come on, then." Mo opened the door, heading towards the break room.

They filed in. Two uniformed constables were inside, feet up on the coffee table. When they saw Mo they pulled them to the floor.

"Can you let us have the TV please, lads?" Mo asked.

The officers gathered up their things and left the room.

"Smashing. Connie, hook it up."

She peered round the back of the TV. Tongue poking out, she fumbled around behind it. After a few moments the leads she'd found in her desk were trailing from the back of the TV. She plugged the camcorder in at the other end.

"Rhodri, stick it on AV," she said.

"Righto." Rhodri grabbed the remote and started flicking through inputs. Mo stood close to the screen, waiting for it to come to life.

Connie was pressing buttons on the camcorder. "There," she said, and looked up. On the TV was an image of Umberslade Road. It wasn't high resolution, but it was a lot clearer than it had been on the tiny camcorder screen.

They stood around the screen, watching as a man came out of the front door of number 240: Rhodri.

"You didn't say you were on this," said Mo.

"I didn't spot meself. Connie, what did you do?"

"Only went back to the beginning."

They all watched as Rhodri drove away in his Saab. Before getting inside, he looked towards the house opposite, which was out of shot.

"This gives us a time," said Mo. "What time did you leave the house?"

Rhodri pulled his notebook out of his pocket. "Nine twenty-six, Sarge."

Mo nodded. He turned back to the screen.

"That was when I thought I saw someone," Rhodri said.

Mo nodded acknowledgement but kept his eyes on the screen.

After Rhodri's car disappeared, the house's front door opened.

Jenson stood in the doorway then turned, disturbed by a movement on the edge of the screen.

"Yes, I was right. I did see someone," Rhodri said. "See? He's looking the same way."

"Yeah." Mo held his breath.

A woman came into shot. She was mid-height, with short dark hair. She wore blue trousers and a purple jacket.

"Who's she?" breathed Connie.

"No idea," said Mo. He looked at Rhodri, who shook his head.

Mo flicked his gaze towards the door to the corridor. Someone was passing, their footsteps loud. He heard a door open and close again.

Onscreen, the woman approached Jenson. She was shouting at him. Her eyes were wide and her mouth moved fast. She waved her arms at him. Jenson put his own arms up as if in self-defence.

"Who is she?" said Mo.

"One of his students?" asked Connie.

"Or a housemate?" said Rhodri.

Mo heard the door along the corridor slam again. It was the door to their own office. Whoever had gone in there wasn't happy. He should go and find out who it was.

He turned towards the door to the break room just as it opened. Zoe stood there, staring at the TV screen.

"What's this?" she said.

"Rhodri got camera footage from the night of Jenson's murder," said Connie.

"It's from just after I left," said Rhodri. "That woman's having a go at him."

"She is."

"We don't know who she is," said Mo.

"I do," said Zoe.

All three of them turned to her. She nodded. "I saw her today. She was with Kayla."

CHAPTER NINETY-TWO

Kayla went back to her desk. It was possible that the lock had broken, that it was an accident.

But Lin had been behaving weirdly, and so had Gina. That detective had cautioned her, she clearly believed Kayla was guilty of something.

This was no coincidence.

Whoever had locked her in was pretty dumb. She still had her phone with her, after all.

She went back to her desk and pulled it out of her rucksack.

Who to call?

She ran through the list of people she would normally call on in a crisis: Lin and Jenson. Not much of a list. Jenson was dead, and Lin might be the one responsible for this.

She had Gina's number. But Gina had been with Lin. What if the two of them had done this together? Kayla shuddered at the memory of Gina guiding her across campus. She'd made out she was being friendly, just a sisterly hand on the arm. But Kayla had felt like she was being taken hostage.

And now here she was, locked in.

She had that detective's number. But she clearly thought Kayla was guilty of something. She wouldn't have cautioned her otherwise.

Kayla took a deep breath and scrolled through her contacts. She had to find out what was going on. She had to face up to what was happening, what had been happening since the moment they'd found Laurence. Maybe since the moment Laurence had tried to rape her.

She gritted her teeth and dialled.

CHAPTER NINETY-THREE

"Who is she, then? What's her name?" Mo asked.

Zoe stared at the screen. "She was with Kayla and Lin earlier today. There was a group of them. I saw them walking Kayla out of her lectures and across campus, when we were all on that phone call."

"So she's a friend of Kayla's?" Connie asked.

Zoe shook her head. "Or maybe Lin's. I can't be sure." She turned to Connie. "OK Connie, I want you to get onto your mate at the university. Show her this photo, see if she can find a match."

"She hasn't exactly got facial recognition software, boss," said Connie.

"No." Zoe sighed. "We'll show it to the Boulton Hall warden as well. And to Kayla."

"Not Lin?" asked Mo.

Zoe narrowed her eyes at the image on screen. "I saw the way Lin was looking at this woman and at Kayla earlier. I don't want to ask her just yet."

"Yeah," added Connie. "I ran into her earlier. She really wasn't in the mood for talking."

"I can run her through the system," said Rhodri. "You never know, we might have arrested her sometime."

"Good thinking. OK, you take care of that. Mo, you call the warden. I've got someone I need to speak to."

Mo frowned. "Someone who can identify this woman?"

Zoe didn't meet his eye. "Something else. I'll be as quick as I can."

Mo looked back at her, eyes narrowed. He would be wondering what she was playing at. They were about to identify a new suspect in a double murder, and the boss was checking out? But she couldn't share what she had with him.

She glanced at him. "I'll be back as quick as I can." She turned and left the room.

She hurried out of the building, anxious to get this over with. The person she needed to see should be at home. As she pulled out of her parking spot, she spotted Mo in the rear view mirror. She braked hard.

Mo ran round the car and banged on her window. He made a winding motion for her to lower the window.

"Trust me, Mo," she said. "I'll be as quick as I can."

"What's going on, Zo?"

She grimaced at the use of the nickname. The two of them had been friends for almost twenty years. He'd been there at the birth of her son. But she couldn't burden him with this.

"You hid stuff from me when we were working the Jackson murder, boss. Please don't do it again."

"You don't have to call me boss. It's just you and me."

"OK. Zo." His hands gripped the upper edge of the

window. "Talk to me. Tell me what's going on. Is it Randle again?"

She felt her chest hollow out. "I can't tell you, Mo. I'm sorry." She stared ahead at the space she'd been trying to reverse out of. Hating herself, she pushed the button to raise the window.

"Zoe!"

"Sorry, Mo." She looked over her shoulder to reverse the car, trying to ignore her colleague banging on the closed window. She hated herself for this, but she had to protect him.

She clutched the wheel as she left him behind, standing in the middle of the car park and staring after her.

CHAPTER NINETY-FOUR

CONNIE GRIPPED THE PHONE, waiting for Rhonda to get back on the line. She knew this was a long shot, but if Rhonda could access student files...

"I'm sorry, Connie. There's no way of checking all these photos. And I can't send them to you. Data protection. You'll have to get a warrant."

"Yeah." Connie slumped in her seat. "Thanks, Rhonda."

"Good luck."

Connie hung up. She had just picked up her phone to call the boss when Mo walked back into the office. He was like a tiger in a cage, his body language tense.

"You OK, Sarge?" Connie put her phone down.

"I'm fine. Get on with the jobs the DI's given you." He slammed into Zoe's office and hurled himself into her chair. Connie watched him through the glass. What had the boss done to piss him off? Was it to do with wherever she was going?

Connie was used to the boss leaving the office at short

notice, rushing off in pursuit of a lead. It was hardly new. But this seemed different.

Where *was* the DI going, anyway?

Connie walked into the inner office, her footsteps slow. At the door she paused, waiting for the sarge to spot her.

"Connie. Sorry I snapped at you."

"It's OK. Anything I can help with?"

He shook his head. He stared at Zoe's computer screen for a moment then stood up, his hand gripping the edge of her desk. "Come on. We've got work to do."

"I got nowhere with Rhonda, Sarge."

"No big surprise there. We'll need to make it official."

"That's what she said. We need a warrant."

Mo dragged a hand through his hair. "We do. I'll speak to DI Dawson."

Connie's eyes widened. "You sure about that, Sarge?"

"He's supposed to be in charge, isn't he? And I used to be on his team."

"What about the DI?"

"She's gone off to see someone. I don't want to disturb her."

Connie felt a chill run down the back of her neck. "OK." She didn't like this. She felt like a child stuck between warring parents.

She turned at a knock on the door. It was Rhodri, a bright smile painted across his face. "Good news."

"We need it, Rhod," Mo said. "Spill the beans."

"I've got a match on the woman. We arrested her for assault two years ago, took place at a demo on campus. She got a caution."

"If she's on the database, why didn't we match her prints already?" said Mo.

Rhodri shrugged. "Gloves, sarge. Not rocket science."

"Well, who is she then?" Mo snapped. Realising what he'd done, he added, "sorry."

"It's OK, Sarge. Her name's Gina Lennon. Lives in Selly Oak. Shall we go see her?"

CHAPTER NINETY-FIVE

Zoe pulled up outside the familiar house. She had no idea if he'd be in or not, but she hadn't wanted to phone ahead.

She watched the building for a few moments, looking for signs of life. The kitchen light was on but she could see no one inside. Maybe they were at the back.

A green Ford Focus drove past and pulled in in front of the house. Ian got out, scanning the road, his eyes wild. Zoe dipped down in her seat. Her car was distinctive, but he wouldn't be expecting her.

She was startled by a thump on the driver's window. *Not again.*

She eased herself up in the seat and looked out. Ian stood outside, his face twisted in a scowl.

She opened the door and squeezed out. "Ian, I need to ask you something."

He looked at the house then back at her. "You shouldn't be here."

"I know. But..."

"What is it, Zoe? You want to get more information out of me so you can pass it on to your mates in PSD?"

"Why don't you get in the car, Ian? I assume Alison's in the house and I'm guessing you don't want your neighbours overhearing this."

He glared at her. "Alison left me."

Her shoulders dipped. "I'm sorry to hear that."

"No thanks to you."

"Come on, Ian. You can't blame me for—"

"Just get on with it, eh? Then you can fuck off." He sped round the front of the car and yanked the passenger door open. He threw himself inside and slammed the door.

Zoe eased back into the seat and closed the door. She looked out at the street: no sign of anyone watching.

"Where have you been?" she asked him.

"None of your fucking business. Just tell me what it is you want to know. And what I get in return."

She took a deep breath. "Ian, I think you're being manipulated. This goes higher than you, much higher, and you and I both know it."

He stared out of the windscreen, his lips zipped tight.

"If you told PSD who you've been working with, who in the force, things might get easier for you."

"Nothing I say will get my job back."

"Yes, but the criminal charges..."

He turned to her. "My wife is with her goddamn mother, who's dripping poison against me into her ear every day. I'll probably not be able to see my kids. All my old mates won't come near me. I've got nothing to lose. I don't give a fuck anymore, Zoe."

"There's always something to hope for, Ian. If you can get

the charges against you reduced, avoid a custodial sentence..."

"What did you come here to ask me? I don't believe you're here to check on my welfare. You didn't help me when you were my boss, and I don't believe you are now."

She pulled out her phone and thumbed to the photo Sheila had sent her. She handed it to Ian. "What do you make of this?"

"It's Detective Superintendent Randle with some woman. So what?"

Zoe eyed him. "The woman's name is Alina Popescu. She was the one who set off the New Street bomb."

Ian took in a sharp breath. "What's she doing with him?"

"That's what I was hoping you could tell me."

He shoved the phone back at her. "Sorry."

"Ian, were you working for Randle? Did he give you your instructions? And how closely involved is he with Trevor Hamm?"

"No idea what you're talking about."

She clenched a fist. "Come on, Ian."

A silver BMW pulled up next to Ian's car, outside the house. A heavily-built woman got out.

Ian jerked the passenger door open. "Sorry, Zoe. Can't help you. I've got a meeting with my lawyer."

CHAPTER NINETY-SIX

Mo GRABBED his coat and stuffed his phone in the inside pocket. "Come on, Connie. The boss says she wants you and me to go and talk to Gina."

"She doesn't want to do it herself?"

"She doesn't want us to waste time waiting for her. Rhod, can you speak to Adi while we're gone? I want to take a swab from Gina if she'll let us, and it'll be good if the forensics team are ready for us."

"Sarge." Rhodri picked up his phone.

Connie was at the door, an expectant look on her face. Mo smiled at her.

Ten minutes later, they pulled up in Raddlebarn Road, a few houses down from the address they had for Gina. Mo stretched out his shoulders.

"Got back pain, Sarge?"

"I need to find more time to exercise."

"You do much of that?"

"I try and take my girls out on their bikes at the weekend."

"Hopefully you'll get your chance tomorrow."

He grunted. "Hopefully."

They got out of the car and walked to the house. Mo rang the bell. A dog started barking inside. He exchanged glances with Connie, thinking of the dog hairs they'd found on both bodies.

He heard a voice inside: a woman. She was talking to the dog, telling it to calm down. He shifted his shoulders, trying to ignore the pain running across his back.

At last the door opened. A mid-height woman with short brown hair and dark purple lipstick stood in front of them, holding a brown terrier by its collar.

"Sorry about Venus, she's a terror for the doorbell. What d'you want?"

Mo held up his ID and introduced himself and Connie. "Gina Lennon?"

"That's me."

"We were hoping to ask you a few questions about Jenson Begg."

Her gaze flicked down to the dog. "I'll have to shut her in the back room. Come inside, wait in there." She pointed to the room at the front of the terraced house. It was lit by the low February sun. A clump of plants in the bay window cast shadows on the walls.

Gina disappeared along the hall and Mo walked into the room. Connie took a seat in a high-backed armchair and Mo wandered the room. The walls were lined with posters of book covers: *Jane Eyre*, *Wuthering Heights*, *Wide Sargasso Sea*.

Gina reappeared. The dog was in the next room, barking through the wall.

"What can I do for you?"

Mo turned to her. "You studying English?"

She scanned the posters. "No. I like to read, nothing wrong with that, is there?"

"Nothing at all." Mo stood in the centre of the room. Gina stood in the doorway, showing no sign of sitting down.

"Shall we sit down?" Mo suggested.

"What d'you want to know about Jenson?"

"Please." Mo gestured to a scruffy green sofa. "Sit down."

"If you insist." Gina took a seat at one end. "What about you?"

Mo nodded and took the second armchair. Gina relaxed, shunting away from the corner of the sofa.

"Do you know that Jenson Begg died?" Mo asked.

"I heard about it."

"On Wednesday night."

She shrugged.

"Did you know Jenson?"

"By reputation. Not personally."

"And what kind of reputation was that?"

"He assaulted my girlfriend."

"You knew him through your girlfriend?"

She shook her head. "Knew *of* him, officer. It's different."

"Who is your girlfriend?"

"Lin Johnson. She's a first year living in Boulton Hall. He was her tutor. He took advantage of her."

Mo glanced at Connie: Lin hadn't told them about this.

"So you're saying Lin alleged that Jenson assaulted her?"

"She got away before he managed anything." Gina bit at a fingernail and spat it out. "Bastard."

"Did Lin raise a complaint against him?"

Gina laughed. "He was the warden's blue-eyed boy. *No,*

she didn't raise a complaint. Right call, given what happened with the Laurence Thomms investigation."

"You knew Laurence as well?" Connie asked.

Gina turned to her. "Of course not. I knew what he did, though."

"How?" Connie's voice was low.

"Lin told me. The whole of Boulton Hall knew it. I asked her to move in here with me, but she said she was happy there. And that her mate needed her."

"Which mate is this?"

A shrug. "Kayla."

Mo shared a look with Connie. He wished the boss was here: she was the one who'd seen the three students together on campus earlier.

He clenched his fists on his knees. "Did you ever meet Jenson Begg, Gina?"

She stared back at him for a moment as if weighing him up. "Yes."

"When?"

"That's why you're here, I guess." Her voice was calm.

"When did you meet him?"

"I met him on the night he died. I went to his house. But it wasn't me who killed him."

"No?"

"Nope."

"Can you provide evidence of that?"

"Look. If you're here, then you've found evidence I was there. I know how these things work. I left the place at nine thirty, came back here. He was alive and being a prick when I left."

"You came back here?"

"I did."

"Was anyone else here?"

She smiled back at him. "My two housemates were, yes. Sharn and Berni."

Mop looked towards the door. "Are they here now?"

"They're at the cinema. You want to talk to them, establish an alibi."

"It would help."

"I'll tell them to call you." She stood up.

"Will you let us take a cheek swab?" asked Connie.

Gina curled her lip at the constable. "Are you arresting me?"

"No, but it would help us to—"

"In that case, no."

Mo stayed where he was, gesturing for Connie to stay seated too. "You knew about Laurence as well, Gina. You knew what he allegedly did to Kayla. And Becca, too."

"Allegedly. People around here like that word. But no, I didn't kill him either."

"You can provide an alibi for Laurence's death too?"

She sighed. "I didn't kill Laurence. Jenson did."

Mo felt his heart pick up pace. They hadn't released the information about Jenson's DNA being found in Laurence's mouth.

"I'm sorry?" he said.

"Jenson killed Laurence. He wanted rid of him cos the little twerp was impinging on his territory."

"How do you know all this, when you didn't know either of the men?"

"You hear things." She looked away.

"Lin told you?"

"She told me some."

"But someone else told you the rest."

Gina yanked the door to the room wide open. "I'm not answering any more questions without a lawyer."

"You're not under arrest, Gina. You're not even under caution."

"I know how you lot can twist things."

Connie stood up and took a step towards Gina. "They were predators, the pair of them. They deserved to die. I don't blame you."

Gina narrowed her eyes at the constable. "Blame me for what?"

"For thinking they got what was coming to them."

Gina stared back at her. She shrugged.

"Why did you go to Jenson's house, Gina? What was it that made you want to confront him?" said Connie.

"It was Lin."

"He attacked someone you care about. I'd be mad as hell if someone did that to me."

Mo watched Connie, thinking of her brother Zaf and the time he'd been kidnapped. Connie didn't flinch, didn't show the emotion she must have felt as she spoke those last words.

"Yes," muttered Gina.

"Lin told you that Jenson had tried to rape her on Wednesday night, didn't she? She told you and you went round to his house to confront him."

"Yes." Gina squared her shoulders. "I went straight round there. But I didn't kill him."

CHAPTER NINETY-SEVEN

"Someone locked me in my room."

"What?"

"Was it you, Lin?"

Kayla sat on her bed, hunched over the phone. If Lin had the keys, she was the only person who could let her out apart from the security guard, and she wasn't about to raise the alarm.

"You're being dumb, Kayla. What makes you think someone would lock you in your room?"

"Because I can't open the door and my keys have disappeared."

"Maybe you left them somewhere."

"The door is locked from the outside."

"It might be faulty."

Kayla took a deep breath. "Lin, will you just let me out, for God's sake?"

"I'll go down the front desk, get one of the security team to let you out. They've got master keys."

"I don't want you to do that."

"It's the best way. Then you can look for your keys."

"I want to know why you're doing this."

Lin was quiet.

"Lin?"

"You're trash-talking, Kayla. You've had a rough week, what with Laurence and Jenson and everything, and it's made you imagine things."

"You were in here before, with that Gina woman. You leave, and then I'm locked in. Pretty suspicious, I'd say."

"You wait there. I'll get someone to let you out."

The line went dead. Kayla stared at the door, unsure what to believe.

CHAPTER NINETY-EIGHT

Mo LOOKED up at the terraced house as he and Connie left. A curtain shifted in an upstairs window.

"She said they were at the cinema," he said.

"Huh?" Connie followed his gaze.

"The curtain moved. Someone else is in there."

"Someone who can give Gina an alibi?" Connie said.

"Why didn't she want to call them down?" He hesitated, turning back towards the front door of the house. "If she doesn't know they're in, we could tell her."

Connie put a hand on his arm. "She might have lied."

He turned to her. "She was at Jenson's house. She says she came straight home. What time did he die?"

"Dr Adebayo said somewhere between ten pm and two am."

"So she could have gone in there with him, killed him and then gone home."

"Except the camera footage shows her leaving after they argued."

"It cuts off ten minutes later. Who's to say she didn't come back?"

Connie stood next to Mo's car. "I'm wondering about why she went there."

"She told us that, she said he was a predator, that she..."

"It was me that said that, Sarge. But she said she went round there cos Lin had told her he'd tried to rape her. No one else has said anything about either of the men trying anything with Lin."

"That doesn't mean it didn't happen," said Mo.

"Maybe Lin wanted Gina to go round there, all guns blazing."

Mo leaned against the side of the car. "You think Lin wanted Gina to kill him?"

"I think she wanted her to go to the house."

"That makes no sense."

Connie shrugged. "Nah. Doesn't make much sense to me. But we've got Lin and Gina both pissed off with Jenson and with Laurence. We've got them pushing Kayla around."

"You reckon the two of them are in it together?"

She shrugged. "Maybe."

"But the DNA on Laurence. It was Jenson's. We didn't find any female DNA there."

Connie deflated. "So maybe Jenson killed Laurence and then these two killed Jenson. Maybe the three of them were in it together."

"Not if Jenson attacked Lin."

"She might have been lying about that."

Mo bristled. "Why would she lie about something like that? To her girlfriend?"

"Dunno."

"We're going round in circles here, Connie. Let's call the boss. I want her take on it."

"Shall we go back and see if we can get that alibi first?"

"We'll stay here, watch the house. If your theory is correct then either Gina will leave or Lin will turn up."

CHAPTER NINETY-NINE

Kayla's phone rang: Lin.

"Are you going to let me out, or what?"

"I've been thinking, and I reckon you're just trying to get attention. All this business about Laurence. You letting Jenson treat you like that. And now this. You locked yourself in, didn't you?"

"No."

"Maybe you just left your keys in the lock."

"I wouldn't do that."

"Maybe you left them at lectures. Or you dropped them on your way back."

"Gina was shoving me along pretty roughly. I could have dropped them, yes..."

"Or you could have imagined the whole thing."

Kayla approached her door, her heart pounding. Was Lin on the other side, keys in hand?

"Lin, where are you?"

"I'm in my room. Where I was when you called me."

"Why aren't you at lectures?"

"I don't feel so good. I've gotta go, got a call on the other line."

Kayla reached out for the door handle. It turned.

That was nothing. It had turned before. Just not far enough to open.

It carried on turning.

She pulled it, her chest tight. The door opened.

After a moment's hesitation she told herself to step into the corridor. It was empty.

She pulled back into the room, her eyes prickling. Was she losing her mind?

CHAPTER ONE HUNDRED

"Hey, Adi."

"Rhodri. How goes it?"

"Not too bad, mate. I need to talk to you about the Jenson Begg case."

"OK."

"We've got a potential suspect and we're hoping to get a DNA swab off her. If we get the swab over to you asap, can you fast-track it?"

"It's Friday afternoon, Rhodri."

"I know, but you're still there, aren't you? FSIs clearly work all the hours God sends, just like us detectives."

Adi laughed. "I'll see what I can do. I had a call from Adana earlier, I think she was trying to get hold of your boss."

"Oh?"

"She found something in the samples taken from Laurence Thomms. Something she didn't spot first time round."

"OK." Rhodri imagined Doctor Adebayo would have tracked Zoe down on her mobile. If this was important, he'd know soon enough. He hoped. "I'll let her know, just in case."

"Cheers. Let me know when you've got those swabs."

"Will do."

Rhodri hung up and stared at the wall over his desk. He dragged his chair back and walked to the board. It needed updating.

He checked the photos: Laurence and Jenson in the centre. Kayla, Lin and Becca to one side. He needed to add Gina.

He printed off the mugshot from when she'd been arrested and placed it on the board. Beneath it he wrote what he knew about her. She'd been arrested two years ago at a demo against a visiting speaker in the English department. She looked older than the others: was she a student, or staff?

They didn't have much.

Maybe he could try what Connie did.

Rhodri sat at his computer and clicked his fingers, eyeing the keyboard. Start with Facebook, he told himself.

How did Connie get into people's private pages?

He brought up Gina's Facebook account. He could see the list of her friends: Lin was one. No sign of Kayla. He checked Gina's relationship status: in a relationship with Lin.

He went to her profile page to see what was public. A string of historic profile pictures. A bunch of them had her snuggling up with a brown terrier.

They'd found hairs like the ones on that dog's back on both bodies.

Rhodri picked up the phone. "Sarge, I've been checking Gina out online, and she had a brown dog. Hair looks like it might match what we found on both bodies."

"Slow down, Constable. We've just been in her house

and we saw the dog. But it looks like she's got an alibi for Jenson's murder."

"She was right there."

"She says she can prove that she went straight home after we saw her leave Jenson."

"She says."

"We're going to check it out. But well done for spotting it, Rhod. You manage to get hold of Adi?"

"I did. He said Doctor Adebayo's been trying to contact the DI."

"What about?"

"Something about the Laurence Thomms samples. Don't know what."

There was silence.

"Sarge?"

"Rhodri, we're watching Gina's house. You call the pathologist will you? Find out what it is she needs."

Rhodri swallowed. The pathologist scared him a little. "OK."

He dialled the mortuary: no answer. At five o'clock on a Friday, that wasn't too surprising. The DI had written a mobile number in the team contact list. He dialled it. Licking his lips.

"Doctor Adebayo."

"Doctor, it's Rhodri Hughes. Have you been trying to contact the DI?"

"She's not answering her phone. Not like her."

"Right. Sorry. Can I help?"

He could sense her expression of surprise and superiority down the phone.

"Might as well," she said.

"OK."

"Have you got a pen?"

He grabbed his notepad. "Yeah."

"Write this down. I went back through the samples we took from Laurence Thomms's body. I found formalin in the throat swabs. I guess I didn't spot it at first because it's such a familiar substance in the mortuary."

"Formalin?"

"Used for preserving bodies."

"Did you use it on Laurence at the morgue?"

"We did not, Constable. And it's not there in large quantities. It wasn't in his digestive system. And it wasn't injected into him. I think it was on the killer's hands, or the gloves they used. And it got onto the inside of Laurence's throat when his killer shoved the drugs into him."

"Who would have access to formalin?" Rhodri asked.

"Well, you can buy it online. But I don't see why the killer would have done so, not if they weren't going to use it as a weapon. I think it got there by accident."

"How?"

"Rhodri, you need to talk to Zoe. Tell her you're looking for someone whose work brings them into contact with dead bodies."

"A pathologist?"

"Or a funeral director. Or a medical student."

CHAPTER ONE HUNDRED ONE

Mo's phone rang. *Thank God.*

"Boss."

"You with Connie?"

"We're outside Gina Lennon's house."

"How did you get on with her?" She asked. "Got the swab?"

"She wasn't cooperating."

A sigh. "Why am I not surprised? What did she have to say for herself?"

"She said she left Jenson and went straight home. She says her housemates can vouch for her."

"And have they?"

"They're out." He looked up at the window. There had been no more sign of movement.

"So she's not off the hook yet."

Connie nudged him and pointed to the phone. He put it on hands-free. "I've got Connie on the line now."

"Connie," said Zoe. "Talk to me."

"Boss, I can't get Lin's behaviour out of my head. Gina

told us that Lin claimed Jenson had tried to rape her. That's why Gina went storming round to his house."

"You think she was lying to Gina?"

"Gina's her girlfriend, boss. She'd have been pretty wound up to hear those things."

"Enough to go round and kill Jenson?"

"Enough to confront him. I think Lin wanted Gina at the house. Maybe she wanted us to find out she'd been there."

"You think Lin was trying to frame Gina? Why?"

"I know it's a bit far-fetched, boss."

"It's just a theory," said Mo. "I know we need more solid evidence."

"Hang on," Zoe said. "I've got Rhodri trying to get through."

Mo heard a bleep followed by Zoe cursing. Then a dial tone.

"Boss?" he said, worried he'd lost her.

"Wait... I've got him. Rhodri's on the call too."

Connie gave Mo a knowing smile. "Well done, boss."

"You taught me well, Connie. Rhod, Mo and Connie are here, too. What's up?"

"I just spoke to Dr Adebayo, boss."

"OK."

"She found formalin in the cheek swabs from Laurence's body."

"When?"

"It was there all along, but she didn't give it the attention it deserved because the stuff is so normal to her."

"Not like Adana."

"She wasn't the one who did the PM on Laurence," said Mo. "That was the other guy."

Zoe whistled. "Brent Reynolds. He's going to be in a

whole heap of trouble when Adana stops covering for him. What's the significance, Rhodri?"

"Formalin is used to preserve bodies, boss."

"By undertakers, yes."

"And in medical schools. They use it to preserve the bodies for the students to dissect."

"Was it used to kill him? Mixed in with the drugs?"

"Dr Adebayo reckons it got there by mistake."

"So we could be looking for a medical student."

"Lin's a medical student," said Connie.

"She is," said Zoe. She winced. "She touched him, after she found him. Said she had gloves on, she'd been in an anatomy class."

"That would explain the formalin," said Mo.

"It might do," said Zoe. "We need to check her out. Mo, one of you stay where you are. The other one head to Boulton Hall. But don't do anything until you get the go-ahead from me."

"What are you going to do?" Mo asked.

He could sense the contempt in her voice. "I'm going to talk to Adana, and then if I'm really unlucky, I'll have to talk to DI Dawson."

CHAPTER ONE HUNDRED TWO

KAYLA SLAMMED her door behind her. She still didn't have her keys but she was confident she knew who did. She ran down the stairs: four flights from her room to Lin's.

As she reached the first floor, she spotted Lin on the ground floor, which was visible from the stairs. She was leaving the building.

Kayla drew breath to call out, then thought better of it. She ran down the remaining stairs and headed towards the door.

Lin was walking up the driveway, almost at the road. Kayla's gut was telling her to call after her friend and confront her. But her head told her to stay quiet and follow.

Lin turned right, heading along Edgbaston Park Road. Kayla followed at a distance, tucking herself into the hedge to avoid being seen. A car pulled up ahead and two men got out, walking between her and Lin.

It meant Lin was harder to see, but would make Kayla less noticeable. Good.

She crept after Lin, her heart racing, until they came to

the Bristol Road. Lin picked up pace and eventually turned into Bournbrook Road.

Where was she going?

The two men had long since turned off. A bus stopped at the junction, a young woman with a pushchair putting herself between Kayla and Lin. Kayla followed, keeping the woman between her and her friend.

CHAPTER ONE HUNDRED THREE

Zoe drummed her fist on her knee as the phone rang out. She was sitting in her car, en route back to Selly Oak from Ian's. She'd parked in the city centre, next to the Peace Gardens.

"Come on, Adana," she muttered. She checked her watch; the pathologist couldn't have left yet, surely.

"DI Finch." Adana sounded as if she was walking.

"Adana. Thank God I got you."

"You've spoken to DC Hughes?"

"He told me about the formalin. I need to know when it got into the victim."

"Sorry?"

"The woman who found him, Lin Johnson. She told me she'd put on gloves and then taken a look at him. She had the gloves with her because she's a medical student and she'd been in an anatomy class."

"Very convenient for her."

Zoe sucked in a breath. "What makes you say that?"

"He breathed it in, Zoe. It was in his lungs. When did she find him? How long after death?"

"Long enough."

"The formalin I found didn't come from a pair of gloves after he was found. It got there while he was breathing his last breaths. If you asked me to speculate, I'd say it was on the hands of the person who pushed the drugs down his throat."

"Or on a pair of gloves they were wearing."

"Exactly."

Zoe had stopped drumming with her fist. She pushed it into her thigh, her skin prickling.

"Thanks, Adana."

She hung up. Now to talk to Dawson.

CHAPTER ONE HUNDRED FOUR

"I'll go," said Connie. "You stay here."

"You sure?"

"I may look like a fat Jamaican woman to you, but I cycle everywhere. I'm fitter than I look. I can be at Boulton Hall in... twenty minutes, I reckon."

"OK. Tell me what you find."

"I will."

Connie got out of the car and started jogging. She knew better than to sprint: she needed to hold her pace.

She rounded the corner into Bournbrook Road. A woman was walking the other way: Lin. Connie sprang back, darting back round the corner so Lin wouldn't see her.

She looked into the front windows of the house nearest to her. They were dark. She crept into the front garden and ducked behind the hedge.

Lin walked past, her footsteps regular. She was muttering to herself.

Connie waited a moment then emerged from her hiding spot just as another woman turned the corner. Connie suppressed a yelp and slammed herself back down behind the hedge.

Had Kayla seen her?

Why was Kayla following Lin?

She waited for Kayla to pass, then peered round the corner into Raddlebarn Road. The chances of a third person following Kayla were slim but Connie wanted to be sure. The road was quiet, just a group of teenagers halfway up.

Connie turned back into Raddlebarn Road, picking up pace to get closer to Kayla. Kayla kept squeezing herself into the hedge. Not the stealthiest surveillance operation, Connie thought. But then *she'd* almost crashed into both the women she was now following.

She reached Mo's car. His gaze was on the house. Lin had gone inside.

"You see them?" Connie panted.

He nodded. "Gina came to the door and let Lin in. Not sure what Kayla's planning."

Connie nodded. She focused on her breathing, trying to bring it back into line. Kayla approached the house, her body hunched.

Connie held her breath.

Kayla stood outside the house, staring up at the windows.

"What's she doing?" Connie breathed. Mo shrugged.

The door opened. Lin emerged, her mouth moving, arms waving.

"I can't hear anything," Connie said.

"We can't risk getting any closer. We've already been accused of harassment."

"But if there's a credible threat to one of them..."

He nodded. "*Then* we go in. Not before."

CHAPTER ONE HUNDRED FIVE

"You've got nowhere near enough for a warrant," said DI Dawson.

"Frank, we have the formalin," Zoe reminded him. "Adana says Laurence breathed it in. Lin Johnson admitted to wearing gloves from an anatomy class. I think she sent her girlfriend round to Jenson's house to cover for her, to throw us off the scent."

Two men walked past her car, glancing in at her. She gripped her phone, her heart racing. She needed to get moving, to be in Selly Oak.

"What about the DNA from the first scene?" Dawson said. "The boot print you still haven't matched up to anything?"

"The boot at the Jenson Begg scene was a woman's boot. If we have a warrant to search Lin Johnson's room, we can check her footwear, it'll help us get closer to a definitive—"

"Exactly. You don't have enough for a warrant. Not yet."

Zoe slammed her fist into the steering wheel. She knew Lesley would have given her the same answer. She was

working on a hunch of Connie's and a single piece of forensics evidence in the middle of a heap of other forensics
pointing in other directions.

"I'm going to question her, Frank. If she consents to talk
to me, you can't stop me doing that."

"Don't go doing anything stupid, Zoe."

She tightened her fist. "I won't."

She hung up just as her phone rang: Mo.

"Zo. Lin and Kayla have turned up at Gina's house. You
need to get over here."

CHAPTER ONE HUNDRED SIX

Zoe parked further along Raddlebarn Road, careful to stay out of sight of the house. She hurried to Mo's car, scanning the street. She wondered if this road had nosy neighbours like Mrs Anderson.

She knocked the window lightly and Mo wound it down. "Boss."

"What's happening?"

"Lin turned up about ten minutes ago. Kayla was following her."

Connie leaned across Mo to speak to her. "I almost crashed into the two of them."

"And they're all inside now?"

"Yup." Mo looked towards the house. "No idea what's going on."

Zoe nodded, following his gaze. "I'll get in the back." She pulled open the back door of the car and slid in.

Mo turned to face her. "How'd it go with DI Dawson?"

She shook her head. "No go. I'm not surprised really."

She gave Connie a shrug. "Sorry, Constable. But we need more than your hunch."

"What about the formalin?" Connie asked.

"Adana says he swallowed it, it didn't get there after Lin found him."

"Surely that's what we need?"

"Lin isn't the only medical student in Boulton Hall," Zoe said.

Mo sighed. "And she may not be the only medical student with a reason to hurt Laurence."

"Yeah." Zoe thought of the women he'd assaulted. The women they didn't know about. The guy was only eighteen. Where did an eighteen-year-old learn to behave like that?

"I saw something," Connie said. "Front window."

Zoe leaned forward to look out of the windscreen. "Can't see it."

"It's gone."

"They might have spotted us. Gina knew we were here. She might have seen us getting into the car."

"Do we have a good reason to go back in there?" Zoe asked.

Connie looked at Mo, her eyes shining. "We do."

"Connie's right," he said. "We need to talk to Gina's housemates to establish an alibi. I believe one of them is in."

"And even if they're not, there's no reason why Lin shouldn't provide her alibi." Zoe opened the car door. "Let's go."

CHAPTER ONE HUNDRED SEVEN

Lin led Kayla into the back room of the house, her hands fidgeting. Gina sat behind a dining table, holding a small brown dog by its collar.

"What are you doing here?" Lin asked her.

"I followed you. I want my keys back."

Lin went to Gina and sat next to her. She put a hand over the other woman's. "Don't be ridiculous." She leaned down and stroked the dog.

"What's going on, Kayla?" Gina asked. She looked concerned, but Kayla couldn't be sure she wasn't faking it. "Are you OK?"

"I'm fine. I just want to know what's up with Lin."

Lin stood up. "Let's talk in private. You and me, we'll get this thing sorted once and for all."

Kayla bit her lower lip. This was her friend: why was she feeling scared?

She nodded. "OK."

Lin turned to Gina. "Can you get some coffees, hun?"

Gina smiled. "Of course." She left the room.

Lin gave Kayla a dry smile. "Let's go upstairs."

"I'm fine here."

"I don't want Gina's housemates walking in on this. She won't mind if we use her bedroom."

Kayla was determined not to show Lin how nervous she was. "OK."

She followed Lin up the narrow stairs to a bedroom at the back of the house. Lin stood to one side, holding the door open.

Kayla span round as soon as she entered the room, checking Lin wasn't about to lock the door. Lin followed, her hands up in a gesture of innocence.

"Take a seat," Lin said.

There was an armchair in the window. Kayla sat in it while Lin perched on the bed. Lin leaned forward, her hands sandwiched between her thighs. The door was open.

Kayla forced herself to breathe. *Stop being so stupid.*

"You've been acting odd lately," she told her friend.

"Odd?"

"You came to the English department with Gina and dragged me across campus. You locked me in my room."

"I didn't lock you in your—"

"And there was the way you reacted to Laurence's body. To finding him like that. You weren't upset by it."

"I'm a medical student, Kayl. I see dead bodies all the time."

"Not ones that have been murdered."

Lin shrugged. "Some of us are squeamish. Some of us aren't. I guess I'm not. Sorry if it disappoints you."

"It's not disappointment. It's..."

What was it? Surely she didn't think Lin had anything to do with Laurence's death?

Lin rose from the bed. She went to the door and pushed it shut. She turned back to Kayla.

"What about Gina?" Kayla asked. "The coffees?"

"We need to be quick, Kayla. I don't want her finding you like this."

"Like what?"

"Like I left Laurence. Jenson, too. Bastards, both got what was coming to them."

"What?" Kayla breathed.

Lin stood over the chair. She reached into her pocket.

She held something out: white, wrapped in a scrap of clingfilm. Kayla shrank back.

"Jenson gave you drugs, didn't he?"

"I don't see what—" Kayla focused on the object in Lin's hand.

Lin grabbed Kayla's arm with her free hand. Kayla tried to pull back but her friend was too strong. Lin's knee went forward, into Kayla's stomach.

She cried out. "Lin! You're hurting me!"

Lin leaned on Kayla with her knee. She had Kayla's arm in a lock, bent round at the side. Pain shot into her elbow.

"Stop!"

Lin pushed her hand into Kayla's mouth, the white object still in it. Kayla sputtered. She shook her head violently, pushing Lin's hand away.

She took the deepest breath she could and screamed.

CHAPTER ONE HUNDRED EIGHT

ZOE APPROACHED THE HOUSE, scanning the windows for movement. Mo was behind her.

As she stepped onto the front path, she heard a scream. She ran for the front door and hammered on it.

"Police! Let us in!"

The screaming came again, muffled this time. Zoe turned to Mo. His eyes were wide.

"Kayla?" he whispered.

"No idea." But whoever it was needed their help.

She bent down and lifted the letterbox. A dog was barking inside.

"Gina's terrier," said Mo. "Not dangerous."

"Don't be so sure," Zoe told him.

"We have to go in there."

"Of course we do."

Connie was behind Mo, her body tense.

"Connie, call for emergency response. Suspected assault under way at 34 Raddlebarn Road."

"Boss." Connie stepped back and took out her phone.

Zoe let the letterbox clatter shut. The house was quiet.

"We need to be quick," she muttered. She turned to Mo. "Stand back."

"We need the enforcer," he said.

"She needs us in there right now. I said stand back."

Mo did as he was told. Zoe took a few steps away from the door, eyeing it, sizing up the best target for her foot. She'd learned to kick in her karate lessons, but knew she could injure herself doing this with a solid wood door.

She ran at the door and raised her leg, aiming her foot at the spot just under the latch. The door didn't budge.

"Damn." She backed up again.

"Zo," said Mo. "It's too heavy. We need to find another way in."

"You do that. Find a window. A back door. Anything."

Another scream, followed by yelling. It came from upstairs. Mo ran off. Connie finished her call.

"Uniform six minutes away, boss."

Zoe nodded. She eyed the door again. She'd strike a little lower this time. She'd felt weakness there.

As she began the run up to it, the door opened. Zoe managed to stop herself from bringing her leg up but couldn't halt her momentum. She crashed into Gina Lennon, who was standing in the doorway.

"I don't know what's happening," Gina said. "There's screaming..." She gestured up the stairs.

Zoe ran past her. She heard a door burst open at the back of the house: Mo.

"Where?" she snapped.

"Back bedroom."

"Stay where you are. And shut that bloody dog up!"

Zoe raced up the stairs and thundered into the door at the back. It gave, thank God. She stumbled into the room.

Two women turned to look at her. Kayla sat in a chair by the window, her eyes wide. Lin stood over her, a wrap of drugs in her hand. Flecks of white ringed Kayla's lips.

"Police!" Zoe shouted. "Don't move." She dived in and grabbed Lin by the wrist. "Lin Johnson, you're under arrest."

CHAPTER ONE HUNDRED NINE

ZOE LEANED AGAINST HER CAR, watching as the flashing blue lights reflected off the house fronts. Kayla had been taken away in an ambulance: she needed to be observed, as neither she nor Lin had been able to say how much of the methamphetamine had got into her system.

Lin was in a squad car parked outside the house. Zoe watched as it pulled out and drove off towards Harborne.

Gina sat on the front step of the house, crying. Connie was next to her, her arm over the blanket that had been placed around the woman's shoulders. Zoe still couldn't be sure if Gina had really known nothing about what Lin had done, but she didn't have the evidence to arrest her.

She sighed and pulled her neck back to stare up at the sky. It was clear tonight, stars peppering the heavens.

She had a call to make. Should have made it hours ago.

She slid into the car as she dialled.

"Zoe, you OK?"

"Hi, Carl." She felt her eyelids droop; the day had caught up with her.

"You sound tired."

"I just made an arrest."

"The case at the university?"

"The very same."

Silence. She stared out of the windscreen, watching two uniformed constables try to keep the neighbours away from the house. Connie squeezed Gina's shoulder and guided her inside. A family liaison officer would arrive soon.

"Zoe. You didn't call me to sit in silence."

"I might have. It's nice, companionable silence."

"I know it is. But you've just arrested someone, you're buzzing with adrenaline. You'll have an interview to do, paperwork to plough through. You're not ringing me to pass the time of day."

"I've been passed some evidence."

"What kind of evidence?"

"I'm going to send it to you now." She had the photo ready to go on her phone. She hit share.

"Who's the woman?"

"Her name is Alina Popescu. She's the New Street bomber."

"Shit."

"Exactly."

"Where did you get this?"

"The Hotel Belvista. Apparently. You'll have to speak to Sheila Griffin."

"She found it?"

"Her team did."

"She should have come direct to me."

"She knew about our relationship, Carl. She was wary of going to PSD, I guess."

"We'll have to talk to her, either way."

"She knows that."

"Zoe? Does this mean you want us to get back together?"

"That depends."

"On what?"

She let out a shaky breath. "On whether you trust me."

"We've done all our interviews. We've dug as deep as we can on Ian and you're right. There's no evidence the two of you were in it together."

"So?"

"So, yes. I trust you. I owe you an apology."

Zoe thought back to her visit to Ian earlier. "Thanks, Carl. In that case, when I've wrapped up what I need to do here, will you be home?"

She could hear his smile down the line. "I will."

She closed her eyes. She wanted to sleep. "Good."

"Does anyone else know about this photo, Zoe?"

She opened her eyes. "I talked to Lesley."

"Why?"

"She's my sounding board."

"I don't see why you'd need a sounding board on this."

"I just did, OK?"

"No one else?"

Zoe swallowed. "No."

"OK. I'll see you later."

CHAPTER ONE HUNDRED TEN

Zoe walked into Café Face to find Mo already there, sitting at the back. She smiled and gave him a brief hug.

"That's unexpected," he said.

"It's how I feel. Dealing with all these students who want to rape or kill each other..."

"I know. I ordered you a full English."

"Perfect." It was Sunday afternoon, not breakfast time, but Zoe didn't care. She was starving.

She sat down just as Fran, the owner of the café, put a black coffee and a plate of food in front of her. She looked up. "Cheers."

"So how did the interview with Lin go?" Mo asked.

"She was so angry." Zoe sipped her coffee then put a slice of sausage on her fork. "I thought I'd need to get Uniform in at one point."

"Angry about what?"

"Rapists. Men who 'prey on' younger women. Sexism. Anyone who wants to hurt her friends."

"But she tried to kill Kayla."

Zoe swallowed a mouthful of beans. "She lost it there. Convinced Kayla knew all about what she'd done and was about to call me."

"And did she?"

"Kayla? She had her suspicions. But she definitely hadn't made the mental leap to thinking her friend was a murderer."

"Poor kid."

Zoe nodded. She gulped down the last of her coffee. "I need another one of these. You?"

"No ta."

Zoe pushed her empty plate away. She fetched another coffee and plonked it down.

"She even confessed to killing Laurence," she said. "All the trouble she went to to frame Jenson for it, and in the end she sang like she was on *The Voice*."

"She was certainly clever."

"Yeah," Zoe replied. "Telling us she'd examined Laurence with those gloves.

"Planting Jenson's DNA," Mo added.

"Medical student. You'd want them to be clever, wouldn't you? And yes, she got Jenson's DNA from his room, managed to get some blood off his razor. She kept it for a week then placed it inside Laurence's mouth."

"And then she made sure she was the one who found him."

"Couldn't have anyone else contaminating her perfectly arranged crime scene."

"Poor Kayla."

"Getting caught up in it all like that," Zoe said. "How is she?"

Mo had been to the hospital to check on Kayla's progress.

"In shock, but not much of the drugs got into her system. She'll be fine for an interview tomorrow."

"Great." Zoe slung the last of her second mug of coffee down her throat and stood up. "What you up to now?"

He smiled. "Bike ride with my girls. We're going to go round Cofton Park."

"Sounds lovely."

"What about you?"

"Nicholas is due home any time. I'd best be back when he gets in."

"Not like you to worry about him."

"It makes me uneasy, him going away with Jim's family like that. I know he finds it hard."

"He's a big boy, Zo."

"An adult, I know. But I'll always be his mum. When Fiona and Isla are grown up, you'll understand."

She pushed the door to the cafe open and walked out, glad to be seeing her son again.

CHAPTER ONE HUNDRED ELEVEN

ZOE POKED her head around the door to see Lesley sitting in an armchair, dressed in jeans and a green shirt. It was the first time she'd seen her boss in anything other than her signature eighties-style skirt suits, or a hospital gown.

"Zoe. Good to see you."

"I've brought company. Hope you don't mind."

"Depends who it is."

Zoe pushed Connie in front of her. "She was worried about you."

Lesley smiled. "Connie. Thank you for your concern."

"The boss has been missing you. Ma'am."

Zoe gave Connie a look. Connie smirked.

"And I've been missing her," said Lesley. "God, it's dull sitting at home."

"When will you be back at work?" Zoe asked.

Lesley stared out of the window.

"You *will* be coming back to work?" Zoe felt her heart pick up pace.

Lesley turned back to her. She wiped under her eye. Zoe fidgeted as she stood.

"Ma'am?"

"I've got news for you, Zoe, and it's not good."

Zoe's stomach dipped. She nodded, her jaw set.

"Sit down, both of you."

Zoe perched on the end of a beige sofa and Connie sat next to her. They both stared at the DCI. Zoe could sense Connie's anxiety, as acute as her own.

Lesley gave them both a smile. "I ain't dying, you two. You look as if you've seen a ghost."

Zoe breathed out. "That's a relief." She forced a tight laugh.

"But I'm not coming back to work. Not for a while, anyway."

"You've got sick leave?" asked Connie.

"Not really."

"Early retirement?" Zoe suggested.

"It'll bloody well feel like it." Lesley sighed. "No, I've been told to take a spell somewhere less... exciting. For the sake of my mental health. Apparently I've got PTSD and I need to distance myself from the source of the trauma." She raised an eyebrow. "It's pretty tough to be a copper in this city and never go near New Street Station."

"Where will you be going?" Zoe was imagining Coventry. Wolverhampton maybe. They had branches of Force CID in both cities.

"Dorset," Lesley said.

"Dorset?" Zoe and Connie spluttered at once.

"I told you it would be dull. I've got to take three months' leave and then report to Dorchester nick, where I'm going to be in charge of the major crimes unit."

"Do they even have major crimes in Dorset?" Connie asked.

"I think that's kind of the point, Constable."

"Is it permanent?" Zoe asked.

"A secondment. Six months, a year if I'm unlucky. I guess I have to wait until the quacks say I'm sane again."

"Ma'am. I'm sorry," said Zoe. "What will your family do? They'll move with you?"

"Sharon's got her GCSEs this summer, we decided it'd be too disruptive. Terry will stay here with her, they'll come down in the holidays. Weekends. Dorset's s'posed to be good for that kind of thing."

Zoe tried to imagine Lesley Clarke in a quiet police station in Dorset, dealing with petty crimes and local politics.

"Dorset is very lovely, ma'am," said Connie. "My sister went there with some mates and—"

Lesley raised a hand. "You don't have to do that."

"I've got a question," Zoe said.

"Of course." Lesley cocked her head.

"Who's replacing you?"

"Frank will be officially acting up for now. Then they'll have to recruit someone. Why, thinking of applying?"

"I've only been an Inspector for six months."

"Stranger things have happened. You should consider it."

"No, ma'am. I like it where I am."

"Fair enough. But you're not keen on having Frank managing you, I can tell that from the way your face went about a metre south when I told you."

"I'll cope."

"You will. Give him the benefit of the doubt, Zoe. He may be an arsehole, but he's a good copper. Now he can drop his seething resentment at you being his equal, maybe he'll stop trying to prove he's better than you."

"Maybe."

"We can live in hope, Zoe."

"We can, ma'am. We can."

READ ZOE'S PREQUEL STORY, DEADLY ORIGINS

It's 2003, and Zoe Finch is a new Detective Constable. When a body is found on her patch, she's grudgingly allowed to take a role on the case.

But when more bodies are found, and Zoe realises the case has links to her own family, the investigation becomes deeply personal.

Can Zoe find the killer before it's too late?

Find out by reading *Deadly Origins* for FREE at rachelmclean.com/origins.

READ THE DI ZOE FINCH SERIES

ALSO BY RACHEL MCLEAN - THE DORSET CRIME SERIES

The Corfe Castle Murders, Dorset Crime Book 1

The Clifftop Murders, Dorset Crime Book 2

The Island Murders, Dorset Crime Book 3

...and more to come!

Lightning Source UK Ltd.
Milton Keynes UK
UKHW042234310122
398002UK00003B/548